W9-CNV-263

Michelle Smart

The Perfect Cazorla Wife

HARLEQUIN PRESENTS®

If you purchased this book without a cover you should be aware that this book is stolen property. It was reported as "unsold and destroyed" to the publisher, and neither the author nor the publisher has received any payment for this "stripped book."

ISBN-13: 978-0-373-13362-8

The Perfect Cazorla Wife

First North American publication 2015

Copyright © 2015 by Michelle Smart

Recycling programs for this product may not exist in your area.

All rights reserved. Except for use in any review, the reproduction or utilization of this work in whole or in part in any form by any electronic, mechanical or other means, now known or hereinafter invented, including xerography, photocopying and recording, or in any information storage or retrieval system, is forbidden without the written permission of the publisher, Harlequin Enterprises Limited, 225 Duncan Mill Road, Don Mills, Ontario M3B 3K9, Canada.

This is a work of fiction. Names, characters, places and incidents are either the product of the author's imagination or are used fictitiously, and any resemblance to actual persons, living or dead, business establishments, events or locales is entirely coincidental.

This edition published by arrangement with Harlequin Books S.A.

For questions and comments about the quality of this book, please contact us at CustomerService@Harlequin.com.

® and TM are trademarks of Harlequin Enterprises Limited or its corporate affiliates. Trademarks indicated with ® are registered in the United States Patent and Trademark Office, the Canadian Intellectual Property Office and in other countries.

Printed in U.S.A.

www.Harlequin.com

"I hate you."

"I know." Raul dipped his head and nipped her earlobe. "Imagine how incredible it will be, all that hate fueling all that lust."

Sensation filled Charley, every crevice of her coming alive at his touch and the whisper of his breath on her skin.

Two years without this...

Somehow she managed to pull her hands free from his grasp, fully intending to use them as weapons to push him off her. Instead, working of their own accord, they hooked around his neck to pull him in for her hungry lips to connect with his. She had no sane comprehension of what she was doing, instinct taking over to seize what her body so desperately wanted.

In that instant, any sort of rationality dissolved from her mind.

In a mesh of lips and tongues, they came together, devouring each other, her fingers digging into his scalp, one of his hands sweeping up her back and nestling into her hair, clasping her head tightly.

His taste filled her, his warm breath merging with her own, sending deeper darts of need into her, every part of her aching for his touch, his kiss, his caress...

Michelle Smart's love affair with books started as a baby, when she would cuddle them in her cot. A voracious reader of all genres, she found her love of romance established when she stumbled across her first Harlequin Presents® book at the age of twelve. She's been reading (and writing) them ever since. Michelle lives in Northamptonshire with her husband and two young Smarties.

Books by Michelle Smart

Harlequin Presents®

The Russian's Ultimatum
The Rings That Bind

The Irresistible Sicilians

What a Sicilian Husband Wants
The Sicilian's Unexpected Duty
Taming the Notorious Sicilian

Visit the Author Profile page
at Harlequin.com for more titles.

The Perfect Cazorla Wife

This book is dedicated to Pippa, my wonderful editor.
Thank you for everything you do—
I couldn't do any of this without you.

CHAPTER ONE

THE MOONLIGHT THAT poured over the mountaintop hotel gave it an ethereal, mysterious quality. From one perspective it looked enticing, welcoming. From Charley's perspective, the shadows it cast spelled danger. The moonlight shouldn't be silver. It should be red.

But this was no time for imagined threats. She was here for one purpose and one purpose only.

Taking a fortifying deep breath, she waited for the barrier to rise then drove through and parked in the main car park. No valet approached to whisk her Fiat 500 off to the secure parking area filled with Ferraris, Lamborghinis, Maseratis and the like.

Ambient music greeted her in the sprawling lobby where hotel guests were lounging around in their finery sipping on pre- and post-dinner drinks. She didn't make eye contact with anyone, intent on slipping through to the function room at the back.

The closer her steps took her, the louder the thuds of her heart grew. By the time she reached the door, the beats inside her were so loud the ambient music was completely drowned out.

A barrel of a man materialised, preventing her entry into the room.

'Your invitation, please,' he said, holding out his hand.

'My husband arrived earlier,' she answered in hesitant

Spanish. She'd lived in the country for over five years but only in recent months did she feel she'd got an actual grip on the language. She still kept her phrasebook in her handbag just in case. 'He left word that I would be getting here late,' she lied.

'Your husband?'

Charley reached into her silver clutch bag, removed her passport and handed it over. 'Raul Cazorla.' She imagined how her soon-to-be ex-husband would react if he were in this situation and tried to channel some of his arrogance. She held her phone up. 'Would you like me to call him so he can come and verify who I am?'

She could see the guard debating what to do. No doubt he had taken Raul's invitation himself. No doubt he had clocked the flame-haired lingerie model on his arm too.

Thinking of that lingerie model...

A host of bitter feelings curdled in Charley's belly, just as they had two weeks ago when the first picture of the happy couple had been spread on the cover of one of Spain's high-end glossies. Raul had looked like the cat who'd licked the bowl dry of all the cream, which Charley supposed wasn't all that surprising. Physically, Jessica was perfect.

She doubted the model was his first lover since she'd left, just the first he'd publicly acknowledged.

Who he saw was none of her business, she reminded herself. In a few short weeks their divorce would be finalised. He would be a free agent.

She inhaled deeply and narrowed her eyes, little signs she had seen Raul perform hundreds of times to denote his displeasure at whatever situation was occurring. 'Perhaps you would prefer to find him yourself and ask him to confirm who I am?'

She knew her words had done the trick when the guard

placed his hand on the door to admit her. Who wanted to be the man to seek out Raul Cazorla, one of Spain's richest men, in the middle of a high-society party, to ask him if the woman bearing his name really was his wife?

'Enjoy the party,' he said, opening the door.

The function room of Barcelona's Hotel Garcia was a mass of glitz and silver and heaving with glamorous bodies. Unlike the easy jazz music of the lobby, here a DJ was playing a set, popular dance music throbbing beneath her already aching feet. It had been nearly two years since she'd last worn high heels and all the bones in her feet were protesting.

Waiters and waitresses armed with trays of champagne and *hors d'oeuvres* mingled discreetly, but close enough for Charley to swipe a flute of champagne and drink it in one swallow.

As she scoured the room she became aware of curious eyes watching her, imagined she could hear the whispers of, 'Is that Charlotte…?'

She tuned them out, focusing her attention on the open French doors that led out into the expansive gardens and the balmy night air.

The garden was alive with revellers sitting on the many iron tables and chairs scattered over the lawn, people talking, smoking, kissing…

Her heart recognised him first, accelerating to a gallop as she spotted the tall, muscular frame standing in the far distance, his back to her, a hand in his pocket. He was deep in conversation with a man she didn't recognise. On the table beside them sat two women chatting between themselves. The redhead took a long drag of a cigarette.

Raul hates smoking, she thought faintly.

For a horrible moment she thought she was going to be sick.

She'd barely taken a step when he turned his head as if sensing eyes upon him.

He tilted his face a touch in her direction then turned back to the gentleman he was talking to and carried on his conversation.

Gathering all her courage, Charley began to walk. She'd only taken a few steps when he turned his head again. This time his eyes fixed directly on her.

He twisted his body round fully to face her.

As she neared him he became more than just a figure in the distance. Step by step he seemed to expand and flesh out, becoming solid. Becoming Raul.

He was as handsome as her tortured mind remembered.

Dimly she noted the dark hair cropped short, the black bow tie loosened around his neck, the perfectly tailored handmade suit hugging his snake hips...

By the time she reached the table, all conversation between his companions had stopped. In particular, she could feel the redhead's eyes boring into her.

'Hello, Raul,' Charley said softly, the anger that had propelled her to gatecrash this party diminishing as she took in the face she had last seen in the flesh almost two years ago.

If her appearance shocked him, he hid it well. He'd always been able to hide his emotions well. Apart from in the bedroom...

'Charlotte,' he said, leaning forward to place a kiss on both her cheeks. 'This is an unexpected pleasure.'

At least, those were the words his mouth said. His eyes spoke a different tale. Even through the tingling on her cheek where his lips had met her skin, she could see the fire spitting from them.

When he next spoke she could hear the tightness of his vocal cords. 'Excuse me, Andres, ladies.' With those polite parting words, he bore her away, taking hold of her arm and clasping it tightly enough to prevent her escaping but not so hard as to hurt.

Eyes followed them as they walked in silence to the far corner of the garden, the part where discreet benches were placed amongst the blooming flowers for lovers to be alone. With every step she took, Charley forced her mind to concentrate, to remember the words she'd spent the day rehearsing.

Being here with him was a thousand times harder than she'd imagined it would be.

The last time she'd seen her husband had been exactly six hundred and thirty-three days ago.

The last time she'd seen her husband they'd been screaming at each other, real hate and fury spilling out like a bunch of fireworks detonating in one big bang. She'd left that night and hadn't seen him since.

She'd thought all the hurt and anger from that evening and everything that had led up to it had gone, that she was over it and moving on with her life. To feel the same maelstrom of emotions stirring within her scared her more than anything she'd experienced since that night.

She could feel him trying to rein in his own fury too, in subtle ways that only someone who'd been intimate with him for a long time would recognise. Someone like his wife.

Only when they were safely out of sight, hidden behind a cherry tree laden with fruit, did he drop her arm and glower down at her. 'What are you doing here, Charlotte?'

'I'm here to speak to you.'

'That much is obvious. The question is why have you wormed your way into this party when I've made it clear I have no wish to see you?'

His words shouldn't feel like a slap to the face. But they

did. They stung as badly as his refusal to take her calls and as badly as when he'd cancelled the appointment she'd made to see him less than an hour after his PA had put it in his diary. Charley had heard the mortification in Ava's voice when she'd called her back with the bad news.

'I need your help,' she said with a helpless shrug, gazing intently into the pale blue eyes she'd once adored. The very first time she'd caught a glimpse of him it had felt as if her heart expanded enough to consume the rest of her. The high cheekbones, the full lips offset by a firm jaw...

She blinked and looked away. Raul's intense masculinity that bordered on beauty had turned her brain to mush before. She needed to keep her head together, not plunge back five years to a time when her libido did her thinking for her. This was her one chance to convince him to help her. 'Did you get my letter and the finance report I put with it?'

His throat emitted a sound of disgust. 'Are you talking about the begging letter I received a couple of days ago?'

She rubbed an eye and immediately wished she hadn't. She'd spent an *age* applying her make-up, unpractised after almost two years of not wearing it, and in one frustrated rub had probably ruined it. But she needed to look the part, not just to gain access to the party but to convince Raul to take her pleas seriously. Image was everything to her estranged husband. Regardless of what occurred behind closed doors, the public face had to be perfect.

'So you've read it?'

Raul had taken one look at the girlish handwriting on the envelope and known immediately who it was from. Charley's writing was undeveloped, as if she were stuck at age twelve.

It suddenly struck him that her handwriting was something she'd always been embarrassed about. She must have been really desperate to get in touch with him in this manner.

At the time he'd received her letter, though, he hadn't been thinking of anything like that. Seeing her handwriting there before him had hit him low in his gut, churning up so many emotions he'd screwed the envelope into a tight ball and thrown it at the wall. A good hour had passed before he'd retrieved it and taken a look at the content of her letter. He'd barely got a third of the way through before screwing it back up again. The finance report—and he used that term loosely—had gone straight in the shredding pile.

'I read enough to know you're after more of my money.' He'd transferred ten million euros into her account not long after she'd left, a reminder to her of everything she was giving up. He'd fully expected her to come crawling back. He'd *still* been expecting her to come crawling back a year later when the divorce papers had landed on his doorstep.

But now those millions had dried up and here she was, dressed to the nines, trying to get her greedy hands on more.

'I'm not after your money. Did you read the bit about the Poco Rio day care centre?'

'Yes.' It was as far as he'd got before the words had blurred in his eyes.

Poco Rio day care centre. Those five words had been the reason his hands had fisted the letter into a ball the second time. It had been his estranged wife's refusal to have a child with him that had killed their marriage.

He'd pumped an endless supply of money into her failed business ventures and now she had the nerve to ask him for money to fund yet another business, this one involving children, when she'd strung him along for three years with the promise of one.

He'd never thought of her as a sadist.

'Then you know how important this is. I've found the ideal premises but the owner won't hold onto them for ever. Either I complete the sale in the next month or he's pulling out. Please, Raul, there isn't time to find new premises. We've got four months left until we're kicked out of our current home and—'

'None of this concerns me. This is *your* problem.'

'But I'm running out of time! The place I've found is perfect. The grounds are enormous and, once all the renovations are done, the building itself will be ten times better than the one we're currently in and we'll be able to double the number of children.'

'As I said, this is your concern, not mine.'

'But without you I can't get the rest of the funding. I've tried everything...'

'Then try harder. Maybe this time you'll actually see something through to the end rather than giving up halfway through.'

She sucked in her cheeks at his home truth but met his gaze head-on. 'I won't give up this time. I *can't*. But no one's prepared to invest.'

'Then either your business plan needs working on or you need to change your résumé. Maybe you should consider changing the truth into lies and hope no one bothers to check it.' He backed away and nodded his head. 'I've given you enough of my time—my date will be feeling neglected. I trust you can see yourself out?'

She blanched at the mention of his date.

He waited for gratification to hit him but all he felt was something akin to guilt, although why that should be the case he couldn't begin to fathom. Charley had left *him*. After three years of his lavishing his money on her, helping her to improve herself, supporting her, giving her everything she desired…she'd refused him a child.

After three years of stringing him along, dangling the promise of a child over his head, she'd finally admitted the truth. She didn't want to have his baby.

Their whole marriage had been a lie, reduced to nothing but a cauldron of recrimination and hate.

And now she had the nerve to ask for his help.

Yet, staring at her now, her skin as pure as alabaster under the moonlight, Raul had to clench his hands into fists and hold them tightly to his sides to prevent them reaching out to touch her.

The first time he'd met her, he'd just taken over the running of the Cazorla Hotel chain, the family business run by his father until he'd suffered a major stroke. Despite having his own successful, unconnected business to run, Raul had stepped up to the plate and taken over. The stroke had left his father physically disabled and unable to speak but he'd perfectly conveyed the disgust he felt at this occurrence. Raul had known it was the thought of *him* taking over rather than his new physical situation his father had hated the most. He knew his father despised the roaring success he'd made of the business since.

Back then, he'd been in Majorca to inspect the Cazorla hotel there, as he'd done in turn with the whole chain, refamiliarising himself with the business. This hotel had been markedly different from the others, having turned into a family hotel over the years rather than a luxury resort as the others in the chain were famous for. Charley had been employed by an outside Spanish company as one of the entertainers there.

He'd first seen her late in the evening, leaving the complex, dressed in shorts, a shimmering top and flip-flops, long honey-blonde hair flowing around her shoulders.

She'd been laughing at something a friend had said, a deep, throaty laugh without inhibition that had made him smile to hear it. He'd spotted her again the next evening. She'd been on the stage running a game show that involved audience participation. She'd been funny and energetic and had the guests, young and old alike, eating out of her hand. He'd sought her out when the show finished, about to head out with her colleagues to party the rest of the night away. It hadn't taken much persuasion to get her to change her plans and join him instead.

Appearancewise, she couldn't have been more different from how she looked now in her expensive tight red dress with the plunging neckline that showcased her creamy cleavage and matching red heels. As soon as she'd been given access to his bank account, her style had changed dramatically, her wardrobe suddenly full of impeccable designer items.

Tonight, her long, thick hair had been dyed a warm blonde but he had no doubt it would be a different colour in a few weeks. Her hair changed more frequently than her ever-shifting career choices.

Her perfectly made up green eyes blinked rapidly as she pulled her generous lips into a tight white line. She reached out an imploring hand before quickly letting it drop. 'You're the only one who can help me. I've finally found a bank prepared to invest in the project but they'll only give me the rest of the funds if you act as guarantor.'

'What the...?' He bit away the oath that jumped on his tongue and glared at her, ignoring the plea ringing from her eyes. 'That's even worse than asking me for money outright. You must be mad if you think I would guarantee money on any business venture you embarked on. After all, I threw away millions of euros during our marriage on your failed ventures—'

A thought occurred to him. 'Why would the bank manager request I act as your guarantor? We've been separated for two years. Our divorce, which I remind you has come at *your* instigation, will be finalised in a few weeks.'

Her teeth sank sharply into her bottom lip and she cast her eyes down in a decidedly shamefaced manner. 'I…'

'What did you do?' His wife was nothing if not impulsive. She could have done anything.

'I…I told him we'd got back together.'

'You did *what*?'

She met his gaze with a cringe. 'I didn't know what else to do…'

'Let me get this straight—you told a bank manager we were back together so you could get investment on your latest hare-brained project?'

'It is *not* hare-brained,' she protested hotly, displaying the first real hint of fire since she'd gatecrashed the party. 'Without the funding, the children have nowhere to go.'

'That is *not* my problem.' The anger that had been simmering within him pushed to the surface. 'I don't care what lies you've told, I want nothing to do with it and nothing to do with you. This is your mess and your responsibility to sort out. Goodbye.'

Leaving her standing there open-mouthed, he strode away. He hadn't got more than a few metres before she called out to him.

'It isn't too late for me to sue for a slice of your fortune, you know.'

He came to an abrupt halt.

Now the truth of this meeting was revealed.

'Our divorce isn't final yet. I can call my lawyer Monday morning and tell him I've changed my mind and now want the large settlement he said I could have.'

Slowly he turned to face her, heart thundering, his brain burning. She dared to *threaten* him?

He did not take threats from anyone, especially not the woman who'd shared his bed for three years and milked him for everything she could before walking out on him.

'Yes, you can call your lawyer and, yes, a court will probably compel me to give you some of what you ask for. I've always been generous with you—it was your choice not to ask for more than I'd already given.' He'd been suspicious to find she didn't want more of his wealth than the ten million euros. Probably she'd seen all the zeros in her account and assumed it would last for ever. He was surprised it lasted as long as it had.

Somehow he found himself right back in front of her with no memory of his legs having moved.

'Any court case will take months, if not years, to settle so will come too late to save your latest business.' He allowed himself a smile as he leaned down to place his face inches from hers so she could follow his lips and their meaning more closely. 'In the meantime, you will have ample time to consider the folly of your extravagant ways and the consequences of your lies.'

This time he walked away without her calling him back.

As he rejoined the party the sight of her hurt, shocked face played heavily on his mind.

His date, Jessica, stared at him coolly, taking a long drag of her cigarette. 'What was that about?'

He looked at her. They'd been dating for almost a month, his first foray into the dating world since Charley had walked out.

Jessica was tall, lithe and beautiful, regularly featuring at the top of sexiest women polls. She was poised, cool and considered, and looked fantastic on his arm.

Charley was inches shorter and considerably curvier.

She was warm and impulsive with a laugh that warmed you to hear it. She smelled of fresh vanilla.

He could still smell her now.

'Well?' Jessica demanded, crunching her cigarette out in the ashtray.

Charley had always smelled gorgeous, especially first thing in the morning when the vanilla had turned to musk and mingled with the scent of their night's lovemaking.

He *hated* the smell of smoke. Was it any wonder he'd been loath to even kiss Jessica?

A dart of red crossed the periphery of his vision. He turned his head to see Charley hurry back into the hotel. Even from this distance he could see the dejection in her demeanour.

Forcing a smile at Jessica, he ignored her question. 'One more drink and then we'll make a move.'

Not giving her the chance to respond, he headed back into the hotel and the heaving function room. As he fought his way to the bar, bypassing the waiting staff and their trays of champagne—he needed something much stiffer than *that* to drink—he kept an eye out for a vision in red but she was nowhere to be seen.

Charley had gone.

CHAPTER TWO

CHARLEY FORCED A polite smile and an even politer *adiós*, and left the bank manager's office. Her chest felt so tight she struggled to breathe. Swallowing in a vain attempt to open her airways, she stepped into the lobby of the enormous building that housed her bank and a dozen other institutions, and headed straight to the ladies' room, locking herself in the nearest cubicle.

It was over.

The manager had been as good as his word. Without Raul to act as guarantor, there would be no loan.

She'd known her chances of getting the manager to change his mind had been slim but had refused to be defeated. Slim was a better chance than zero.

And now it was all over. That last glimmer of hope had died. Zero chance had become reality.

Clamping a hand over her mouth, she stifled a sob.

Despite all her efforts, Poco Rio would lose its home and close.

Those poor children. Whatever she felt was nothing in comparison to how it would affect them and their families. God alone knew they'd already suffered enough in their short lives.

She had to hold her hands up and admit defeat. There were no avenues left to explore. She'd done everything she could, even turning to Raul for help.

Another sob formed in her throat as she recalled how he'd thrown her desperate plea back in her face. She'd never have believed he could be so heartless, had had no idea he was still harbouring the fury that had underpinned the end of their marriage. Then, his fury, his loss of control, would have been frightening if her own anger hadn't matched his.

How clearly she remembered the reasonable tone he'd always adopted when discussing her failings. '*Cariño*,' he'd said, 'it is time for you to accept you are not business-minded. You have tried but now it is time for us to make the family we once talked of having.'

She remembered even more clearly how her blood, her skin, her bones—every part of her—had chilled at his words.

Bring a baby into this marriage?

Up until that point, having children was something she'd looked forward to having but in the future, after she'd found her niche in life.

Her own mother had worked hard to put food in Charley's belly. The fact she'd thrown away all her mum's hard work in her teenage years was something she'd become deeply ashamed of and determined to rectify. When she had a child of her own, she wanted her baby to look up to her. She didn't want her own children comparing their parents and seeing a father who was a roaring success and a mother who was a dismal failure. She wanted her husband and children to be proud of her, to see her as a successful woman in her own right.

It hadn't been on her mind to leave him but when she'd tried to explain why this still wasn't the right moment to have a baby, everything had turned on its head and somehow they'd been in each other's faces, shouting words she no longer remembered in detail but remembered the meaning behind.

Gold-digger and *failure* were two of his choice accusations that still rang clear and still had the power to make her stomach contract with pain. Those accusations had hurt terribly. She'd tried so *hard* to make a success of those businesses, had been desperate to impress him with something other than her body. But she had reached too high, she could see that now. Desperation had clouded her judgement; she had reached the stage where she couldn't see the wood for the trees. The trees had become so thick she couldn't see a way out either.

And then he'd told her to leave.

It had been like a light bulb going off in her skull. All the things she'd been in denial about had come to the forefront and with them had come the realisation that she couldn't do it any more. She couldn't be the woman he'd tried to shape her into being.

By the time she'd finished packing, he'd calmed down enough to tell her, not ask her, that he wanted her to stay. But it had been too late. Raul wanted perfection and she was far from perfect. She'd known as clearly as she knew her own name that their marriage was dead.

So why did she feel so heartsick to think about him? Why did she feel not just upset that he'd thrown her pleas for help back at her but a bone-deep misery that had stopped her eating more than a slice of toast since the party two days ago?

Only when she was certain she could keep the threatening tears at bay long enough to return home did Charley leave the ladies' room, making sure a smile lay on her lips. That was one of the things the decorum tutor Raul had employed had drilled into her: always show a pleasant demeanour whatever the circumstances. Image was everything to the Cazorlas.

Her head ached, hurting much worse than the time she'd swallowed too large a lump of ice cream and got brain-freeze. The brilliant Valencian sunshine magnified it and she shielded her eyes as she stepped outside.

Her car was parked around the corner but before she could walk to it her vision cleared and she made out the tall figure leaning against an illegally parked silver Lotus at the front of the building, arms crossed over his broad chest.

'Raul?'

For a moment she was too stunned to move or say anything else.

Seeing him in full daylight, gorgeous in a dark blue suit and light blue shirt that made the colour in his eyes gleam, threatened to knock what little stuffing she had left out of her heart.

This wasn't a coincidence. It couldn't be. Over the years Raul had wined and dined all the major players of the Spanish banks. He had all the best contacts. His web covered everywhere.

He'd probably known the outcome of her meeting before she had.

Suddenly it became clear what he was here for.

She marched over to him. 'Here to gloat, are you?'

He unfolded his arms and straightened, his pale blue eyes fixed on her without expression.

'No, *cariño*.' The faintest of smiles tugged at his sensuous lips. 'I'm here to offer you a lifeline.'

She studied him carefully, trying to read his face.

'What kind of lifeline?' she asked, not hiding her wariness.

'The kind of lifeline that will save your centre.'

Raul watched a dozen emotions flitter over her pretty face as she digested his words.

'You're going to help me?'

He allowed himself another smile and opened the passenger door of the Lotus. 'Get in and we'll discuss the matter.'

'Tell me where to go and I'll meet you. I've got my own car here.'

She could drive now? That was news to him.

'If you want the lifeline for the centre that means so much to you, I suggest you get in. This is a one-off discussion. When I leave, the offer of my help leaves with me.' Not waiting for a reaction, he sidled round and got into the driver's side.

It was only when he shut his door and fastened his seat belt that Charley galvanised herself into action, jumping in beside him and shutting the passenger door with a slam.

He put his sunglasses on before turning to face her, taking stock of the designer black suit she wore and the way her hair hung loose around her shoulders. It surprised him to find her make-up-free bar a touch of eyeliner and mascara. His wife normally made her face up so artfully that not the slightest imperfection showed; at least she had after she'd been given access to his bank account and had hit the high-class department stores. When he'd first met her she'd been as fresh-faced as she was today.

His loins tightened as he caught her vanilla scent. He'd been imagining that scent since she'd gatecrashed the party.

She stared right back at him, confusion and suspicion vying in her look.

He experienced a surge of satisfaction.

He had her exactly where he wanted her.

With a half-smile on his face, he shifted the car into gear and joined the rest of the traffic on the street.

'Are you serious about helping me?' she asked in the throaty tone he remembered so well.

'Why else would I be here?'

On Saturday night, his only intention had been to let her stew in the mess of her own making and get on with his life.

Charley had left him. She was nothing but a gold-digger who'd played him for a fool. She deserved *nothing*.

He'd dropped Jessica home after the party and returned to his own house alone, just as he'd slept alone since Charley had left him.

He'd lain awake, his mind drifting back to the nights he'd spent with his wife, remembering the curves of her body, the softness of her skin, the scent of their sex…for the first time in two years, his libido had awoken.

One short, angry conversation with his wife and his body—every part of it—had come back to life in a way it hadn't in the whole of their two years apart.

He'd recalled their conversation in minute detail, over and over, Charley vivid behind his eyes. He couldn't block her out.

When the sun came up he'd still been lying there, his mind still racing in a hundred different directions.

Not caring that it was a Sunday morning and that they would likely be in bed, he'd used his contacts to learn more about the finances behind her venture, including speaking to a businessman she'd pitched to.

He learned Charley only had the personal funds to pay for half the building costs. He dreaded to think what she'd blown the rest of the money he'd given her on.

Financially, her name was toxic. No investor would

touch her. Her own bank wouldn't touch her without his name as guarantor.

She'd explored all other avenues and now it was down to him and him alone to save her project.

Well, she would damn well pay the price for it, starting today.

'You're going to lend me the money?'

'Better than that—I'm going to give it to you.'

He let that sink in, letting her realise in her own sweet time that he alone had what was needed to make her dream a reality.

'Are you seriously serious?'

He almost laughed. He'd forgotten the way she had with words. 'Yes.'

'I'm assuming this offer comes with a catch.'

'Nothing in life comes free, *cariño*.' He felt her bristle at the use of his old name for her. Good. By the end of the day she would be doing a lot more than bristling beside him. By the time the sun went down she would be back in his bed beneath him.

Celibacy had not been a conscious decision. It was only as he'd lain in his bed thinking about her that he'd realised why he'd not found another bedmate.

How could he be with another woman when his wife still lived in his blood?

Charley hadn't just gatecrashed the party, she'd gatecrashed her way straight back under his skin. And he knew just the way to exorcise her once and for all.

'What's your catch?'

'We will discuss the terms when we get home.'

'You're taking me to Barcelona?'

'*Sí*. And when we get to my home we will share a civilised lunch and discuss the terms of the deal in detail. For now, you can rest your mind knowing that if you agree to my terms, the building you want to buy will be a done deal.'

Charley bit into her bottom lip and balled her hands into fists, digging her nails into the palms of her hands. If her nails were as long as she'd kept them when she'd been with Raul, she would have inflicted pain upon herself. Now they were short and practical and produced only the dullest of aches. Nowhere near enough to distract from the turmoil playing in her belly.

'Can you at least tell me why you changed your mind about helping me?'

'We will discuss everything when we get home.'

She wanted to demand answers but forced herself to think rationally. Right now he was being cordial towards her, his attitude a marked improvement to the loathing he hadn't bothered to hide at the party. He was here and, if he was as good as his word, prepared to help her. At that moment, that was all that mattered. Anything else she could worry about later. Antagonising him would accomplish nothing.

If she had to suffer his company then for the children's sake she would gladly accept it.

Her head might term it as suffering, but her body had a different word for the reaction provoked by being in the close confines of the car with him. It was familiar torture: her lungs tight, her pulse loose, her skin alive with awareness.

She breathed out slowly and peeked at him from the corner of her eye. Her heart swelled to see his sleeves rolled up, his tanned left arm resting on the ledge of the open window. Unlike most people with his wealth, Raul preferred to drive himself unless he was drinking. The first of his birthdays that they'd celebrated together, she'd bought him a day's racing at a racetrack. He'd been too well-bred to tell her he'd already raced on it a dozen times, happy that she'd bought something that actually meant something to him.

They'd been happy then. *She'd* been happy then.

She blinked the memories away and fixed her gaze on the road ahead.

A few minutes later they were at the heliport where his pilot awaited them, ready to take them back to Barcelona.

Charley stared up at Raul's home with a definite sense of awe and trepidation.

'When did you move in here?' she asked.

'A year ago,' came the curt reply.

In direct contrast to the old villa, which had been set in a private enclave by the beach, Raul's new villa was located in the exclusive neighbourhood of Avenida Tibidabo. Surrounded by high-security gates that in turn were lined with palm trees, the villa was three-storey, with cream outer walls and turrets, all topped with terracotta roofs.

Intuition told her she was walking into a trap, although she couldn't fathom what it could be. Once she knew exactly what he wanted from her she'd deal with it. It was the not knowing that made her feel so tense, that and being back in the company of the man whose masculinity she'd always found so very potent. It shamed her that even now, after so much water had passed beneath the bridge, her body was as alert to him as it had always been.

The villa's differences internally were as marked as the location. The home they'd shared by the beach, although just as grand, had been modern. This villa was steeped in splendour, with mosaicked floors and high, arched frescoed ceilings, a sense of history breathing through the whitewashed walls.

Here was the evidence, if she hadn't already guessed it by his two years of silence, that Raul had moved on.

She swallowed the acrid taste that had formed in the back of her throat. 'Where are the staff?' At this time of day the house should be teeming with activity, especially on a Monday.

'I told the household staff to take the day off.' Raul's eyes gleamed with something she couldn't interpret. 'I thought it best for us to be alone.'

Low, down in the juncture of her thighs, heat pulsed and licked through her veins.

How *could* she still react to him like that, as if the past two years had never happened?

She rubbed her arms, her trepidation growing with each passing second. 'What are the terms you want to talk about? Only, I'm working at the centre tomorrow and want to get back to Valencia before it gets late.'

'We can talk while we eat.'

She followed him through to a dining room with huge windows that looked out onto the villa's gardens. The sun shone down, beaming on the manicured lawn and the abundance of flowers and shrubs.

A long dark wood table had been set for two. Raul pulled a chair out for her. 'Lunch has been prepared for us. Make yourself at home.'

Home? She gagged at the thought. This would never be her home. In a few weeks they would be officially divorced. She was almost counting the days.

She sat gingerly, running her fingers over the silver cutlery in silent contemplation.

Any moment now and his real motive for bringing her here would be revealed. She doubted it was to do with the money. Unlike Charley, who'd proven herself to be a spectacular failure in business, her husband had a habit of turning whatever he touched into gold. Much as she tried to avoid reading media reports on him, it was like telling a child not to touch the nice shiny toy in the corner. Already worth hundreds of millions, he'd sold the technology firm he'd founded and run before his father's stroke had forced him to take over the running of the Cazorla luxury hotel chain. The sale had earned him a reported two and a half billion euros. Since taking over the family firm he'd added a fleet of aeroplanes and half a dozen brand spanking new cruise liners to the stable.

Simply speaking, her husband was worth more than entire countries.

If she'd taken her lawyer's advice she could have taken a good slice of his wealth, far exceeding the ten million he'd transferred into her account without consulting her. She hadn't wanted to take even that, had left it untouched for months. It was Raul's money, not hers. She'd contributed nothing to it so why should she have a claim to it?

She'd spent enough of his money during their marriage as it was.

He came back into the dining room carrying a platter of antipasto: deli meats, marinated vegetables, roasted peppers and sundried tomatoes, olives, cheese, rustic breads... all her favourite bites. And to think this was only the first course...

He poured her a glass of the red wine that had been left to breathe on the table, then raised his glass in a toast before swallowing half his wine and taking the seat beside her.

Charley couldn't bear it a moment longer. 'This all looks delicious and I thank you, but I can't eat anything until you tell me what your terms are.'

Helping himself to a little of everything before them, Raul took a bite of some bread then fixed his eyes on her as he ate. Once he'd swallowed and taken another drink of his wine, he answered. 'I am prepared to give you the money you need to buy the building and for all the renovations that will be needed to make the day care centre fit for purpose.'

She returned his stare, waiting for the catch that was surely coming.

'When do you have to get the renovations done by?' he asked. 'Four months, was it?'

'Yes. The new owners agreed to give us six months to relocate.' She watched him with caution. 'Two of those months have already gone.'

The owner of the building that housed Poco Rio had died unexpectedly, leaving the team who worked there rudderless. Worse still, his family had not shared his sentimentality and opted to sell to a developer, only telling the staff about it when it was a done deal.

'Four months to complete the purchase and the renovations?'

'It sounds like a long time but it isn't. We need to make it as safe and as suitable for the children's needs as it can possibly be. Walls need to be knocked down, doorways need to be extended...'

Raul made a dismissive motion with his hand. 'All of that can be discussed when we have reached an agreement.'

'But what is it you want me to agree to?' she asked in bewilderment. 'The centre receives sufficient funds to repay any loan.'

His lips curved upwards. It was like looking at a sensuous shark. 'As I said earlier, I will not be giving you a loan. With your track record, who knows when I will get it back?'

Her ire, already simmering at his mocking attitude, rose. 'I already told you...'

'You have the business acumen of a child. I trust your figures as much as I trust your judgement.'

'My judgement must have been seriously off when I married *you*.'

She regretted her hotly spat words before they'd left her tongue. So much for not antagonising him until the deal was done.

Raul's smile remained but his eyes had turned to ice. 'It is a shame you feel that way but it's not a sentiment I happen to share.

'When I say *giving* I do not mean it in the literal sense. I *will* require a form of payment but not one of monetary value.'

She'd known it. From the minute she'd got into his car she'd known there was a catch involved.

'My condition for giving you the money and for giving your project all the skills and expertise at my disposal is modest. I want you back in my bed and living with me as my wife until the work on the new building is complete.'

CHAPTER THREE

THE COLOUR DRAINED so quickly from Charley's face that Raul braced himself to steady her should she faint.

Then the colour returned, her cheeks staining a dark, angry red.

'What do you mean, *live as your wife*? We're getting a divorce.'

'Which we can put on hold.' Deliberately he drained his wine. 'If you want this new home for the centre, then that's the payment I require.'

'But *why*? Of all the things you could want, why that? Until Saturday night we hadn't spoken in almost two years. Our marriage is dead.'

'Our divorce isn't finalised.' He swallowed a plump black olive. 'We will put it on hiatus until the renovation work is complete and the centre reopened.'

'I don't see why that means we have to pretend to be back together.'

'There won't be any pretence about it. But to answer your question, I will be donating a considerable amount of money to your project and I want to be there to make sure you don't give up on it halfway through.'

'I would never do that.'

'You founded three different businesses in our time together. They all failed because you lost interest, failed to take the good advice I gave you, and let things slip. I won't just be backing this project; I'll be taking control of it.'

She winced at his cold assessment of her failures but understood his meaning immediately. 'You haven't the faintest idea what the project entails or what's needed for the renovations.'

'You will be by my side to assist me. Think of it as a learning curve. Four months to learn how to run a business properly rather than rely upon guesswork. After all,' he continued, 'it won't be my bank balance that suffers if you fail but the children and families you've made promises to.'

More angry colour flooded her cheeks. Her green eyes darkened, her fury as easy to read as a book.

He refused to feel any sympathy.

Charley loved children. He'd seen that from the first. They'd discussed starting a family of their own and he'd shown great patience in her request that they wait a few years so she could make something of herself first.

He'd lavished her with everything she desired.

In return she'd denied him what *he* desired: the baby she'd promised.

Together they would have created the perfect family.

He'd imagined their unborn child a thousand times, imagined how different a parent he would be from his own father. Not for his child the feeling of being worthless. His children's achievements would be celebrated, their failures whether minor or major understood and forgiven, their opinions valued. He would have shown his father what being a father was *really* about. It was everything his father hadn't been.

'Take control of the project if you must,' Charley said, a tremor racing through her voice. 'Be the big alpha man you are and throw your weight and money around as you always do. So long as the centre reopens in four months' time I don't care how it's done, but there is no need to go through a charade of us being back together.'

He clenched his hands into fists, straining not to react to her inflammatory words. Taking control of situations where he was the most suitable person to take charge was not akin to throwing his weight around. She made him sound like a tyrant, which, he was certain, was deliberate. His wife might be uneducated but she was not stupid. Regardless, he would keep his cool even if she couldn't.

'I fail to see what your issue is,' he said, channelling his composure. 'You were happy to tell your bank manager the barefaced lie that we're back together when it suited you. This arrangement suits *me* but in this case it will not be a lie. For four months you will live with me as my wife and then you will be free to resume your life. But this time our marriage will end on *my* terms.'

Already he could taste the satisfaction that would bring. It might even taste as sweet as having his wife back in his bed.

The wildness he'd sensed in her from that first look had translated into the bedroom. Making love to her had always been out of this world. Whether it was hard and fast or slow and sweet, their passion for each other had been unquantifiable.

'This is your pride talking, isn't it? Because I had the nerve to leave you? You want to humiliate me?'

'Not at all,' he answered with deliberate smoothness, counteracting the vibrations emanating from her delectable frame. A charge flickered through his loins to see her face become the same colour it rose to when in the throes of passion. 'You want my help and I'm prepared to give it to you but in return I want payment—and the only form of payment you are in a position to make is with your body.'

She pushed her chair back as if she'd been scalded and got to her feet. 'You want me to prostitute myself?'

'I'm merely requesting that you, my wife, return to the

marital bed for a fixed period and in that period you make yourself available to me wherever and whenever I require.'

The charge in his loins tightened at the thought of her doing whatever pleased him. All those years when he'd done everything in his power to please her, in bed and out...now the tables had turned and it was her subjugation he required. For a limited time.

Yes, four months should serve him perfectly. During their marriage they'd spent a substantial amount of time apart, the distance always stoking the flames of lust so when they were together they made the most of every minute. This time, he would keep her by his side continuously so the lust they shared would finally be slaked and he could walk away from her without a backwards glance. Just as she had walked away from him.

Charley's legs felt wobbly. *Everything* felt wobbly. She hadn't touched a morsel of food, knew she wouldn't be able to swallow it past her throat.

'In all the years I've known you, I've never hated you.' Her body trembling, she forced her eyes to keep their gaze on his cool, unflinching stare. 'I hate you right now, more than I thought it was possible to hate another human being.'

He rose and, although he smiled down at her, his eyes were like ice. 'I don't care for your hate any more than I care for your love.' He reached out a hand and slipped it under the open top buttons of her blouse to rest on her collarbone.

She didn't want to react to the feel of his warm fingers on her skin...

She held her breath, his touch setting off a charge within her, certain he must be able to feel the hammering of her heart.

It was the first time he'd touched her in so, *so* long.

His voice dropped to a murmur. 'I am willing to give

you what you want. Are you willing to give me what *I* want? Because, let us speak frankly, it's the only thing you're any good at.'

If his thumb hadn't found the exact spot on her neck that always sent tingles of need and delight rippling through her, Charley might have reacted to his words a little quicker. As it was, it took a few moments for them to sink in and when they did she wrenched his hand away and pushed at his chest.

'How dare you reduce me to nothing but a plaything? I'm not a sex toy.'

The ice in his eyes melted into a gleam, as if he'd accepted a challenge. He reclosed the gap between them, trapping her against the table. 'You never had a problem being my sex toy before.'

Heat streamed through her at the feel of him pressed against her, all the memories she'd spent six hundred and thirty-five days trying to forget pouring into her mind.

She had lusted after him from their first conversation.

He'd been like no one she'd met before. Outrageously handsome, ridiculously wealthy…everything a young woman of twenty could wish for in a man. Prince Charming had come to life and it was *her* slipper he wanted. Was it any wonder her head had been turned?

And the sex… Never had she imagined such carnal responses existed within her, the same responses that were flashing back to life now, at the time when she needed her head clear to deal with what he was demanding of her.

It had been her own misfortune that she'd mistaken lust for love and married him. What they'd shared should never have been more than a summer fling.

As hard as she'd tried to fit in—and she'd tried *so* hard—she didn't belong in his world. She was a badly educated south-east London girl; elocution lessons paid for by her husband had knocked most of her mild cockney accent out of her. She'd come from a broken family where finances were erratic. Raul had grown up with wealth and social standing and had all the arrogance such an upbringing instilled.

They couldn't have been more wrong for each other if they'd got a computer program to determine their worst matches.

But the computer would have got their desire for each other right.

'That was when I loved you,' she said hoarsely. For love *had* grown from the lust, a greater love than she'd ever imagined could exist. Leaving him had been easy. Staying away had been almost unbearable.

And now that love had twisted into hate. But the desire was still there, however deeply she'd thought she'd buried it. 'If you ever felt anything for me you wouldn't ask for such a…a *despicable* thing from me.'

'Oh, I still feel a great deal for you.' He swept his fingers up her neck, pressing even closer.

She smothered the gasp that wanted to break out at the feel of his hardness against her.

Take control, Charley. Don't show your weakness for him.

'You can't force me.' The words she'd intended to come out forcefully were expelled with a whisper. Every inhalation brought *him* into her tight lungs, that masculine smell that had become as familiar to her as the scent of her home.

Her body remembered. His scent made it sing with delight.

He laughed softly into her ear and traced his fingers up her side. 'I don't need to force you.'

As if proving his point, he cupped her breast over her blouse and ran a thumb over a nipple straining against the suddenly restrictive bra she wore. The heat that had pooled low within her deepened, and she pressed her thighs together in denial.

He could demand all he wanted, but she would never give herself to him willingly, not now he was showing his true colours, the colours her love-blinded eyes had forgiven for far too long.

Mortified at her lack of self-control, she tried to wriggle out from beneath him but he was too strong.

'See, *cariño*,' he said, smothering her hands in his own and resting them on the table by her sides, his grip unyielding. 'The desire between us is as strong as it ever was, however much you try and deny it. When I ask you to open yourself for me, your head might want to say no but your body will be begging for it.'

That his words were true only served to shame her further, which she knew for certain was his intention. She'd humiliated him by leaving him and this was the price he was forcing her to pay.

The worst of it was, her treacherous body was eager to pay the price.

'I hate you.'

'I know.' He dipped his head and nipped her earlobe. 'Imagine how incredible it will be, all that hate fuelling all that lust.'

Sensation filled her, every crevice of her coming alive at his touch and the whisper of his breath on her skin.

Two years without this...

Somehow she managed to pull her hands free from his grasp, fully intending to use them as weapons to push him off her. Instead, working of their own accord, they hooked around his neck to pull him in for her hungry lips to connect with his. She had no sane comprehension of what she was doing, instinct taking over to seize what her body so desperately wanted.

In that instant, any sort of rationality dissolved from her mind.

In a mesh of lips and tongues, they came together, devouring each other, her fingers digging into his scalp, one of his hands sweeping up her back and nestling into her hair, clasping her head tightly.

His taste filled her, his warm breath merging with her own sending deeper darts of need into her, every part of her aching for his touch, his kiss, his caress…

The hand not cradling her head so possessively swept up her thigh and under her skirt, his mouth still hot on hers, his tongue swirling in her mouth. His finger found the band of her knickers and slid beneath it to feel the heat and dampness at the heart of her.

When he found her, already swollen and aching for him, she gasped…

And then he pulled away, releasing his hold so quickly her legs would have given way if the table hadn't been there to support her.

There was the tiniest moment when she caught Raul's own dazed incomprehension before his composure snapped back into place.

He smoothed his shirt down and nodded at the window. 'The gardener,' he said tightly.

A rumbling sound played in the distance and through the glass she caught a glimpse of a figure on a ride-on mower just metres from where they were…

It was enough to bring her to her senses.

What on earth had possessed her?

She tugged her skirt back down before straightening.

A taunting smile now played on his lips. 'See, *cariño*? I was right. All that hate fuels lust beautifully.'

She wiped her mouth defiantly, loathing herself for being the one to instigate the kiss as much as she loathed him for the mocking tone of his voice and his unscrupulous mind and the power he held over her.

'It won't happen again,' she promised through ragged breaths.

'I think you've told enough lies this past week, don't you?'

Raul sat back down and reached for a breadstick, waiting for the thunder beneath his ribcage to abate.

How had things got out of hand so quickly?

He'd been taunting her, teasing her, asserting his control, spelling out to her how much he held the upper hand. He'd enjoyed it but had kept his mind firmly on the seduction in hand.

She'd been the one to kiss him, a fact that, from the look on her face, she regretted hugely.

She'd hooked her arm around his neck and his mind had gone blank, desire overshadowing everything else.

The chemistry between them had always been explosive but that…

It had felt as if a coil locked in a too-tight box had finally sprung free.

He'd been seconds away from taking her on the table.

In his haste to free the house for them, he'd forgotten about the ground staff. If he hadn't heard the sound of the mower, who knew how far they would have taken it?

She still stood by the table, her green eyes firing their hatred at him.

Who did she hate the most? Him for compelling her back into his bed? Or herself for wanting it?

'So, *cariño*, do we have a deal?' He was gratified to hear his voice functioning as normal. He would *never* allow himself to show weakness in front of her. 'The day care centre, signed, sealed, delivered and renovated in exchange for four months in my bed?'

Four months. That would surely be enough to get her out of his system once and for all.

Maybe it was fortuitous that she'd walked back into his life at this moment. He needed to move on, not just from the dissolution of their marriage but from the sexual hold she still held over him.

Her chin rose, her pretty nostrils flaring. 'Yes. I accept your terms but with one condition of my own: I won't be sharing your bed until the deeds of the building are in my hands.'

'The building will be in the Cazorla name by the end of the week.'

'Then you'll have to wait until then before you can touch me again.'

'You are not in a position to make any demands, *cariño*.'

'Of course I am.' She swallowed but didn't waver. 'You can always go running back to your girlfriend if the frustration of waiting four days gets too much for you.'

'That relationship is over.' It hadn't even started.

Her lips curled into an expression that most closely resembled a sneer, but it was a fleeting look, quickly replaced by the loathing he was becoming familiar with.

Another four days?

He could force the issue if he wanted. It wouldn't be hard. All he had to do was touch her and she'd be putty in his hands.

Another four days?

The anticipation would be delicious.

He knew his wife and what an earthy, sexual creature she was. The chemistry between them was just as potent— if not more—as it had always been.

After four days of living together, Charley would be begging him to take her.

He'd managed almost two years. Another four days would be nothing.

'What time do you finish?' Raul asked when he pulled the car to a stop outside the building that currently housed the Poco Rio day care centre.

'Five o'clock,' she answered shortly. 'Wait for me to call—I might be late.'

'I'll be here at five o'clock and you will be ready.'

Not bothering to argue or say goodbye, she shrugged a shoulder, grabbed her bag and got out, slamming the passenger door behind her. She might not be able to see his face but could easily imagine her handsome husband's wince at her treatment of his precious Lotus.

When they'd first met, her manners had been somewhat rough around the edges. She'd been taught to say please and thank you, and not speak with her mouth full, but that had been the extent of it and those few manners had been drilled into her by her primary school headmistress, not her parents. Her mum had been too busy holding down two jobs to find the energy while her dad had hardly been there, flitting in and out of their lives as and when it suited him, which had never been enough, not for her.

She'd never lived with her father, had never spent a night under his roof and had lived for the days when he would visit his only daughter.

She remembered once begging her mum to move so they could be closer to him, remembered the anxiety on her mother's face at this impossibility. Her mum would do anything for her but to move the fifty miles would mean uprooting from the support network of her own loving and hardworking family.

Before they'd married, Raul had employed various people to 'help' Charley assimilate into Spanish high society. At the time it had felt as if she were starring in a rags-to-riches film and she'd been happy to embrace the elocution and deportment lessons, the drills on social niceties.

When she was growing up, meals at home had been spent beside her exhausted mum, with trays on their laps in front of the television, the pair of them happily arguing about whatever reality television programme they'd been into at that time. They'd hardly tasted the food. Their one proper meal of the week had come every Sunday when they would go to her grandparents' for a roast dinner, everyone squashed around the small kitchen table with huge mugs of tea in front of them.

Raul's world, with meals around a fully laid dining table with jugs of iced water, expensive wine, the savouring of food and the correct order of cutlery...it had been a different world. A fantastical dream come to life. Learning all these new things had been fun! At first.

It had taken a long time for her to realise that Raul had set out from the off to improve her so he could stand beside her without her being an embarrassment to the Cazorla name.

Their whole marriage had been about him moulding her into the sort of woman he believed she should be, the perfect wife he so desired.

She might have missed him terribly these past six hundred and thirty-six days but she had also been able to reclaim herself.

Leaving him had let her breathe again. She didn't have to introduce herself to people as Charlotte any more. She could simply be who she'd always been: Charley, the name Raul had never once addressed her by.

Whatever happened over these next four months, she

would not allow herself to lose sight of who she really was. Charley. Charlotte was merely the name on her birth certificate.

Inside the centre, she was greeted by Karin, a nine-year-old girl who'd been in a car crash as a baby. The crash had killed her father and left her with one functioning lung and severe brain damage. Yet, however locked in her own world Karin seemed, she always appeared to know when Charley was on the rota to work and would hang around the door of the day room until she arrived.

Charley scooped the skinny child up and planted a kiss on her cheek then gently set her back down and took her hand. Karin would be her shadow for the rest of the day, her easy affection something that warmed her heart.

A lump came to her throat as she looked at the dozen children in the day room, many locked in their own worlds, most of them here and alive against all the odds. *This* was what she was fighting for, these beautiful children. This was what she had to hold onto over the next four months.

For these children she would do anything. Even suffer living with her husband again.

CHAPTER FOUR

RAUL SAT IN his car scowling at his phone. It was almost five-thirty and Charley hadn't yet come out. Nor was she answering his calls.

He looked at the building again, debating for the tenth time whether or not to go inside and get her. To his eyes the place looked like nothing but a load of concrete blocks slapped together. The only spot of colour was a faded sign above the door that read Poco Rio. Little River. The name would have amused him—for a start, the Turia had run nowhere near this part of Valencia even before the devastating floods of 1957, which had caused the authorities to divert it to skirt the city rather than run through it—but instead he shuddered. Who would want their child to spend their days in a place like this? Far from the sunny exterior most day care centres projected, this building, with its drab grounds…everything about it shouted 'institution'.

His mind flickered to the care home his father had spent time in after his stroke while his mother had turned a wing of the family home into a facility able to manage his twenty-four-hour needs. That care home had been more akin to a hotel, a beautiful villa set in luscious grounds with first-class staff.

The care home could have been as opulent as the very first Cazorla hotel, built by Raul's grandfather, Nestor Cazorla, in 1955, and Eduardo Cazorla would still have hated it, even if he couldn't vocalise his thoughts or feelings. That hotel, built in Madrid, had been a shot in the eye to the Ritzes and Waldorfs of this world, a statement that anything they could do, the Cazorlas could do too.

Under Eduardo's reign, the Cazorla Hotel Madrid fell from its lofty heights, as did the other thirty-eight hotels in the chain. Investment became a dirty word, Eduardo preferring to spend the dwindling profits on maintaining his lifestyle.

Raul clearly remembered the day when he'd sat down with his father to discuss the shocking decline of the family business. He'd graduated from university with a mile-long list of ideas for improvement. He'd mistakenly thought that gaining a first-class degree from MIT would finally garner his father's respect. If not respect then at least something more than the distaste that seemed to be his father's default emotion towards him.

His father had calmly sat at his desk and flipped through the pages and pages of analysis and reports Raul had completed, then, still calm, had walked to his office window, opened it, and thrown the pages out onto the street below.

Then he'd turned back to his son and said, 'That's what I think of your ideas.'

After twenty-two years of Raul's being on the receiving end of his father's relentless criticism, something inside him had snapped. He'd walked out of his father's office without a word, returned to the family home, packed his bags, and left, using the small cash inheritance he'd received when Nestor died to rent an apartment and invest in a friend's fledgling technology business. He'd recouped his investment in three months and immediately set out to invest in another.

He'd spent his entire life striving to be the perfect son his father wanted; now he was going to be the man *he* wanted to be. What he wanted above all else was to be *nothing* like his father.

As his business had grown, not once had his father asked any questions about it. Raul had no idea whether he had been pleased or disappointed that his only son had bailed on the family firm. When they had been together as a family no one had spoken of or alluded to it; not even his mother, who came from a wealthy, high-society family in her own right. So long as Raul had still played at being the dutiful son, kept the perfect Cazorla face intact, joined them at important family functions and kept the family name away from the scandal rags that had been good enough for her.

He was pulled out of his reminiscences when a dark blue minibus drove into the grounds and pulled up beside him. He paid little attention to it until he caught the figure getting out of the driver's side.

While he was processing the image of Charley driving a minibus, she spotted him and, unsmiling, held up a hand and mouthed, 'Five minutes.'

He shoved his door open. 'We need to leave now. You're late enough as it is.'

'I did warn you,' she replied with a nonchalant shrug. 'I need to drop the keys back in and sign off. I won't be long.'

She hurried off in her jeans-clad legs and disappeared through the double front door.

He could still hardly believe his wife was wearing jeans. He didn't think he'd ever seen her in a pair before.

When he'd refused to take her back to her house in Valencia the night before, although promising to get her to work on time that morning, she hadn't argued. He'd been quietly satisfied that she was adapting to his authority well, right until he'd discovered her missing. She'd returned a couple of hours later with a bag of shopping, saying, 'You can hardly expect me to go to work wearing Chanel.' Thus she had proceeded to take herself off to one of the spare rooms she'd appropriated for her own use, locked the door, and refused to come out until the morning.

He'd been sorely tempted to kick said door down but had refrained from losing his cool in any fashion. He'd left her alone, dining on marinated fillet of pork while she stayed hungry, stewing in her own righteousness.

Come Friday she would be in his bedroom with him. If she refused, she knew what the consequences would be. No more funds for her pet project.

When she reappeared exactly five minutes later, she got into the car and slammed the door.

'You're doing that deliberately, aren't you?' he said through gritted teeth.

'Sorry.'

She didn't sound in the least bit sorry.

Grinding his teeth some more, he reversed, turned round and drove out of the car park.

'Why were you driving that thing anyway?'

'I was taking some of the kids home.'

Now he recalled her mention of her car the day before. 'When did you pass your driving test?'

'A year ago.'

'I always said there was nothing to be frightened of and that you were capable of driving over here.' She'd learned to drive in England but had never taken a test. Despite all his cajoling and his offer to buy her any car she desired, she'd always flatly refused to get behind the wheel of a car in Spain.

It felt like a slap to know she'd waited until she was out of his life before trying for her licence.

'You're always right,' Charley said shortly, thinking of all the times she'd heard the words 'I told you' from his lips, before quickly adding, 'I needed to be able to drive for the job. We take it in turns to collect the kids and drop them back, at least for the ones whose parents don't drive.'

Looking back, she couldn't believe it had taken her so long to take her test. She'd been even more surprised when she'd passed first time. She'd been *convinced* she was going to fail.

When the examiner had told her she'd passed, her first impulse had been to call Raul and share the news with him. Finally she'd passed something—it had been a heady moment.

'I assume you charge extra for the taxiing service?' he said.

She shot him a look. 'Of course we don't.'

'That's something that will have to change. You're throwing money away.'

Charley breathed deeply, biting back every nasty name she wanted to throw at him.

She'd always known her husband was materialistic but this was something else. How could he have such an attitude towards those poor children?

'Do you know where I live?' she asked, deliberately changing the subject before she gave in to the urge to punch him.

'Your address was on the divorce papers.'

They lapsed into silence for the rest of the short journey to her home.

'*This* is your house?' Raul asked when he pulled into her driveway.

'Not what you were expecting?'

'I was expecting something more lavish.' His lips formed a mocking smile. 'What happened? Did you have to sell up when the money started to run out?'

She kept her gaze on him even. 'I bought this house six

months after I left you. Lavish is your style, not mine.' Her two-bedroom villa was modest but more than adequate for her needs. It might not have its own swimming pool or a beach at the bottom of the garden but nor did it have so many rooms she needed a map to find her way around.

'That's not how I remember things.'

Oh, yes. That was right. He thought she was a gold-digger. 'I don't control your memories.'

'And neither do you control your finances.'

Fighting the rising anger, Charley tugged at her bag and rummaged through for her keys. 'Let's get this done.'

Inside, she headed straight to her bedroom and began to pack, carefully placing her clothes into the same Louis Vuitton suitcases she'd used when she'd left him. She could hear Raul giving himself a tour of her home. It was a very short tour. Minutes later he was in her room watching her put the last of her stuff into the cases.

'Are you nearly done?'

'Yes. Whatever we can't fit in the car today I'll collect on Friday.' On Friday they would be coming back to Valencia. She would work at the centre while Raul finalised the purchase of the new building. As far as Raul was concerned, her shift at the centre would be her last. She wasn't prepared to argue about it until the deeds were signed and in her hands.

Raul heaved her cases off the bed and carried them to the car. Charley slipped into the spare room she used as an office and gathered all her plans together.

'What's that?' he asked, entering the tiny space a short while later, standing behind her and immediately making it feel even more cramped than usual.

'The plans for the redevelopment of the new centre.'

'Don't bother with them,' he said dismissively. 'I'll get my own architect onto it.'

She placed everything into the briefcase she'd taken to the bank manager only the day before, sliding it on top of the financial aspects of the loan she had pored over for hours. *Do not bite,* she warned herself. *Raul still has a number of days to change his mind. Do not bite.* 'Your architect can use these plans to guide him.'

'You think you know better than an architect with twenty years' experience?'

'I think this is something to be discussed when the deeds have been signed.' *Until then, do not bite.*

'*Cariño*, do not forget, this project is now under my control.' He stepped closer to her, close enough that she could feel his heat warm her back. His voice dropped to a murmur. She could feel his breath in her hair. 'As are you.'

Charley froze, keeping herself ramrod straight, and swallowed the moisture that filled her mouth.

How did he *do* this? How did he make her want him so much while simultaneously making her want to scratch her nails down his face?

'I'm not yours until Friday,' she reminded him in a strangled voice. 'No touching until then.'

'I don't think you'll make me wait that long.'

'I hate you.'

'I know.' His breath whispered through the strands of her hair, heating her scalp. 'It must be awful for you, hating me so much but wanting me even more.'

'I don't want you.'

'I never realised when we married what a liar you are.' The tip of his nose nestled into her hair. 'If I hadn't been so blinded by lust I would have known your words of love and your promise of a child were nothing but lies to access my fortune.'

His tone was playful but when Charley spun round to face him she saw the darkness in his eyes.

'I didn't lie to you and I didn't marry you for your money.' She *hated* that he thought of her as a gold-digger, making out that the times when they'd been happy together—and there had been times when she'd been delirious with happiness—were nothing but a lie.

'Then what did you marry me for? My wit and personality?' he taunted in that same playful way, as the darkness in his eyes turned cold.

'You.' She felt heat creep up her neck. 'I married you for *you*. I thought you were wonderful.'

He feigned injury. 'You don't think I'm wonderful any more?'

'I think you're cruel. You're using those poor children as pawns to get me back into your bed and all because of some ridiculous notion of revenge because I wouldn't have your baby.'

Where her words came from she didn't know and she would gladly have swallowed them back if she could, but they spurted out as if they had a force of their own.

His eyes had gone cold enough to make her shiver. But the smile hadn't dropped. He leaned forward and brushed his cheek to hers. 'It's not revenge, *cariño*. I'm giving you what you want. In return you're giving me what I want.'

'My body.'

'Exactly that.' He nuzzled against her cheek. 'But if it *was* revenge I sought, then having you back in my bed would be the sweetest-tasting revenge there is.'

'I think you're cruel.'

That was what Charley had said.

Was he being cruel?

Raul didn't like to think of himself as cruel. His own father, when he'd been in good health, had had a great capacity for cruelty and it was a trait Raul had sworn he would never adopt. He was prepared to accept that he was forceful and direct, arrogant even, but never cruel. Not until the woman he'd lavished everything on thought she could come to him for help as if nothing had passed between them.

He forced his mind back to their marriage. He'd been happy to indulge her when she'd announced she wanted to run a luxury chauffeur hire for travelling business people. He'd had his doubts from the off—for a start, Charley couldn't drive, but, as she'd pointed out, she would employ drivers. Despite his misgivings, he'd given her the money to buy a handful of limousines and premises from which to run the business. With his extensive contacts book at her disposal, he'd seen no reason why her fledgling business should be anything other than a success.

A year later, the company had folded. Contracts had dried up and instead of coming to him for help she had thrown in the towel.

He'd tried to be understanding. It was a big thing she'd undertaken, starting a business of her own, especially coming into it with no qualifications or business experience.

The next venture she'd embarked on, he'd supplied her with both his financial backing and a team of his personal staff to help her with it all. It had gone bust within four months. The third—which he couldn't even remember—had lasted only a month longer.

It was after that third and final venture that he'd sat her down and insisted it was time for her to stop playing at business and time for them to start the family she'd promised him.

His stomach soured as he recalled her reaction. It was as if he'd thrown a pot of boiling water over her.

He took a breath and pushed her bedroom door open.

She was in the adjoining room, sitting at the large desk below the window, papers spread out before her.

'We need to leave in an hour.' He'd informed her over breakfast that morning that they would be dining out with friends that evening.

She didn't look at him. 'I'll be ready.'

'Charlotte, it takes you at least two hours to get ready for a night out.' And that was if he was lucky. She had a tendency to try on her entire wardrobe before deciding on an outfit, then she would tease her hair into a dozen different styles before deciding which was the 'right' one. It didn't matter how many times he told her, she never seemed to believe him when he said she was beautiful in whatever she wore.

A sudden memory brushed through him, of their honeymoon, where he'd flown her to a private island in the Caribbean. It had been the last time he'd truly seen her full of spirit and abandon. One night, when he'd been gently chivvying her to get ready for dinner, she'd stripped her clothes off with glee and charged off to the private cove the island's staff were banned from, splashing naked in the water with such joy it had compelled him to strip off his own clothes and join her, and make love to her.

His chest filled as he recalled how special that moment had been, the freedom he'd felt with the sun bathing down on his naked form and his wife's supple limbs wrapped around him.

Of all the good moments within their marriage, this was the memory that stood out for him, the vivid remembrance of the belief that they were the happiest, most perfect couple in the world.

'I'll be ready,' she repeated.

'What are you doing?'

'Going over the plans for the development.'

'What for? I told you, I'll be using my own team.'

Her shoulders raised stubbornly. 'I've put hundreds of hours into this. It's stupid not to at least take it into account.'

'I'm sure my architect will be delighted to have your input,' he drawled.

Shoving her chair back, she got to her feet. 'I'm going to take a shower,' she said, her voice tight.

'One hour.'

'So you keep telling me.' She closed the adjoining door firmly behind her. He heard the lock slide into place.

Raul flexed his fingers and took a deep breath.

The past four days had been like living with a sullen teenager. He'd given her a little leeway, which had been decent of him under the circumstances, but from now on he would not put up with it.

Tomorrow, the deeds would be signed and she would be indebted to him.

Curiosity made him look at the papers sprawled over her desk.

A few moments later he sat on the chair still warm from her body heat with a frown on his face.

Peering more closely through the stack before him, he saw she'd taken each room of the new building and committed to paper her ideas for the renovations. Each drawing was done to scale.

Charley had said she'd done these plans.

Had she been lying in an attempt to impress him?

But no—the notes in the margins, the numbers indicating the measurements, these were all in her girlish writing.

He rubbed at his temples, his chest tightening as he imagined her sitting in that tiny study in the tiny home she'd been living in, working diligently on these plans. Alone.

* * *

After a quick shower and shave, Raul found Charley in the living room.

'You're ready?' he asked, astonished to find her waiting for him. He was equally astounded at what she was wearing: a pair of cropped grey figure-hugging patchwork trousers and a sheer black blouse. On her feet were a pair of flat black strappy sandals.

'Yes.' Rising from the sofa, she passed the window, the low early evening sun shining through to allow him to see perfectly the lacy black bra she wore beneath the seemingly modest blouse.

'What?' she asked, a scowl forming.

'Are you really intending to go out for a meal with friends wearing that?'

'Yes, Raul, I am. Why? Is there something wrong with it?'

'I'm surprised, that's all.' She looked good—she looked beautiful—there was no denying that but he could not recall a single time after they'd married when she'd worn trousers or jeans. Now, other than the party she'd gatecrashed and the morning of her meeting with the bank manager, he'd not seen a single sign of her legs. The Charley he'd been married to wouldn't have dreamed of going out for dinner in anything less than a designer dress and five-inch heels. She would hardly *breakfast* in anything less.

'This is what I have in my wardrobe.'

'What happened to the rest of your clothes?' Charley had had a wall at the back of her walk-in wardrobe filled with shoes alone. Thinking about it, he couldn't see how her tiny Valencian bedroom would fit even a fraction of her clothes in it.

'I gave most of them to charity shops.'

'What did you do that for?'

She shrugged. 'There's not much call for Dolce & Gabbana at Poco Rio.'

'I'll give my sister a ring and see if she's free to go on a shopping trip with you over the next few days.' He reached into his pocket for his phone.

Charley folded her arms and shook her head, but the scowl disappeared, replaced by a look that was almost... sad. 'I don't want to go on a shopping trip. I like my wardrobe just fine as it is.'

'Charlotte,' he said, striving for patience, 'over the next four months we will be dining out and socialising as we always used to do. The clothes you have are fine for what you've been doing at the centre but those days are currently over. You're my wife and you know what that means.'

'That I have to dress up like a doll?'

'No.' She was being deliberately obtuse. 'But being a Cazorla does mean projecting a certain image—'

'Why?'

He rubbed the nape of his neck and whistled air through his teeth. 'We discussed this when we first became engaged. My family is highly respected here, our hotels some of the finest in the world. People look up to us.'

It had been for her sake that he'd wanted her to fit in. He knew what it was like to be judged as not good enough and had never wanted that for her. He hadn't wanted the woman he loved to enter a social situation and feel insecure about *anything*. He'd done his best to give her all the tools she'd needed to assimilate into high society as if she'd been born into it.

'I still don't understand why that means I have to dress like a doll.'

'You don't have to "dress like a doll",' he said, his jaws clamping together. 'I really don't understand what the problem is. You loved dressing up when we lived together before.'

He remembered the light in her eyes after that first shopping trip with Marta and their personal shopper and Charley's bursts of laughter as she'd carefully taken each item out of its box for him to look at and comment on. Her happiness hadn't been fake, of that he was certain.

The corners of her lips curved into a whimsical smile, the closest thing to a real smile he'd seen all week, although there was nothing happy about it.

'I did at first, yes. But what twenty-year-old *wouldn't* love being let loose in one of the most exclusive shopping arcades in Europe with an unlimited credit card?'

'So you admit, you *did* marry me for my money?'

She shook her head, her blonde hair brushing over her shoulders. 'I won't lie; your wealth turned my head. Your whole lifestyle did. But I would have married you if you'd lived in a shack.'

He laughed humourlessly. 'It is lucky your nose is not like Pinocchio's or it would be sprouting leaves as we speak.'

Her eyes held his. 'If I'm such a gold-digger, why did I walk away and leave it all behind?'

'You left with ten million euros.'

'Money I never asked for,' she pointed out. 'And you know as well as I do I could have asked for a whole lot more.'

'And you know as well as I do that until our divorce is final, you still can.' He reached out a hand and traced a finger down her cheek, not liking the disquiet prodding at him.

She was right. She *hadn't* asked for his money. He'd given it freely.

Nor had she asked for the credit cards and everything

else he'd given her when he'd wanted nothing more than to see that smile from her first shopping trip replicated.

None of that mattered any more. The only smile he wanted to see on her face now was the smile of pleasure.

One more night of sleeping on his own and she would be his again.

'It is hardly coincidence that you returned to my life when the money had almost run out,' he pointed out.

She made to speak but he cut her off by rubbing his thumb over her lips. 'If you play your cards right over the next four months, you will find my generosity knows no limits. Play your cards right and I will give you so much money it would take you a lifetime to spend it.'

She slapped his hand away, angry colour heightening her cheeks. 'Once the centre has been redeveloped, the only thing I will want from you is my freedom.'

'Your freedom will be guaranteed.' Unable to resist dropping his face into her neck and inhaling that musky vanilla scent that turned him on so much, he added, 'And so will mine.'

CHAPTER FIVE

CHARLEY WAS OUT of the centre before Raul's watch registered her being even one minute late. She hurried to the car, her excitement tangible. She'd been the same that morning, unable to keep still for a second, downing coffee as if it were going out of fashion but unable to eat a morsel of the eggs his chef had cooked for them.

She pulled the passenger door open. 'Is it done?'

'Yes.'

She punched the air. 'Thank God.'

'You're welcome. But Raul will suffice.'

She pulled a face at him and laughed. 'Right now, I'm so happy and grateful I'll call you anything you like.'

He bit back the quip forming on his tongue, not wanting to break the moment. Seeing the delight on her face lightened his blood.

It had been a long time since he'd seen that smile.

A skinny, balding man poked his head out of the building. Abandoning Raul, Charley hurried over to him, hurled her arms around his waist and kissed his cheek. The man disappeared back inside with a beaming grin of his own.

She rushed back to the car, jumped in, shut the door without slamming it and yanked out the band holding her hair in a ponytail. Tidying her hair with her fingers, she looked at him, her eyes bright with excitement.

'Who was that?' he asked in as nonchalant a voice as he

could muster. Watching his wife throw her arms around another man had felt...disturbing, like having pins stuck into his flesh.

For the first time, he confronted the possibility that there had been another man in her life since they'd parted.

Two years was a long time to be alone.

'Seve—he runs the centre. He'll be sharing the good news with the others.' Charley's happiness was so infectious even the car seemed to react to it, an upbeat song playing out from the radio.

But what was she so happy about? Raul's purchase of the building? Or the fact she'd spent most of the day with *Seve*?

'I hope they enjoy the moment.' He killed the radio and put the car into gear. It was only three p.m.; if traffic was kind, they could be back in Barcelona within a couple of hours. His helicopter pilot was primed for take-off.

'I'm sure they'll celebrate all night.'

'Do you wish you were celebrating with them?'

'I would *love* to.' The longing was clear in her voice.

If she was hoping he'd relent and let her stay in Valencia for the night, she was doomed to disappointment. They'd made a deal. From this moment on, Charley was *his*.

'This Seve, he is a good friend of yours?'

'Yes.'

'Is that all he is to you? A friend?'

She twisted in her seat to stare at him. 'Are you trying to find out if Seve and I are lovers?'

'Are you?'

'He's married.'

'And so are *you*.'

Her cheeks tightened. 'I wouldn't be if you'd signed the divorce papers when you'd first got them, but even if I wasn't, I wouldn't mess about with a married man.'

'And what about single men? Have you "messed about" with many of them since you left?'

She was silent for a moment before answering, her voice as taut as her features. 'I will tell you how many men I've messed around with after you tell me how many women you've been with. Obviously I know about Jessica, so that's one. How many others?'

If she only knew the truth.

How would she react if he were to tell her that since she'd left there hadn't been anyone else? He would visit his hotels and cruise liners, be surrounded by semi-naked women flirting outrageously with him, and feel nothing. He might as well have been dead from the waist down. Jessica was famed as one of the sexiest women in the world but even she'd left him cold.

He wouldn't give Charley the satisfaction of the truth.

But neither did he want to hear if she'd had other lovers in their time apart. Nothing good could come of it.

Four months was ample time to get her out of his system. By the time those months were over, his libido would surely be begging for variety.

'Giving numbers is vulgar and unbecoming,' he said smoothly.

'I quite agree.'

His gaze darted briefly to her. 'But to be clear, while you are back in my bed, there will be no other men in your life.'

'I'm only yours until the renovations are complete,' she reminded him with a pointed look. All the euphoria she'd displayed when she'd got into the car had now gone.

'But until then, *cariño*, you are *mine*.' To reiterate his point, he put a hand on her thigh and squeezed it lightly, before moving it to change gear.

He heard her suck in a breath and hold it for the longest time.

'Have you got the deeds?' she asked, her voice now flat.

'I have a copy of them in my briefcase. You can have them when we get home.'

Soon enough they would be back.

Soon enough she would be back in his bed, right where she belonged.

If she'd had any lovers in the time they'd been apart he would ensure they were obliterated from her memory, leaving only him.

Yes. Tonight she would be his again. All his.

Charley entered the villa feeling as if the weight of the world had landed back on her shoulders.

For a few brief minutes, when Raul had confirmed the purchase of the new building, she'd felt so light-headed she wouldn't have needed the helicopter to fly.

Then he'd ruined it all by implying there was something romantic going on between her and Seve. This, from the man who'd been bedding a hot lingerie model.

Raul had carried on with his life as if she'd never been a part of it. All her paranoia from their marriage had come true, her secret fear that, as had always been the case with her father, when Charley was out of someone's sight she was out of their mind. Forgettable. Replaceable.

Raul had moved on. New home, new lover, new everything.

If only it had been as easy for her to move on too.

Her life had become rich with friends—real friends; their meal with Diego and Elana the previous night had brought home to her how wonderful it was to *have* true friends. Elana's friendship had been foisted upon her when she and Raul had first got together. Originally a receptionist for Diego's world-famous plastic-surgery practice, Elana was now the epitome of high-society goddess with a perfectly straight nose, sculpted cheekbones and inflated breasts. All of the other 'friends' Charley had made in their time together had been of an identical mould.

Far too well-mannered to say anything derogatory about Charley's outfit, Elana had been unable to hide the flicker of shock when she'd cast her eyes over her. For her part, Elana had been dressed from top to tail in the required designer label, her gold shoes so high Charley had felt sorry for her feet. Not even the red stilettos she'd forced her feet into on Saturday night had been that high.

Looking back, Charley struggled to understand how she'd allowed herself to suffer such self-inflicted torture. She'd thought nothing of wearing five-inch heels for a full day at work.

But it had been expected of her. She had been the wife of Raul Cazorla and she had been expected to dress and act the part, including cultivating friendships with like-minded women.

The only real friendship she'd made had been, funnily enough, with Marta, Raul's sister, who was an incredibly smart and amusing woman.

The strange thing was, while they'd been eating last night, she'd noticed so many new things: the way Elana picked at her food as if scared to consume a calorie more than was good for her, the way she deferred to her husband before offering an opinion...all the things Charley had once done. And just like that, she'd seen all the insecurities running under Elana's surgically lifted skin. Being the trophy wife of a successful, rich, handsome man wasn't all it was cracked up to be. Charley should know. It had broken her in the end.

Even so, there was no hiding away from the knowledge that for the past two years she'd been empty inside, as if a big hollow had opened up in her belly. She hadn't so much as looked at another man.

Raul called out to her from the living area.

She found him pouring a bottle of red into two glasses. He handed one to her.

'To us,' he said, raising his glass.

'To the new centre,' she corrected, chinking her glass against his.

'You can't have one without the other.' His eyes gleamed. 'I have given you what you want. Now it is time for you to fulfil your end of the bargain.'

It didn't take Einstein to know what he meant, or a mind-reader to read his thoughts.

He took a sip of wine, his full lips pressing together as he swallowed, his blue eyes holding hers in the way that had always made her melt.

She did the same now, a rush of heat pooling low in her belly and spreading out to her limbs.

Her mind ran amok as she took a steadying sip of her own wine, remembering all the nights they'd come together, devouring each other, loving each other...

Don't go there, Charley. He never loved you, only loved who he wanted you to be. You were never good enough for him as you were. You're worth even less now, nothing more than a warm body for him to use to sate himself whenever and wherever the mood strikes.

She was good for only one thing. He'd spelled that out loud and clear. And now he wanted his payment.

It was the reminder she needed.

The reality of making love—no, *having sex*—with him for the first time in such a manner had the effect of making her libido nosedive to her toes.

Whatever wrongs he might believe she'd done to him, she deserved more than to be taken at his command and only for his pleasure. Whatever gratitude she might feel for him saving the centre plummeted with her libido. The financial cost to Raul was so tiny in comparison to his wealth it would be akin to a normal person buying a bottle of wine.

She cleared her throat, determined to stall the moment for as long as she could. 'I would like to take a look at the deeds.'

The strangest expression came into his eyes. 'As you wish.'

He stepped over to his briefcase, which he'd placed on the bureau, and unlocked it. About to open it, he was distracted by his phone vibrating. He grimaced and shrugged before pulling it out of his pocket, looking at the screen, and deciding whoever was on the other end was worthy of his attention.

He left the living room and disappeared, she assumed to his study.

Relieved for a few more minutes' grace, she pulled her own phone out of her bag and answered the dozens of messages that had come through from overjoyed staff and the children's parents alike, all of whom had been waiting on tenterhooks like her.

Done, she stared at Raul's briefcase, which was still where he'd left it, unlocked.

Unable to wait a moment longer, she opened it and pulled out a hefty brown envelope lying on the top. She had a quick peek to make sure it was the deeds and not another business-related document that was none of her concern.

A fresh wave of excitement swept through her when she saw the address of the new centre in the middle of the cover page. She pulled the thick sheath of papers out of the envelope and rifled through them, her mind awhirl with all the plans she had for the centre, plans that would now become a reality.

Her grasp of Spanish had increased greatly in the past two years but legalese was a whole new ballpark. All the same, she persevered, right through to the last page. By then she'd finished her wine and was ready for another glass, but, rather than pour herself one, she stared at the pages with a frown.

Something bugged her. She couldn't think what it could be but her intuition told her something was off.

She started scanning the pages again, fiddling with a lock of hair as she forced herself to concentrate...

The bastard!

Now she knew what was wrong.

Sucking on her little finger, she skimmed through all the papers one more time looking in vain for her name.

In a maelstrom of anger and indignation, she stormed to his office and shoved the door open.

Raul was sitting at his desk, phone in one hand, a pen twirling between the fingers of his other.

'You lying, manipulative...' she said, throwing the deeds onto his desk.

He stilled for a moment, then spoke quietly into the phone and disconnected the call.

'Has something upset you?' he asked with steely calm.

'These deeds are in your name.'

'Yes,' he agreed.

'You said the building would be mine.'

'No, I said the building would be in the Cazorla name and that is exactly what I have done.'

'You know perfectly well I thought it was being put in my name. I was going to form a trust and hand it over to the centre!'

He laughed. 'Then it seems I made a wise decision to

put it in *my* name. What do a bunch of childminders know about managing a project such as this?'

'Don't speak so...so derogatorily about them,' she snarled, pulling the word out after having it trip over her tongue. She hadn't even known what derogatory meant five years ago. 'Besides, they weren't going to manage the project, *I* was, and I know a lot more than you credit me for. I didn't go into this lightly.'

'Maybe you did, maybe you didn't; it doesn't change the fact that you couldn't get the financing for it and for the very good reason that your track record in business is abysmal.'

'You're *sick*,' she seethed. 'You've done this deliberately, haven't you?'

He shrugged. 'Does it matter? The end effect is the same—the building will be used for a new centre.'

'But under your control.'

'I am not a team player, *cariño*. I don't deal with collaboration. You will get your centre but you will not have the opportunity to mess up the renovations.'

'I am not going to mess this up!' she shouted.

He gave her a measured stare. 'Control your temper. It is most unattractive.'

'Do you think I care what *you* find attractive?'

'You should, considering the project hasn't even started yet.'

She knew exactly what he meant. 'Are you seriously serious? If I don't toe the line then you'll pull the plug?'

'If necessary. But as I've said numerous times, if you fulfil your side of the bargain then I will fulfil mine.'

'You *lied* to me.'

'No. You made assumptions.' He rose from his seat and rested his hand on the desk, leaning forward. 'I made it very clear that I would be taking control. I will be in charge and you will be by my side. Look at it from a positive perspective—this time you'll see how a project is conducted properly all the way to its conclusion.'

The anger inside her had risen so high it threatened to choke her. The worst of it was that she knew he was right. She *had* made assumptions.

But, damn him, he'd let her.

She'd known from the start that her husband was a competitive man who had to be the best at everything he did. He wasn't satisfied until he'd mastered whatever he'd set out to do. In this case he'd set out to master *her*, to punish her for her refusal to have the child he thought was his due.

Unable to be in the same room as him for a moment longer lest she throw something at him, she stormed out and ran up the stairs to the sanctuary of the room she'd made her own.

The room was empty.

She checked the wardrobe, the dresser and the bathroom. Every single one of her possessions had gone. The bed had been stripped, the white mattress and plump pillows lying there uncovered as if in forlorn sympathy for her.

'Your belongings have been moved into my bedroom.'

She spun around to find Raul pressed against the doorway.

'Nice to know you didn't waste any time,' she said, not bothering to hide her contempt.

He smiled lazily and stepped over to her, placing his hands on the tops of her arms and leaning down to breathe into her hair. 'Your anger is a waste of your energy.' His voice dropped as he slid his hands down her sleeved arms and covered her balled fists. 'Come, let me show you where you'll be sleeping for the next four months.'

'I'd rather sleep in a box,' she hissed, somehow managing to hold back the burn of angry tears that had welled in her eyes.

'*Cariño*, are you deliberately trying to rouse my anger?' he asked in a caressing tone that contained an edge of warning.

'Why should I be the only one to be angry?' she demanded. 'You've hoodwinked me.'

'I'm investing a great deal of money in your scheme and I want to protect it.'

She forced her voice to remain calm. 'Will you sign the deeds over to me when the renovations are complete?'

He contemplated her silently and his blue eyes narrowed. '*If* you can prove yourself to be focused, and by that I mean that you *keep* your focus until the renovations are complete, then I might consider signing it over to you.'

'Might?'

'I will not make a false promise, *cariño*.' His voice dropped to a purr and he dipped his face into the curve of her neck and traced his lips gently over her skin. 'Enough talk about deeds and renovations. I can think of a much better way to pass the time.'

She dug her still-too-short nails into her palms, far too aware of his warm fingers holding her, his hot breath sensitising her skin... How *could* she still want him?

Something hot flickered in her belly, a resolve that pushed through her fury, taming it enough so she loosened her fists and laced her fingers through his.

So he wanted her, did he? Well, let him have her.

CHAPTER SIX

WITH CHARLEY'S FINGERS linked through his, Raul led her out of the empty room, down the wide landing and up a set of narrow wooden stairs to the top floor.

As soon as they stepped over the threshold into his bedroom she dropped his hand, kicked her sandals off then marched over to stand in the centre of the room.

Her eyes fixed on his, she tugged her top up and off.

No sooner had her top hit the floor than she was undoing the buttons of her shorts and letting them drop to her feet, where she stepped out of them and kicked them away.

He stood, transfixed at the scenario playing out before him, his eyes drinking in the unexpected striptease his wife was performing for him.

Her green eyes flashing, she unclasped her white bra, which went the same way as the rest of her clothes, then pinched the sides of her matching knickers, skimming them down her hips from where gravity took care of the rest.

When all her clothes were lying in a pool beside her, she put her hands on her hips and jutted out her chin.

He made to step towards her but something held him back.

Her eyes burned, but it wasn't with desire. It was with defiance. Her whole body vibrated with it.

'Well?' she said, the challenge in her voice clear. 'I'm here. I'm ready. I'm willing. If you want me, then *take* me.'

Her figure was exquisite, with her full breasts and succulent nipples, the feminine swell of her abdomen and the rounded hips that topped long, shapely legs. At the juncture of her thighs lay the soft dark brown curls he'd once loved running his fingers over.

He remembered the first time he'd seen her naked. At the time she'd been platinum blonde. He'd laughed when he'd pulled her knickers off and seen the dark hair there, the only evidence of her natural colouring. He'd especially liked kissing her there, that first time and all the others, feeling her excitement mount as she'd press upwards and into him, her gasps of pleasure seeping through his skin.

Memories flooded him, vivid and colourful. His wife had always been putty in his hands. It would be so easy to kiss all that defiance away. The sweetest, easiest thing in the world.

The heat running through his loins had turned the ache inside him into a form of pain.

He ignored it.

Folding his arms, he shook his head and clicked his tongue against the roof of his mouth.

She trembled as he walked to her but her chin didn't drop, not even when he reached an arm round to cup her bottom.

'You want me to take you now, do you?' he whispered, pulling her flush against him, tracing his fingers up her bare back, then gathering her thick mop of hair together and spearing his fingers through it.

'You can do whatever you like,' she whispered back, her breaths coming in shallow hitches.

But when his lips met hers, he found her mouth unyielding.

'You said I could do whatever I like.'

'And you can. But that doesn't mean I have to participate or enjoy it.'

He tugged her hair back and stared into her insolent eyes. Anger flooded through him at the confirmation of the game she was playing. But he tempered it.

She wanted to play?

Nothing would give him greater pleasure.

And she would learn that whatever game she played with him, she would never win.

He released his hold on her and swept his fingers over her shoulders, down over her breasts, lightly pinching those gorgeous nipples, already hard with the arousal she wished to deny, in the way that had always made her moan.

There were no moans this time, but her lips parted a fraction, her cheeks heightening with colour. The defiance remained.

'Sit on the chair,' he commanded, indicating the armchair in the corner of the room.

'What?'

'Sit on the chair. You said I could do whatever I like, and what I would like is for you to sit on that chair.'

She swallowed, looking at the chair as if it might be a trap.

'I can carry you if you'd prefer?'

Her eyes dilated at his words but her chin rose. She turned and walked to it, her back straight and her head high, goddess-like.

When she sat down, her eyes met his. *You can make me do anything you like but you won't make me enjoy it,* they said.

Smiling, he stalked towards her and dropped to his knees. Without a word, he gripped her thighs and pulled her towards him so that his face was level with the place he so desperately wanted to taste. Just the thought of it made him want to plunge deep inside her.

Instead, he mustered all his discipline and spread her thighs, waiting, teasing.

She didn't move, her body rigid.

Whatever fight was occurring between Charley's mind and body, her body was winning. He rubbed his thumb along the delicate folds, his eyes gleaming as he found her hot and moist. When his tongue finally found her, he gave a growl of appreciation.

Her body remained unyielding, right until he found the rhythm he knew she loved. The tiniest of moans escaped from her.

Keeping the pressure light but firm, his hands stroking the soft skin of her thighs and stomach, slowly but surely he felt her relax into his ministrations.

He felt fit to burst himself, especially when her hands finally gripped his head, her fingers scraping at his scalp. She raised her hips to increase the pressure. Only by the skin of his teeth did he keep himself in check, intent only on her pleasure. Her moans deepened breath by breath until her body went rigid all over again…but this time in ecstasy.

He kept his mouth and tongue exactly where they were, absorbing the shudders that racked through her right until she dropped her hold on him and lay back.

His heart thumping painfully, Raul raised his head to look at her.

She was staring at the ceiling, her chest rising and falling as if she were struggling to get air into her lungs.

Not until he got to his feet did she deign to look at him. Her eyes were wide and dazed but he could see the defiance creeping back into them.

How easy it would be to take off his trousers and free

himself, to enter her, to obliterate the rising insolence in her eyes and bring her to a second climax.

But that would be to let her win.

In this game of desire there would only be one winner.

When she opened her legs for him, he wanted her screaming his name not fighting it, and if he had to suffer to achieve that aim then so be it. He was a big boy. He would cope.

'I'm going to take a shower. Get dressed. We'll be going to dinner in an hour.'

Without looking back, he strolled into one of the en suites, shut the door firmly behind him and stripped off his clothes.

His erection hadn't abated a touch.

The Cazorla family home was in a private enclave as exclusive as the one Raul's current house was in. As they neared it the coil in Charley's belly pulled ever tighter.

Of all the times to have to dine with her in-laws, now had to rank as the worst possible. All she wanted to do was lock herself away in a dark room, go to sleep, and pretend what had happened between her and Raul a few short hours ago had never occurred.

Her skin felt as sensitised as she'd ever known it, the movement of her clothes against her body heightening the sensations. Try as she might, she couldn't stop her eyes flittering to Raul's hands, those long, dark fingers holding the steering wheel like a caress, and imagining them running over her body and dipping between her legs...

When he'd gone for his shower, leaving her naked on the seat, the humiliation of it all had been almost too much to bear. That his intention had been to humiliate was all the spur she'd needed to drag herself up and into the other en suite. This had a surprisingly feminine feel to it with its soft, muted creams and whites; a total contrast to the rest of his vast room, which covered the entire top floor and was masculine to its core.

It was bad enough having come undone so thoroughly at his hands, or tongue to be precise, but she would not give him the satisfaction of thinking he'd bested her emotionally too.

Raul wanted her total subjugation. Hell would freeze over before she gave it to him. The only good thing she could cling to was that he hadn't bothered to tell her of their destination until they'd got into the car. Dining out was a way of life for him and she'd assumed they were off to yet another restaurant. On the nights he was home, which when they'd been properly married had been around fifty per cent of the time, they would both dress up and head out for the evening, sometimes with friends, sometimes just the two of them. It had reached the stage where she didn't think there was a restaurant in the whole of Barcelona she hadn't dined in.

'They do know I'm coming with you, don't they?' she asked for the second time, unable to believe how nervous she felt at the thought of being with his family again.

'I have no wish to provoke my mother to a heart attack,' he replied with a lazy smile. 'I can assure you, there is nothing for you to worry about. My family are nothing if not polite.'

That was true. One thing the entire Cazorla family did well was putting on a good front in any given situation.

The butler greeted them at the door, a discreet Englishman who had been with the family for years and had never once made any reference to the shared country he and Charley came from.

Lucetta and Marta Cazorla, Raul's mother and sister respectively, were in the drawing room awaiting their arrival. Both were dressed impeccably, as if they were heading off to a night at the opera, something Raul had once taken Charley to and which, to her shame, she had fallen asleep through.

She wondered when Raul would comment on her own attire. He'd given her a sharp glance but hadn't said anything.

If she'd known they were coming here before she'd got in the car, she would have made a greater effort than the casual inky-coloured silk trousers with the tapered legs and the silk blush-pink roll-neck top. On her feet were flat snakeskin-effect sandals. She knew her outfit would hold its own at any restaurant but in the Cazorla household... she might as well have come dressed in her pyjamas.

It shouldn't matter to her. In the days after she'd left she'd gone through her wardrobe and removed every item that had been purchased for its suitability for Raul Cazorla's wife and not for personal style or comfort. She'd donated ninety per cent of her wardrobe to charity and vowed never to wear anything again that wasn't *her*.

All the same, Lucetta and Marta had always been good to her, especially Marta, who, when Charley had first come into Raul's life, had been tasked with the job of turning Charley into a mini version of herself. Under Raul's directive, Marta had taken her to Barcelona's most exclusive shopping arcade and had taken great delight in finding a brand-new wardrobe for her.

Although not as direct in her enthusiasm for Raul's new bride, Lucetta had gone out of her way to make Charley feel a valued member of the family. Charley had never been able to shake the feeling that Lucetta's friendliness towards her was motivated by what she thought to be an acceptable way to behave towards a daughter-in-law, rather than out of any real affection. She would have treated the

Bride of Frankenstein with the same graciousness. But she had done her best to be welcoming and, for that, Charley would always have affection for her.

Dressing up and looking the part was something that mattered greatly to both Cazorla women, and for them Charley would have put on a dress and heels. Not silly heels that would leave her feet begging for mercy though. Three inches would have sufficed. Something to show she'd made an effort.

As it was, both faces lit up to see her walk through the door. If either was disappointed in her outfit or at seeing her again, it was hidden under a wave of perfumed embraces and air kisses.

An Adonis, a dry-sherry-based cocktail that was wonderfully moreish, was thrust into her hand by Marta, who linked her arm through Charley's with a grin.

'It is so good to see you,' she said, resting her head on Charley's shoulder. 'I always knew you'd see sense and come back to him.'

Charley met Raul's eyes and read the warning contained in them.

'It's lovely to see you too,' she answered, brushing aside the comment. She didn't want to lie to Marta, who had become a good friend, the two of them keeping in touch secretly after Charley had left Raul.

She took a sip, the taste reminding her of the time she and Marta had drunk so many of the cocktails before a meal they'd been unable to eat a bite, collapsing in giggles on a sofa much to the amusement of Raul and Marta's fiancé at the time, Fabio. Lucetta had been away, which had no doubt explained Marta's low inhibitions.

Raul had really taken care of her that night, she remembered. In the morning he'd handed her a glass of water and a couple of painkillers without a word of reproach, then climbed back into bed and held her, making sure not to squeeze her too tightly.

The tender memories sent a jolt through her.

Sometimes it was easy to only remember the bad stuff but there had been good times too, especially at the beginning.

Watching him now, chatting with his mother, she noticed the physical distance he kept between them. There was respect there but little affection.

After a few minutes of small talk, the wide diningroom door opened and Eduardo Cazorla, Raul's father, was wheeled through.

He looked exactly the same as when she'd last seen him, the left side of his face sagged and his hands arranged for him on his lap. Only his eyes, the same blue as his son and daughter's, showed any sign of life, letting you know that behind his infirmity lay a mind as sharp as the day the stroke had robbed him of his body.

When he caught sight of Charley, his eyes flickered to Raul, who did nothing but stare at his father with an expression that sent a shiver running up her spine. Goosebumps broke on her skin to see the same expression mirrored in his father's eyes.

Lucetta broke the ice, strolling to her husband and speaking to him in Spanish, her words too fast for Charley to understand anything but the gist of it, which seemed to be something along the lines of, 'Raul and Charley are back together.' As she explained the situation the butler entered the room to announce that dinner was ready.

Charley was placed opposite Raul and next to Marta, Lucetta next to her son. Eduardo sat in his usual place at the head of the table, his nurse, a young, dark-haired woman, by his side feeding him.

Seven courses were served in total. That was nothing;

if Lucetta hosted a 'proper' dinner party, a minimum of a dozen courses would be served. They started with gazpacho, which was followed by *calamares en su tinta*, squid in their own ink, which was far tastier than it sounded. As they ate, Raul, as he always did at these family meals, gave them a rundown on what was happening with the family business, the staff he had hired or fired, the hotel he'd closed for decontamination after an outbreak of the norovirus, the profit from the air fleet that was almost double the projected estimate...

And as he spoke, his words washing over her, Charley noticed how it all seemed to be aimed at his infirm father. And, for the first time, she noticed the challenge in the tone of his voice.

Because this was surely how he had always spoken to him. She'd just never noticed before how barbed his tone was or how pointed his stance.

For the first time it occurred to her that the Cazorlas, for all their outward respectability, were as dysfunctional as her own family.

There was Lucetta, the pillar of society.

Eduardo, the infirm head of the house.

Marta, the daughter with a mischievous streak that only came to the forefront when away from the stifling presence of her mother.

And Raul. The man who had to be the best at everything.

It was like observing a cleverly crafted game of manners in which everyone wore masks that hid anything resembling real emotion.

After a two-year absence from this table, it was as if Charley had sat down with a brand-new pair of eyes.

During her marriage she'd always felt intimidated in this house, terrified one of them would point a finger at her and expose her for being an imposter that no amount of expensive clothing or cosmetics could hide. Her fear had left her blind to what surrounded her.

The past two years had been a chance for her to find herself again and, no matter what happened in the future, she was determined never to lose herself again.

CHAPTER SEVEN

'WHEN DID YOU see my sister?' Raul asked, as soon as he had driven clear of the house.

She made no attempt to play innocent. 'Which time are you on about?'

So his hunch had been correct. It had been Marta's lack of curiosity about what Charley had been doing these past few years that had roused his suspicions. Even when their mother had left the room, Marta hadn't asked any of the questions he'd expected. It was because she'd already known the answers.

'It has been more than once?'

She sighed. 'I've seen her a handful of times since we split.'

'Am I correct in thinking this is something my mother is unaware of?'

'We thought it best not to tell her because we knew she'd feel obliged to tell you.'

That his mother certainly would have done.

'Who instigated it?'

'I did but it wasn't deliberate.' She turned her head to look at him. 'I went to see my father…'

'Your *father*?'

'He moved to Spain not long after we separated. He's living in a town on the Costa Dorado.'

'When you say he moved to Spain, how was he able to afford a property?' The last Raul had heard about his useless father-in-law was that he'd declared himself bankrupt after his latest get-rich scheme had failed.

'I bought a villa for him.' She didn't sound contrite about it. If anything, she sounded bullish.

'You bought a villa for him out of my money?'

'Technically it was my money. You gave it to me.'

'I can't believe you spent my money on buying that man a home.' Her father deserved nothing of the kind.

'I know you don't like him but he's my father.'

Raul took a deep breath. They were going off on a tangent here and he wanted to bring them back to the original thread of their conversation. But first he needed to make something clear. 'I do not dislike your father.'

Charley snorted her disbelief.

'What I have an issue with is the way he treated you and your mother when you were a child.' His fingers tightened on the steering wheel. 'He took advantage of your mother when she was seventeen years old and left her to raise you on her own giving little money and even less support.'

It used to infuriate him to think of how Graham Hutchinson had behaved towards his young family. The man had been fourteen years older than Charley's mother and, when he'd learned of the pregnancy, instead of doing the decent thing, had dumped her. He'd then flitted in and out of their lives as and when it had suited him, prioritising the two sons he had from a prior relationship. Charley and her mother had lived on the poverty line while Graham had taken exotic holidays and driven a sports car, thinking all his parental neglect could be made up for with expensive presents when he could afford them.

In truth, it still made him furious but he'd learned over the years that any criticism of Charley's father would be met with fierce indignation.

'That's all in the past,' she said now. Even through the

darkness of the night, he could sense her eyes blazing. 'I know he's no angel but he's still my dad and I love him. He needed a home and wanted to live closer to me. I had the money so I bought the villa for him.'

'So, he just happened to get in touch when he learned you'd left me and gave you his latest hard-luck story?'

'We've always kept in touch.'

There was that defensive tone again, but she made no comment about his guess that her father had gone to her cap in hand.

When they'd married, Graham had acted as though all his luck had rolled in at once, fully expecting his new son-in-law to support him. Raul had given him short shrift. After that, he'd kept his distance. As soon as Raul was out of the picture he'd swooped straight back in.

'So how does your father moving to Spain coincide with you visiting my sister?' he demanded to know, pulling them back on track.

'I went to visit my dad when he moved in and I dropped by to give Marta her books back,' she said.

'When did you borrow books from Marta?' He didn't think he'd ever seen Charley with a book in her hands.

'Lots of times. She thought it would help me learn Spanish if I read books in the language.'

'Why did you never tell me this?'

'I thought you'd laugh at me.'

'Why on earth would you think that?'

'You laughed at me whenever I tried to speak it.'

Had he? He'd always thought her attempts at speaking his language were cute. If he'd laughed it had been with pride that she was trying to master it. Had she really interpreted it as him making fun of her? 'I wasn't laughing at you.'

She didn't answer.

What did it matter anyway? Those days were gone.

'And after you dropped the books back, then what? You decided to carry on seeing each other?'

'It wasn't like that. I just got in the habit of meeting up with her whenever I visited my dad, that's all. We'd have a coffee and something to eat and then I'd leave. We were hardly conducting a high-level conspiracy.'

'Yet you kept it a secret from my mother. And from me.'

Raul shook his head, unable to believe the treachery conducted between his wife and sister. To think they'd been conspiring to see each other behind his back made his brain burn.

Where did family loyalty come into his sister's thinking? When Fabio had ended his relationship with Marta, Raul had been ready to kill him, not suggest they share cosy lunches together.

But then, Marta hadn't had loyalty drummed into her as he had. For Marta, childhood and life itself had been a charm; she'd been doted upon by the father who only spoke to his son to pick fault with him.

'Marta didn't want to upset you,' Charley said softly. 'She said you would think she was being disloyal.'

'You're damn right she was disloyal. But I'm not upset.'

'Then what are you?'

He forced his features into neutrality and glanced at her. 'I'm not anything.'

Silence rang out, not even a whisper of sound to be heard until Charley said, 'Nothing changes, does it?'

'What are you talking about?'

Her voice was sad. 'Nothing is allowed to be less than perfect, not even your own feelings.'

The silence suddenly filled with a roaring noise. It took a moment for him to realise the sound was in his own head.

His grip on the steering wheel tightened.

'How much did you have to drink tonight?' he asked, his voice tighter than he would like.

'See? Rather than confront what I've said, you deflect it.'

He expelled a long push of air from his lungs and flexed the tension from his fingers. He would not allow her to provoke him into an argument. All arguing did was bring about a loss of control, which solved nothing. Raul had learned that at a young age. His father had seen to that.

He remembered once sitting at the dining table while his father had read through his school report, slowly picking it apart, demanding to know why he'd only received the second highest grade on his end-of-year maths exam. Raul had argued his point that he'd spent the month leading up to that exam in bed with a bacterial infection but his reasons had been met with a fist thumped on the table and the school report had been ripped into pieces and burned. For his nerve in arguing back he'd received a two-week grounding. Nothing was mentioned about the top grades he'd received in all his other subjects.

Marta's report had been less than glowing academically but had been received by their father as if it were the best report ever written. Raul had been incensed at this double standard and, although Marta had begged him to keep quiet, he'd asked, reasonably, why they were being treated so differently. His insolence had been rewarded with an extra fortnight's grounding.

He'd been eleven.

'There's nothing to deflect,' he said, his vocal cords loosening under the force of his will. 'I'm perfectly in tune with my feelings.' To compound his point he flashed her a grin. 'Especially my baser ones.'

Charley undressed and quickly readied herself for bed while Raul made a phone call in his study.

She stared at the emperor-sized bed, at its plush seductiveness with the black sheets and plump pillows, inviting her to enter.

She wondered how many other women had been invited to enter it, before she could turn the thought away.

Turning the sheets back, she climbed in and lay down on her side of the bed. Strange to think that since leaving him she could have slept dead centre when in her own bed but had still favoured 'her' side.

She turned off the bedside light, flattened her pillow and burrowed herself into the sheets. The Spanish summer was hitting its stride but you wouldn't know it in this room where Raul had set the air conditioning to arctic.

Hopefully he would be kept busy making his phone calls and she would be fast asleep when he came up.

As was the contrary nature of sleep, it wouldn't come, her brain far too wired to switch off.

She found her mind turning over the evening's meal with his family. Maybe it was because she knew there was a time limit to the number of times she would share a meal with them but tonight she'd observed everything like a distant spectator, the fear of doing something wrong, something less than perfect, gone.

In all the years of their marriage she'd always thought Raul lucky to have such a close family and had envied him. How had she never noticed the undercurrent of poison there, especially between Raul and his father? Polite, gracious poison for sure, but poison all the same.

Her stomach clenched when she thought of her own family, the half-brothers she so wished would accept her as one of their own. What would Raul say if he learned she'd bought *them* a home each too? He'd accuse her of trying to buy their love and he would be right because that was exactly what she'd done. Except, as with everything else she did, she'd failed. She was more like her father than she'd ever thought possible. But she didn't want to be like him. She wanted to be like her mum, her sweet, naïve, hardworking mum who deserved everything good life had to offer.

She shut her eyes, trying to shake the direction of her thoughts and all the misery she'd thought she'd escaped when she'd married Raul, the man who'd made her feel like a princess even if only at the beginning...

A noise caught her attention and she heard the tread of his approach, followed by the creak of the bedroom door opening.

Squeezing her eyes together even more tightly, she concentrated on making her breathing deep and even. Hopefully he would assume she was asleep and leave her alone.

She heard him go into the bathroom, listened to the muffled sound of water running as he brushed his teeth. A slant of light came into the bedroom when he stepped back in, and she opened one eye a fraction. It took a few seconds for that eye to adjust to what it was seeing—Raul stripping off.

In the beat of a moment her mouth ran dry.

In no time at all he was down to his snug boxer shorts, his beautifully defined chest silhouetted against that tiny beam of light in all its glory; broad and hard, a smattering of dark hair running across his pecs and thickening the lower it ran...

Forget deep and even breathing. When his fingers hooked the sides of his boxers and tugged them off, pulling them past his strong thighs, all the air in her lungs went into hibernation.

His silhouette moved back to the bathroom and turned the light off, plunging the bedroom into darkness.

Too late she remembered her plan to feign sleep.

The bed dipped, the sheets rustled and a large, warm figure slid in beside her.

The dryness in her mouth became a memory as moisture filled it…and a lower part of her anatomy.

Immediately she pressed her thighs together in a futile attempt to counteract the heat filling between them and closed her eyes, anticipating the moment he reached out and pulled her to him.

Did she have the strength to even pretend lack of interest, when every part of her felt so heightened?

It felt as if she waited for ever for him to make his move, every passing minute dragging on to the next.

Nothing.

He lay on his side facing her, making her scold herself for not having faced the wall rather than the centre of the bed. She might have her eyes shut but she could feel his gaze upon her.

'Well?' she said, before she could stop her tongue from speaking. 'Isn't this the moment when you take your next payment?'

He shifted closer to her, his face near enough for her to feel the warmth of his minty breath.

'My payment is your body, whenever and wherever I require,' he said in a tone that washed through her skin like a caress, moving even closer so the tip of his nose pressed against hers.

Her lips parted in anticipation of his kiss.

'But tonight I will put my payment on hiatus.' Suddenly he twisted away and turned his back to her. 'Unless you wish to make a payment to me of your own accord?' he added, pulling the sheets over his shoulder and edging away from her.

'That will never happen,' she whispered, goosebumps covering her at the abrupt withdrawal of his warmth.

'Never say never.' He laughed quietly. 'If you change your mind…'

'Dream on.'

'Oh, I will.'

Raul smiled into his pillow and closed his eyes. He could practically smell her frustration.

When he *did* make love to her, she would be desperate for his touch. All her defiance would be smothered by desire.

He let his mind run free, imagining all the ways he would take her and she would take him; imagined her tongue snaking its way down his chest…

But something else fought for space in his head, the same something that had been jarring in his throat since the journey back home.

Her words echoed within him, becoming louder the more he tried to push them away.

'Nothing is allowed to be less than perfect—not even your own feelings.'

Was there some truth in it?

No. Of course there wasn't. Charley was trying to needle him.

A memory flashed in his mind of one time he *had* allowed his emotions to get the better of him. It had been the night Charley told him she didn't want his baby.

His anger had been bubbling at the surface, impossible to hide and, for the first time in his adult life, he'd given into it, lashing out verbally, cruelly. He'd called her a gold-digging bitch and told her to leave, not meaning it and never for a moment imagining she would.

It hadn't been one-sided. The recriminations had flown both ways, Charley screaming back at him with furious tears streaming down her face that their marriage had no basis in reality, that he patronised her and treated her like

a child, that he should find himself another wife, someone who could breed a dozen children for him, look perfect and run a multinational company and all in her sleep.
That he was a cold, arrogant control freak.

By the time the anger had notched down to a simmer,
both of them visibly calmer, her bags were packed.

'This is ridiculous,' he'd said. 'You're not going anywhere.'

'You told me to leave,' she'd replied with a face so stony
it was like looking at a statue.

'That was in the heat of the moment and now I'm telling you to stay.'

'But I don't want to stay.' She'd looked straight at him
with eyes that were a red, raw mess, black streaks of make-
up splotched down her cheeks. At that moment she had
looked exactly as he'd felt. 'I can't live like this any more.'

And just like that, their marriage was over.

He almost laughed at the irony. The one time in his
adulthood that he'd truly given into his feelings, his wife
had walked out on him.

If that didn't tell him he was right to keep his emotions
controlled and locked away, nothing did.

The grounds of the building Raul had purchased to rehome
Poco Rio were filled with overgrown weeds dying in the
heat and parched grass. Charley didn't care; all she saw
in her mind's eye was how glorious it would be when the
renovations were complete.

The architect, a middle-aged man with a shock of
white hair called Vittore, had travelled from Barcelona
with them. Other than Raul's introduction, the two men
had conversed between themselves during the short helicopter trip and even shorter car journey, discussing other
business projects they were working on together. If Vittore

was bothered about travelling to Valencia on a Saturday morning there was no sign of it in his relaxed demeanour.

She itched to get back inside the sprawling one-storey building; she had been dreaming of this moment for two long months. Of course, her dreams hadn't involved Raul buying the place in his name. In her dreams it had been in her name and, when all the renovations were complete, she'd intended to sign it over to Poco Rio so they never need worry about losing their home again.

He'd said he *might* give her the deeds if she proved herself to him. All she could do was try.

The main thing was that so long as she kept her side of the bargain and stayed with him for four months, Raul would keep his and Poco Rio would have a new home. That much she trusted him on.

The interior of the pretty red stone building, which was so much nicer than the institutionalised building Poco Rio was currently homed in, was as ramshackle as she remembered, but that was only decoration. The rooms were large and, once new windows had been installed, would be airy.

'I'm going to look around and see what my money has bought,' Raul said, leaving her with Vittore.

The moment he was out of sight, Charley sat on the dusty floor, opened her briefcase and pulled out her plans. 'Please don't feel I am treading on your toes,' she said, speaking in hesitant Spanish, 'but here's a guide to what the centre needs.'

Vittore squatted beside her and took the plans. After he'd perused them for a while, he said, 'Is there a reason the doorways need to be so wide?'

'A lot of the children have wheelchairs,' she answered carefully, scared of things being lost in translation.

He nodded thoughtfully, then asked her some more questions.

They were deep in conversation, Charley pointing out where she thought a wall should be knocked down to make a large soft-play area, when Raul rejoined them.

Her Spanish died on her lips.

He regarded her for a moment, his eyes drilling into her with something that looked like cold suspicion, before turning to Vittore. 'Has Charlotte explained the brief?'

Vittore nodded and stretched back up. 'Her plans are very impressive.' He turned his attention to her. 'Be proud. You have done well.'

Charley's cheeks flushed at the unexpected compliment. She hadn't expected *that*.

She became even more flustered when Vittore carefully refolded her plans along the seams she'd made and tucked them into his large carry-case. 'Next time, you roll them.'

'Sorry?' She didn't have the faintest idea what he was talking about.

'Next time you create plans, roll them, don't fold.'

She bit into her bottom lip to stop the smile that fought to spread over her face. Vittore was a renowned architect with over twenty years' experience and he was complimenting and advising her as if she were, if not an equal, then a promising student.

So stunned was she that the rest of the conversation passed her by, right until the moment came for them to leave.

While Raul and Vittore headed outside, she gave the place one last look, imagining how bright and fabulous it would be when the renovations and subsequent decoration were complete. Her heart swelled to think of the children's faces when they saw it for the first time.

The humidity outside hung heavy like a damp cloak and Charley was grateful to get back in the helicopter, where the air conditioning ran at full blast. She caught the tail end of the men's conversation and Vittore saying he would bring a team over on Monday. He smiled encouragingly at Charley and added to Raul, 'Your wife's plans have made our job much easier.'

'You are going to follow them?'

'As much as we can. They make a lot of sense.'

Raul's gaze caught hers. 'My wife has hidden talents.'

His tone and expression were so inscrutable she didn't know if he was being serious or mocking her.

CHAPTER EIGHT

Soon they were back in Barcelona making the short drive
to the villa. Saturdays in the city were always busy, especially in summer, and today was no exception, so, while
traffic was calmer during the weekend, the number of pe-
destrians more than made up for it.

The villa was empty when they got in; the household
staff all took weekends off.

During their marriage Charley had lived for the weekends. Sharing a home with staff was something she'd
never got used to. One of many things she'd struggled
with. Going from a tiny two-bedroom flat in a high-rise
block of flats in south-east London to an eight-bedroom
villa by the sea would have challenged anyone.

She thought of Raul's parents' household with a shudder. They had live-in staff on call seven days a week.

'Vittore was impressed with your plans,' Raul commented as he headed into the kitchen and found the cap-
sules to slot into the coffee machine.

She managed a nod, still stunned at the praise she'd received from the architect.

Other than entertain kids, she'd never done *anything* in
her life that warranted praise before. It was a heady feeling to know she didn't have to fail at everything she set
her mind to.

She thought back wistfully to the businesses she'd tried

so hard at but for which she'd never been able to find the magic quality Raul possessed with all *his* businesses. She'd so badly wanted to make him proud and for him to see her as his equal, and all she'd done was mess it up, over and over again. The pressure had been too great to bear.

'Where did you learn how to do it?' he asked.

'I did a search on the Internet on how to create plans. The estate agent did a scale floor plan so I worked from that.'

He pulled two china cups out of the cupboard, placing one in the slot of the machine. 'I'm sorry I dismissed your plans the other day.'

Her heart jolted at this unexpected apology. She hadn't thought the word sorry was in his vocabulary.

'That's okay,' she said with a shrug. 'I'm used to it.'

He looked at her curiously. 'What do you mean by that?'

'You used to cross-examine me about everything to do with my businesses. I always knew you didn't take my plans or ideas seriously.'

'I took them seriously enough to give you a lot of money to pay for them.'

She sighed. 'But I always knew you were humouring me.'

Raul punched the button on the machine at the same moment a swell of anger cut through him. 'I was not humouring you. I wanted you to succeed and I believed you could. But, Charlotte, you left school without any qualifications. All I did was give you the benefit of my knowledge and experience. It was when you chose to ignore my advice that your businesses floundered.'

It had been hard for him to watch her throw them all away, discarding them as if they were toys that had lost their sparkle after their first few uses. But he'd kept his patience, as hard as it had been. A part of him had admired her guts in dusting herself off and starting again.

It wasn't until he'd lost that tolerance and witnessed her immediate horrified refusal to have a child that he'd realised her businesses had failed *because* she'd treated them like toys. They'd been something for her to play with so she could put off the moment she confessed to not wanting his child that bit longer, enabling her to milk him and their lifestyle for all it was worth.

He'd understood all this the night she'd left him and still he'd asked her to stay.

What sickened him more than anything was knowing he would have taken her back, right up until the divorce papers had landed on his doorstep.

He'd almost lost control of himself that day too, had taken his car for a drive, not knowing where he was going and somehow ending up in Valencia. Before he'd known it, he'd been at the street listed on the divorce papers.

The fog had lifted and he'd slammed on his brakes before he could seek her house out, a cold sweat breaking out on his skin.

He was certain the tyre marks at the entrance of her street had been made by him when he'd spun the Lotus round and screeched away.

Thinking about how she'd played him sent another spike of fury through him. He tempered it by the skin of his teeth.

'It was hard for me,' she said quietly, leaning against the wall by the door and folding her arms across her chest. 'I was desperate to impress you.'

'What for? You were my wife. I wouldn't have married you if I wasn't already impressed by you.'

'You were impressed with my body,' she answered with a hard laugh.

'It was more than that and you know it,' he cut in. 'I admired your spirit.' Something which, he had to admit now he thought of it, had disappeared during the latter years of their marriage.

How had he not noticed?

Seeing that spirit return now, that zinging feistiness, sent the most peculiar feeling of déjà vu tearing through him.

'I wanted you to be impressed with my mind and my abilities,' she said, a rueful twinge to her voice. 'But it was so much harder than I thought it would be. Call me naïve but I wanted to do things my own way, to prove I could do it, but I put so much pressure on myself that I crumbled. It didn't help that I didn't speak the language.'

'You've mastered it well enough since we separated.' He'd employed a tutor to help her with Spanish but after a few months she'd put a stop to the lessons, saying they were too hard. Like driving a car, she'd mastered Spanish after she'd left him and without his help. 'I suppose reading Marta's books helped.'

'Not much. It was working at Poco Rio that really did it. The kids hardly speak Spanish never mind English so I had to learn fast if I wanted them to understand me.'

Raul didn't answer, his teeth clenching together as they always did whenever he thought of her surrounded by small children on a daily basis.

Charley loved children.

But not as much as she loved money...

Was that really true? All the evidence pointed to her leading a frugal existence without him. And she hadn't asked for any money for herself...

She'd lapsed into silence, her head bowed. Then suddenly she lifted her chin and stared at him with enough force to keep his focus on her and not the coffee machine.

'Marrying you was all wrong,' she said, her eyes wide. 'You were the shining star turning the family business from silver into gold—*everything* you touched turned into gold. Everything I touched turned into rust. I couldn't compete.'

'Our marriage wasn't a competition.'

'I know, but for me...'

'For you, what?' he asked, when her words tailed off.

'I wasn't equipped to deal with any of it. I tried, really, I did, but I knew you wanted perfection. Never mind learning Spanish, you wanted me to speak proper English, to wear the right clothes, to be a wife you could be proud to have on your arm...'

'That was *not* how it was,' he retorted, irked she could twist things round to make herself seem like some kind of victim. 'I was trying to help you fit in with my world.'

'I wanted to fit in too and it took me a long time to realise that I couldn't because I *don't* belong. The world I come from is just too different. You make everything you touch turn into pure gold, but all you could do with me was add gold-plating—underneath I was still Charley, not the Charlotte you tried to create.'

'That's a good story you've spun there but my memory tells it differently. In all the time we were together not once did you say you were unhappy. Not once.'

'That's because I was terrified that if I said how I felt, you would agree with me. I spent most of our time together waiting for the day you realised I wasn't up to scratch and replaced me with a better model.'

She looked and sounded so sincere he almost believed her. 'Answer me this. In all the time we were together did I *ever* give you cause to think I would cheat on you?'

She shook her head. 'I always knew you'd never cheat, you're too honourable. But,' she added, before he could retaliate, 'you spend a huge amount of your time in hotels and on cruise liners surrounded by beautiful, well-bred women throwing themselves at you. Knowing you wouldn't cheat didn't mean I was stupid enough to believe someone else wouldn't catch your eye and you'd want to get to know them better. I knew I was disposable, just as Jessica was disposable when I came back on the scene.'

Dios, she could not be serious.

'Why would you even *think* such a thing?' he demanded to know, not giving her time to answer before adding, 'I never once looked at another woman in the whole time we were married.'

Doubt reverberated through her curvaceous frame.

The incongruity was laughable. Charley had been the one to walk out. She'd left *him*. Their marriage vows had clearly meant a damn sight more to him than they had to her.

'Why would I have looked at another woman when I had you to come home to?' he said, striding over to her and pressing a hand against the wall by her head. 'You, *cariño*, are all woman.'

She tensed, her jaw becoming rigid as she swallowed. 'You've just proven everything I've said. You really *do* think I'm only good for one thing.'

'And that, I can assure you, you are superb at.'

She grabbed his wrist and tried to yank it down, but he twisted his hand and caught her own wrist, pinning her without any effort, then snaked an arm around her waist and pulled her flush to him.

Her head tilted back, her green eyes staring at him with the strangest mixture of contempt and desire. 'When did you become so cruel?'

'When I realised the woman I adored was playing me for a fool.' And with that, he brought his mouth down to hers, drowning out the voices in his head clamouring to argue with this assessment of her.

Charley tried to resist. She closed her mouth as tightly as she could, tried to shut her senses off, but it was like fighting the tide.

His heat, his scent, filled her, creeping through the pores of her skin and down into her blood.

She could push him away. All it would take was one hard shove and she'd be free. Raul might be many things but he would never use his physical strength to force her to do anything she didn't want.

But they had a deal. She was here for his pleasure and no other reason.

And, if she was being honest with herself, she was here for her own pleasure too because her husband set her alive in a way she would never have known if they'd never met.

Rationality fighting with her senses, she put a hand to his chest, still uncertain if she was going to push or pull. Her fingers splayed against him and before she knew it she'd gripped his shirt. Her lips softened and parted as she melted into him.

His kiss was hard, demanding, his tongue moving within her, her own dancing against it.

Her grip on his shirt loosened and she wound her arms up and around his neck, her fingers pressing into the back of his head, leaning against his strength as he kissed her so thoroughly she doubted she would have been able to stand if he weren't there supporting her.

Time became nothing. All she knew and all she cared about was now, this moment, and the heat burning through her.

His kisses deepened, then he broke away long enough to dip his head and nip her neck.

Then his hands clasped her bottom and she was pushed against the wall while simultaneously lifted off the ground.

Wrapping her legs around his waist, she pressed kisses over his face, tasting him, inhaling him, rubbing her nose into the smooth skin of his cheeks that roughened as she nuzzled his jawline.

He held her tightly to him, as if her weight meant nothing, and carried her through the kitchen to the narrow stairs. She had no idea how he managed to make it up the two flights with her in his arms, could only assume the fever burning through them drove him onwards until he kicked open their bedroom door and threw her effortlessly onto the bed. Stepping back, Raul gazed down at her, his handsome features taut, his chest surging. Her heart thrummed painfully, pulses racing through her as she stared right back.

Without a word, his eyes holding hers, he pulled at his belt to undo it then opened the buttons and dropped his trousers.

In reply, she raised herself enough to tug off her top and throw it onto the floor.

Working methodically, Raul undid the buttons of his shirt while Charley fumbled with the zip of her denim shorts before kicking them off and sending them sailing towards the other clothes that were forming a messy pile by his feet. His shirt joined them, leaving him in nothing but boxer shorts that stretched over his snake hips and tight buttocks, the strain of his erection visible through the fabric...

Heat bubbled deep within her, a sweet yet torturous sensation that begged for attention, and she dragged herself to her knees, taking in every part of him from his toes to his cropped dark hair as she unclasped her bra and threw it to one side, not caring where it landed. Then, finally, she pulled her underwear down past her hips, as Raul's eyes watched every move she made, his strong throat moving as he swallowed.

'Lie down,' he instructed, his words guttural.

She did as she was bid and laid back, posing provocatively for him with one arm hooked over her head, a hand clasping a breast that was practically crying for attention, deliberately encircling a hard nipple.

A muted groan came from his throat and he yanked at his boxers and tugged them down past his muscular thighs, freeing his erection.

More moisture filled her, the heated ache in the apex of her thighs now nothing but a mass of sensation begging for his touch.

A warning thought rang out, breaking through the haze.

'I'm not on the pill any more,' she managed to gasp, beyond caring if this gave away her total lack of sex-life since their parting.

His blue eyes widened a touch before darkening, his desire as easy to read as anything she'd ever seen before.

Wrenching his gaze from her, he took the three steps to his dresser and opened the top shelf, rummaging for a moment before producing a packet of condoms.

She couldn't deny the relief at seeing the box still in its seal.

Raul used his teeth to rip the clear seal off, then pulled a foil square out of the box and ripped it open.

They hadn't used condoms since their engagement. Her heart twisted to see him struggle with it, as if he were out of practice...

All thoughts vanished when he turned to her and feasted his eyes on her naked form. 'Spread your legs.'

Parting her thighs, she exposed herself to him, thrilling in the dilation of his eyes as he drank her in, then strode over to her and climbed on the bed, grabbing her hands and pinning them beside her head, his fingers entwining in hers.

His mouth crashed down on hers, crushing her lips, his tongue sweeping into her mouth while the tip of his erection found the heart of her and, with one long thrust, he pushed into her, filling her whole.

Charley could no more hold back her cry of relief than she could swim to the moon.

Raul's hold on her hands tightened as he moved within her with no hesitation, no lingering caresses, just pure carnality.

She parted her legs ever wider, her pelvis tilted so they ground together, taking everything he gave and giving it back with sobs of pleasure. Sensation fizzed and built within her, heightening with every stroke.

The feel of him on her and inside her, his powerful thrusts, the way his chest crushed her breasts, everything fused together to form one whole sensitised buzz forming into a tight ball that, with one long final stroke, exploded within her. Raul's groan of release toppled her over the edge.

She clung to him, her hands, freed from his hold, clasping his head as she buried her face in his neck, whimpering into his skin as pulsations rippled through her.

For the longest time they lay together, her legs wrapped around his waist, Charley savouring the feeling of release and the weight of his body upon her.

But all too soon he shifted off her and padded to the bathroom, leaving her alone for long enough that the glowing feeling deep inside her dimmed.

This means nothing. He hates you. He thinks you're a gold-digger. He didn't even want to hear how you felt during your marriage, he cared only about getting you naked.

She pushed the thoughts away, refusing to acknowledge the way her heart felt as if someone had grabbed hold of it and given it a mighty squeeze.

Silently he returned, climbed back under the sheets and pulled her into his arms. He dropped a kiss to her forehead.

Her heart twisted as she listened to his deepening breaths, his hand remaining buried in her hair as he fell into sleep.

It didn't matter what he believed or that he hadn't listened to her. It wasn't as if they were intending to give their marriage another go in the proper fashion.

She was here for his pleasure, nothing more. And that meant *her* pleasure too.

Things were already different between them. It *felt* different and not just because she'd been blackmailed into being here. The dynamic between them had changed. In a sick kind of way, it was better like this, more honest. She didn't have to mask who she was any more; her fear of disappointing him was gone.

She should be celebrating. Four months of physical bliss without having to pretend to be someone she wasn't?

In other words, exactly what their marriage should have been.

Charley was sitting at her desk in the office adjoining Raul's, trying to read a book on finance while nibbling at a biscuit.

'You look as if you have a headache,' he said, walking through the open doorway to join her, two cups of coffee in his hands.

'Just trying to get my head around it all.' She wiped the crumbs off her blouse onto her desk, then swept them into her hand and into the bin.

Raul had been as good as his word. All week she'd been

chained to his side. Monday and Tuesday had been spent in his office, Wednesday and Thursday in France where he was involved in negotiations to have a base for his air fleet in Paris. He'd been incredibly busy, in and out of meetings, most of which he'd insisted she come along to, working at a pace that made her dizzy.

Today they were back in Barcelona and, while the pace seemed no less frantic, there was an air of calm about the place, his staff more relaxed. It was probably that Friday feeling, she guessed. It had infected her too, that sense of the working week being almost over and a couple of days of relaxation to look forward to.

She hated to admit it, but the thought of a weekend alone with him sent a thrill through her.

Making love to Raul was as addictive as the packet of biscuits she'd been munching her way through. Having his throat, so strong and golden, in her eyeline right now as he took the seat opposite her...

'This book might as well be gibberish,' she said, closing it with a snap and pushing it over to him.

He raised a dark brow and loosened his tie. 'The main reason your businesses went bust was because you didn't take care of the bottom line. Unless you want the same thing to happen at Poco Rio, I suggest you pay attention carefully.'

'But Poco Rio is different,' she protested.

'A business is a business. Catering for children is no different from any other business—the bottom line is still the same.'

'Not in this case...'

Her phone went off, jumping with the vibrations from the alert. She snatched it up.

'Who is it?'

'My dad.'

'What does he want?'

'He's replying to a message I left for him last week.' She winced at her slip that she'd been waiting a week to hear back from him and hurriedly added, 'I wanted to know when he's free for lunch.'

His expression was even. 'Are you forgetting our deal? Your place is by my side.'

She rolled her eyes. 'Not for a second. That's why I suggested he choose a weekend.'

'You're still by my side at weekends.'

'Even prisoners are allowed visitation rights.' She took a sip of her coffee.

A pulse worked at his jaw.

'You're not seriously thinking you can stop me visiting my family?' she asked. 'Because that would make you even more hateful.'

His eyes crinkled at the edges. 'You didn't think I was hateful last night when I made you come with my tongue.'

'You're very talented,' she responded sweetly, wishing her face didn't flush at the memory.

'Why don't you sit on my lap and I'll show you how talented I am with something other than my tongue?' He placed his chin on his hand and held his blue eyes on her, a lascivious glimmer in them.

'Why do I get the feeling you're trying to distract me again? We were talking about my dad, not about having sex in your office.' She had to admit, the thought of doing something *here*, in the heart of his empire, sent the most erotic charge racing through her.

He clicked his tongue on the roof of his mouth and settled back in his chair, cradling his cup to him, that same glimmer still there in his eyes. 'No, I wouldn't try and stop you seeing your father, even though I could.'

Oh, yes, he could. Of that Charley had no doubts. But

she wondered if he would still hold the kids of Poco Rio over her head like a weapon if he actually met them and spent time with them.

'It concerns me to see you give up a day for something that might not happen,' he continued. 'Your father is hardly the most reliable of people.'

'Your concern for my emotional well-being is touching.'

Something dark glittered across his features. 'I know you dislike criticism of him but I spent three years watching you be disappointed by that man.'

Her hackles rose. 'That *man* is my father.'

'And if he had ever acted like a father towards you I would be more forgiving of him. Charlotte, he was an hour late for our wedding. Your mother had to walk you down the aisle.'

'He was stuck in traffic,' she snapped, her belly knotting at the remembrance.

'If he'd left earlier traffic wouldn't have been a problem.'

'You have no right,' she said, red-hot fury pushing through her. 'No right at all, not when your own family is more screwed up than mine.'

'My family is—'

'Perfect,' she finished for him. 'The famous Cazorlas, practically perfect in every way, apart from the only son clearly hating the infirm father and having a strained relationship with the mother, the only daughter hiding the essence of herself when with the parents so as not to fall off the pedestal they've put her on, everyone putting on a front when they step out of the door because nothing's more important than showing that *perfect face*.'

The tendons on Raul's neck were straining, his jaw clenched. 'I warn you now, Charlotte, stop.'

'Oh, I get it—it's okay for you to pick fault with *my* family but I'm not allowed to criticise yours?'

'You don't know what you're talking about.'

'Yes, I do—I lived with you for three years, remember? The difference now is that I'm not wrapped up in my own insecurities. I can see it all clearly.'

He got to his feet and placed his hands on the desk, looming down over her, his face a mask. 'My family is none of your business, not any more. You lost that right when you walked out on me.'

'Then consider my family off limits too.'

His eyes bored into her, his lips now a tight line. 'What date has your father given for you to meet?'

Her answer was just as terse. 'A week on Saturday.'

'I will check my diary and let you know if we're free.'

'Thank you.'

He straightened and reached for his cup, his breathing heavy. 'I've arranged for a member of the finance team to sit down with you for the afternoon and go through some accounts with you.'

'Now?'

'Now.'

He strode back into his adjoining office and closed the door behind him.

CHAPTER NINE

RAUL PASSED THE living room on his way outside for his daily swim and paused.

Charley was sprawled on the sofa thumbing through a Spanish magazine, dressed in a thigh-length white T-shirt, her hair pulled back into a loose ponytail, not a scrap of make-up on her face. She was working her way mechanically through a bar of chocolate.

Deep in concentration, she didn't notice his presence, allowing him to gaze at her unhindered.

His guts twisted.

Walking away before she noticed him, he stepped out into the swimming-pool area, placed his towel on a sun lounger, and dived in.

As he powered his way through the water he waited for the usual calm to envelop him and empty his mind.

Today, it didn't happen. Length after length, his mind was filled with his wife. Not the heated discussion about their families that had taken place two days ago and which had settled into a strange kind of truce, nor their lovemaking, the potency of which still showed no sign of abating, but the vision of her sitting on that sofa eating the chocolate bar, just as she'd been eating those biscuits at her desk.

It was that sense of déjà vu again, that feeling of staring at the Ghost of Wife Past.

For the first time, he properly considered if there could

be any truth in her words that she had spent their marriage unhappily striving to be the person she thought he wanted.

When they'd first met she'd had an innate sunniness. Smiles and laughter had come easily. They were what had drawn him to her, along with the earthy sexiness that came off her in waves.

While the smiles and laughter were no more evident now than they had been by the end of their marriage, the earthiness had returned.

He'd assumed the casual way she'd dressed when they'd first met had been due to her lack of money, had assumed that all women wanted personal shoppers, hairdressers, beauticians and dieticians on speed-dial. His mother and sister did; all his exes had. He'd never met *any* woman who didn't.

But then, he'd never met a woman like Charley before. His inner circle was insular, he acknowledged, filled with like-minded people with the same wealth and outlook on life.

Charley had embraced it all, he reminded himself, right down to the rationing of chocolate.

All he'd wanted was for her to be happy and fit into his world and, with a little help, she'd fitted in perfectly. With his help she'd never had to feel that anyone was judging her. Or so he'd believed...

To see her eating a bar of chocolate...it was such a small thing, but enough to shift his perspective even more. Enough to make him question...

Gone was the haute couture. Gone, the immaculately coiffured hair. Gone, the rigid diet. Gone too, were the rock-hard abs she'd developed during their marriage, replaced with the luscious softness he recalled from their early days.

When he'd completed his daily two hundred lengths,

he hauled himself out of the pool. For once there were no hunger pangs. Everything felt tight inside him, far too tight to eat.

He grabbed his towel and rubbed it over his hair and face. As he towelled the water from his back Charley came out into the morning sunshine and walked over to him, her phone in hand.

'Have we got anything planned for tomorrow?' she asked, keeping a respectable distance from him although he noted with some satisfaction that her eyes lingered on his chest for longer than was respectable. All at once, the disquiet within him evaporated. He closed the distance and reached for her hips.

'You'll get me wet,' she scolded but with definite half-heartedness. After a week of erotic lovemaking, he knew her resistance was nothing but a measure to prove her own self-control against him.

'That's the idea,' he murmured. Unable to resist, he pulled her in for a kiss, delighting in the sweet, chocolate taste of her mouth.

She sighed into him, slipping her tongue into his mouth and sliding her arms around his neck, before her hands balled into fists and she stepped away. A dark, wet stain now marked her top.

'Tomorrow?' she reminded him.

'You will be with me.'

'Doing what though? Anything important or am I going to be stuck in my office again?'

'Doing whatever I require.'

'Seve's just messaged me.' Her speech came in a rush. 'Two of the staff at Poco Rio have caught a sickness bug.'

'And that involves you how?'

'They're going to be short-staffed.'

'No.'

'I haven't asked for anything yet,' she protested.

'Do I have to remind you that our deal is for you to stay by my side?'

'No, but if they don't have the staff, the centre won't be able to open and the children…'

He did not want to hear a single word about children, not from her lips.

Every time she uttered the word he was reminded of her treachery.

'I'm not prepared to debate the matter. We have already agreed that your day-to-day work at the centre is over.'

Her face darkened, her eyes ringing with obvious contempt. 'But—'

'Shh.' He placed a finger to her lips. 'It's a beautiful day with no work or anything else to worry about. Let's not waste it by arguing about things we have already agreed on.'

Gently he moved his finger off her mouth and traced it down her neck.

He could see her thinking, her eyes moving as she deliberated his words. When his fingers found the band holding her hair back and carefully tugged it out, to let her hair fall down across her shoulders, her breath hitched. When his lips reclaimed hers, there was no more protest. Only willingness. Followed by ecstasy.

After a day spent making love and a night spent doing the same all over again, Raul awoke on Monday morning to an empty bed and the distant sound of a helicopter flying close by.

He stretched and looked at his watch, surprised to see he'd overslept by a good hour. He could have sworn he'd set his alarm.

Wondering where Charley had got to, he showered and

dressed quickly. He had a meeting with the MD of his air fleet at ten a.m. and if there was one thing Raul did not appreciate, it was tardiness, either from others or himself.

The scent of fresh coffee and newly baked *bollos*— sweet rolls—pervaded the air: morning aromas that never failed to lift his spirits. The household staff worked at their chores with their customary zeal. The dining table had been set...

Set for one.

On the placemat sat a folded letter.

Eyes wide with disbelief, he read it.

Gone to the centre. Back some time this evening.
Charley.
PS: Have borrowed the helicopter.

Of all the reactions provoked by the note, the one that came to the forefront the quickest was laughter.

He could scarcely credit her nerve.

That feeling of witnessing the Ghost of Wife Past consumed him again. The Charley he'd first met had been impulsive, living for the moment...

But surely she must know what the consequences would be?

The laughter died as quickly as it had come. By the time his *café con leche* and *bollos* were brought through to him, all amusement had gone.

Did she seriously think she could take off to the centre in direct contravention of his wishes?

Was she seriously serious, as she herself would have put it?

Did she think that now she was back in his bed she could do as she pleased and he would be as forgiving as he had always been?

It was time his wife learned a lesson. If she refused to learn it then he would cancel their agreement and to hell with the day care centre. It meant nothing to him anyway.

Raul parked the Lotus next to the minibus Charley had been driving the week before and stared at the institutional-looking building with the same distaste as when he'd first been there.

When he'd called his helicopter back to Barcelona, his pilot had been full of contrition.

It hadn't taken Raul long to put the pieces together. Charley had got the pilot's number from the household directory and said she wanted to go to Valencia. The pilot hadn't thought twice about the instruction. He would think twice if Charley tried the same stunt again.

Raul assumed she'd turned his alarm clock off at some point during the night in the snatches of sleep he'd managed between bouts of lovemaking.

He had to press his thumb on a buzzer at the door and wait for someone to approve his admittance before he could enter. When he was finally granted entry, his initial reaction was that he'd walked into a clinic.

To his mind, day care centres were supposed to be bright and colourful places full of squealing children. The exterior might have an institutional feel to it, but he'd expected the interior to be more fitting, not grey and lifeless.

The man he recognised as Seve greeted him at the door of a large room that looked more as he'd imagined, filled with colourful drawings and bright furniture. He could smell food cooking and the aroma was not at all unpleasant.

Seve shook his hand enthusiastically, treating Raul as if Elvis himself had walked into the building. 'It is an honour to meet you. We are all so grateful for what you have done for the children here. It is an amazing thing.'

As Seve droned on Raul took stock of what surrounded him. The harder he looked, the harder his heart pumped and the lighter his head felt.

Of the dozen or so children in the room at least half were in wheelchairs. All of them sat in a horseshoe around a woman dressed in a bright yellow all-in-one outfit, bright red curly wig and a round red nose. The woman was juggling soft balls, while standing on a plank of wood atop a football. Her balance looked precarious, her juggling atrocious—she dropped more balls than she caught—but it made no difference to the children, all of whom watched with rapt attention, some of them squealing their laughter loudly.

It took a few moments for his brain to comprehend that it was Charley in the ridiculous clown outfit.

A small hand tugged at his arm and he looked down to see a young boy gazing up at him.

'This is Ramon,' Seve said, with a benevolent smile. 'I think he wants you to watch the show with him.'

'I'm not here for the entertainment,' Raul said, intending to add, 'I'm here to take Charley home.' But when he opened his mouth to say the words, he caught Ramon's eye and was rewarded with a smile that could melt the entire Arctic Circle.

Somehow Raul allowed himself to be guided over to the floor by the child who, it was obvious, had Down's syndrome. As he looked at the other faces one thing was abundantly clear—every single one of these children was severely disabled. One other thing was clear though too: every single one of these children was enthralled with the performance Charley was giving them.

Suddenly she spotted him and for a moment she faltered. When the balls fell out of her hand this time, there was nothing feigned about it.

A girl who looked to be no more than eight, who had the most beautiful curly white-blonde hair, toddled over to Raul, her head turned to one side, and stared with curiously vacant eyes, then prodded a finger into his cheek.

'Leave the nice man alone, Karin,' Seve said, scooping the little girl up into his arms. Karin thus proceeded to poke Seve in the face.

'Sorry about that,' Seve said, gently taking Karin's hands to stop any more incessant prodding. 'She doesn't know what she's doing.'

'It's no problem.' Other than a slightly tilted head, there was nothing Raul could see physically atypical about the little girl. But something clearly wasn't quite right.

Charley had stopped juggling and was now making balloon animals in the same slapstick manner that had most of the children, those who could, laughing. When she spoke it was in precise Spanish without any of the inhibitions she'd displayed when speaking the language to Vittore.

She finished her act with a bow, then Seve and two other workers took on the task of wheeling and walking the children into an adjoining room that looked, from where Raul sat, like a dining room, while Charley gathered her props together in a battered old suitcase.

She didn't say a single word to him. If he hadn't caught her eye during her little show, he would have thought she hadn't noticed him.

Done packing, she picked up the suitcase and carried it off. Raul followed her out of the room and into the entrance hall, where she turned off down a connecting corridor and opened the door into a large storeroom.

'I'm sorry, okay?' she muttered, stacking the suitcase

upright next to a shelving unit crammed with waterproof paints, non-toxic glues and all manner of child-friendly crafts.

For once, he was at a loss for what to say.

Charley pulled her red nose off, followed by the wig, which was making her scalp itch.

A part of her had known Raul would turn up. Never mind her defiance, borrowing his helicopter would have tipped him over the edge.

A part of her had *wanted* him to follow her, to see the children for himself, to understand how important the project was on a humane level.

As vain as she knew it to be, another part of her wished he had come when she hadn't been dressed as a clown in pyjamas.

She wished he would say something.

She unzipped the yellow onesie and stepped out of it with relief. With no air conditioning in the building, it had been like wearing a portable sauna.

'What is this place?' he finally asked, his voice heavy.

'I thought you said you'd read my letter,' she said, deliberately keeping her tone breezy. She opened the cloth sack in the corner and folded the onesie into it, stuffing the wig and nose in its pockets.

However this conversation went, she would not allow it to affect her. The children were very sensitive to undercurrents of mood.

'I read what I thought was enough.'

'What did you think it was?'

'A crèche.'

'Really?'

His jaw tightened. 'You look pleased.'

'I am.' She crossed her arms and gave him a rueful smile. 'Your reaction is more forgivable if you thought this was an ordinary day care centre for ordinary kids from ordinary families.'

His lips tightened, his throat moving.

Unbelievably, she felt a pang of sorrow for him and his cynical view of her.

'Do you understand why I had to be here today? If I hadn't, the centre wouldn't have opened. It's a lifeline for their families as well as for the kids.'

'Who are these children?'

'Children who, whether by birth or accident, will never lead a normal life but who have enough awareness to *want* a normal life.'

She wished she could read his eyes and know what was happening in his brain.

'Stay for a few hours.' Reaching out, she brushed her fingers on his hand before placing them down her side. 'See what we do here and what your money is saving.'

After a beat he said, quietly, 'We'll leave when you're ready.'

Her heart lighter than it had felt in a very long time, she walked by his side back to the day room.

Lunch was in full swing so she went through to the dining room to help. As was usual, it looked as if a food war had broken out. She glanced at Raul, whose attention had been taken by a board with smiling pictures of all the staff.

'You're a volunteer?'

'Yes.'

He nodded slowly, his eyes narrowing but not in a way that made her skin go cold. This time there was no contempt in that look, only contemplation. 'What do you want me to do?'

She stared at his Armani suit and grinned. 'Help the kids eat.'

A tug on her shorts had her lowering herself automatically to take Karin into her arms, whereby the little girl immediately prodded her then covered her face in sloppy kisses.

'Come on, let's get you fed,' she said, carrying Karin to her own special seat at the table and opening her lunch-box for her.

She looked to where Raul had brought over a chair to help Ramon eat his dinner, quietly sniggering at what she knew would happen next. Ramon, possibly the messiest eater of them all, was eating a centre-cooked hot meal of carbonara.

Oh, well, she thought cheerfully, Raul could afford the dry-cleaning bill.

Once back in Barcelona, the sun setting on the horizon, they stopped at a pizzeria for something to eat, wedging themselves on an outside table inches from the pavement.

One thing Charley had always appreciated about Raul was his lack of snobbery when it came to food. His tastes were refined towards everything else but he would happily wolf down anything put in front of him. When she'd suggested they eat here rather than somewhere fancy, he'd shrugged his shoulders and agreed.

Fancy food was something she'd had to get used to when they'd married, having been raised on a diet that consisted mostly of microwave meals or baked beans on toast. A chocolate bar or ice cream had been their usual form of dessert.

How simple everything had been back then. Her mum had been young and naïve but incredibly hardworking. She'd held down two jobs for as far back as Charley could remember but had always made sure she was home to have dinner with her only child. Half the time she was unaware her daughter had skived off school again and had spent the day watching music videos on the television.

Charley had never doubted her mum's love for her.

It was her father's love she'd always doubted, a thought she shoved firmly from her mind, feeling disloyal to even *think* it. Of *course* her dad loved her—he told her so every time he saw her.

She just wished she could have seen more of him but he had always been so busy, running his latest get-rich-quick scheme and being with her half-brothers. This had been completely understandable; her half-brothers had lived in the same town as him. A visit to his daughter every few months had been the most time he could spare. And he *had* visited her home on a whim once, when she'd been at school. He'd left a note for her saying he'd been there. If that didn't prove he loved her and carried her in his thoughts, what did?

And if her days skiving off school, watching music videos, had been spent hovering on the sofa by the window that had overlooked their flat's car park, and every time she'd seen a dark blue estate car pull into it her heart would accelerate with excitement that maybe he was paying her another unannounced visit…well, it was hardly his fault that he'd never made another unexpected trip, was it? Her dad hadn't known she'd been sitting there in hope, waiting for him.

'How did you get involved with the centre?' Raul asked once their order had been taken.

'I went there as a volunteer to entertain the children…'

'Yes, but *how*? Did you see an advert?'

'Kind of. I decided to do some voluntary work to pass the time while deciding what to do with my life. I've always liked children and keeping them entertained is about the only thing I've ever been good at.'

All those teenage years sitting alone in the flat in the hope her dad would eventually turn up instead of knuckling down at school had left her with nothing to show for over a decade of education. It was only after she'd left school and seen how severely limited her options were that she'd understood what she'd thrown away: her future. She'd never given the future any real thought; the present had been enough to cope with. Her mum had been so disappointed too, although she'd tried to cover it up with an understanding hug. That one hug had spurred Charley on more than any career advice she could have been given.

She might have no qualifications but she *would* make something of herself. She'd always loved kids, had danced along to enough music videos to have gained some decent rhythm, so being an entertainer at family resorts had seemed the logical thing to do.

But meeting Raul and his brilliant mind had only served to magnify her past mistakes and she'd been determined to rectify them, to make her mum's sacrifices worthwhile, to make Raul proud and to make their future children proud. She'd clutched at business ideas that had looked good on paper but held no emotional appeal. She hadn't thought it mattered. All that had mattered was proving herself a success.

All she'd proved was that she was a failure.

How could *anyone* respect her, let alone her husband and future children?

'I went to the children's hospital first to see if they needed or wanted any volunteers and through them I met one of the kids who went to the centre,' she continued, forcing brightness into her voice. 'I went along once to see if they had any need for me, fell in love with the place and ended up volunteering on a permanent basis.'

'Could they not pay you?'

'They could barely afford the staff they did have.' A whimsical smile crossed her face. 'Besides, I had the money to support myself.'

While he tried to digest all this and process the shifting sands of his opinion towards her, their pizzas were brought to their table.

'Where does the centre get its money from?'

'Are you telling me you bought the new building for us without looking through any of the financial reports I'd made?'

'There hasn't been the time.' It didn't strike him as the right time to confess he'd assumed her financial reports would be worth less than the paper they were written on. He'd fished them out of the shredding pile but was still to sit down and read them.

He had misjudged her terribly.

From the knowing look in her eyes, she knew it too.

'The parents who can afford it pay a day rate,' she said. 'But most of the funds come from donations and grants. It's enough to keep the place ticking over but not enough to build a healthy reserve.'

'Do you do much in the way of fundraising?'

'As much as we can. We'd hoped to devote more time to fundraising and awareness this year but obviously recent events put the brakes on that.'

Raul chewed in silence, thinking.

He'd spent less than five hours in the centre but that had been long enough for him to know he wanted to help.

'Why didn't you come to me?'

'I did.'

'I mean before, when you first learned the building was being sold out from under your feet.'

She dropped her gaze from his and picked up a slice of spicy pizza. 'I thought I could do it myself.'

The same way she'd always thought she could run her businesses on her own even though she didn't have the tools. In the end it had become a battle of wills between them. The more he'd tried to help, the more she'd pushed him away.

'Is that why you wanted to do it in your own name? For the glory?'

He knew the answer even as her eyes shot back up to him and her cheeks tightened in on themselves. 'No! I wanted to *help*. Poco Rio has no assets, no back-up capital. I thought I had enough money left to pay for it all. All I could think was *let's get this done*, but I had it in my head that once it was complete I would get some kind of charity established and hand it all over so Poco Rio would always be guaranteed a home.'

She put her pizza down without taking a bite and took a large sip of her lager.

She'd drunk lager on their first date. It was only after he'd brought her to Barcelona that her palate had taken an immediate preference to fine wine.

All along he'd made assumptions but if his assumption that Charley was a gold-digger had been wrong—and today had only confirmed what his senses had been trying to tell him for weeks—what else was he wrong about?

He thought of all the lengths he'd gone to throughout his childhood and adolescence in his increasingly desperate bids to impress his father, working so hard on his studies, often studying until the early hours, regularly turning down invitations that took him away from his books, determined to be the top-ranked student in his private school. He'd succeeded in that aim, leaving school with the highest grades possible and a personal recommendation from the headmaster. His father's response had been an uninterested grunt and the words, 'Let's see how you get on at MIT when you're competing against the best brains in the world.'

Had he somehow caused Charley to feel the same inadequacies his father had caused him?

Dios. No. He had loved her. He hadn't wanted to change her, just make her adapt to his life with ease so she *didn't* feel those inadequacies.

But that strange feeling of witnessing the Ghost of Wife Past whispered through him again, a hollow ache expanding through his chest.

'With my contacts and media presence, we can raise awareness and funds,' he said, before draining his own lager.

'That would be amazing.' The emotion in her eyes sparkled into joy, her cheeks widening into a smile. 'The more funds we raise, the more staff we can employ and the more kids we can take in.'

As he peppered her with more questions about the project, her animation grew.

It was an animation he'd never seen when she'd been planning her own businesses.

She looked magnificent, her green eyes swirling, her hands gesticulating.

When he suggested doing a fundraising cruise on his brand-new liner, her pizza almost flew out of her hand in her excitement.

Eventually their plates were empty, desserts consumed along with coffee to finish.

Raul checked his watch and was surprised to find they'd been sitting there for three hours. If not for the sun having set, he would have said no longer than an hour. He called for the bill then threw Charley a lazy smile before covering her hand. 'Let's go home.'

Her eyes brightened before cooling. 'Am I still expected to stick to our pact?'

'Of course. We have an agreement, *cariño*.' He leaned forward to place his cheek against hers, inhaling the scent of faded vanilla. 'Nothing has changed.'

Inside, though, he knew that *everything* had changed.

If he had any kind of decency, he would make their pact void.

They would stay together, he decided, until the renovations were complete. He would give her all the support he could to see it through to its conclusion. They would work together, just as he should have insisted in their marriage's first incarnation.

The simple truth was that he wasn't ready to say goodbye to her. Not yet.

He never had been.

A whispering voice inside him told him he never would be.

CHAPTER TEN

CHARLEY STOOD IN her dressing room, nose wrinkling as she tried to decide what to wear. If she was going to the centre she would wear something casual, which food and paints could be splattered all over. Dressing for a day in Raul's HQ required an entirely different form of dress. It required the kind of attire she'd shunned since she'd left him.

High-powered business outfits left her cold.

So far she'd mixed and matched anything suitable she could find but was quickly running out of options.

She sighed. She supposed she should take a shopping trip to stock up. Mixing and matching wouldn't see her through the four months she was supposed to be at Raul's side learning the ropes of business she'd shunned all those years ago.

Why had she shunned his advice?

Had she really been so scared that allowing him to help would give him undeniable proof of her stupidity? The sad answer to that was yes. She had been scared. She hadn't wanted to give him evidence that she was less than perfect.

She'd been honest about her past and lack of education but had tried to romanticise it, to insist she had the know-how and savvy to build her own business. She'd tried to convince herself as much as him, starting her businesses with bags of enthusiasm. But she'd been faking it.

The sad fact, one she'd never been able to bring herself to admit, was that business left her as cold as the high-powered suits she'd worn. Working at Poco Rio made her feel warm.

Hearing movement in the bedroom, she turned and found Raul with a pile of papers in his arms. He'd risen early, long before she'd hauled herself out of bed.

He put the papers on her dressing table and handed the top sheet to her. 'Here's a list of my schedule for the next month. The dates highlighted are when I won't need the helicopter. You're welcome to use it on those dates to get to and from Valencia.'

She eyed him warily. She'd thought during their meal at the pizzeria last night that they were reaching an understanding, that his time at the centre had softened his attitude towards her. He'd been quick to put her straight on that.

Nothing has changed, he'd said.

And while their lovemaking when they'd returned home had been long and tender, that counted for nothing. Raul was nothing if not a generous lover. Even when he hated her.

'Are you saying I can work at the centre?'

'Yes.'

'I thought I was supposed to be glued to your hip?'

A glimmer of a smile curled on his lips. 'I would much rather have you glued to a different part of my anatomy.'

She couldn't help the burst of laughter that escaped and she almost responded with, 'So would I.' Almost.

As he'd said only the evening before, nothing had changed. He hadn't entirely reclaimed his humanity, not when he still had her in his bed as a form of punishment.

'I've been on the phone to Pierre Binoche,' he said, re-ferring to the interior designer he used for his hotels and cruise liners, 'and have arranged a meeting with him at the end of the month at the new building. I assume you will want to be there?'

'Pierre's going to do the interior design?' she asked in amazement. 'That's incredibly good of you but, really, it's not necessary. Once all the renovations are done, all we'll need to do is give the place a lick of paint.'

'Pierre won't be discussing colour charts; he'll be looking to create the right mood for the centre. He'll take your lead, *cariño.*'

'Really?'

'You know the brief better than anyone. Think of it as PR. His name will help in the awareness drive we're going for.'

'There is that,' she conceded. This, on top of the fundraising cruise trip, would raise so much awareness and funds for the children she felt like pinching herself to make sure it wasn't all a dream.

A thought crossed her mind. 'When at the end of the month are we meeting him?'

'The last Wednesday.'

'Oh.'

'Why?'

'The last Wednesday of August is La Tomatina. We're planning on taking some of the kids to it.'

'You're taking the children to a *tomato fight*?'

From the look on his face she might have said they were taking the children to watch bareknuckle boxing.

'Just to watch. We took five of them last year and they loved it. We sat on a roof terrace with a box of tomatoes to throw at the crowd.' La Tomatina was an annual festival in the Valencian town of Buñol.

He eyed her thoughtfully. 'Have you already got your name down to go?'

'Yes, but don't worry, I wasn't planning on stealing your helicopter again to get there.'

'You wouldn't have had any luck if you did—my pilots now know not to take you anywhere without my express permission.'

Only Raul could give with one hand and take with the other, one minute sounding human and reasonable, the next reminding her of her current position in his life. The difference now was that he said it with good humour rather than the horrid cold tone she'd hated so much. It made her hope he was thawing towards her.

She grinned mischievously. 'I wasn't going to steal your helicopter. I was going to steal your Bugatti.'

'I am going to assume you're joking or my blood pressure might combust.'

'You should come with us,' she said, speaking on impulse.

'I think not,' he said drily.

'Why not? Worried you might get your clothes dirty?'

'No.' He shook his head.

'Then why not?' Her eyes were on him, peering intently. 'Is it not becoming for a man of your standing to have a tomato fight?'

'You know perfectly well it isn't.' Raul couldn't think of anything more abhorrent than pictures of himself covered in gunk surfacing in the press and on the Internet.

'Go in disguise.'

'Charlotte, I'm not going to take a whole day off work to watch a lot of people throw tomatoes at each other.'

'Don't be such a snob. It's fun.'

'I'm not a snob.'

'Not consciously,' she conceded.

Her phone vibrated loudly. She read the message and sighed, the smile leaving her face.

Raul knew before she said anything that it was her father.

'Dad can't make it.'

He kept his features neutral. 'Why?'

There was that defensive look he recognised. 'He has a business meeting.'

'On a Saturday?'

'*You* have business meetings on Saturdays.'

'I run a multibillion-euro company. Your father is currently jobless.'

'Well, this is something to do with him finding a new job. You should be pleased he's trying to find one.'

'I am.' Raul's issue was that he simply didn't believe it. Graham had most likely found himself a date and concocted a story for his daughter's benefit rather than admitting the truth. The only good thing was that he'd had the decency to cancel in advance rather than at the last minute as he had done on numerous occasions.

The problem was, Charley didn't want to hear it.

Shaking his head, he strolled back to her dresser and picked up the rest of the papers. 'While you were sleeping, I also had the chance to look through the financial report you produced.'

'And?'

A pang shot through Raul's chest to see trepidation immediately fill her eyes.

'You did a good job.'

The trepidation was pushed out by a ray of beaming light. 'Really?'

Pulling her into his arms, he kissed her lightly and murmured, 'Really.'

He'd been astounded at how good a job she had done.

All throughout their marriage he'd believed in her innate abilities, had known she needed to harness them and focus to achieve something substantial. And now he'd been proved right.

But *she* hadn't believed it.

Why had he not recognised before that his wife had no confidence in herself?

She'd put on a good front, that was for certain. But they'd been married. How had he not seen her insecurities?

'Come on,' he said, giving her one last kiss before stepping back. 'Get dressed—I've got a meeting in half an hour.'

Before leaving the room, he turned back to her. 'Don't feel you have to dress up for the office any more. You're coming with me as my sex toy, remember?'

His heart lightened to see the grin spread across her face. 'Shall I dress as a dominatrix?'

'Now that I would *love* to see.'

Her cackle of laughter followed him out of the room.

'You've hardly stopped for the past month,' Raul said. 'Take the day off—go and see Marta.'

'Are you sure?'

'Yes.' His voice dropped. 'Unless you want to come here and take me in my office.'

Even with Raul a mile away, just the suggestive sound of his voice whispering down the phone set a frisson of heat through her.

'I'll see you when you get home,' she said firmly. 'Goodbye.'

Swiping her phone to end the call, she padded over to the window and looked out at the lashing rain and palm trees swaying in the growing wind.

It was the height of summer and Barcelona was under a deluge of water.

She was supposed to be working at the centre but the

circling storm had forced the pilot to ground the helicopter. She'd been on the verge of jumping in one of Raul's cars and driving the three-hour journey there when Seve had called, insisting he had it covered and forbidding her to go in. She could only hope the weather cleared by Wednesday. She and Raul were meeting Pierre first thing, then Charley would head over to the current centre as part of the team taking the children to La Tomatina.

But today, for once, her time was her own.

A bath. That was what she needed.

It had been ages since she'd last had a long soak.

Filling the bath until it was a steamy mass of foamy water, she climbed in and lay back, closing her eyes, happy to listen to the heavy thud of rain.

When had she last felt so content?

The past few weeks had passed in a blur. She'd travelled with Raul to St Lucia to see the development of a new hotel complex, to Madrid where the headquarters of his air fleet was located, dined out with business colleagues and friends, and still managed to work a couple of days a week at the centre.

It was amazing how different everything felt. Before, when she'd travelled with him and witnessed his burgeoning empire, her inadequacies had felt strong enough to eat her whole. So she'd stopped accompanying him, using the excuse of her own businesses to keep her rooted in Barcelona. The side effect had been the jealousy that had gripped her on their nights apart, the fear of him meeting someone more suitable that had plagued her.

Now, her inadequacies didn't matter. Her imperfections didn't matter. She and Raul were together for a strict time period. This wasn't permanent and, as a result, she no longer had to put on the pretence of being perfect. If he was concerned that she was less than perfect, he wasn't saying, and, really, why would he? Come November, they would go their separate ways. They would divorce and he could then find himself the perfect wife he needed.

A lance of pain shot through her chest as she thought of him with another woman on his arm. She sucked in her breath, holding it tightly, waiting for the feeling to pass as it always did, although it seemed to be taking longer and longer for it to pass as the days went by.

She would *not* make the same mistakes as she had before.

Mind-blowing sex did not equate to love. That was what had got her into trouble in the first place, mistaking the lust she'd felt for him for love, then, when love truly had come, it had been too late and she'd been trapped. Worse, she'd become a stranger to herself.

But this time she knew better.

This time...

Unless you want to come here and take me in my office...

She'd told herself hell would freeze over before she made the first move. As if she would give herself willingly to the man who'd blackmailed her back into his bed.

And yet...

There would be no consequences if she walked away. Raul would never back out of the centre, not now. She'd known that since he'd turned up there and been pulled into the magic of the place.

And Raul knew it too.

She could walk away and there wasn't a thing he could do or threaten her with to make her stay. Something told her that even if there were, he wouldn't use it.

For over a month she'd been telling herself that she stayed because they'd made a deal, as hateful as it had initially been.

Her eyes opened with a snap as the truth hit her.

She'd stayed because she wanted to.

Raul had done a terrible thing blackmailing her back into his bed. A *terrible* thing. He'd believed—possibly still believed—awful things about her that she could never disprove without a lie detector but over the past month he'd treated her with something he'd never shown her in all the years of their marriage. Respect.

She hadn't even known the respect had been missing until she'd found it.

Adrenaline coursed through her, her heart hammering as powerfully as the rain pouring like sheets against the window, her mind a train wreck of careering tracks.

Could their marriage work...?

No, it would be no good to think that way. Things had started well when they'd first met, when it had been all about the lust holding them together, before he'd dropped to one knee and pulled out the enormous diamond ring now locked securely away.

Their time limit meant this could be the fling their relationship should have been, the fling that should have ended with the summer and remained a beautiful memory.

A peace settled on her as she came to terms with the fact that she was no longer a hostage against her will but a full participant. Did she really want to waste the next few months, holding a part of herself back from him out of a sense of outrage that served nothing?

She lay back again and allowed her mind to drift away, images of their lovemaking filling her senses. If she concentrated really hard, she could feel the weight of his body upon her, the flicker of his tongue...

Suddenly she sat back up, sloshing water over the sides of the bath in her haste, as a deliciously naughty thought came into her head.

'Unless you want to come here and take me in my office...' Raul had said.

If she was going to be a full participant in this, then it was time to let Raul know, to put their relationship on the equal footing it deserved.

And she knew *just* the way.

Raul sipped at his water, forcing himself to concentrate on the letter he was dictating straight into his laptop for his PA and trying not to think of Charley at home alone, trying to rid himself of thoughts of finishing early to return to her.

The phone on his desk buzzed.

He paused mid-sentence and frowned down at it. His executive team knew he was dictating and not to disturb him.

He pressed the offending buzzer and spoke into it. 'Is there a problem?'

'Your wife is here,' came the voice of Ava. 'She says it's important she speak to you.'

Immediately his mind went into overdrive, imagining all the things that could have driven her here, something icy clutching at his heart. This could not be anything good.

'Let her in.'

The past month, things had been good between them. Better than he'd dreamed they could be, even when they'd first exchanged their vows and their whole future had been a blank canvas waiting for them to paint with glorious colour.

Too good. Highs were always followed by lows.

The door opened and Charley stepped in, dressed for the awful weather in a long black trench coat.

He rose from his seat. 'Whatever's the matter?'

A serene smile on her face, she closed the door quietly behind her.

'Sit down,' she said softly.

Raul would be the first to admit that confusion rarely entered his vocabulary, but right then... 'What?'

Her hands went to the belt of her trench coat.

'I said...' her voice was quiet but knowing as she tugged the belt loose '...sit...' her hands went to the lapels and pulled them apart '...down.'

Under her coat she was as naked as the day she'd been born.

Shrugging it off, she sashayed towards him in high black heels, her breasts moving with the motion, her nipples drawing his attention.

He blinked, suddenly certain he'd fallen asleep at his desk.

She placed a hand to his chest and pushed him back onto his chair, the height of her heels lifting her so his face was almost level with the top of her thighs.

The effect on him was instantaneous.

Her smile had lost its serenity, had become something heavy and sensual.

Placing a hand on his shoulder, she hooked a leg over his lap to straddle him, keeping her shoes on the ground so she was elevated over him. The only part of her touching him was the hand on his shoulder and her inner thighs. Not a single inch of her touched his bare skin yet he felt scorched by her touch.

Her hand slipped round his neck and she leaned forward to breathe into his ear. 'I thought I would take you up on your offer.'

With the heavy weight of her breasts pressed against his chest and her warm scent clinging to her like a cloud, coherent thoughts were a world away.

'Which offer?'

She moved her lips across his cheek until she reached

his mouth while tracing a hand over his shirt-clad chest and down to the belt of his trousers.

'To take you in your office.'

Her mouth didn't move from his as she worked at his belt then unzipped him, with just a whisper of her lips touching him. He placed a hand on her waist, the warmth and softness of her skin deepening the burn in his loins.

He didn't think he'd ever been aroused so quickly and so deeply as he felt right now or ever been as aware of the sound of his blood pumping.

A sudden urgency rippled through him and he reached down to help tug his opened trousers and boxers down enough to free him. Immediately she took hold of him.

He inhaled deeply to stop the groan that wanted to escape.

Her breaths coming out in shallow pants, she guided him to her opening, and sank down on him.

This time his groan could not be held at bay and as his mouth parted she moaned into him, the sound of their pleasure muffled.

She broke away from his mouth and raised herself, placing her hands on his shoulders to steady herself, then sank back down.

With a hand on her back and the other on her hip, Raul began to move with her, bucking upwards to meet her downward thrusts, unable to tear his gaze from her eyes.

They were filled with wonder and ecstasy and it was all directed at him.

But the urgency was there too, for both of them, the movements quickening, pressing closer and closer together until he had her crushed against him and her mouth and tongue were twined with his.

He felt her tighten around him and fought to hold on,

right until she sank one final time and shuddered, clinging to him.

And then it was time for his release.

It ripped through him, blinding him with its savage force, his whole body shuddering as he fought for every last drop of the pleasure consuming him.

He had no idea how long they sat there afterwards, fused together, faces buried in each other's necks, the only sound their ragged breathing.

It was only when she raised her face to kiss him that some form of sanity came back to him.

'I need to use your bathroom,' she murmured, climbing off him. She grinned, then sashayed on obviously unsteady feet to his adjoining restroom.

Alone, he blew out a burst of warm air and got to his feet, sorting out his clothes, his dazed brain slowly clearing.

That had to count as the most unexpected and erotic experience of his life.

In no time at all, Charley slipped back into the office and scooped her coat from the floor.

She met Raul's eye and grinned again as she slipped her arms into the sleeves and tightened the belt around her waist.

Stepping back over to him, she slid her arms around his neck and reached up to kiss him. She made to leave but he caught her wrist and pulled her back to him, cupping her cheeks to give her one final, deep, passionate kiss.

The serene smile lighting her face, Charley left his office as silently as she'd come.

Raul flopped back onto his chair and rubbed his eyes.

Had that really happened?

In all the years of their marriage, Charley had never done anything like this. Not once. The closest had been her dressing up for him in sexy lingerie and seducing him in their bedroom.

He felt a twitch in his loins as he saw again her opening that long coat to reveal her shimmering nakedness.

Dios.

She'd been so ready for him.

Dios.

Dragging a hand through his hair, he tried to force his concentration back on the work before him but knew he was fighting a losing battle.

She'd be back home soon.

He felt the twitch in his loins again and gritted his teeth.

Would she get dressed or would she stay naked?

He punched the buzzer of his phone. 'Get me a coffee,' he ordered, forgetting his usual pleasantries. 'And make it a strong one.'

Only through ruthless control did he manage to get any more work done that day. His libido never quite returned to dormancy, a dull ache there that he studiously ignored, determined to get his work complete as quickly as possible so he could return home to his wife waiting there for him. Not just waiting for him but openly wanting him.

His heart felt so full and weighty he could feel it pressing against his chest.

CHAPTER ELEVEN

RAUL FASTENED HIS seat belt wondering what exactly he'd agreed to.

They'd met Pierre at the new centre, along with Vittore and Pablo, the project manager. Seve had also joined them, enthusing about all the renovation work being undertaken.

Charley had been in her element, eyes shining, her happiness as bright as the sun blazing in the sky.

The storm that had covered great swathes of Spain over the past few days had lifted. His spirits had turned with it.

'It would be better if I drove,' he said, watching as she adjusted the driver's seat. He'd never been a passenger with his wife behind the wheel.

'You're not insured,' Charley said blithely, switching the engine on.

'It will take one minute to get me on the insurance.'

'I'm driving.' And with that, she put the minibus into reverse and they were on their way, ambling towards the town of Buñol.

Five of the children were strapped in the back with two of the other workers and another volunteer, all the children in a heightened state of excitement. From what Charley had said, they displayed the same level of enthusiasm towards trips to the local swimming baths and the supermarket.

The plan had been for him to drive Charley to the centre

then head back to Barcelona, but then she'd turned those gorgeous green eyes on him and said, 'Come with us.'

He still didn't understand why he hadn't just refused as he had when she'd first suggested it. Said *No, I've far too much work to do to spend time watching a bunch of people throw tomatoes at each other.*

Most likely it was curiosity, to see for himself the event regarded as the world's biggest food fight.

It wasn't, he assured himself, because being away from Charley was becoming a physical pain.

There was no doubt though that their relationship had shifted dramatically since her seduction in his office. The last of her reserve towards him had vanished.

When they made love now nothing was held back. She laughed easily and walked as if she had springs implanted in her shoes.

She was happy. Being with *him* made her happy.

Being with her was like being with the woman he'd first fallen in love with…

When they arrived at the tiny hotel that overlooked Plaza del Pueblo, where most of the action would be taking place, they were greeted by the manager who led them straight up to the small roof terrace. From what Raul could see, their spot was one of the only ones that allowed spectators to actually see what was unfolding.

And what a sight it was. Tens of thousands of men and women were crammed in the plaza and the surrounding narrow streets, haulage trucks filled with crate upon crate of ripe tomatoes placed strategically alongside water cannons. Many of the shop fronts and homes had been protected with huge plastic sheets. Scores of mostly young men were attempting to shimmy their way up a two-storey pole with what looked like a hock of ham at the top, but he guessed it must be greased for the men got no further than a couple of feet before sliding back down on top of each other, only to immediately try again.

Chairs had been laid out for them; the terrace was safe enough for the kids to jump up and down with the excitement of it all.

Never in his wildest dreams had Raul imagined he would take a day off work to watch a tomato fight, and he imagined the look on his father's face if he were to learn what his son had done. The disapproval would be as clear as the juice of the ripe tomatoes.

'Next year I'm going to try and spend the week here and join in with the whole festival,' Charley said, shouting over the chants of *'Olé, olé, olé, olé!'* bellowing from the crowd. Her cheeks were flushed with excitement. Karin climbed onto her lap and she automatically put her arm around her waist to secure her. 'I bet you'd love it too.'

Before he could respond, the roar of the water cannons signalled the start of the fight.

Carnage ensued, joyous, messy, glorious carnage.

Charley and the kids were in fits of laughter watching overripe tomatoes being thrown and squelched in all directions, the streets and the people that filled them soon a river of red juice.

He could hardly credit that he, Raul Cazorla, a man who enjoyed the finest of all the world had to offer, was enjoying something so...unrefined.

When he'd been growing up, his mother would have rather gone without her weekly pedicure than allow her children to attend something so messy and unbecoming. The Cazorlas had an image they protected fiercely; they were seen at the right places in the right clothes. The annual tomato fight at Buñol, preceded by a week-long festival, would most certainly have fallen onto the 'unbecoming for a Cazorla' list.

Something wet and squelchy slapped into his back. Turning his head, he saw that one of the children had thrown a tomato at him and was laughing so hard tears were falling down his face.

He saw the box of tomatoes, feet away from him, right at the moment Charley placed Karin on her seat and ran for it, grabbing a couple of tomatoes. Grinning widely, she squished them in her hands, then lobbed them at him.

He gazed down at what seconds before had been an immaculately pressed white silk shirt and was now dripping in juice and pips.

The others had got in on the act, except for Karin, who was clapping her hands, not knowing what was happening but reacting to the sounds of delight ringing out.

Charley dipped back into the box, her eyes sending out a clear challenge.

Raul never turned down a challenge.

Charley couldn't remember ever having experienced such a magical day.

By the time the tomato fight had finished, they'd been as red as the people in the streets. The hotel manager had appeared with a hose to wash them all down. They'd returned to the centre wet and exhausted but happy.

'You looked like you enjoyed yourself today,' she said as they left the car park. It had surprised and delighted her how Raul had really got into the spirit of things on that little terrace, accepting the splatters of tomatoes from the children with good humour and retaliating with the gentlest of throws. His retaliation of her own throws at him had been markedly different; at one point he'd pinned her arms behind her back and encouraged the kids to use her as a target before squishing one right under her T-shirt.

She was certain there were tomato pips stuck in the wiring of her bra.

He nodded musingly, bringing the car to a stop at a junction. 'It was fun.'

'Wasn't it? Saying that, my arms are killing me after all that tomato throwing.' She eyed him suggestively. 'I think I need a good massage.'

His hand drifted over to her thigh and gently squeezed. 'I'm sure I can think of a good masseur.'

'I'm sure you can.'

With his hand resting on her thigh, she rested her head against the window and closed her eyes with a contented sigh. 'Do you know how the ticket sales for the fundraiser are going?' she asked.

Raul had got a team of his people to organise the fundraiser, for which they were charging obscenely rich people obscenely high ticket prices. Charley was fully involved in the practicalities but not with the ticket sales.

She heard the clicking of his tongue on the roof of his mouth. 'I was waiting for the right moment to share this with you,' he said in a chiding voice.

'Oh, just tell me!'

'We've sold out.'

'No way!' If the traffic hadn't chosen that moment to start moving again, she would have thrown herself at him. 'That's amazing.'

'I have a good team.'

She hugged her arms, doing the maths in her head. 'Ticket sales alone will guarantee everyone's salary is paid for the next two years.'

'By the time the fundraiser is over, you'll be able to guarantee salaries for the next decade.' He laughed.

That made her sit up. 'Wow. Just think, with those kinds of funds we'll be able to afford more staff and start taking teenagers in. The builders are dividing the building into two separate parts so there can be adolescent quarters, but we never thought we'd be able to start taking them this soon.'

'You can start paying yourself a salary too,' he said lightly.

'I don't know about that.' She shook her head. 'It doesn't sit right. I've got enough money left that, if I'm careful, should last me a long while yet.'

'You have two hundred thousand euros, which you were prepared to give to the new centre, not loan. If you'd been successful in raising the rest of the money by other means, you would have been left penniless.'

'How do you…? Oh, yes, you read my finance report.' She'd listed on it how much of her own money she'd intended to contribute to the project, which had basically been everything in her account and her jewellery, all of which she'd sold with the exception of her wedding and engagement rings. As sentimental as she'd known it to be, she hadn't been able to bring herself to part with them.

'So you are intending to stay at the centre?'

'What else can I do?'

'You can start by drawing a salary. God knows, you work hard enough.'

'Hardly. I just joke around and make the kids laugh.' That was about all she was good for, she thought, her mood suddenly darkening.

'You do a lot more than that.'

She shrugged.

'Charlotte, if it wasn't for you, the children wouldn't have a new centre to look forward to and the staff would be job-hunting as we speak.'

'If it wasn't for *you*, you mean.' While she had spent two months beating at doors to get the funding, putting an immediate freeze on personal spending other than on the bare necessities, selling anything of value, boiling her brain over design plans and finance reports, Raul had swept in and taken care of everything as easily as if he were taking a shower.

He drove them through the gate to the hangar. The Cazorla helicopter sat ahead of them, gleaming in the early evening sun. 'You did all the hard work. The renovations are being done according to your plans. Vittore has adapted them a little but it's still your work. Take the credit for it. You've earned it.'

'Twaddle. I didn't do anything that anyone else couldn't have done.'

He banged his fist on the steering wheel, making her jump.

'When,' he said tightly, 'are you going to stop putting yourself down?'

'I'm not putting myself down,' she protested. 'I'm just saying that anyone else in my position would have done the same.'

He pulled the car to a stop and gazed at her with an intensity that sent a not unpleasant shiver running up her spine.

'No,' he said slowly. 'I don't think many people in your position would have done the same.'

She swallowed, staring at him, trying to read what lay behind the intensity.

'Sometimes, Señora Cazorla, I look at you and I remember exactly why I fell in love with you.'

A loud buzzing played in her ears. Her throat ran so dry no amount of swallowing could moisten it.

She cleared her suddenly arid throat. 'Your pilot's waiting for us.'

His gaze held a moment longer before he smiled and shook his head.

* * *

'More wine?'

Charley blinked. She'd been a thousand miles away.

She breathed deeply and fixed a smile to her face. 'Go on, then. We might as well order our food too.' They'd been in the restaurant for an hour and still there was no sign of her dad. Neither was he answering his phone.

'Are you sure?'

She gazed back at the menu open on her lap. She didn't want to look at Raul or the sympathy radiating from him.

He was only an hour late. For her dad, that was nothing. As a kid she'd often spent whole days waiting for him to arrive.

'Definitely. The minute we order is the minute he'll arrive,' she said brightly. 'You wait, he'll be here any second.'

'Of course he will,' Raul agreed with eyes that said he thought the total opposite.

She snatched up her glass and downed the last of the red liquid. Forget bouquets of blackcurrant and cinnamon and whatever else it was reputed to have, the only attribute she cared for was its anaesthetic quality.

She was an adult now, she reminded herself, and had long ago accepted her dad for who he was: a man who had certain reliability issues.

Yet waiting for him as an adult still made her feel like the little girl who would wait for hours for his car to pull into the car park, and the adolescent who would skive off school for fear of missing out on an unexpected visit from him.

He would be here.

They ordered their dishes and more drinks were brought over.

Her phone vibrated.

She knew what it would say before she opened it.

'Has something come up?' Raul asked carefully, while she read her dad's brief message. He didn't need to be psychic either.

She forced a cheerful smile to her face and nodded. 'There's something wrong with his car—it's making strange noises. He doesn't think it's safe to continue the drive.'

She'd *known* she should have travelled to him and would have done if she hadn't been spending the day at Poco Rio. When she was the one to make the effort there was less chance of some emergency cropping up at the last minute.

But…since her dad had moved to the Costa Dorado, he hadn't made the effort to visit her once. The intention had been there though, she reminded herself. They'd made plenty of dates for him to come to her. She'd even bought him a car so he could get around and not be stuck in his beachside home.

She should have arranged to meet him in Barcelona, not here in Valencia. Barcelona was much closer to him.

'That's a shame,' Raul said.

'There'll be another time.'

Another time for him to stand her up.

It had been bad enough worrying that Raul was going to be late for the meal too. He'd travelled to Brazil on Wednesday, only arriving back that afternoon. Two nights of fret and worry.

Sometimes, when she let her mind wander too far, she heard his words echo in her head. *'Sometimes, Señora Cazorla, I look at you and I remember exactly why I fell in love with you.'*

She'd laughed it off but under the bonhomie she'd turned into a wreck. His words had terrified her.

If he'd loved her so much then why had he given up on her so easily? Two years of silence had said it all.

He'd made her into the perfect Cazorla wife but as soon as she'd denied him what he wanted, a child, he'd given up on her.

Just as her father only wanted her when he needed money. Charley was disposable.

Nothing similar had been mentioned in the subsequent weeks but those words had stayed with her.

Then he'd gone off to Brazil, the land of beautiful women, leaving her alone for the first time since they'd got back together—got back together *temporarily*, she reminded herself—and found herself alone in *his* huge bed with a brain that refused to switch off.

They were only temporary, her brain had screamed. In less than a couple of months they would head their separate ways.

Oh, why had he said it? Why had he mentioned the L word?

He hadn't said he loved her now. Just that he'd loved her then.

But he didn't love you then. If he had he would never have tried to change you.

In defiance, she'd rolled over to the middle of the bed.

Come the morning and after a few hours of broken sleep, she'd been back on her own side with his pillow in her arms. She'd had to stop those same arms throwing themselves around him when he'd arrived at Poco Rio late that afternoon, as they were clearing up after a long day. She'd wanted to hug him even harder when he'd taken her briefly to the new centre so she could see how all the renovations were going.

'Oh, stop pretending to be nice about it,' she snapped now, suddenly and unbelievably on the brink of tears. 'We both know my dad couldn't give a stuff about me.'

To her horror, she only noticed her hands were shaking when Raul took one of them in his own.

'Do you know my dad's the only person not happy that we're back together?' she said, speaking the words before she could call them back. 'He'll want to meet up when he knows you're out of the picture. Either then or if he runs out of money before our time's up.'

He didn't answer, his blue eyes holding hers, sympathy and not a little anger in them.

Raul had got the measure of her dad right from the start.

She jerked her hand out of his grasp, picked up her re-filled glass and held it aloft. 'Happy birthday to me, eh?'

'Charlotte…'.

'Don't worry about it,' she dismissed, putting her glass back down. 'This isn't the first of my birthdays he's missed and I'm sure it won't be the last.'

Twenty-six birthdays and her dad had only made two of them.

'Charlotte,' he repeated, speaking quietly, 'this isn't your fault.'

She attempted a smile, now really scared that she would cry. 'I know.'

At least, it wasn't her fault she'd been born a woman. She'd always known that if she'd been born with male genitals her father would have wanted to spend more time with her, just as he did with her half-brothers. Deep down she'd always known it, just never acknowledged the painful truth.

She was a mere woman. Disposable.

A waitress arrived at their table with their first course.

Charley stabbed a piece of chorizo with her fork. Before she could pop it in her mouth, more unbidden words spilled out. 'I've never mattered to him. I look back on my childhood and all I can clearly remember is the waiting. I used to get so excited when I knew he was coming over. Half the time he'd be late—at the very least an hour—the other half he wouldn't turn up at all. When he did bother, he'd always have a great big present for me that cost the earth, then tell my mum he didn't have the money to buy me a new pair of school shoes.'

She took a breath and another sip of wine, wondering why she was rehashing a tale Raul was already familiar with. But there was one story she'd never shared...

'I have never spent a single Christmas with him,' she said, keeping her eyes on her glass of wine, 'and I only got invited to celebrate one of his birthdays—his fortieth. I was about nine, I think, and Mum and I went together. I remember being really excited about meeting my two half-brothers. Dad had told me *all* about them. I knew he lived close to them and saw them a lot.'

Now she dared look at Raul. 'They didn't know who I was.'

'I suppose that's understandable, seeing as they'd never met you.'

'No—I mean they didn't know *of* me. My dad had never told them they had a sister.'

Raul tried to keep his features composed, not to let Charley see the anger her words were provoking in him.

He had little doubt that if her father should walk into the restaurant at that moment he would connect his fist to his face with all the force in his possession. How that man had the nerve to call himself a father...

How Charley had managed to grow up into the warm, compassionate woman she was today stumped him too.

'Can we go home?' she asked. 'I've got a headache.'

She did look pale.

He called for the bill and discreetly told the waitress to cancel the cake waiting in the kitchen that was to have been brought out when their meal had finished. Getting to his feet, he felt in his pocket for the square box. He would give Charley her present when they got home, after a relaxing massage and a bottle of champagne. He would spoil her rotten and make this a birthday to remember for all the right reasons.

But first he had to get them home.

CHAPTER TWELVE

THE STREETS SURROUNDING the restaurant were gridlocked, the pavements packed with people spilling out of the nearby theatre, Teatro Olympia.

Wedging them comfortably in the stream of the traffic, Raul put the car in neutral and rested his head back.

His chest filled to see Charley gaze out of the passenger window, chewing her little finger, her silent pain pulling at him, making him want to hold her tight and stroke all the heartache away.

'How much money have you given him over the past few years?' he asked quietly.

She raised a shoulder but didn't look at him. 'I didn't keep track. A quarter of a million in all, I think.'

'On top of the house?'

A sharp nod.

He sighed, feeling even more strongly for her.

A cacophony of beeping cars broke through the silence and, with a start, he realised they were beeping at him.

He put the car into gear and pressed gently on the accelerator. 'What did you do with the rest of the money?'

'What do you think I did with it?' she asked, turning her head to look at him, a curious expression on her face.

'I don't know.' Every single one of his assumptions about her had been wrong, that much he did know. 'I don't think you spent it all on yourself.'

'I bought some houses.'

'You went into property?'

She let out a muted bark of laughter. '*No.* I didn't *go into* property. I bought houses—one for my mum...'

'*I* bought your mum a house,' he interjected. Unlike Charley's father, who he wouldn't spit on if he were on fire, her mum he did like and he'd been happy to buy her a decent place to live. He'd bought it as a Christmas present for her, keeping it a surprise from both her *and* Charley.

He knew Charley's mood would be lighter if her mum could have been here to celebrate her birthday too, but Charley's grandmother had had a hip replacement the week before and Paula was staying with her.

'That was in England. I bought her a holiday home here in Valencia so she could visit whenever she wanted and have a place to stay; my home is a little cramped for two. Also,' she added as an afterthought, 'I thought it unfair my dad was getting a Spanish home when she couldn't have the same.'

He grinned, liking her way of thinking.

'Who else did you buy houses for?'

'My half-brothers and—'

'Why on earth did you buy them homes?' Raul had never met her half-brothers and had no wish to. Like her father, they only bothered with her when they wanted some money. 'Let me make an educated guess—your dad told them we'd separated and that you had some money in your own right so they took the opportunity to get in touch and played you with a good sob story?'

'Wrong.' She scowled at him. 'I bought them because I wanted to. They might keep their distance but they're the only siblings I've got.'

'Did you buy them cars too?'

She nodded.

'Who else?' he asked, with a sigh. There was no point in arguing about the wrongs or rights of it. There was truth in the saying that blood was thicker than water. Charley had been right in her criticisms of his own family but that hadn't stopped them needling him like barbs in his skin.

'My grandparents and my auntie Beverley.'

'Is that it?'

'Isn't that enough?'

She wasn't being facetious. Her question was genuine.

'Enough? Charlotte, that money was for *you*.'

'And I did spend some of it on me. I wasn't completely selfless, you know. I bought myself my villa and a car, and until recently I've been taking monthly visits to the hairdresser. They all needed homes of their own far more than I needed another exotic holiday.'

'Why didn't you tell me you wanted to buy your family houses?'

'I couldn't have asked you to do that,' she said, clearly horrified at the idea.

'Why not? We were married.' He didn't know what was worse: knowing he'd thought the worst about her or learning that she hadn't felt secure enough in their marriage to think she could ask him for anything.

He'd thought he'd given her everything she'd wanted and needed.

Suddenly it hit him with force, like a punch to his solar plexus. It had *all* been a lie.

'You never opened up to me at all, did you?'

She must have caught something in his tone because her eyes became wary. 'What do you mean?'

'In the whole of our marriage you never trusted me, did you?'

'I did trust you. I told you before I knew you wouldn't cheat on me...'

'That is *not* trust!' A fraction too late, he saw the flashing brake lights of the car in front and slammed his foot down, missing the car in front by inches. 'You trusted me not to cheat but you didn't trust me with what was going on in your head.' He took in a breath. 'I loved you but you were never honest about anything, were you? You started all those businesses without having any real interest in any of them but didn't have the guts to tell me. If you'd had an ounce of the passion for them that you have for the centre, they would have succeeded.'

He took in her red checked silk top, black crepe trousers and short black heels, a classy combination that, with her blonde hair twisted in a simple knot, looked stunning on her but was markedly different from the clothes she used to wear.

'You even wear different clothes.' He shook his head and breathed deeply, struggling to comprehend.

Dios. Even her clothing had been a lie.

'What did I do that was so bad you couldn't trust me with the truth about yourself or your feelings? Did I ever mistreat you in any way?'

'Of course you never mistreated me…'

'Then *what*? I loved you.'

Her eyes became pincers. 'If you loved me as much as you say you did, then why did you try to change me?'

'I didn't try to change you.'

'Well, that's what it felt like,' she said, a tremor carrying in her voice. She rubbed her forehead. 'Before we'd even exchanged our vows you'd thrown tutors at me to teach me elocution and all that other stuff. You got your sister to take me shopping to all the best places, you hired me my own personal trainer and dietician… The only reason you went to all that effort was because I wasn't good enough for you and your perfect family as I was.'

'For the last time, I was trying to help you fit in.'

'And why was that? It was because I *didn't* fit in.'

He slammed his fist on the steering wheel. 'I was trying to protect you!'

Astonishment crossed her features. 'Protect me from what?'

'From my world and the people who live in it. I didn't want you in social situations where you felt intimidated or unable to hold your own.'

Silence rang out between them, the only sound their ragged breaths and the pounding in his head.

'From now on, no more lies,' he said when he felt more in control of himself.

'They weren't deliberate lies,' she whispered. 'I was just so desperate to fit in and make you proud. I was terrified you would meet someone more suitable and drop me like a hot rock.'

'That would never have happened. When I married you it was for ever, not until someone better came along.'

'But I didn't believe it—how could I when I spent my whole life believing I was so insignificant my own father only wanted to see me when he had nothing better to do? That I wasn't good enough to even deserve a mention to his other family?' She blew air out of her mouth and rested her head back to gaze at the roof of the car. 'How can you understand what that feels like when everything you touch turns into gold?'

He swallowed, her words like claws gripping at his skin.

Not understand how she'd felt? The boy who'd grown up having every tiny mistake and digression magnified under his father's totalitarian disapproval?

'I know what it looks like on the surface but my life hasn't been totally charmed. I know what it's like to feel useless and inferior.'

'When have *you* ever felt inferior?' she asked, twisting to face him, her eyes wide.

'My father...' He cut his words off and attempted to gather his thoughts. If he was demanding honesty from her, then it was only right he give it in return, however hard it was to get the words out. Without honesty, they had no future. 'I could never please him. Nothing I did was ever good enough.'

Her brows drew together.

'He was a cold, cruel man—a hard taskmaster. He had exacting standards he expected me to live up to and if I failed in any aspect then he made his displeasure known. I don't remember doing anything that pleased him or raised a smile to his face. If he felt any affection for me he didn't show it, whereas Marta could do no wrong. He doted on her.'

'Is that because she's a woman?'

'Probably,' he admitted with a sigh. 'Just as your father treated you differently to your brothers. I struggled for a long time to live with the double standards and his disapproval of me.'

'And now?'

He shrugged, clenching his teeth together. 'And now he's infirm. For years I wanted to take him aside and demand answers about his treatment of me but now it's too late and I will never know.'

'Can't you ask your mum?'

'There isn't any point,' he dismissed. 'My mother always turned a blind eye to it. She turns a blind eye to anything that can be construed as negative. When I left home and set up on my own, her only concern was that I wasn't going to do anything that would bring shame on the Cazorla name.'

'That's a huge assumption you're making about her,' Charley said softly. 'She might surprise you.'

'We'll see,' he said, non-committal. 'The reason I've shared this with you is because if we're going to have any kind of lasting future, we need to always be honest with each other. If you'd been honest about your feelings before, I would have understood, but I'm not a mind-reader.'

A wary, almost frightened expression came into her eyes. 'What do you mean about having a "lasting future"?'

'If we talk and keep the lines of communication open, then these problems won't occur again.'

'You make it sound like we're getting back together properly.'

'Would that be such a bad thing?' he asked in a much calmer tone than he felt. Ever since La Tomatina he'd experienced an awful sickening in the pit of his stomach whenever he thought of the day they would say goodbye for good. Those couple of days away in Brazil, when he'd called her a dozen times just to hear her voice, had convinced him they had what it took to make a new start. He'd missed her so badly he'd been on the verge of jumping into his jet the first night and demanding to be flown home.

Being with Charley felt very different this time too. Easier somehow. Stripped back.

'Get back together?' she asked in a tiny voice.

'We've proven these past few months how good we can be together with a little compromise and sacrifice on each side. We understand each other a lot better too—you must feel that.'

'And would I still be expected to have a baby?'

He could hear the edge in her voice but couldn't place it.

'*Cariño*, you will make a wonderful mother.' And she would. Whatever motherhood threw at her, she would handle it magnificently.

'Are you *mad*?'

His head reared back at the vehemence of her words.

'I can't believe you're talking like this.' The colour had drained from her face to leave her ashen.

A bang on his window brought them both up short.

He turned to find a man there, gesticulating and hollering abuse at him, and saw that traffic was moving again, had most likely been moving for a good few minutes, all bar the cars stuck behind them.

Raising a hand in apology, he was about to put the car back in gear when Charley opened her door.

'What are you doing?'

'I don't know. Going for a walk. I need to clear my head.'

He heard her words but couldn't comprehend them. 'What are you talking about? It's the middle of the night.'

All the colour that had drained from her face came back in a dark flood that reached into her eyes. Her words were a rush. 'I'm sorry, I'm sorry, but I can't do this again.'

Grabbing her bag, she slipped out of the car and slammed the door with so much force the Lotus shook.

Raul stared at her rapidly retreating figure, his heart thumping, something sharp tearing at his throat.

What the hell had just happened?

It took a few heartbeats before the shock of her reaction dislodged and his body unfroze.

He unbuckled his seat belt, jumped out and, ignoring the dozens of angry drivers honking and waving their fists at him, slammed his own door shut.

For a moment he couldn't see her and there were seconds when his heart seemed to stop with the panic of it all. Then he spotted her, already far in the distance in the middle of a crowded pavement.

Charley slipped through the crowds and into a narrow side street where cars were banned, not knowing and not caring where she was going. All that mattered was escaping...

A hand grabbed her arm. Her throat opened to scream but then she saw it was Raul who had hold of her.

She yanked out of his grasp. 'Raul, please, leave me be. I want to be on my own.'

'It's dark—it isn't safe to be out here on your own.'

People shuffled past giving them curious glances.

Raul muttered something and tried to steer her away from the middle of the street. She shied away from his touch.

Under the dim light of the streetlamp, she watched him run his fingers through his hair, his face a dark mask of grimness.

'What is *wrong* with you?' he asked roughly.

'Everything!' And with that, the tears came, not huge sobs or little wails, but a sheet of water pouring out from her eyes over which she had no control. 'Don't you see? Nothing's changed. How can you even *think* we should get back together on a permanent basis and have little Cazorlas when everything that drove us apart in the first place is still there? How could we bring babies into a marriage like that? How can we *ever* bring a baby into a marriage like that?'

'But it isn't the same. We've been better together this time. You know that as well as I do.'

'But that's because we've known it's only temporary.'

He held his hands aloft in an imploring manner. 'It could be for ever this time.'

'We spent *three years* together thinking it was for ever and, you're right, it was all a lie. I was so desperate to meet your expectations of perfection that I lost sight of who I was, and that person is not someone who fits into your world.'

'I have *never* expected perfection from you.' His breathing had become ragged. 'When I met you I lived in a bubble. All my life had been spent in it, a life of wealth and privilege where the most important thing was to keep up the public face. You were the first person outside of that bubble that I noticed. I fell for you the first moment I saw you. All I wanted to do was scoop you up and pull you into the bubble with me and protect you. Can you understand that?'

'Yes, I can, but can't you understand that your bubble suffocated me? I wanted so desperately to make you proud, to be the perfect wife, to hold my own beside you, to give you the beautiful mini Cazorlas we both wanted—and I *did* want them too, I really did, but I needed to find my self-respect first. I never found it with you because the pressure of living up to the perfection of your life was just *too much*.'

The walls of the surrounding buildings seemed to close in on her, crowding her, squeezing her, like creatures from the horror film her fairy-tale marriage had turned into.

She gazed at him, feeling an almost unbearable sadness loom down on her. He looked haggard, as if he'd been told his entire fortune had been lost for ever.

'Raul, your whole life is about perfection. Perfect business, perfect house, perfect car, perfect wife, perfect *everything*. Perfect, perfect, perfect. Look at the new centre for Poco Rio—when it's done it will be perfect and that will be down to *you*.'

She wiped the tears away only to find a fresh torrent pouring down. 'I'm sorry. We're just too different, don't you see that? What we had should never have been more than a summer fling. I can't do it. I can't live that life again. I can't live permanently with *you* again.'

God forgive her, she knew she was being unfair and cruel but fear had caught her in its grip so tightly she would have said anything to relinquish it.

And Raul…forget losing his fortune, he looked as if he'd had all the stuffing knocked out of him.

'Answer me this,' he said, his voice hollow. 'If you don't want me, what *do* you want?'

That brought her up short.

'I don't know. All I know is I don't want to lose sight of who I am again. I just want to be *me*, Charley.' She raised her shoulders and stared at him. 'I want to be happy.'

'And you don't think you can be happy with me?'

'No. I can't be happy with you.'

A shudder ran through her at the same time his face blanched.

She wished she could take it back, all her words, or soften them somehow. But she couldn't. The words wouldn't form.

Raul shoved his hands in his trouser pockets and straightened, visibly composing himself. 'If that's how you feel, there's no point in prolonging this conversation any further. I'll drive you home'

'To my house here?'

He gave a sharp nod, not looking at her. 'If that is what you want.'

'I think that would be for the best.'

On shaking legs, Charley walked back to the Lotus, which was still abandoned in the middle of the road, headlights still beaming.

Not a single word was exchanged until they pulled up onto her small driveway, the outside lights switching on automatically and bathing them in colour.

His gaze fixed ahead, Raul said, 'I'll arrange for your stuff to be couriered back to you.'

'Thank you.'

'And I'll get Ava to liaise with you about the cruise fundraiser.'

All she managed was a nod, her throat so tight it felt as if she were choking.

When she got out of the car she shut the door softly, sending a silent apology for all the times she'd slammed it in anger.

Don't look back. Don't look back.

She fumbled in her bag for her door key, having a moment of panic as she wondered if she'd taken it out at some point over the past few months. Her fingers gripped on the cold metal…

'Charley.'

She looked back to see Raul standing by his door. 'The new centre… It was you, not me. Everything it is and everything it will be is because of you.'

It wasn't until she stepped into her home and locked the front door that her legs gave way.

He'd called her Charley.

Back to the wall, she slid onto the floor, curled into a ball and sobbed so hard her broken heart shattered all over again.

Raul let himself into the villa and threw his keys on the sideboard.

The house sat in silence, the staff having long retired for the night.

He rubbed his temples and headed to the bar. After fixing himself a neat Gin de Mahón, he sat on a stool, used the remote to turn the television on, and flicked through the sports channels until he found the highlights of the evening's La Liga games.

Sipping at his drink, he concentrated on watching Barcelona demolish Celta Viga. There were some good goals to enjoy and ordinarily he would have been cheering his home team on. Football. His guilty pleasure.

Tonight, though, he was distracted. Something in his trouser pocket was digging into the top of his thigh. He should pick it out.

Instead, he waited for the adverts to finish, swallowed his drink and poured himself another.

The damn thing still dug into him.

With a grimace, he shoved his hand into the pocket and fished the small square box out. Without looking at it, he stuck it on the bar and shoved it away from him. He heard it slide across the marble.

Another game had started. He had no idea which teams were playing.

His eyes kept flitting to the box, still in its wrapping paper. It had landed right at the edge of the bar, part of it overhanging.

When he next picked up his glass his hand had gone clammy. All his skin had dampened, as if he'd caught a fever of the flesh his brain hadn't registered. Just as he thought it, his forehead began to burn and pound and his stomach contracted.

I've eaten something that doesn't agree with me.

But he hadn't eaten. Charley had wanted to leave before they'd really started on their first course.

Charley...

He was off the stool and reaching for the box before he could stop himself. Feeling as if his heart could burst through his ribcage, he ripped the wrapping paper off and popped the lid open.

For a moment he couldn't see for the film that had formed over his eyes. He blinked it away and stared at the contents of the box. The longer he stared, the greater the nausea formed inside him until he could bear it no more and, using all his strength, threw the box at the optics behind the bar, hitting the vodka, the power behind the throw enough to smash the bottle.

He laughed as the smell of alcohol immediately filled the space, was still laughing when he swallowed his Gin de Mahón in one and threw the empty glass at the bottle of single malt whisky. Only the glass smashed.

The laughter died as quickly as it had formed as he surveyed the shattered glass around him.

He couldn't make her happy.

All his attempts to protect her had backfired. He'd suffocated her.

All Charley saw when she reflected on their marriage was unobtainable levels of perfection she didn't believe she could reach. Just as he'd always known he would never be able to reach the levels of perfection his own father had demanded of him.

He clutched at his hair so tightly small strands were locked between his fingers when he pulled them away.

Had he really become his father?

All he'd wanted was to please her and make her happy but all he'd done was drive her away just as his own father had driven *him* away.

The happy ending he'd envisaged for them and had dared hope could be a reality had been cut out from beneath him.

He couldn't make her happy. She didn't want for ever with him.

Holding onto the bar to steady himself, he breathed deeply.

It would pass, he told himself. It had passed last time, it would pass again.

But the pain...

It was intolerable.

The shattered glass was nothing compared to the shattered mess that was his heart.

CHAPTER THIRTEEN

CHARLEY FLOPPED ONTO her sofa and buried her face in her hands.

She didn't think she'd ever felt so exhausted. It wasn't even as if she'd had a particularly busy day. She'd worked at Poco Rio but it hadn't been strenuous, not like some days there could be. She'd then had dinner at her mum's house as her grandma's hip was much improved. They'd had a microwave meal for two, just like the old days.

She should be happy. She had a roof above her head, food in her belly, her mum back on her doorstep and the new centre was progressing nicely, the fundraising cruise was days away...

Oh, but she was going to have to see Raul.

She'd debated not attending, but when she'd told Ava she thought she should stay away Ava had clearly ratted her out to the boss because she'd received a terse email from Raul saying that if she didn't attend he would call the whole thing off.

The email had ended with a postscript: Charley, this is a result of your hard work. Enjoy it, please—you've earned it.

His words had played in her mind since she'd received them.

He'd addressed her as Charley.

He'd also called her that from his car.

Oh, but she *missed* him, a pain like nothing she'd experienced before, not even when their marriage had fallen apart the first time.

She'd spent over two months practically glued to his side. In that time they'd spent only two nights apart, when he'd travelled to Brazil. Right before she'd left him a second time...

Her head began to swim. All the thoughts and feelings she'd studiously avoided and denied these past few weeks crowded in on her with a force that could no longer be ignored.

Was it coincidence she'd broken their relationship on the very day her dad had stood her up again, on her birthday, and after she'd spent two restless nights missing Raul, imagining all the beautiful women who would be on his radar?

Could she...?

Was it possible...?

She straightened.

Was it possible she'd sabotaged their relationship deliberately, out of fear? Because Raul had been right, this time round, once they'd got over their loathing of each other and started to forgive the past, their relationship had been better than she could have dreamed. It had been everything she could have wanted. *Raul* had been everything she could have wanted. They'd been completely at ease with each other. Honest. Without pretence. Equals.

And she'd thrown it all away.

What the *hell* was wrong with her?

Was she really going to let *fear* ruin the rest of her life?

Was she really going to let Raul pay for the sins of her father? Because surely that was where it all originated? A lifetime of feeling replaceable had crept into her psyche and made her believe it to be gospel. Rather than wait for

Raul to leave her for someone more suitable, someone less replaceable, she'd run away.

But he didn't *want* someone more suitable.

He wanted *her*.

He loved *her*.

She sat up straight, suddenly as certain of something as she'd ever been in all her life.

Raul loved her with all her imperfections.

She jumped to her feet, bouncing, then slumped back down as another thought occurred to her.

He might love her but she'd hurt him badly. His pride was enormous and she'd wounded it, not once, but twice.

He might not want to listen to her. Even if he did listen, he could still walk away.

Oh, get some backbone, she snapped at herself. *If he walks away it'll be nothing less than you deserve. You'll still live.*

Better to try than spend the rest of her life wondering what if.

But before she could do *anything,* she realised there was something that needed to be taken care of first.

She'd spent the years of their marriage searching for her self-respect. Somewhere in their short second time together, she'd found it. She didn't know where or when but it had nestled inside her. And now she needed to claim it. Until she claimed it and embraced it, she would never be free to love Raul properly, as he deserved to be loved, and nor would she be free to accept his love as *she* deserved. Because she *did* deserve love. They both did.

Reaching for her phone, she dialled. After a few rings it went to voicemail. She dialled again. The same thing happened.

She would keep trying until her dad answered. After all, he kept his phone on him all the time when he was with her, holding it in his hands while they chatted, or on the table by his cutlery while they ate.

On the fifth attempt her dad answered. He sounded breathless. 'Charley?'

'Hi, Dad.' She took a deep breath and plunged straight in. 'I just wanted to let you know I won't be coming to visit you on Thursday. I'll wire the money you asked for but that will be the last of any money you'll get from me. If you need any more, get a job.'

He spluttered down the line, his words unintelligible.

'I've spent my whole life waiting for you,' she continued. 'I love you very much but I won't wait any more.'

Swiping at her phone to end the call, Charley closed her eyes. After a few moments she opened them and expelled a long breath.

That had felt good. Sad, but good.

How could her father or *anyone* respect her if she didn't respect herself?

Respect had to be earned and that included self-respect.

And as she thought all this, something else struck her, something that made her sit bolt upright and clutch at her heart...

Raul stood in the golden atrium of his new cruise liner, smile fixed to his face, shaking the hands of his guests as they were led through by his crew.

Charley was here somewhere. She'd been aboard since early morning, working with Ava and other members of his executive team to ensure everything was ready.

He hadn't seen her yet.

He hadn't seen her in the three weeks since he'd dropped her back at her tiny house.

He hadn't spoken to her either. Other than the one email he'd felt compelled to send her when Ava had mentioned

Charley was thinking of not coming, there had been no direct contact.

Soon the atrium was full, ladies beautiful in their fanciest dresses, the men dashing in their tuxedos, the heavy scent of perfume and cologne filling the air. He gritted his teeth and forced a welcoming smile as he saw his parents and sister arrive, Marta pushing their father's wheelchair.

He cut through the crowd to them, kissing them all. It was the first time he'd seen them since he'd dropped Charley back at her house in Valencia. He'd cancelled the meal he was supposed to attend at his family's house last weekend.

It was the first time he'd been anywhere other than to work since she'd dropped out of his life.

'Is Charlotte here?' his mother asked.

'She's around somewhere,' he said, his heart clenching as it did every time her name was mentioned. Her name had been mentioned a *lot* in his office, especially by Ava, who seemed to have developed some kind of girl crush on her. Raul found this completely understandable.

'So this thing is for her charity?'

He nodded, not trusting himself to speak.

It was at this moment that they were called into the main restaurant where the first part of the proceedings, the meal, would begin.

Turning away, he followed the crowd to the large board displaying the table plan. As was proper, he'd been placed at the top table with the captain, his parents, sister, and... Where was Charley?

Scanning the other tables, he finally found her name at a door near the entrance, as far from his table as it was possible to get.

He caught Ava's eye and beckoned her over. 'Why has my wife been placed down there?' he demanded to know.

'She's sitting with the children and their families—she thought it best for them to be by the door so if any of them get upset they can take them out and calm them down. She's fabulous, isn't she?' she added reverentially.

Seven children, the same ones who had gone to La Tomatina, plus a couple of others, had been selected to attend with their families. Raul would have had all the children there but for the majority of them it wasn't possible. Rather than being a night they could enjoy, the unfamiliarity and break from routine would have distressed them too much. All their families had been invited, though, as had all the Poco Rio staff and their partners.

He was planning on getting every euro he could from the other guests but for the children, their families and the staff, the night was on him.

He spotted little Karin, the beautiful white-blonde-haired girl who had such an attachment to Charley, and a tall boy in a wheelchair whose name escaped him...

And then he saw her.

She was walking in his direction, deep in conversation with another child's mother.

She must have felt his eyes upon her for she paused and lifted her gaze to meet his.

His chest clenched.

Beautiful. She was beautiful. Glowing.

She was wearing a royal-blue lace dress that fell to mid-thigh and displayed her gorgeous curves, her now even lighter blonde hair loose around her shoulders. She wore black heels, which made her fabulous legs appear even longer.

Even with the distance between them he could see the animation in her eyes.

A tall man he recognised—possibly a famous American singer—stepped in front of her and the contact was broken.

Everyone took their seats.

Wine was poured and the evening began.

Course after course was brought out to them by an army of attentive waiting staff, laughter filling the room, overshadowing the piano player in the corner.

Through it all, through all the conversations he had with the others at his table, Raul's eyes didn't stray far from his wife.

Her table of twelve looked as if they were enjoying themselves immensely, Charley chatting away happily as she ate her food. Every so often she would look over to him and catch his eye and he would feel that pull that had always been there between them, right from the very start. The pull he knew deep down in his soul would never leave him.

He gazed at the children on her table. To her left was the boy in the wheelchair, being fed by his father.

A wave of sadness washed through him to think that boy would never be able to feed himself or do anything for himself. With the sadness came a tiny flicker of pride that he was doing something to make that boy's life a little brighter.

Then his eyes flittered to his father, sitting opposite him in his own wheelchair, being fed by Marta, locked in his own version of hell.

For the first time he felt a wave of compassion for him.

His father had been a hard man. He'd been cruel and demanding of his only son. But no one, not even Eduardo Cazorla, deserved this. And neither did his mother, who could easily have left him in that plush care facility but instead had turned their home and life upside down so he could remain part of the family.

Charley would do the same, he knew. Forget about keeping up appearances, which he knew had played a part in his mother's decision; Charley would never abandon someone she loved. Not unless she had to—or felt she had to.

While all these thoughts were filtering through his mind, the empty dessert dishes were being cleared away and from the corner of his eye he saw Charley head to the corner of the room where a microphone stand and booth had been set up.

After fiddling with the microphone for a few moments, she tapped it, the thuds of her finger reverberating through the packed room.

'Can everyone hear me?' she asked in Spanish.

Cheers rang round the room.

'Okay, then.' She cleared her throat. When she next spoke, her voice was clear, fluent and full of warmth. 'Before I start the auction, I would just like to say, on behalf of all the children, their families and the staff of Poco Rio, the most enormous thank you to each and every one of you for being here tonight and for spending your hard-earned money on our centre. I promise you, every cent will be spent wisely.'

Even more raucous cheers carried around the room. She stood there beaming, waiting for quiet. 'I would like to extend especial thanks to the wonderful man who made this night happen.'

Suddenly her eyes were on him.

Prickles ran up his spine.

Her smile faded a little but the warmth in her voice grew. 'If it wasn't for Raul, we wouldn't be here and nor would Poco Rio. Please, everyone, raise your glasses. To Raul.'

The word, 'Raul,' echoed around the room, everyone staring at him and drinking to him.

He wanted to smile and accept the toast with good grace but he couldn't do it. It was all wrong. They were toasting the wrong person.

Before he could get to his feet, Charley had started talking again and the auction was up and running.

Once the auction was over, Charley disappeared. He was about to seek her out—he knew she couldn't go far, not with the ship being in the middle of the Mediterranean—when his mother rose and took hold of his father's wheelchair.

'Can't you ask your mum?' Charley had said. He'd dismissed her suggestion out of hand.

But, since he'd driven her out of his life the second time, he'd had time to reflect and suddenly the conversation became imperative.

He followed his parents through to one of the lounges, where he helped his mother settle his father in a quiet corner.

Raul waited until drinks had been served to them and they were all comfortable before talking.

'Why did you just let me walk away from the family business?' he asked, addressing his mother. His father's reaction hadn't been any surprise but it had always played on his mind that his mother's reaction had been negligible.

A look of surprise crossed her Spanish features. 'Could I have stopped you?'

'No.'

'There is your answer.'

He stared at her. 'You didn't even try.'

'But I knew you would be okay whatever you did.'

'How?'

'Because you are just like your grandfather, Nestor.'

'I am?' Nestor had created the Cazorla empire but his name was one seldom mentioned in the privacy of the Cazorla home.

'Of course.' She nodded at her husband, who was gazing at the pair of them, his eyes flashing as if he was desperate to join in with the conversation, then sighed. 'Your father never got on with Nestor any more than he got on with you.'

'But why?' Now he addressed his father directly. 'I always felt as if I were a huge disappointment to you. There were times when I felt as if you hated me and wished I'd never been born. Nothing I did was ever good enough and I need to know why.'

A grunting sound came from his father's throat. His mother patted his knee with a manicured hand, and smiled at Raul. 'I thought you would have worked it out by now; you're an intelligent man. Too intelligent, just like Nestor. He will hate me for saying this but your father had to work hard for what came naturally to you. He struggled with the business. He knew there would come a time when you took over and it would show up the failures he'd made. You intimidated him.'

Now there was a flash of pain in his father's eyes. Suddenly Raul wished he'd chosen to have this conversation out of his earshot. His father couldn't defend himself.

'*I* intimidated *him*? He treated me like *dirt*.' He shook his head and looked at his mother. 'And *you* allowed it to happen.'

'Allowed what to happen? For your father to correct you, as was his right as your father?'

At least she wasn't pretending not to understand.

'My own father was far harder on me than Eduardo ever was with you.' She lifted the sleeve of her arm and showed him the old silvery scar that ran along her biceps. 'My father did this to me in a drunken rage when I was seven. For all his faults as a father, Eduardo never once lifted his finger to you.'

He felt as if he'd been punched. She'd always shrugged it off as a childhood accident. 'I never knew.'

'It was a long time ago when such things weren't spoken of, especially amongst people like my family. Personal problems were kept behind closed doors. We both suffered at the hands of our parents and we tried not to repeat that with you and Marta.'

He laughed without any trace of humour.

'You think your father was hard on you?' his mother said, a sharpness in her voice. 'Nestor would *beat* him when he failed at anything or disappointed him in any way. I accept we didn't always get it right with you but it's those mistakes you will try to avoid when you have your own children. But know, you will make mistakes. We all do.'

The irony almost made him laugh again.

His own children? The only person he wanted to have children with was Charley, and he'd damaged her. Just as his father had damaged him.

Looking back at his father, he could see a whole heap of emotion playing in his eyes and suddenly he knew exactly what the expression meant.

His father wanted to apologise.

A part of him wanted to turn around and walk away and leave the unsaid apology unacknowledged.

Instead, he leant over and covered his father's limp hand and squeezed, then pressed his lips to his cool cheek.

Life had punished his father enough. What kind of man was he to condemn him for eternity when his own actions had driven away the woman he loved?

For the first time he had an understanding of what his own parents had lived through and, while it was too soon to speak of forgiveness, he knew the road to healing—for all of them—had begun.

CHAPTER FOURTEEN

LOT NUMBER FIFTEEN, a week's holiday on Aliana Island, donated by Pascha and Emily Plushenko, went for a hundred thousand euros—but that was by no means the highest-selling lot of the evening. That honour went to lot number twenty-one, a portrait by the artist Grace Mastrangelo, which sold for a quarter of a million. Those of an artistic bent nodded wisely and said the winning bidder had got themselves a bargain.

The numbers were enough to make Charley dizzy. In one evening, they had raised over a million euros, and that was without adding the ticket sales. Looking at the dazed faces of Seve and the other Poco Rio staff, she could tell they were having trouble processing the figures too.

Now the auction was over and everyone was free to do as they pleased, be it head to the nightclub to dance or go to the casino to gamble or to make their way to the theatre where a top musical was being shown with the original cast...or they could head outside as she had done and stand at the railings looking out at Barcelona in the distance, a mountainous city illuminated magically under the black sky. She squinted, trying to remember where on the shoreline their old home had been. When she looked up, a million stars twinkled down at her.

She inhaled the salty air and tried to capture her thoughts. What she wanted, more than anything, was to find Raul and talk to him. She'd planned it all out, everything she wanted to say, but the look on his face after she'd raised the toast to him had stopped her in her tracks. He'd looked furious.

Doubt and her old friend fear had crept back in.

What if he rejected her? What if...?

What ifs didn't matter. She would speak to him before the night was out. She had to.

'May I join you?'

She turned her head with a jolt, her heart immediately racing off at a canter to find him standing there behind her, dazzling in his black tuxedo, carrying two glasses of champagne.

He held one out to her. 'I thought you might be thirsty after all that talking,' he said drily.

'Thank you.' As she took it from him her fingers brushed against his and her stomach somersaulted.

He stood level with her, his body almost touching hers, and gazed out at the same view.

'You were wrong, you know,' he said.

'About what?'

'That speech you made, toasting me. I didn't deserve that. You did.'

'No...'

'Yes. Without you none of it would have happened. This was your vision, your passion. All I did was put your hard work into motion.'

'But without you doing that it wouldn't have happened.'

'Without you doing all the hard stuff at the beginning there wouldn't have been anything for me to do.'

'We can argue over who should receive the praise all night,' she said softly. 'How about we accept it needed both of us to make it happen?'

A faint smile crossed his face and he raised his champagne flute. 'To teamwork.'

'Teamwork,' she echoed, chinking her flute to his. She didn't drink any of it.

'You look beautiful.'

'Thank you.' She made her voice sound cheerful. 'I couldn't go back to dressing up every day but it's nice to do it for special occasions.'

'You always look beautiful, no matter what you wear.'

A lump formed in her throat.

'I want you to know I've signed the deeds for Poco Rio over to you.'

'But the renovations aren't complete yet.'

He dropped his head with a sigh. 'I should never have done what I did. It was a nasty stunt that I pulled and one I am deeply ashamed of. I just hope you can one day find it in your heart to forgive me.'

'You had your reasons,' she murmured, her head swimming.

'No, I didn't—not any reason that makes sense now I think back on them.' He breathed heavily. 'All it needs is your signature to make it official. You can either drop by the office to sign it or I can arrange for it to be delivered to you, whatever makes your life easier.'

'Thank you,' she whispered.

He shrugged, turning his face back out to the illuminated city in the distance. 'I've been thinking. With the amount of money raised tonight, there's more than enough to fund another Poco Rio. How would you feel about scouting out suitable premises in Barcelona for me?'

'For you?' she asked, confused at the turn of direction.

'I'll pay for the building and any renovations that need doing. The funds raised can pay towards staffing and day-to-day running costs.' He must have caught her dumb silence. 'I'm happy to pay outright for it all, staff costs, upkeep, everything. The money raised tonight has been earmarked for the centre and it's only right it be spent on it, but it can also be used to help other children in the same position. If we keep fundraising we can raise more awareness of what these children are living with and help even more of them.'

'And you want me to help you?'

'I want you to run it all for me. I'll pay you a salary—'

'I don't want a salary.'

'I know but I'll pay it anyway. That's if you choose to accept my offer.'

She opened her mouth, not sure what to say, but he spoke forcefully before she could make a sound.

'Don't make a decision now. Think it over. Let me know when you come to a decision.'

If Charley had felt dazed before, that was nothing to how she felt at that precise moment.

He really did trust her. He truly did believe in her.

'I wish I could turn the clock back.'

Her heart skipped.

Sadness had spread over his handsome features. 'It's that bubble we spoke of before—I'm used to living in it but I never thought of how it would be for someone like you, because you're right, it *is* a different world from the one you knew. I just thought you would adapt and fit in, not thinking that I needed to adapt too. It put—*I* put—so much pressure on you it's no wonder the weight of it was too much. I see you now, living back outside the bubble just as you did when we were apart for those two years, thriving.'

Charley stayed silent, letting him say what was on his mind.

'I know my standards are high. Too high,' he admitted ruefully. 'I spent my whole life having every fault picked over by my father. I was always striving for perfection in the hope of making him proud and getting one word—that's all I wanted, one word—of praise from him.'

'Being less than perfect doesn't diminish you,' she said. 'It just makes you human.'

'I know. Being with you has taught me that.' He bent his head and forked his fingers through his hair. 'That's what I hate the most about myself. I swore I would never be like him but in my pathetic attempt to punish you for not wanting my child and having the nerve to leave me, I became the very thing I despise the most. Because you were right—that marriage was no place to raise a child. Can you ever forgive me?'

She smiled wanly. 'I already have.'

He straightened and brushed a finger down her cheek. 'I used punishing you as an excuse. The truth was I'd missed you so much that when the opportunity came to have you back in my life I grabbed it.' Leaning down, he brushed his lips to her ear and whispered, 'You're the best thing that ever happened to me, Charley Cazorla. Whatever you decide to do in the future, be happy.'

With one last brush of his lips to her own, he stepped back and turned, placed his champagne flute on a small fixed table, and walked away.

'I lied,' she blurted out to his retreating figure, shoving her flute next to his.

He stopped mid-step.

'When you asked if I could be happy with you, I lied. The truth is the two months we just spent together were the happiest of my life. The past fortnight without you has been the most miserable.'

He didn't move, standing as still as the marble statues that encircled the atrium.

Her confidence almost deserted her but she was determined to plough on to the bitter end. He'd put his heart on the line two weeks ago and she'd rejected him. Even if he rejected *her*, she needed to say it. She would not spend the rest of her life regretting that she'd let this one chance of happiness slip through her fingers.

'I've been a scared, stupid idiot. I've left you twice now and I wouldn't blame you if you told me to get lost but, Raul…' She took what felt like the deepest breath of her entire life. 'I love you. I love you so much it hurts and I know I don't deserve it but if you ever wonder if it could be third time lucky for us…'

She got no further. Raul spun round and in the blink of an eye had her up in his arms kissing her as if there were no tomorrow.

Joy and relief filling her, she wrapped her arms around his neck and burrowed herself into him.

For an age they stood there, Raul holding her securely, his mouth hot on hers, until he gently placed her back on her feet and clasped her cheeks in his hands to gaze intently into her eyes.

'I thought that was it for us.'

She shook her head and clutched at his tuxedo jacket. 'Never.'

'I thought I'd lost you.'

'Never. My heart has been yours since the day I met you.'

'Cariño…' Now Raul was the one to shake his head.

'I love you. Totally.' She smiled and traced her fingers across his jawline. 'That bubble you were talking about? Do you think it's possible to live straddling it? One foot in your world, one foot in mine?'

He laughed, a big, deep roar that filled her with such happiness she just had to kiss him again.

Disentangling himself, he stuck his hand into his trouser pocket and pulled out a small square box. 'This is for you. It was supposed to be your birthday present.'

'What is it?'

'Open it and see.'

She flipped the lid open and immediately her heart jumped into her mouth. Nestled in the box was a white-gold and diamond eternity ring.

'It's beautiful,' she whispered.

'I bought it to show you that my love for you is for ever,' he said, taking it out of the box and sliding it onto her empty ring finger.

It fitted perfectly.

'See—now you are mine again.'

She beamed, happiness radiating through her.

'*Cariño*, we will build our own bubble to live in,' he said, placing a reverential kiss to her hand, 'and we will love and celebrate all our imperfections in it.'

'You, me and our babies?'

The laughter died, a serious expression forming in his eyes. 'We will have children when you're ready and not a day sooner. I don't care for the perfect family any more—perfect is *boring*,' he added with a crooked grin. 'Our children will be an expression of our love and commitment, nothing else.'

'How does seven months from now sound to you?'

The shock ringing from him was so palpable that Charley was the one to burst into laughter. 'Yes, you wonderful man, you're going to be a father.'

His eyes were so wide she feared they would pop out. 'How?'

'Do you remember that time in your office…?' She laughed again at the widening of his eyes, relieved to have it out in the open, unable to keep the excitement and joy contained. 'I didn't even *think* about using contraception then.'

'Nor did I,' he admitted, looking completely dazed.

'I took the test yesterday so it's early days. I can't tell you how happy I am...' Her happiness dimmed a fraction. 'You *are* happy too, aren't you?'

'Happy? Charley, I've just got the woman I love more than anything in the world back and I've learned I'm going to be a father. Happy doesn't even come close.'

And there they stood on the deck of the ship, smothered in each other's arms and kisses, oblivious to the passengers milling around them, oblivious to the envious smiles at their obvious, deep love for each other.

EPILOGUE

RAUL PLACED THE scissors to the pink ribbon tied across the front door and said proudly, 'I declare the Poco Rio Madrid open.'

This was the third Poco Rio they'd opened; two more were in the pipeline.

Enthusiastic applause rang out from the crowd around him, the happiest face of all that of his beloved wife, who was leaning against his father's wheelchair, tapping her thigh with one hand rather than clapping with both. Her other hand was holding the base of her enormous belly that strained against the maternity dress she wore.

Passing the scissors to the manager Charley had appointed to run this centre, he hurried over to her side, scooping up two-year-old Sofia on his way. Sofia's face was covered in chocolate. He dug a tissue out of his pocket and wiped it as best he could.

It made him laugh to think that three years ago he would have been horrified to have a child so messy.

Marta had an arm around Charley's waist.

Charley grinned at him but there was a pained expression in her eyes. 'You know I said this morning I felt fit to burst?'

He felt his eyes widen. 'Is it time?'

She nodded.

'Give me my granddaughter,' his mother said, bustling through and tugging Sofia from his arms. She held her up in the air and made silly clucking noises at her. Raul debated for all of a second about telling his mother of the chocolate Sofia had been caught scoffing with the little gang of friends she'd made that morning, before wickedly deciding against it.

'Can Sofia go home with you?' he asked, taking Charley's hand. She squeezed it so hard he winced and he swore he could feel the contraction run through her. 'It looks like grandchild number two is on its way.'

His mother's eyes lit up. 'Of course.' Keeping a firm hold on Sofia, who was screaming to be put down, she kissed them both, rubbing a hand over Charley's belly as she did so. Marta looked as if she were about to go into shock with excitement, while Raul's father's eyes were wide with emotion.

Since their talk on the cruise ship, Raul's relationship with his parents had changed greatly and all for the better. Sofia's birth had cemented the new bond between them. His father loved nothing more than having his wriggling granddaughter placed on his lap so she could smother him with sloppy kisses.

'Call my mother,' Charley said, her words coming in little pants. She managed a pained smile. 'I think this one's in a hurry.'

Exactly one hour and thirty-eight minutes later, Mateo Eduardo Cazorla arrived safely into the world. His mother was tired but delirious with happiness. His father was just delirious, unable to decide who to kiss the most—his beautiful wife or his beautiful son. His big sister was fast asleep after crashing with exhaustion from her chocolate overload. Her dreams were filled with all the happiness she'd known since her own birth.

* * * * *

COMING NEXT MONTH FROM

HARLEQUIN *Presents*®

Available August 18, 2015

#3361 THE GREEK COMMANDS HIS MISTRESS
The Notorious Greeks
by Lynne Graham
Making billions and bedding women couldn't make Bastien Zikos forget the lustrous and defiant Delilah Moore. So Bastien has gone to great lengths to ensure that the one—*and only*—woman to have ever refused him returns to his bed!

#3362 BOUND TO THE WARRIOR KING
by Maisey Yates
Untamed Tarek al-Khalij was never meant to rule Tahar. More familiar with a sword than a crown, this warrior must now heal the suffering his brother's rule inflicted. To do it, he needs his most precious weapon yet...a royal bride!

#3363 TRADED TO THE DESERT SHEIKH
Scandalous Sheikh Brides
by Caitlin Crews
In the desert, Sheikh Kavian's word is law. So the defiance of his promised queen, Amaya, who flees after their betrothal ceremony, is intolerable! Kavian's already tasted her sweetness—perhaps his reluctant bride-to-be needs reminding of the pleasure *he* can give...

#3364 HER NINE MONTH CONFESSION
One Night With Consequences
by Kim Lawrence
The merest *glimpse* of handsome and sophisticated Benedict Warrender was enough to make wallflower Lily Gray blush. Until a twist of fate allows her to enter his orbit for one life-altering night...with consequences!

HPCNM0815RA

#3365 A PAWN IN THE PLAYBOY'S GAME
by Cathy Williams
Alessandro Falcone is notorious for winning in *every* pursuit. Being forced back to Scotland on business is an inconvenience for the billionaire bachelor—until the delectable Laura Reid becomes a welcome distraction on the long, cold Highland nights...

#3366 A BRIDE WORTH MILLIONS
by Chantelle Shaw
Innocent Athena Howard can't believe she escaped The Wedding of the Year only to fall *straight* into Luca De Rossi's arms! It must be fate. The cutthroat businessman needs a wife, and fast...will Athena accept his offer worth millions?

#3367 VOWS OF REVENGE
by Dani Collins
Melodie Parnell has always wanted to experience insatiable passion, and she thinks she's found it in Roman Killian's bed. But in the aftermath of their lovemaking, Melodie is catapulted back to reality when Roman reveals his true plans...to ruin her!

#3368 FROM ONE NIGHT TO WIFE
One Night With Consequences
by Rachael Thomas
Three months ago, Serena James had her heart broken by a man she'll never forget, especially not the fury in his eyes the night they parted. Now she's back in Santorini to tell him that their summer fling had unexpected repercussions...

YOU CAN FIND MORE INFORMATION ON UPCOMING HARLEQUIN® TITLES, FREE EXCERPTS AND MORE AT WWW.HARLEQUIN.COM.

HPCNM0815RB

REQUEST YOUR FREE BOOKS!

HARLEQUIN *Presents®*

2 FREE NOVELS PLUS
2 FREE GIFTS!

PASSION GUARANTEED SEDUCTION

YES! Please send me 2 FREE Harlequin Presents® novels and my 2 FREE gifts (gifts are worth about $10). After receiving them, if I don't wish to receive any more books, I can return the shipping statement marked "cancel." If I don't cancel, I will receive 6 brand-new novels every month and be billed just $4.30 per book in the U.S. or $5.24 per book in Canada. That's a saving of at least 13% off the cover price! It's quite a bargain! Shipping and handling is just 50¢ per book in the U.S. and 75¢ per book in Canada.* I understand that accepting the 2 free books and gifts places me under no obligation to buy anything. I can always return a shipment and cancel at any time. Even if I never buy another book, the two free books and gifts are mine to keep forever.

106/306 HDN GHRP

Name	(PLEASE PRINT)

Address	Apt. #

City	State/Prov.	Zip/Postal Code

Signature (if under 18, a parent or guardian must sign)

Mail to the **Reader Service:**
IN U.S.A.: P.O. Box 1867, Buffalo, NY 14240-1867
IN CANADA: P.O. Box 609, Fort Erie, Ontario L2A 5X3

Are you a current subscriber to Harlequin Presents® books and want to receive the larger-print edition?
Call 1-800-873-8635 or visit www.ReaderService.com.

* Terms and prices subject to change without notice. Prices do not include applicable taxes. Sales tax applicable in N.Y. Canadian residents will be charged applicable taxes. Offer not valid in Quebec. This offer is limited to one order per household. Not valid for current subscribers to Harlequin Presents books. All orders subject to credit approval. Credit or debit balances in a customer's account(s) may be offset by any other outstanding balance owed by or to the customer. Please allow 4 to 6 weeks for delivery. Offer available while quantities last.

Your Privacy—The Reader Service is committed to protecting your privacy. Our Privacy Policy is available online at www.ReaderService.com or upon request from the Reader Service.

We make a portion of our mailing list available to reputable third parties that offer products we believe may interest you. If you prefer that we not exchange your name with third parties, or if you wish to clarify or modify your communication preferences, please visit us at www.ReaderService.com/consumerschoice or write to us at Reader Service Preference Service, P.O. Box 9062, Buffalo, NY 14240-9062. Include your complete name and address.

HP15

TWILIGHT

Sherryl Woods

Zebra Books
Kensington Publishing Corp.

http://www.zebrabooks.com

ZEBRA BOOKS are published by

Kensington Publishing Corp.
850 Third Avenue
New York, NY 10022

Copyright © 1997 by Sherryl Woods

All rights reserved. No part of this book may be reproduced
in any form or by any means without the prior written consent
of the Publisher, excepting brief quotes used in reviews.

If you purchased this book without a cover you should be
aware that this book is stolen property. It was reported as "unsold and destroyed" to the Publisher and neither the Author
nor the Publisher has received any payment for this "stripped
book."

Zebra and the Z logo Reg. U.S. Pat. & TM Off.

First Printing: December, 1997
10 9 8 7 6 5 4 3 2 1

Printed in the United States of America

Prologue

The brilliant late afternoon sun could only do so much. The orange blaze shimmered on the Gulf of Mexico like a scattering of gemstones. It warmed the wide stretch of sandy beach. But it couldn't touch the cold place deep inside Dana Miller's heart.

She had never felt so totally empty, so thoroughly alone. Even with her sons whooping and hollering and splashing a few feet away at the water's edge, she was gut-deep lonely. Even knowing that her parents were there for her—that they shared her anguish and understood her pain—couldn't erase the horrible sense that she was facing a bleak and empty future.

Her husband, her sweet, gentle, kind husband, was dead. Murdered by a person, or persons, unknown, according to the cryptic police report that she read over and over, alone in her room at night, trying to make sense of it, trying to find acceptance of the cold, hard truth.

It had been over a month since that terrible January night, and there were still no answers—not for her, not for the Chicago police, who seemed to dread her daily calls almost as much as she hated making them. But she couldn't stop. She desperately needed answers and no one had them. Until she did, there could be no tears, no healing.

"Put it out of your head," her mother had pleaded more than once. "You may never know why it happened. What does it really matter, anyway? Knowing won't bring Ken back. The boys need you. You have to move on for their sake."

Dana wished she could do as her mother asked. The boys did need her. If only she had something left to give.

Every night she prayed for some sort of peace, some small measure of the kind of serenity she had always felt in Ken's arms. He had brought so much into her life. As a private investigator, she had seen a lot of ugliness. She had seen people at their worst, but Ken had changed that. He had shown her how to find the goodness in everyone. He had taught her about joy and laughter and the kind of oneness with God that few mortals ever felt. Ken had felt it, though, and he had known how to communicate it to others—even a doubter such as she had been before they'd met.

Her lips curved into a sad half-smile, as she remembered how he had loved the church, the rituals and the hymns and the prayers. He had loved ministering to his congregation, loved sharing his strength and his beliefs with those whose faith had been tested by tragedy. Rich or poor, saint or sinner, Ken had been there for them, generous with his time and with his unconditional love.

And now that he was gone, Dana had no one to bolster her shattered faith as her husband would have done. From the moment the police had come to her door, from the moment they had tersely described Ken's senseless slaying in the middle of Chicago gang turf, her faith had been destroyed. A benevolent God could not have allowed that to happen, not to Ken, not to one of His most ardent believers.

And since Ken was very much dead, Dana bitterly accepted the fact that God had abandoned him and her and their three precious boys. If there was some sort of divine purpose behind such an act of madness, she couldn't discern it. She doubted she ever would.

She shivered as the sun ducked behind a cloud and the sensation of emptiness returned. Where once there had been hope and happiness, now there was only this huge, gaping wound where her soul had been.

Time promised to heal eventually, but Dana had never been a patient woman. She'd always been decisive and quick and instinctively curious. She'd had daring to spare. Those traits had made her one of the best private investigators in the Midwest, but she'd given it all up when her first son was born. The same danger that brought a satisfying rush of adrenaline also came with a warning: do not mix with parenting.

She had made the sacrifice willingly and never looked back. Ken and the boys—first Bobby, then Kevin, and finally Jonathan—had fulfilled her in a way she'd never imagined possible. The challenges had been vastly different, but just as rewarding. After a surprisingly brief period of adjustment, she had been thoroughly content with her decision, as fiercely protective of their safety as she had once been lax with her own.

Until now. Now those old urges to pursue truth taunted her late at night, when the loneliness was at its worst. She needed answers and the police weren't getting them. She had the same investigative skills they had, but more important, she had the passion for this particular hunt. She wouldn't relegate it to some cold case file drawer, content to let it remain unsolved until, years from now, some street thug confessed or some witness uttered a tip from his deathbed.

With the boys already settled in a new school for the rest of the year to give them time away from Chicago to heal, with her plans half-made to move to Florida permanently, as her parents wanted, there was only one thing keeping her from making the decision final. She had unfinished business back home.

More and more, she saw going back to Chicago, taking charge of her life and the search for the killer, as the only way she would ever be at peace again. Staying in Florida now without knowing was as good as quitting, and she had never been a quitter.

She dreaded telling her parents, though. They were already worried sick about her. She was too quiet, too lifeless, even for a woman in mourning. She'd caught the troubled glances, the whispered exchanges, the helpless sighs. They would be terrified that in her state of mind she would take dangerous, unnecessary risks. She doubted she could make her reassurances convincing enough to soothe their fears.

Yet she knew, if she asked, that they would keep the boys with them, give them a sense of stability that she couldn't with her heart in turmoil. They would protect them and love them, while she went home to do the only thing she could. The only thing.

She would find the cold-blooded, violent person who had ripped her heart and her life to shreds. She would find answers for the unceasing questions asked by her sons, answers they all needed, if they were ever to move on.

And though the police claimed to have followed up on, then dismissed, her repeated suggestions, she thought she knew exactly where to start.

One

The blasted sofa must have belonged to the Marquis de Sade in another life, Rick Sanchez thought as he shifted his body in a futile attempt to find a more comfortable position. Between the oddly solidified lumps and protruding springs, he was lucky he hadn't gouged out a vital organ. He was very careful to avoid lying on his stomach.

This was the fourth night he'd gone through this same torture, and he was beginning to wonder if he was wasting his time. Whoever had been breaking into the *Yo, Amigo* headquarters either knew he'd moved in to guard the place or had simply decided that there was more fertile turf for theft elsewhere.

Lord knew, that was true enough, he thought as he cautiously rearranged his body once more on the worn-out, too-short sofa. The program he'd founded two years earlier was perpetually short of funds and equipment. The sole, ancient computer he'd hoodwinked a friend into donating had been an early victim of daring neighborhood thieves. Now about the only things of value lying around were the TV and VCR in the lounge. They were bolted down, though not so securely that anyone intent on nabbing them couldn't manage it with a little time and diligence.

They were also in pathetic condition, but at least they'd been obtained legally, unlike the collection of state-of-the-art electronic equipment a few of the boys had offered him the week before. He'd really hated turning them down, but *Yo,*

Amigo was all about taking a moral stance and teaching values. Accepting stolen property would pretty much defeat the very message he was trying to send out.

Exhausted but wide awake, he closed his eyes and tried counting confiscated weapons, instead of sheep. He'd turned over a dozen to the police two days earlier, another seven the week before. It was a drop in the bucket, but each gun or knife he managed to get out of gang hands and off the streets was a small victory.

Rather than putting him to sleep, though, the mental game left him more alert than ever. Images of boys killing boys, of babies being shot by accident in a violent turf war crowded into his head. He wondered despondently if the program he'd founded would ever be more than a tiny, ineffective bandage on the huge problem.

Such thoughts led inevitably to memories of Ken Miller, the decent, caring man who had been his friend and, some said, had lost his life because of it. Rick knew he would never have a moment's peace again, if he allowed himself to share that conviction. His conscience, which already carried a heavy enough burden of guilt from the sins of his youth, would destroy him, if even indirect responsibility for Ken's death were added to the list.

He shifted positions and felt the sharp jab of a metal spring in the middle of his back. He muttered a harsh expletive under his breath and sat up.

Just as he did, he thought he heard a faint whisper of sound, an almost imperceptible scratching from the back of the old brick firetrap that had been condemned until he took it over and began restoring it room by room with the help of the boys in his program. He went perfectly still and listened intently.

The second subtle scrape of metal against metal had him on his feet in an instant. He grabbed the baseball bat he'd kept by the door and eased from the office.

Slipping quietly through the shadowy rooms toward the increasingly persistent sound, he wished for a moment that he hadn't sworn off guns. He also wished the budget had been large enough to pay for a cell phone, rather than the lone, ancient phone that suddenly seemed very far away on his desk. He might as well have wished for a fleet of shiny new vans to transport the teens to the job assignments that were a part of the program. All were out of reach on the shoestring *Yo, Amigo* budget.

Just as he closed in on the back door, he heard the heavy-duty lock give. Whoever had conquered it was skilled with lock picking tools, he concluded with grudging admiration. It hardly narrowed the field, since most of the kids he knew had been breaking and entering since they could reach a door handle or heave a rock through a window. Most, however, didn't have the finesse or patience to work at a lock with the tedious determination that this person had.

The heavy steel door inched open silently on its well-oiled hinges. Pressed against a wall, Rick waited in the shadows. There was no point in risking his neck until he knew exactly what he was up against. One thief. Two. Or a whole damned gang, in which case his goose was cooked and he could kiss the TV and VCR goodbye.

To his relief, the lone person who slipped inside was slightly built and dressed in black from head to toe. Black baseball cap, long-sleeved black T-shirt, trim black pants, even black sneakers. Vaguely taken aback, he concluded it was the working gear of a pro, not some daring kid intent on mischief. The kids he knew wore the baggy clothes and colors of their gangs. Solid, form-fitting black like this would have appalled them.

More on edge than ever, and itching for action, he studied the person creeping slowly and unwittingly toward him in the narrow hallway. Rick figured he easily had a fifty pound advantage over the intruder, plus several inches in height. Even so, he forced himself to wait patiently and watch for accomplices.

When none appeared, he bit back a sigh of relief and considered his options. The bat seemed unnecessary. He propped it cautiously against the wall. Then he slipped up behind the increasingly confident and fast-moving thief and, without uttering a word, slammed the jerk onto the hardwood floor in a full-body tackle that knocked the breath out of both of them.

Rick recovered from the fall first, latched onto a pair of skinny wrists and brutally wrenched the would-be thief's arms behind him.

He received a blistering earful of curses for his trouble. The words didn't shock him. He'd heard far worse. Used far worse, for that matter.

What flat-out stunned him, though, was the fact that the voice uttering such foulmouthed language was so evidently and self-righteously outraged. More startling yet, it was also very clearly feminine.

"If you don't let me up right this instant, I will slap you with a lawsuit that will take away this building and every dime you have to your name," the woman vowed furiously.

Rick was intrigued despite himself. Not intrigued enough to let her go, but fascinated enough to pursue the conversational direction for a bit.

"Is that so?" he asked, unexpectedly amused by her gambit. "And how do you figure you're the injured party here?"

"Because I've been attacked by an idiot with more muscle than sense. I wouldn't be at all surprised if half my ribs were cracked."

"You did break into private property," he reminded her.

"A technicality," she insisted.

"Some technicality. You a lawyer?"

"Sweet heavens, no," she said with such heartfelt distaste that Rick grinned.

"I'm not overly fond of them myself. I guess that gives us something in common, dollface."

"Dollface?" she repeated with more of that misplaced indignant outrage. "No one calls me dollface or honey or sweetheart."

"Too bad," Rick said sympathetically. He decided he could

really enjoy deliberately aggravating this woman. "Mind telling me why you dropped by, dollface? Since you chose not to use the front door or to come during business hours, I have to assume your mission is less than legal."

"That's not true," she said.

"The facts say otherwise."

"To hell with your so-called facts. Are you going to let me up or not?"

"Not just yet," he said, wondering abruptly if the decision was the security precaution he wanted to believe or merely an attempt to prolong the distinctly provocative contact. Worry over his motives kept him silent for so long that his captive jumped back in with her two cents.

"If you're figuring on copping a feel, you'd better think again," she said in that imperious way that amused him so. "I'll slap you with sexual battery charges while I'm at it."

Rick chuckled. "Dollface, I do not need to get my kicks from accosting total strangers. In case you've missed the point, I am subduing a thief who broke into this building. I'm within my rights, believe me."

"I am not a thief," she retorted.

"Maybe not technically, since you never got a chance to lay your hands on anything of value," he agreed. "But you seem to be in deep denial of the seriousness of your position. Now, how about giving me some answers?"

She hesitated for a very long time, probably evaluating her alternatives, before asking, "Such as?"

"Who are you and what are you doing here?"

"Who are you?" she countered. "For all I know, you're just a thief who got here first."

She had audacity. Rick had to give her that. She was the kind of smart-mouthed handful who'd drive a man crazy. He wished he could get a better look at her to see if she'd be worth the trouble, but the lighting in the hallway was virtually nonexistent. The only thing he knew for sure was that she wasn't local. She had no accent. All of the girls in this neighborhood—and some of them were indeed tough as nails—were Latinas.

Based on her shape, though, this one definitely had promise. His own body had picked up on that without his brain even having to kick in. Another couple of minutes of close contact and he'd be dangerously aroused. Hell, he was already aroused. For a man who'd vehemently sworn to remain celibate through all eternity after his very brief and ill-advised marriage had gone sour, it was a troubling turn of events. He'd better settle this nonsense in a hurry and extricate himself from a dangerous situation.

"Let me assure you, dollface, I belong here," he said. "I run the place."

The announcement had an odd effect on her. Though she'd remained relatively still since he'd taken her captive, it now seemed that the remaining breath whooshed right out of her. She was utterly and absolutely motionless. That didn't strike Rick as a good sign.

"Dollface?"

"You're Rick Sanchez?" she asked in a broken whisper.

Rick couldn't tell if her voice was choked by tears or was shaking with some inexplicable anger, but he definitely got the feeling she knew a whole lot more about *Yo, Amigo* than he'd assumed. He also realized that he was the very last person she'd expected to encounter here tonight.

"That's me," he told her. "Which leaves us with you. Who are you, dollface?"

Several seconds ticked by before she answered.

"I'm Dana Miller."

She said it in a tone so stiff and cold that it sent goosebumps chasing over Rick's body. Dismay slammed through him as the name registered. Ken's wife? Dear God in heaven, he'd tackled Ken's wife as though she were a common criminal. Which, of course, at the moment she appeared to be, but that was beside the point.

He released her wrists at once and leapt to his feet, holding out his hand to help her up. She ignored it and rose with a grace and dignity that belied the situation.

"I'm sorry," he said, trying to convey a month's worth of emotions in those two simple words. "For everything. For Ken. For just now."

"Save it," she said harshly. "Save it for someone who'll buy your phony sympathy."

Anger radiated from her in almost palpable waves. Rick had known she blamed him for Ken's death. A half-dozen people had told him exactly how bitter she was toward him and *Yo, Amigo*. In fact, he had stayed away from the funeral for that very reason, out of consideration for her feelings, justified or not. He'd figured Ken's graveside was no place to force a confrontation. Later he'd tried to see her, but she'd been gone, off in Florida to recover from the tragedy, her best friend had told him.

Now he realized that he should have seen her sooner, should have gone at once to offer his condolences, to explain how deeply he too was grieving over the death of her husband. He doubted she would have believed him any more then than she did now, but he knew how wounds could fester unless they were cleansed right away. This soul-deep wound was no different than one to the flesh. It had had more than a month to worsen dangerously.

Ironically, he had anticipated that sooner or later, she might come after him. He just hadn't expected it to be in the middle of the night.

Gazing into her bleak expression, he tried to tell her now what he would have said weeks ago, if he'd had the opportunity.

"Your husband was the best friend . . ."

He never got to finish the sentence. Her open hand connected with his face in a stinging slap that rocked him on his heels.

"Don't you dare say that," she said. "Don't you dare."

Rick fell silent, uncertain how to cope with such anguish

and outrage. Used to coping with broken teenaged dreams with words and hugs and timeworn platitudes, he could think of nothing that would touch Dana Miller's hurt, or calm her fury. Obviously, she needed to lash out at someone and she'd picked him.

Since the topics of Ken Miller and his death were clearly off limits, despite their obvious connection to tonight's break-in, he decided to focus on why Dana Miller was at *Yo, Amigo* headquarters in the middle of the night. It didn't take a genius to figure that one out.

"You expected to find answers here, didn't you?" he asked softly.

The direct question seemed to surprise her. Her gaze clashed with his. "It's the obvious place to start."

"The police thought so, too," he reminded her. "They've searched through every file, talked with every one of the kids who comes here regularly, questioned every potential eyewitness. They've almost destroyed the program in the process." He regarded her defiantly. "I won't let you start the whole thing all over again."

"You don't have a choice in the matter," she told him coldly. "I will do whatever I have to do to find Ken's murderer. You can't stop me."

He found her resolve chilling, but it bolstered his own commitment to salvage *Yo, Amigo,* at any cost. "Oh, but I can. These kids need a safe haven. They need one person who believes in them. That's me. They had Ken, too, but he's gone now."

"Because of you," she accused bitterly.

"Not because of me or these kids," Rick insisted. "I'd stake my life on that."

"Then you're a blind fool," she said. "He was here, in this neighborhood, because of you. Week after week, he risked his life by coming here. Eventually the odds caught up with him." That said, she turned her back on him and headed for the door.

Rick couldn't let her go, not like this. "Dana?"

Her determined footsteps faltered, but she didn't look back.

"I will do anything to help you find Ken's killer, but I will not let you destroy *Yo, Amigo*. There's too much at stake."

"You can't stop me," she said again.

"I'll report what happened here tonight, if I have to," he said, catching her attention. Her eyes blazed when she turned to face him. He went on with his warning, hoping to scare some sense into her. "I will let the police know that you're on a vigilante's mission. They'll stop you."

She choked back what sounded like a sob, but her voice was steady when she said, "Do what you have to do, Mr. Sanchez. And I will do what I have to do."

Before he could think of anything to say to that, she slipped out into the night and vanished even more quietly than she had arrived.

More shaken than he'd ever been by an encounter with a rival gang, Rick sighed at her leaving. She was a handful, all right, everything Ken had ever described her as being.

And he had a terrible feeling that tonight had just been the first skirmish in what was likely to turn into all-out war.

Dana climbed into her car a half-block from *Yo, Amigo* and leaned back against the seat. Her whole body was shaking, not from the very real danger that existed all around her in this neighborhood, but from that face-to-face confrontation with Rick Sanchez.

How could she have been so stupid, so careless? Obviously she'd lost not only her mind, but her touch. She'd been so anxious to begin her search for answers, so determined not to stay away from the boys one second longer than necessary, that she'd gotten off the plane and plunged ahead on her first night back in Chicago. She'd done it without thinking things through, without so much as a day's surveillance of how the stupid program operated or who was likely to be in the building. She'd just assumed it would be empty at night. Assumptions had been the downfall of more than one private eye. She knew that, and she'd acted impetuously, anyway.

Now Sanchez knew she was after him or, if not him directly, then one of those precious criminals he defended so arduously.

"Damn, damn, damn," she muttered, hugging herself to ward off the chill that came from getting caught on her very first attempt to gather information.

She drew in a deep breath and made a promise to herself that tonight's foolishness would be the very last mistake she'd make. She couldn't afford another one, not with a man like Rick Sanchez. Ken wouldn't have admired him so if he'd been anything less than brilliant and committed. That meant he would be every bit as passionate in his defense of his boys and his program as she would be in her search for the killer.

His offer to help echoed in her head. Of course, he wanted to help. He wanted to steer her as far from *Yo, Amigo* as he possibly could. She couldn't afford to be taken in by the compassion or the sorrow he'd expressed. He had his own agenda and it was not the same as hers. Far from it, in fact.

For a moment she allowed herself to wish it were otherwise. The next days and weeks promised to be lonely, albeit frantically busy. It would have been nice to have someone with whom to share theories, as she once would have with Ken.

But Rick Sanchez was not that man. She thought of the powerful, barely leashed strength he'd radiated, the taunting arrogance as he'd held her down before he'd learned who she was. The memory made her shiver, this time with unwanted awareness of just how dangerous a man he was.

She shook off the sensation that she was flirting with disaster. She couldn't afford to be scared off now. Tomorrow, when she'd had some rest, had a chance to compose herself, she would plot out her strategy. And no one—not even the formidable Rick Sanchez—would stand in her way.

Two

The greatest act of courage Dana had ever performed wasn't breaking into *Yo, Amigo*. It wasn't fighting off an assailant that had turned out to be the man she held responsible for her husband's death. It was walking back into the house she and Ken had shared for most of their marriage.

With her heart thudding dully, she hesitated on the tiny cement stoop, unable to push the key into the lock. Her fingers, so nimble earlier, felt stiff and awkward now. Her key ring seemed to have tripled in weight, as if every key had been coated with lead.

"Come on, Dana, it's just a house," she told herself sternly. "A few walls, a roof, some putrid gold carpeting you never liked anyway. How can you be scared to face that?"

Because with Ken there, it had been home. It was as simple as that, proof positive that it wasn't the appearance of a place that turned it into a home, but love. She had felt it every time she had walked through the front door.

Now she faced only emptiness. For one brief second she regretted leaving the boys in Florida. They would have filled the place with noise and laughter. Their presence would have kept loneliness at bay, at least until the darkest hours of the night.

How pitiful was that? she thought ruefully. How pitiful was it to even consider using her kids to buffer the pain? Besides, she had come home for one reason and one reason only: to find Ken's murderer. That was the best thing she could do for all of them, the only thing that would give them any peace. She couldn't afford any distractions if she intended to solve things quickly so that they could move on with their lives.

That reminder was enough to stiffen her resolve. Revenge was a powerful motivator. Even though her hand shook, she managed this time to get the key into the lock, even to walk through the front door.

Perhaps it was better that it was the middle of a moonless night, pitch dark so that she couldn't see the collection of family photographs sitting on top of the upright piano that Ken had played with more enthusiasm than skill, couldn't see the eclectic stack of books beside his favorite chair, or the notes he had been making for his last sermon, still scattered across his desk.

But even though the room was cast in shadows, she could imagine it all, could visualize it as clearly as if every light blazed. It was as if he had just stepped away for a moment or an hour, not forever.

She dropped her luggage inside the door, tossed aside her jacket. Guided by pure instinct, she made her way to his chair, the overstuffed one where she had often sat cradled in his lap, content just to be held as the strains of Brahms or Beethoven surrounded them at the end of a long day.

She reached out, traced the buttersoft leather, and smiled at the memory of how appalled he'd been by the indulgence when there were so many more practical things they could have used. It had gone against his frugal nature to waste money on luxuries. But even as he'd protested, he had settled into the chair, sinking into the deep cushions, caressing the leather as sensuously as he might have traced the curve of her hip or the weight of her breast. He had fallen in love with it, just as she'd known he would.

It was a wonderful memory, one to cherish, she thought as she plucked an afghan from the back of the nearby sofa and settled into the chair. The coldness of the leather was a shock, snapping her back to reality like a slap. Even this, it seemed, would never be the same. The warmth was gone.

Still, she craved the sense of connection that sitting in Ken's favorite chair gave her. It was personal, something he'd used daily, yet it lacked the intimacy of their bed. She wasn't sure when she'd be able to sleep there alone, if ever. From the night she had learned of his death until she had left for Florida, she had slept in this chair. It had brought her a small measure of comfort.

Now, once again, she wrapped the afghan around her and curled up, cradled by leather now, instead of Ken's strong arms. Even so, the restlessness that had plagued her in Florida eased. For better or worse, her journey to find the truth behind Ken's murder had begun.

Finally, as dawn turned the sky grey, then mauve, and at last a pale, winter-weary blue, she slept, more soundly than she had in weeks. It was as if her body were preparing for whatever lay ahead.

Her dreams, though, were disturbing. They were not of the man she'd loved so fiercely, but of a shadowy gunman, his face tantalizingly obscured.

Dana awakened at midday to find her best friend staring down at her, hands on generous hips, a worried frown puckering her brow.

"How'd you get in?" she muttered groggily.

Kate Jefferson waved a key ring under her nose. "I found these in the front door. Even if I hadn't, I have the one you gave me so I could bring in the mail, remember? When did you get home? You were due in at eight. The plane was on time. I checked. I called until all hours, but you never answered. I finally decided you'd changed your mind or missed the plane."

"I got here in the middle of the night," Dana said without elaborating. She struggled awake. Her back ached. Her neck was stiff and she was freezing. She'd forgotten to turn the heat up when she'd come in the night before. It couldn't be much more than fifty-five in the room, the temperature her father had decreed would at least keep the pipes from freezing.

"Where are the boys?" Kate asked. "Didn't they come with you?"

"No. I enrolled them in school in Florida for the rest of the year. They're with my parents."

Kate stared at her in shock. "You've enrolled them in school? Have you decided to move to Florida, after all?"

Dana sighed. "No, not for sure. I haven't decided anything definitely. I can't think that clearly. I just wanted them to get some sense of normalcy back into their lives." She stood up and headed toward the kitchen. "Any more questions will have to wait until I have coffee."

"It's already made," Kate said, proving once again that she had an admirable, take charge attitude. Dana had often told her it should have been put to use running some company, instead of being wasted on her often unappreciative friends or two typically rebellious teenage daughters.

"An hour ago, in fact," Kate added pointedly. "I've been banging pots and pans ever since, hoping to stir some sort of a reaction from you. I thought maybe you were planning to sleep into the next century."

"Would if I could," Dana told her as she filled a mug with the gourmet blend she hadn't been able to give up, despite Ken's conviction that instant served the same purpose. Leaning against the kitchen counter, she carefully avoided looking outside toward the small church where Ken had preached and beyond to the cemetery where he was buried. She drank deeply, one long swallow, then another. Finally she met Kate's worried gaze. "Stop frowning. Aren't you glad to see me?"

"Of course, I am. You just gave me a fright when I found the keys in the door and you didn't answer after I knocked or rang that awful, screeching bell."

Dana figured it was a testament to Kate's anxiety that she'd touched the bell at all. The sound was more appropriate for some creaky Addams Family domicile than a parsonage. Kate shuddered every time she was forced to ring it. Dana had always thought it was a hoot, which probably showed just how perverse her sense of humor was.

"If the boys are in school in Florida, why are you here? I thought you'd be down there a few more weeks at least," Kate said. "I thought the plan was for you to get some rest before you came home to tackle everything that needs to be done here."

Dana shrugged. "Plans change."

Kate's brow puckered again. "Meaning?"

"There are things that can't wait."

"What things?"

"The house, for one thing. Sooner or later, I'm going to have to get out of it. It belongs to the church."

"Lawrence Tremayne told you it was yours for as long as you needed it," Kate reminded her. "Local pastors are taking services for now. If they hire a new pastor, they'll make temporary arrangements for him, if they have to." She gave Dana a penetrating look. "So, what's really going on?"

"You know, you'd make a great private eye," Dana observed. "You poke and prod with the best of us."

"I thought you'd retired."

"I did."

Kate's frown deepened as she apparently guessed what was going on in Dana's head. "Dana, you can't investigate Ken's murder," she protested. "Leave it to the police."

"Who said anything about me investigating?"

"I know you. You're impatient. You're frustrated with the lack of answers. Anybody would be. But it's harder for you, because you think you could do the job better. Plus, you've been evading every question I asked. How am I doing so far?"

Dana thought about denying it, but couldn't find the energy. "On the money."

"Bad idea," Kate shot back. "You're too close to this one.

I know you were one of the best private eyes in the business. That's how we met, remember? You found the proof I needed to take that lowdown ex of mine back into court and show that he had hidden assets in half the states in the country, even though he claimed he couldn't come up with child support. I know you have contacts up the wazoo, but this is personal. You can't be objective. You won't be cool and rational, the way you need to be. You won't be able to analyze the risks. You can't very well sashay around gang turf asking questions. You'll stand out like a sore thumb."

Dana wasn't about to be dissuaded. "I'll just have to work even harder to keep my emotions out of it. . . ." The way she had last night, busting into the *Yo, Amigo* headquarters without a plan, she thought dryly. If Kate ever heard about that, she'd be muttering, *"I told you so"* for the rest of Dana's days.

"What about the boys?" Kate demanded.

"What about them? They're perfectly safe with my parents," she said. "They like the new school well enough. Best of all, there are no sad memories for them in Florida. They're adjusting, better than I am, as a matter of fact."

"That's all lovely, but they need you. I don't care how well-adjusted they seem."

Dana sighed. "I know, Kate. And they'll have me, they'll have my full-time attention just as soon as things are taken care of here."

Kate clearly wasn't satisfied. She leveled another of those penetrating looks straight into Dana's eyes. "This could wait. They should be with their mother, so they won't start to worry that they've lost her, too."

That last one cut. It stirred guilt that she'd worked damned hard to bury. "You've made your point," Dana said tightly. "Now drop it."

Kate was a wonderful friend—compassionate, thoughtful, levelheaded. She was also tenacious. Dana figured she was wasting her breath trying to shut her up. Kate's next words proved it.

"I will not drop it. You can't put yourself into danger, Dana. It's not fair to your sons. What if something were to happen to you? Their sense of security is already shaken by losing their dad. As for your parents, they're great people, but they're older. How long will it be before three rambunctious boys get to be too much for them?"

It wasn't as if she hadn't considered everything Kate was saying. She had, over and over again. In the end, it had been outweighed by her conviction that finding Ken's killer was the first step in healing for all of them. She would be no good to her children, if she weren't at peace with herself.

"It's not fair to Ken that he's dead and that no one knows who did it," Dana retorted stubbornly. "Look, you can fight me on this, but it won't do any good. I've been over every single argument, time and again. Believe me, my mother and father repeated most of them morning, noon, and night, up until the minute I got on the plane. The bottom line is that I have no choice."

"We always have choices." Kate stepped closer and wrapped her arms around her. "Sweetie, I know how much all of this hurts, but getting yourself killed isn't the answer."

Dana returned the fierce hug, then stepped away. "I'm a professional. I know how to minimize risks."

"Oh, really?" Kate retorted skeptically. "Is that why I got a call at the crack of dawn from Rick Sanchez, telling me to keep an eye on you, suggesting that you were behaving irrationally?"

Obviously she'd been saving that little tidbit for its shock value. It worked, too. Astonishment left Dana speechless for thirty seconds. Then her temper kicked in. She snatched up the wallphone, glanced at the list of numbers posted next to it, and punched in the one for *Yo, Amigo* headquarters. Kate reached over and cut off the call. Dana whirled on her, furious.

"What do you think you're doing?"

"Keeping you from making a fool of yourself. He called

me because I asked him to let me know if you showed up there."

Dana's mouth gaped, unsure which stunned her more, Kate's foresight or her betrayal. "Why?"

"Because I know you. It was only a matter of time before you decided to charge in there, demanding answers. Of course, even I didn't expect you to sneak in in the middle of the night like a common thief. It's nice to know you haven't lost your touch with a set of lock picks," she said with more wry humor than genuine admiration.

"Thanks," Dana responded anyway, recalling the surge of adrenaline rushing through her as she'd felt that lock give way to her touch. She hadn't realized just how much she'd missed living on the edge until that moment.

"I'd feel better, though, if you hadn't gotten caught." Kate scowled. "What is wrong with you? Didn't that prove that you're too rusty or muddleheaded to be doing this?"

"Rusty, maybe," Dana conceded. "Right now, though, I'd prefer to know just how cozy you and Rick Sanchez have gotten in my absence. I didn't even know you knew him."

"I didn't. He came around looking for you one day when I was here to bring in the mail and water the plants."

"What the hell was he doing here?"

"I imagine he came to offer his condolences."

"Yeah, right."

"I liked him," Kate said. "I also thought he was being sincere. He thought a lot of Ken. I could tell. He walked out to the cemetery and stayed for the longest time. When he came back, he had tears in his eyes."

"Big, fucking deal!"

"Dana!" Kate protested.

She was clearly as shocked at hearing such language as Dana was at having uttered it. She'd learned to temper her tart tongue the day she'd fallen in love with a minister. Ken had never voiced his disapproval of her tendency to curse, but she'd seen the disappointment in his eyes whenever a particularly foul word slipped out. She'd been home less than twenty-four hours and she'd been cursing a blue streak ever since. She doubted that Kate had ever said anything harsher than darn in her life.

"Okay, I'm sorry," she apologized. "I can't help it. It's just that the thought of Rick Sanchez brings out the worst in me. He got Ken killed."

Kate was shaking her head before Dana could complete the sentence. "You know better than that. Ken was at *Yo, Amigo* because that was the kind of compassionate, caring man he was. He saw the good in those kids. He wanted them to have a chance. You wouldn't have loved him, if he hadn't tried to live up to his own ideals, if he hadn't put himself on the front line, no matter the cost to himself. Ken believed in that program. He believed in Rick Sanchez."

"And he died because of it," Dana repeated. "I can't forgive Sanchez for that. I won't."

"Is he the one you can't forgive, or is it yourself?" Kate asked quietly. "Are you sure you're not taking risks to punish yourself?"

Dana's eyes brimmed with stinging tears and her throat clogged up at the softly spoken question. That was the trouble with having a friend who knew your deepest, darkest secrets. All those confidences could come back to haunt you, Dana thought.

"I should never have told you," she whispered.

"Yes, you should have," Kate contradicted, automatically handing Dana a pristine hankie from her pocket. "If you hadn't told me that you and Ken had fought that night, it would have eaten away at you. You have to forgive yourself, sweetie. Ken was going to *Yo, Amigo* that night, whether you two had argued or not. He'd made up his mind, and he was every bit as stubborn as you are. It wasn't your fault he got killed."

"No," Dana agreed, clutching the handkerchief and ignoring the tears that streaked down her cheeks. "But I shouldn't have let him leave when he was so angry. Maybe that's what made him careless. Maybe that's why he didn't see that there was someone there with a gun."

"And maybe he just got in the way of some drug-crazed kid," Kate said. "That's what the police think."

"One of the kids Rick Sanchez protects," Dana countered bitterly, bringing the argument full circle.

Kate sighed. "There's nothing I can say to talk you out of this, is there?"

"Nothing," Dana agreed.

Kate's expression turned resigned. "Then tell me what I can do to help."

"Just be my friend."

"No, I want to do something constructive. You helped me when my life was a mess. Now it's my turn. I can work a phone with the best of them. You've always said I could talk anyone into doing anything I wanted. Let me put those powers of persuasion to work for a good cause. We'll be a team."

Dana laughed at the excitement sparkling in her friend's eyes. "Kate, you are not a private investigator," she pointed out.

"Technically, neither are you."

Dana was taken aback for a minute, until she realized that Kate was right. She had long since let her license lapse. Hopefully her skills were a bit more up-to-date, though after last night's disaster, she had to wonder. Not that she'd ever admit to such a thing.

"What about your kids? What about the risks?" she asked, throwing Kate's earlier arguments right back into her face.

"One's seventeen, the other's nineteen," Kate said dismissively. "They barely know I exist anyway. Besides, I'm just going to be chatting on the phone, like I always do. How much danger can there be in that?"

"Famous last words," Dana retorted. "Are you really sure you want to help?"

"I really want to help. Just tell me what you want me to do."

"I will," Dana promised. Unfortunately, without any of the clues she had hoped to find at *Yo, Amigo,* she had no clear-cut idea just yet what the first step ought to be.

Three

Rick couldn't decide whether he'd done the right thing by calling Kate Jefferson first thing in the morning. Obviously, she and Dana Miller were close friends. He had found the slightly plump, angelic-looking blonde at the Millers' house when he'd finally worked up the courage to stop by to see Ken's wife and try to make peace with her. Besides, she had made him promise to call the minute Dana turned up.

Knowing how Ken's widow felt about him and about *Yo, Amigo,* at first he hadn't expected that to be necessary—not for a long time, anyway. Only after careful thought had he realized that she was not the type of woman to let things lie. Obviously Kate knew her friend very well.

Even now his lips curved as he thought of the audacity Dana Miller had shown, first in breaking in, then in accusing him of assault when he'd tackled her. She was a handful, all right. Ken had always told him that and now he'd seen her in action firsthand.

She was going to be trouble. He knew that, too. She had the same sort of passion for her particular cause that he had for his, which put them at cross-purposes, for the moment. Oddly enough, they both wanted to find Ken's murderer. She would destroy *Yo, Amigo* in the process, if she had to. He was convinced that no one connected to the program had had anything to do with the shooting.

The kids he worked with weren't saints. Far from it. They'd been handling knives and guns and wearing gang colors starting at a frighteningly early age. Most of them had been touched by tragedy and violence more often than white, middle-class America could imagine. They'd responded the only way that made sense to them, by seeking protection in numbers, by arming themselves. Only a few had learned the lesson that violence only spawned more violence. It solved nothing. As injustices mounted and anger deepened, the violence only escalated, unless they learned another way. He'd tried to teach them that.

Even so, even knowing that his message had convinced only a handful of the teens he worked with, Rick knew in his gut that not one of them would have harmed Ken Miller. They had respected the *Padre,* as they called him. The youngest ones had clustered around him, desperately seeking the warmth and love he radiated, the father figure he represented. The older boys grudgingly admired his straight talk and his jump shots. Ken had run circles around them on a basketball court, playing with a ferocity that had been startling in a man normally so placid.

Rick hadn't relied solely on his gut in reaching the conclusion that no one he knew would have harmed Ken. He was a little too cynical for that. He'd asked questions, gently most of the time, forcefully when necessary. He'd laid it all out for these tough kids who were trying to find their way. One of their own was down and he wanted to know the names of the people responsible. The future of *Yo, Amigo,* their future, was on the line. He believed so strongly that any one of them would have ratted out their best friend for Ken's sake, that he would have staked his reputation and his life on it.

When no one had stepped forward with so much as a whiff of innuendo—much less a solid clue—it convinced him that his kids were innocent. That left a whole lot of unanswered questions. He was as frustrated as Dana Miller had to be. He was also convinced that the answers had to lie outside the 'hood.

The difference was, she was going to tear his fragile grasp

on the souls of these boys to shreds trying to find those answers. She was going to put herself at risk by poking and prodding and turning up in every dangerous nook and cranny until she found something. For every boy in the program who'd respect her for trying, there were a dozen on the streets who would take advantage of her. Some would only take her money for leads that would merely take her down blind alleys. Some were capable of doing far worse.

Rick figured he was either going to have to trail along behind, protecting her, or he was going to have to find some way to join forces with her—for the program's sake and for hers.

Of course, that meant seeing her again, trying to cut through the pain and the hatred and the anger to convince her that they were on the same side. His pulse raced predictably at the prospect. His quick rise to any challenge was both a blessing and a curse. After the way he'd responded to the woman struggling in his arms the night before, he figured this time it was downright suicidal. His body apparently didn't have the same high moral standards his head did, standards that said a man shouldn't be intrigued by his best friend's wife. Ken's death hadn't changed that. In his eyes, Dana Miller still belonged to her late husband.

"Que pasa, Señor Rick?"

At the sound of the softly spoken question, Rick's gaze shot up. "Maria, you have to stop sneaking up on me," he told the teenager with the huge brown eyes and shy, dimpled smile. "My heart can't take it."

The shyness faded, replaced by a knowing twinkle. "Oh, I think your heart can take quite a lot, *Señor* Rick."

"And how would an innocent girl like you know a thing like that?"

"The others talk," she said, then shook her head. "As if you didn't know that already. They think you are *muy* sexy, a how-do-you-say it, a chunk?"

Rick laughed. "That's *hunk,* as if you didn't know that already. Your English only fails you when it suits your purposes."

"No, no," she protested. *"Para me, anglais es muy difficile."*

"Maria, you were born right here in Chicago."

Her chin rose a defiant notch. "But my parents, they speak only Spanish at home," she protested, her expression all innocence. "I heard no English until I went to school."

It was a common enough story in certain immigrant neighborhoods, including this one. Rick happened to know, however, that Maria could speak and understand English like a native, unless it seemed inconvenient to do so.

"The way I hear it, you were a quick study. I've seen all your transcripts. Straight A's. That's why the *padre* was trying to help you get a scholarship to college."

At the mention of Ken, she immediately sketched a cross across her chest and her eyes turned sad. "I miss him every day," she said softly. "He was very good to me and the others, especially my brothers."

"He loved you all. He wanted you to succeed."

Maria perched uneasily on the edge of the chair opposite Rick's desk. She folded her hands in her lap in the pose of a proper young lady, but it was only seconds before she began to fidget nervously. "What do you think will happen now? Will they find the person who killed him? They don't seem to try very hard anymore."

Rick couldn't deny that. It was one reason he could understand Dana Miller's determination to take matters into her own hands. "I don't know whether the police have given up," he told Maria honestly. "But I haven't."

"Do you have any leads?"

"No, but I think someone knew exactly what he was doing that night." It was the first time he had voiced that particular opinion, but he was forced to temper it by acknowledging the other possibility, the one Dana Miller and the police shared.

"On the other hand, if the killer is from the 'hood, I'll find him."

Maria looked shocked. "You think one of us could have harmed him?"

"No one in the program," he said firmly. "But others, who knows? Others believe anything is possible here. The only way to prove them wrong is to find the person responsible. Have you heard anything, Maria? Anything at all? Is anyone bragging a little."

"Who would brag about such a thing?" she demanded indignantly.

"We both know there are people who would like to see the program fail, who would gloat if we lost our funding. They might even commit murder to bring us down."

"But why? What you do here is good."

"Not for those who want to recruit every young child into a gang. They're afraid we might cut into their power."

"They are fools!" she declared dismissively. "And I have too much work to do to waste time on them."

As she left his office, Rick smiled at her vehemence. There was no chance that Maria would become one of the lost souls. Raised by two strict, doting, Catholic parents, she and her brothers had been taught right and wrong. Unlike so many others, they had been surrounded by love. They had been taught the value of hard work, grit, and determination. There would be no shortcuts, no straying from the straight and narrow.

When Juan Jesus, the youngest, had gotten too friendly with members of the toughest gang in the area, the entire family had come to Rick for guidance. Dollars had been scraped together for the tuition to a private school in Ken's suburb. A family in Ken's congregation had taken Juan Jesus in as one of their own weekdays. Ken had brought him back to his family on Friday afternoons and picked him up again at dawn on Monday mornings for the trip north of town. Those days away from the 'hood had been the boy's salvation.

Only Maria knew that the small pittance the family had raised was a fraction of the actual tuition. Had the others known, they would have been too proud to accept the arrangements.

Ever since discovering that Rick and Ken had chipped in to pay the rest, Maria had been coming to the program headquarters every morning to do whatever jobs needed doing. She typed. She answered phones. She cleaned. She bullied Rick into eating, when he would have forgotten. She stayed as long as he did, sometimes longer.

Unofficially, she counseled the teenage girls who trusted her with secrets they might never have shared with Rick. All in all, Rick knew he'd gotten the better end of the deal when he'd made the contribution to Juan Jesus's education. And when Maria had her college scholarship, he guessed she would study psychology or social work and make an even greater contribution to his program, or another like it.

Now and again, when he saw the flash of passion in her eyes for *Yo, Amigo's* goals, when he heard her sweet voice of reason working its magic on a potential backer, he could envision her in the state capital or in Washington, making a difference for all of the teens who seemed intent on sacrificing their youth, or their lives, to gangs. For now, he might be the brains and the drive behind *Yo, Amigo,* but Maria, and a few others like her, were its heart. Ken Miller had been its soul.

Not a day passed that Rick didn't miss him. Not an hour passed that he didn't contemplate his own inadvertent complicity in bringing Ken into the barrio, where he died. Not a minute passed that he didn't want to avenge his friend's death.

Thinking of that brought him full circle, back to the fury he'd read in Dana Miller's eyes the night before. She was trouble all right, and it was way past time he faced it. His warnings last night weren't nearly enough to make her back down.

"Maria, I've got to go out for a while," he said as he passed the desk where she was trying to make sense of the piles of paperwork that accumulated on a daily basis, paperwork that Rick had no patience for, even when he understood the necessity for it.

"I'll be here," she told him with a wry expression. "You haven't touched this in a week. It will take me most of the day to see which is important and which could have been tossed into the trash, if only you'd bothered to read it."

"Gracias. What would I do without you?"

She shook her head. "I cannot imagine."

"Neither can I, *nina.* Neither can I."

"Then it is good you won't have to find out."

"Until next fall," he reminded her. That was when he was convinced she would have the full scholarship to Northwestern that she deserved.

"Even then, I will be here to worry you every day," she insisted.

It was an old argument and one they wouldn't resolve today or even tomorrow. Maria Consuela Villanueva was a woman who knew her own mind, probably had from the time she was two, Rick guessed. There had been times he regretted the age difference between them. She was barely eighteen to his thirty-four. Had she been a few years older, she might have been a good match for him. As it was, he thought of her only as the kid sister he'd never had. Even when she was at her nagging, pestering worst, he would have protected her with his life.

"When will you be back?" she asked.

He thought of the likely battle that lay ahead. Either Dana would slam the door in his face and he'd be back in no time, or she'd listen. He was counting on the latter. He held no illusions, though, that he could persuade her easily to accept his help.

"I'm out for the day," he said, "unless there's an emergency."

"What constitutes an emergency this time? Fire? The arrival of the mayor? A delegation from the capital?"

"Those would do," he agreed.

"Where will you be?"

"With Ken's widow." He shrugged, then added realistically, "Or nursing my wounds beside Lake Michigan with a hot dog in one hand and a beer in the other."

"Better you should take bandages," she retorted.

Rick stared at her suspiciously. Something in her tone alerted him that she knew something about what had gone on here the night before. "Why would you say that?"

"People talk," she said enigmatically.

"Maria! Spit it out. What are people saying?"

"They say that bruise on your cheek is the work of Mrs. Miller. Since it was not there when I left last night, I assume you've seen her since then." She tilted her head and studied his face. "She must not have been glad to see you."

"I'm sure she wasn't," Rick agreed.

"And you think today will go better?"

"Probably not."

Maria opened a cabinet behind the desk and plucked out a handful of Band-Aids and a bottle of peroxide from the stock kept on hand for the multitude of kids with minor wounds that turned up on their doorstep nearly every day. They were all too practiced at coping with major wounds as well, at least as long as it took to send for an ambulance.

"Then these may come in handy," she said. "Of course, people say she is also a trained private eye, like Magnum." Maria was a very big Tom Selleck fan. She thought he was even "chunkier" than Rick.

"She was a private detective," Rick corrected. "What does that have to do with anything?"

"She knows how to use a gun, yes?"

"Very amusing, Maria. You seem to forget that I have at least a vague familiarity with guns myself."

"The difference is that you have vowed never to touch another one. Can you say the same for Mrs. Miller?"

Rick could only say that he knew, with relative certainty,

that she hadn't had one with her the night before. She would have found some way to use it on him.

Of course, that didn't mean she wouldn't grab a gun the second she realized who was on her doorstep. Another adrenaline rush raced through him at the prospect. Disarming her could prove to be absolutely fascinating.

Four

The screeching of that damnable doorbell brought Dana to her feet at once. It had to be a stranger. No one she knew liked the sound of it any better than Kate.

"Want me to get it?" Kate offered.

"I'm still capable of answering the door," Dana said dryly, pushing aside the virtually untouched slice of the pecan coffee cake that she had made when she could no longer sit still. "I haven't lost all my wits yet."

She stepped into the foyer and paused. She could see the large shape of a man through the glass panels on either side of the door. Tall, broad-shouldered and wearing an ancient football jacket from one of the Catholic high schools in Chicago, there was no mistaking Rick Sanchez.

"Oh, boy," she muttered under her breath.

"Dana, who is it?" Kate whispered, slipping up behind her.

"Rick Sanchez."

"*Oh, boy,* is right. Has he brought the police with him?"

"I doubt that Mr. Sanchez is any fonder of the police than I am at the moment."

"Were you counting on that when you broke into the *Yo, Amigo* headquarters last night?"

"No, I was counting on not getting caught," Dana said, keeping a wary eye on the man outside.

He seemed to be growing more agitated by the minute. When he turned and leaned on the doorbell, filling the house with the squealing sound, she decided there was no point in postponing the inevitable. He was here to see her and he'd probably break down the door, if he had to. She was in no position, at the moment, to complain about a little breaking and entering on his part.

"Okay, okay, I'm coming," she shouted as she unlocked the door. When it was open, she glared at him and said, "Mr. Sanchez, you really need to work on your patience."

A twinkle lit his brown eyes, softening his hard, unyielding expression. "Isn't that the pot calling the kettle black?"

Standing squarely in the doorway, Dana refused to concede the point. "Why are you here?"

"To talk."

"I'd say we both made our positions completely clear last night. Anything we said today would be a waste of breath."

"Then I guess you haven't seen the error of your ways," he said with exaggerated regret. "Too bad. I was hoping this was going to be easy." He glanced over her shoulder. "Hello, again, Mrs. Jefferson. Good to see you."

Dana shot a warning look at Kate, whose love life was such that a potent man like Rick Sanchez might be able to charm her with little more than a smile. "Don't think you can use my friend to get to me."

"I wouldn't dream of it. I'm an up-front kind of guy. My friends say I'm direct."

"And your enemies?"

"They say quite a lot of things about me," he conceded.

With his hands shoved in his pockets and his hair tousled by the wind, he had a look of pure innocence about him. Clearly it was deceptive. "I can imagine," she said.

"I'm hoping you and I will become friends."

"Not in this lifetime," she said fiercely.

"That's what Ken would have wanted," he added with quiet conviction.

Dana wanted to hit him for dragging Ken into the conversation, even though he was obviously the reason Rick Sanchez was here. "Do your friends know that you hit below the belt, Mr. Sanchez?"

He didn't look half as insulted as Dana might have liked. In fact, he looked her squarely in the eye.

"I'm a product of the streets," he reminded her. "I fight any way I have to for what I believe in."

The penetrating, brown-eyed gaze, the softly spoken words sent a chill washing through her. For the first time, she fully accepted just how dangerous an adversary Rick Sanchez could be. Knowing the enemy could sometimes be as important as arming against him. With that in mind, she stepped aside and gestured toward the kitchen.

"Kate and I were just having coffee, if you'd care to join us."

There was nothing gloating in his expression, no hint of smug arrogance. In fact, if she'd had to describe what was going on inside him, she would have had to say he looked relieved. Obviously, he hadn't expected her to capitulate so easily. Good. That meant she'd thrown him off guard.

In the kitchen, she poured him a cup of coffee, then refilled her own and Kate's. She deliberately didn't offer him any of the coffee cake. It didn't matter. His gaze landed on her slice, then lifted hopefully. "Aren't you planning to eat that?"

"No," she said resignedly and pushed it toward him. "There's more on the counter."

"I can smell the cinnamon and nuts. Just baked, isn't it?" he asked, sounding as eager as a kid.

"Yes."

"Why'd you bother if you didn't intend to eat it?"

"For something to do. What difference does it make?"

He shrugged. "None, I guess. Just making small talk."

"Don't waste your time."

He accepted the advice without comment and pulled out a chair. When he was seated at the round oak table, Dana suddenly wished that she'd suggested the living room instead. This table, bought at an auction the first year of her marriage, had been at the heart of her family's life. Every breakfast and every dinner, they had gathered here, no matter the other demands on their time. This was also where she and Ken had discussed the future, made plans for vacations, argued over finances. It was at this table, lit by the soft glow of candles, that she had first told him she was pregnant on three different occasions.

It was also where they had lingered over coffee, gazing into each other's eyes with yearning, both of them regretting for just a moment that there were boys underfoot to keep them from acting on the desire that always simmered just beneath the surface of their relationship.

Seating Rick Sanchez here, of all places, seemed to defile the memories. She had never wanted this man to touch the intimate portions of her life with Ken. That was why she had stubbornly refused for so long to include him in family dinners, in holiday celebrations. Ken had accepted her decision, had even understood its roots, but it had been clear that he thought less of her for her inflexibility.

Even then, she realized, Rick Sanchez had found a way to come between them. Now he was doing so by replacing her memories of Ken sitting across from her with his own powerful and very masculine presence. She added that to the list of things to hold against him—the fact that he was so virile, so alive, while just outside her husband was cold in his grave.

She could feel the patches of angry color burning in her cheeks as she scowled at him. "Why are you here?" she asked for the second time that morning. There was nothing gracious or even polite in her tone. Kate glanced at her sharply, subtly warning her to back off. Dana sighed and forced a smile. "That is, what did you want to talk about?"

"You and me," he said.

She scowled at that. "Oh?" she said, her voice a lethal warning against assuming any kind of intimacy was possible between them.

His perfectly sculpted lips curved ever so slightly. *"That was not what I meant, Dana."*

Despite the denial, her name on his tongue was like a caress. Heat crept up her neck and inflamed her cheeks again. "Of course not," she said stiffly. "But I think you'd better explain exactly what you did mean."

Without answering, Rick pushed himself away from the table and stood. Half of the coffee cake remained. Obviously, his appetite had fled, too.

Still silent, letting her demand for answers hang in the air, he moved toward the window, as if he couldn't stay away. She knew precisely what he was seeing—the cold, barren earth, the simple marker, the place where Ken would rest for all eternity.

"He deserves to rest in peace," he said so quietly that she had to strain to hear him.

When the words registered, she realized it was as if he had read her mind. For a brief second, there was a connection between them, a fragile thread of understanding that she hadn't expected. It shook her to discover that she could feel that, despite the overwhelming hatred she felt toward him.

When he finally turned back, his eyes glistened with unshed tears. As Kate had warned her, it was a devastating sight in one so strong. Dana had to steel herself against that image, as she had against so many others lately. She couldn't afford to feel any compassion for this man. None. Ken had been nothing to him, nothing more than someone to be used for the good of his cause. She believed that of Rick Sanchez, because she had to. The hatred, the need for revenge, was all that anchored her these days.

Rick leaned against the counter, propped one sneaker-clad foot on the rung of a chair and cradled his coffee mug in hands that, despite their nicks and scars, looked somehow graceful. Sure and competent hands. Hands that could caress a woman's body and bring it alive.

Dear heaven, where had that last come from? She glanced

at Kate and saw that she, too, was fascinated with Rick Sanchez, fascinated the way a woman would be with a devastatingly attractive man who radiated sexuality from every pore.

That, of course, was his single most potent weapon, Dana realized. If she weren't careful, if she weren't strong, he would weave that easy magic over her, as well. She was lonely now and, like too many lonely women, she was vulnerable. She could not, *she would not,* allow anything to happen between her and this man. She would keep the hostility alive as protection, as a duty.

"I'm waiting," she said, keeping her voice icy, her expression remote. "Unless you have something specific to discuss, I'd like you to go."

His lips curved again. "Patience, Dana."

"I don't have time to be patient. I have things to do."

"Planning more break-ins?"

She scowled at him. "Possibly."

"Not at *Yo, Amigo,* I hope."

"If that's where the answers are, then I'll be back."

"I've already told you that the program and its boys are not the key to Ken's death."

"How can you possibly be so confident of that?"

"Because everyone at *Yo, Amigo* loved Ken," he said.

The simple declaration shook her as more vehement statements might not have. For just a moment, she wished she hadn't remained so adamantly opposed to what Ken had been doing. She wished that she had accepted one of his repeated offers to take her with him, to let her see for herself why these lost kids mattered so much to him.

Instead, she had clung to the long-ago betrayal of a boy very much like those in Rick's program. She had been trying to help him and his lawyer fight armed robbery charges he claimed had been unfairly brought. She had believed in him. Only after they had successfully fought off a conviction had she discovered he was guilty, that he had played on her sympathy and used her clever investigative skills to win his case.

Weeks later, released from jail, he had shot and killed another storekeeper in yet another robbery attempt. A scared sixteen-year-old boy had been his accomplice. He had been shot by police arriving at the scene. She had vowed right then never to trust her instincts again, never to trust vows of innocence and remorse from the very kind of boys Ken and Rick believed capable of change.

Had she put aside that vow and gone with Ken, would she have shared Rick's belief that his teens were incapable of harming Ken? She doubted it. Her own experience would have warned against it.

In fact, she would have grabbed onto any possible motive, any possible suspect, just as she was doing now. She was too desperate for answers to exclude anyone on blind faith alone.

"What do these kids know about love?" she countered.

"Precious little," Rick agreed. "But they experienced it with your husband. Ken showed them what it meant to be accepted unconditionally, to be forgiven. He taught them they were worthy of God's love. Every one of them was blessed to have known him." His gaze locked on hers. "And they knew that."

Dana shuddered under that unwavering gaze. In his own way, Rick Sanchez was as fervent in his beliefs as Ken had been in his. She, to the contrary, believed in nothing anymore, not even in the generous, compassionate, forgiving God who had guided her husband.

Despite their opposing views of his boys, she couldn't help being swayed just a little by Rick's faith in them. "Okay, Mr. Sanchez. Say I were to take your word for the moment that no one connected to the program had anything to do with Ken's death. Where would you start to look for answers?"

"Closer to home," he said at once.

He said it with such quick certainty that she was startled.

"What on earth does that mean? Surely you don't think I? . . ."

"Of course not. I was talking about the people Ken dealt with right here, in his own congregation, in his own community. He told me there was a faction who wanted him removed."

Dana stared. "If there was, this is the first I've heard of it."

"It had just come up. He didn't want to worry you. He told me it was the sort of nuisance thing that arises every now and then. A few people don't like the way their minister thinks, or they respond to some imagined slight. In Ken's case, he suspected there were some who disapproved of his work with *Yo, Amigo*. They feared he was already dragging the gang problem into their backyard."

It was easy enough to make the connection, then. "This came up after he brought Juan Jesus here to live with the Wilsons, didn't it?" she asked.

Rick nodded. "That would be my guess."

"But he is such a sweet young man. How could anybody fear him?" Kate demanded.

It was the first time she had said a word in so long that both Dana and Rick turned to stare at her. Rick smiled at the fiercely protective tone of voice. Obviously, all of her motherly instincts had been aroused. And unlike Dana, she hadn't been a holdout, fighting Ken's commitment to the kids in the barrio. She had gotten to know Juan Jesus and any of the others he had brought around from time to time. Kate's soft heart hadn't been touched by the kind of tragedy that had made Dana so terribly wary.

"Taken individually, most of our boys are just like Juan Jesus," Rick responded. "They're tough on the outside, but if you look beyond that, you find a scared, vulnerable kid. Put him in the right environment and he will flourish."

"Put him in a gang, he becomes dangerous," Dana pointed out.

"Yes," he said. "Some do."

"Most," she countered.

He studied her intently, assessing her. "Would you have joined with the faction who felt threatened by Juan Jesus's presence in the community?" Rick asked.

Dana didn't like the immediate response that formed. She bit back the instinctive yes that formed in her gut. She and Ken had argued over that very subject more than once. They had argued about it again on the day he had died. She had wanted their boys to live in a safe environment. She hadn't wanted outside influences to change their protected world. It was petty and selfish of her, but there it was. She was a mother first and she'd seen firsthand the very real danger that came with trusting a kid with a record.

Intellectually, she had understood that boys like Juan Jesus deserved a chance. Give them their chance, she had argued— just not here. Not here, where a failed experiment could be so terribly costly to their own children. She hadn't realized there were others in the church who'd said the same thing.

Nor had she considered that such feelings might run hot enough to do harm. For a brief moment, with Rick's knowing gaze studying her, she allowed herself to feel ashamed at her unwitting complicity with narrow-minded, hurtful people, who would have ruined her husband's career out of fear.

"Would you?" Rick asked again.

"I would like to think I'm better than they are, more open-minded, fairer, but the truth is I had said many of the same things to Ken myself," she confessed reluctantly.

"Dana, you hadn't!" Kate protested.

Dana nodded. "Yes, I had. I didn't want that kind of influence around my kids. I'm sorry, but that's the truth, and you know why I feel that way. I've seen firsthand just how destructive an influence kids like that can be."

Rick regarded her with disturbing intensity. He seemed to be weighing something.

"You know, Dana, I've changed my mind. I think the best

place for you to start this investigation would be at *Yo, Amigo,*" he said eventually.

She stared at him in amazement, torn between gratitude and suspicion. "You'll open the doors to me? Let me look at your files, talk to the kids?"

He nodded.

"Why? You said the answers weren't there."

"Maybe not to Ken's murder," he agreed. "But I think you might learn quite a lot about your husband."

She found the suggestion that she hadn't really known Ken to be insulting, but she couldn't afford to turn down the offer. Once again, she and Rick Sanchez would be operating at cross-purposes. But whatever his motives in offering, she had to take advantage of the opportunity.

"I have no idea what made you change your mind, but thank you. I will be there first thing in the morning," she said, meeting his gaze evenly.

"Why not now? You could come back with me."

The prospect of being confined in a car with this man rattled her, but she could see the sense of taking him up on this offer, as well. Despite her determination to take whatever risks were necessary to get answers, there was no point in being foolhardy. Going into that neighborhood in broad daylight with Rick Sanchez as her escort made sense. His acceptance of her presence might smooth the way for her, might make others speak to her more openly.

"I'll get my purse."

"Just your keys," he countered. "You won't be needing your purse."

"What if I get a hankering for something to eat?"

"I can afford to treat you to lunch, Dana. Dinner, too, for that matter."

Something in his eyes, a flash of heat, a suggestion of sensuality, told her she would be wise to stay away from cozy meals for two with this man. He'd persuaded cold-hearted politicians to part with city money for his pipe dream. He'd sweet-talked tough, streetwise kids out of their weapons. If he put his mind to it, would he be able to convince her to leave *Yo, Amigo* out of her investigation?

Hell would have to freeze over first, she vowed silently, her gaze clashing defiantly with his. To her regret, he looked amused, not intimidated.

He would learn, though. She vowed that he would discover very soon that Dana Miller was a formidable enemy.

Five

Rick had regretted his impulsive offer to take Dana into Chicago the instant the words were uttered. Was he out of his mind to consider giving Dana Miller full access to *Yo, Amigo*? He'd seen no evidence of a kinder, gentler side to her. Yet for some reason, perhaps Ken's frequently expressed faith in his wife's essential goodness, Rick had to believe that her ingrained attitude of distrust wouldn't come back to haunt him.

Still, what would the kids think when they realized she was there to investigate Ken's death, when they saw that they were the target of her suspicions? It could unravel every shred of progress he'd made with them over the past couple of years. It could shatter their trust.

He couldn't renege, though. One way or another, she would be underfoot, snooping. He owed it to Ken to keep Dana where he could watch over her, where he could protect her. Somehow, he'd have to make the kids understand that.

Maybe it wouldn't be as difficult as he imagined. They were bright. Maybe they would see how much pain Dana was in and would cut her some slack, especially if she managed to keep that tart tongue of hers in check. Maybe it would be a good lesson in tolerance for all of them.

And maybe they'd hang him for bringing the enemy into their midst, he thought wryly.

Oh, well, there was nothing to be done about it now. Dana was upstairs, probably tucking some sort of wire into her blouse and a gun into her back pocket, if he read her correctly.

She might leave her purse at home, but she wasn't about to go with him unprepared for her own style of battle. She had the determination of a pit bull. As angry as she was, she was also likely to be oblivious to real danger.

He glanced across the kitchen table to find Kate Jefferson studying him intently, a frown knitting her brow. "What?" he demanded.

"If you allow anyone to harm one hair on Dana's head, I'll come after you, personally," she warned. She leaned closer and repeatedly jabbed a finger into his chest. "I may look like some sweet, innocuous, little suburban homebody to you, but nobody is more ferocious than a woman like me when someone we care about gets hurt."

Because she sounded so serious, Rick held back the grin that threatened to emerge. "I don't doubt it," he said solemnly and fought the urge to rub the spot she'd been assaulting. He'd probably have a bruise there to match the one Dana had left on his cheek. "Believe it or not, I want her to find what she's looking for."

"Ken's killer?"

"That," he agreed, then added, "and peace of mind."

Kate sighed heavily. "I'm afraid the last won't come easily."

"Where I come from, Mrs. Jefferson, very little comes easily."

Rick's car was old and battered and nondescript. The outside seemed to be held together mainly by beige paint and rust. It would be an unlikely target for young thieves, Dana concluded. Inside, however, it was immaculate, and it ran like the car of a man who tinkered possessively with its engine.

"How fast does it go?" Dana asked as they made their way into Chicago.

He slanted a look in her direction. "Fast enough. Why?"

"Just making small talk, Mr. Sanchez," she said, mimicking

his earlier claim. The truth was that a part of her wondered if he'd tuned it for quick getaways, but for once, she managed to keep the deliberate insult to herself. Somehow she had to find a way to meet the man halfway.

He glanced over at her. "Can't you call me Rick?"

Dana debated before answering. That would mean taking one brick out of the wall of defenses she'd built between them. She wasn't sure she dared risk it. Refusing, though, seemed churlish. Not that he had a particularly high impression of her anyway, but she hated to add to the negatives. For the time being she needed his cooperation and goodwill.

"I'll try to remember," she said eventually.

He seemed to be fighting a smile. "That'll do," he said, then added pointedly, "For now."

Dana let that remark go unanswered. He was only trying to provoke her, a trait that obviously came naturally enough to him. Perhaps, if she failed to rise to the bait a few times, he'd give up and settle for the uneasy truce they'd reached. She still wasn't exactly sure why he'd suddenly agreed to her meeting the kids at *Yo, Amigo.* Clearly he had a point of some sort to make.

As they neared the *Yo, Amigo* headquarters, the signage in the neighborhood was more frequently in Spanish than English. The *taquerias,* the *bodegas,* the promise that those inside spoke Spanish made Dana feel as if she'd unwittingly entered a foreign land. This world of immigrants, who clung to the past, to old ways and their old culture, seemed totally alien.

"Are most people here from Mexico?" she asked, her natural curiosity stirring.

"Most. Many are Cuban, a few from Central America."

She nodded, absorbing that and the fact that in broad daylight, the streets seemed less menacing. Bundled up against the freezing wind and bitter cold of early March, people were simply going about their daily business, pausing only briefly to chat with neighbors, their breath visible in the icy air.

Strains of rapidly spoken Spanish filtered through the car's windows. Latin music blasted from passing boom boxes, the salsa beat cheerful and provocative.

It seemed so . . . She searched for the right word, then settled for *normal.* Except for the language, the street could have been any other ethnic neighborhood in Chicago, rich with color and surging with life. Where was the danger in this? she wondered.

"It changes at night," Rick said quietly, once more displaying that uncanny knack for reading her mind. "These people stay inside after dark, even in summer. Kids aren't allowed to play in the streets because of the threat—no, the certainty—of drive-by shootings. Children here see more violence up close than yours will see on TV. They'll know it as a reality, as the loss of a brother or sister or a friend. It's no way for a kid to grow up."

Dana thought of Juan Jesus, whose presence in her neighborhood had stirred such controversy and wrath. As worried as she'd been about his influence on her kids and others, would she have wanted this life for him, instead? He was just a boy who'd already seen too much, experienced things no child should have to endure. Gazing around her, she gained a tiny bit of insight into Ken's perspective.

And Rick's, she conceded reluctantly.

Leaving her to her thoughts, he turned the corner into the alley behind *Yo, Amigo.* Dana recognized it. She had crept down it just the night before, staying in shadows, filled with determination and rage. She was calmer now, but no less determined.

Rick stopped the car just a few feet from the back door in a spot clearly marked as his by the scrawled name in bright yellow paint on the brick wall of the building. It was surrounded by fading graffiti. If she'd been paying attention, as she should have been the night before, would she have spotted his car there? She thought back carefully. She couldn't summon a single image of any car being in the alley. Surely she would have noticed it and checked it out. Her skills weren't that rusty.

"Where were you parked last night?"

He regarded her innocently. "You were in a very big hurry. Are you so certain I wasn't right here?"

She thought about it once more, then nodded with more certainty. "I'm positive."

"Very good," he praised, though his tone was mocking. "Actually, I left the car at home and hitched a ride over."

"Why?"

The question seemed to make him uncomfortable for some reason, so she asked it again.

"Because we've had a few problems."

She could see that the admission cost him. "What sort of problems?"

"Unwelcome visitors," he said tersely.

"Other than me?"

He smiled at that. "I wasn't expecting you, at least not last night."

"Truthfully, you weren't expecting me at all, were you?"

"Your friend seemed all but certain you'd turn up here eventually."

Dana persisted. "But you didn't believe her, did you?"

"No," he admitted. "At least, I didn't think you'd have the guts to come creeping around here in the middle of the night, since you'd never been inclined to show up with Ken during the day."

"I didn't stay away out of fear," she protested.

"Just disapproval," he guessed.

She realized that in his eyes that was far, far worse. Compared with her compassionate husband, she had to seem cold and hardhearted. She didn't want Rick's opinion to matter, but oddly enough, it did. Even so, she refused to waste time right now trying to change it. Even if she'd explained about the boy she had once trusted, would he have understood? Or would he have said that was just one boy, that others shouldn't be condemned for his mistakes? Ken had said that often enough, but it hadn't swayed her. She hadn't had his capacity for forgiveness or his willingness to risk a second, more dangerous betrayal.

Now, though, she needed to get inside, to start looking at files and talking to people. She had to do something, find at least one solid piece of the puzzle. The compulsion that had brought her back from Florida was stronger than ever. Once again, she had allowed Rick to deliberately distract her. She wondered how many more times she would come up against the tactic, as he tried to protect his precious program.

"Are we going to go in or are we going to sit here all day analyzing my psyche?" she inquired testily.

"Analyzing your psyche might be fascinating," he said. Before she could respond, he added, "But you're clearly too impatient to get on with your agenda to cooperate."

She reached for the door handle, but before she could open it, his hand closed over hers. The shock of his touch, the heat of it, stilled her. He waited until she turned to look at him before he said a word.

"One bit of caution: proceed slowly in there. If you go in like a private detective, they won't talk." His gaze locked with hers. "I've taken a huge gamble by bringing you here. I won't let you hassle them."

"You promised—" she began, only to be cut off.

"I promised to bring you here, to let you get to know what we're all about. If you get answers as a result of that, fine. If you can't live with that, I'll take you back home right now."

She didn't like the rules. Nor was she certain how she would operate within them. "How will you explain me?"

For a moment he seemed to be weighing the alternatives. "I'm going to tell them who you are," he replied eventually.

Her gaze narrowed. There was more. She could read it in his eyes. "And then what?"

He smiled. "And then I'm going to say that you're here to take up where your husband left off."

She stared at him, aghast by the suggestion—no, the command—that she was going to become a part of the *Yo, Amigo* program in some way. She felt manipulated, though no doubt the signs of his intentions had been there from the moment he uttered his invitation.

"I can't do that," she protested.

"You will do that," he corrected, then added more gently, "It's the only way to find the answers you're after. You'll have to blend in, become one of us."

"I don't shoot hoops," she grumbled.

"Then tutor them in reading, teach the girls to sew. We have a kitchen here. You can teach them to cook. It won't matter what you do. It'll matter more that you're here."

Dana didn't like the gender based suggestions. More importantly, she wanted to move her investigation along far faster than the snail's pace he was suggesting. And yet, she conceded reluctantly, she could see the sense of what he was saying. She knew just how distrustful these toughened street kids were likely to be. If she came on too forcefully, demanded too much, they would walk away without a backward glance.

But Rick's way would also risk getting involved, putting her emotions on the line. She didn't want to know these ex-gang members. She didn't want to take a chance that she might actually come to feel something for them as Ken had.

No, she didn't like his plan at all, but she would do as he was demanding. She could tell from his unrelenting expression that he wasn't giving her a choice.

"Let's go," she said through gritted teeth.

This time he didn't try to stop her from getting out of the car. But when they reached the door that she had used the night before, he blocked her way. Once again, she felt the power of his presence, the heat of his body, his taut strength.

"If you find out anything, anything at all, you will tell me about it first," he said, his gaze locked with hers.

"You told me I wouldn't find anything here," she taunted.

"I don't believe you will, but there's always an outside

chance I'm wrong. I don't want you tearing off half-cocked and getting yourself killed."

"Why? You'd be rid of a serious thorn in your side."

"No," he corrected. "I'd have one more death on my conscience. Ken's already keeps me awake at night."

There was just enough torment in his voice that Dana had no choice but to believe him. She knew all about that kind of guilt and anguish. She hadn't had a decent night's sleep herself since the murder.

Even so, she was far from ready to forgive him, even further from being willing to trust him. He was a means to an end at the moment. He was giving her entry into a world that she might never have been able to penetrate on her own. She would use him, as he had used Ken. If she destroyed him and *Yo, Amigo* in the process, it still wouldn't be enough to compensate for the loss of her husband.

Six

Apparently it was too early in the day for a big crowd. Inside the *Yo, Amigo* headquarters, Dana spotted only a handful of boys and even fewer girls. Perhaps it was part of Rick's tactic to bring her here when there would be only a few people to talk to.

But it was a starting point, she reminded herself sternly, and, right now, that was all she needed.

She watched as Rick strolled through the cavernous building with the confidence of a man who was in charge. She overheard him tease and taunt in a surprisingly lighthearted manner, saw the playful exchange of punches and handclasps. There was respect here and trust.

There was none of that in the hard, cold gazes that turned on her. She was eyed with obvious suspicion. Even when Rick explained, first in quiet Spanish, then in English, who she was, there was only the slightest softening of attitudes, the faintest mellowing of distrust.

The boy Rick had called Marco was the first to speak directly to her. With chiseled features and thick black hair, he had classic good looks, plus plenty of attitude. He surveyed her with an insolent, assessing gaze, then muttered something in Spanish that had his friends chuckling, until a stern look from Rick cut them off. He spoke sharply to them in such rapid Spanish that Dana caught only an occasional word and even then, her long-ago lessons in the language failed her.

Whatever he'd said, though, seemed to alter the charged

atmosphere. First one girl and then another smiled and shyly introduced herself. There was Rosa with the huge dark eyes and curly hair and the thickening waistline of pregnancy. Then came Ileana, with the tattoo of a scorpion on her wrist and half her head shaved. Dana forced herself not to react to the eccentricities, but to the hesitant welcome in their eyes.

There were more, but Dana knew she would never keep the names straight and apologized for it. She added in faltering Spanish that she was glad to be there, glad to meet them.

Her attempt to speak their language gained her another grudging point or two. She could see the first vague hint of acceptance in their eyes. She knew, though, that it was only a beginning. There would be many more steps before she could ask the questions that plagued her, that much was clear. One wrong step and the distrust would return, stronger than ever.

She had tiptoed through many an awkward interrogation, smooth talked her way around deep suspicions in the past, but she was out of practice, and no one she had ever encountered was as deeply distrustful as these kids clearly were. How had she ever imagined that she could blithely waltz in here and demand answers? The past few minutes had shown her the folly of that thinking.

When an awkward silence fell, Rick stepped in. "You guys can spend time with Mrs. Miller later. We have a few things to take care of first in my office."

Dana knew he was right to hustle her along, to give them time to absorb the idea of her presence, but she hated the prospect of even so minor a delay. Still, she said her goodbyes and dutifully followed him to the open door on which his name had been painted by the same artistic hand that had inscribed it on the wall out back.

When they walked inside, a beautiful, dark-haired teen looked up from the piles of paper in front of her, started to say something, saw Dana, and gaped. She had barely recovered, when Rick's introduction had her gaping again.

"You are the *padre's esposa?* I mean, his wife?"

There was such awe and reverence in the girl's voice that Dana could do no more than nod.

"This is Maria Consuela Villanueva," Rick said. "She keeps things in order around here."

Dana surveyed the chaos doubtfully.

"I know, *señora,*" Maria said with a shrug. "It does not look as if I have achieved much, but you should have seen it before I came."

Dana could not imagine it being worse than it was now. File folders lined the walls in stacks that were waist-high. There were no file cabinets to hold them. A rickety table in the corner held a coffeemaker, a mismatched assortment of mugs, and some sort of pastries. All of it looked ready to topple to the floor if so much as a breeze stirred.

Then there was the general decor. It seemed to Dana as if someone had gotten a deal on seconds at the paint store. The old metal desk with its fresh coat of bright red paint looked incongruous against the buttercup yellow walls. The backbreaking metal chair in which Maria sat was a vivid blue. Even the trash can had received a coat of new paint—lime green.

"Who's your decorator?" Dana inquired.

"That would be Maria," Rick said with obvious pride. "She thought it was too dull around here before."

"It was grey," Maria said, wrinkling her nose in disgust. "Everything grey. It was enough to make a person depressed."

Dana glanced at Rick. "I assume the grey had been your choice."

"No, it was here when we took over the building from the county. Institutional grey. Very bland and non-threatening."

"And your office? Did you allow Maria to change the decor in there? Or were you happy with your bland environment?"

Rick opened the door. "See for yourself."

Dana stepped inside and promptly had to hide a chuckle. His walls were fire engine red, his desk yellow. His chair was lime green. Those for his guests were a startling shade of purple.

"It's very . . ." She hesitated, then settled for ". . . bright."

"Cheerful, yes?" Maria said, gazing around the room happily. "Everyone helped. We did it as a surprise."

Dana searched Rick's face. "And were you surprised?"

"Stunned is more like it," he muttered. "I'd really grown rather fond of that grey."

"Too boring," Maria said, ignoring his plaintive expression. "This is better. People leave this room feeling happy."

"Or dizzy," Rick countered.

Maria's brow crinkled worriedly "You hate it?"

Dana waited to see just how diplomatic Rick Sanchez could be when the situation required tact. Sure enough, he reached out and gave Maria's hand a quick squeeze.

"It's a beautiful office," he reassured her. "Everyone who comes here says so."

She gave a nod of satisfaction. "We could do something wonderful with your apartment, too, if you would just allow us." She glanced at Dana. "Beige, floor to ceiling, nothing but beige and brown. It is worse than the grey, I think. It feels as if you are already in your grave with the dirt closing in."

Dana shuddered at the imagery.

"It is not beige," Rick protested. "It's Navajo white. I picked it out myself."

"Call it what you like. I know beige when I see it. And the carpet is brown, yes? And the sofa? And that disgusting chair you love so much?"

Rick threw up his hands. "Okay, yes. But I'm not wasting money to change any of it. It's livable. Besides, I'm never there."

"True enough," Maria agreed, "especially since . . ." A warning glance from Rick silenced her. "Never mind. Would you like coffee, *Señora* Miller?"

Dana shook her head.

"Okay, then. I will leave you to your meeting." She retreated hurriedly.

Dana had listened to the exchange with fascination. She had watched the casual, affectionate teasing and wondered if there was more to their relationship than boss and secretary. Maria seemed to know an awful lot about Rick's home.

"If she's not crazy about your decor at home, maybe you should let her change it," Dana said when Maria was gone.

Rick stared at her blankly. "Why would I do that?"

"If you expect her to spend any time there . . ."

Rick's immediate chuckle stopped any further speculation. "My, my, you do have a vivid imagination, don't you? I thought private detectives were supposed to look for evidence, not jump to conclusions."

"In this case, the facts add up."

"What facts?"

"She's a beautiful young woman. You're a healthy male. Both of you are single and unattached. She knows exactly what your apartment looks like, so obviously she's spent time there."

His gaze locked with hers. "I *am* a healthy male," he confirmed softly. The mood suddenly shifted as he stepped closer. "You're a beautiful widow." One finger stroked lightly, provocatively along her jaw. "I know exactly what your house looks like, so obviously I've spent time there."

Dana swallowed hard, but she couldn't seem to make herself look away. She knew he was just trying to make a point, but she was too caught up in unexpected sensations to reason out what it was.

"So, Ms. Private Detective, would you say you and I are having an affair?"

She should have anticipated it, but she hadn't. The taunting, softly spoken suggestion shocked her. Dana scowled at him, even as a traitorous tingle of awareness and anticipation shot through her. She forced herself not to back away, not to show any sign at all that he had shaken her with that slight caress.

"Touché," she said, her voice husky and uneven, despite her best efforts. "Sometimes the facts may not add up."

"Maybe it would be best if you and I stick to the things we can prove," he suggested, his tone astonishingly casual considering the level of electricity that had been humming through the air just seconds before.

Dana could only nod.

"Have you thought about what you'd like to do here?" he asked as if the conversation up until that moment had been about nothing more consequential than the weather.

For once, she was grateful for the quick change of subject. "Poke through the files," she said readily.

"I meant with the kids."

She sighed. "You're really going to make me go through with this, aren't you?"

"It's part of the deal. Reading, cooking, sewing, whatever. It's up to you."

She thought over the choices he'd offered and rejected all of them. She wanted something that would potentially reveal more of their personalities. "How about photography?" she said impulsively. "I have some experience with that." Of course most of it had been snapping shots of errant husbands in the arms of the other woman. She supposed she could translate that and her two formal classes into an impromptu course of some sort.

Rick looked doubtful. "I don't know."

His lack of enthusiasm only fueled hers. "Why not? It's a skill that they might be able to use."

"But to get the equipment they'll need, they might resort to theft," he said realistically. "We can't afford to buy the cameras, the film, or the darkroom supplies."

Dana wasn't sure whether it was real enthusiasm for the idea or just plain perversity that made her say, "I have several old cameras at home and I can pay for the supplies."

"You would trust these kids with your cameras?"

His doubting expression had her hesitating, but only for an

instant. She didn't want him to think she wasn't willing to put herself on the line in exchange for the information she so desperately wanted. "Until they give me reason not to," she said firmly.

A grin spread across his face. "Well, well, Mrs. Miller, now you're beginning to sound just a little like your husband. There may be hope for you yet."

The hard won, if somewhat mocking, compliment pleased her more than it should have. She forced an indifferent shrug. "One small step at a time. What should we do? Put up an announcement of some kind?"

"Just set a time for the start of classes and tell Maria. Believe me, word will get around."

"And if no one shows up, do we still have a deal?"

He shook his head. "You have to win them over. That was the deal. If photography doesn't work, I guess you'll just have to come up with something else, won't you?"

The challenge was unmistakable. Dana resolved then and there that she would make the photography class work. She would teach these kids the skills they would need to take first-rate snapshots. Maybe, with a little luck, she'd even find one who could become a professional. Catching herself, she realized she was actually getting carried away. She saw how easy it was to become excited about possibilities.

She was also, once again, getting distracted. She eyed Rick suspiciously. Was that what he really intended? Had he hoped that she would get so caught up with these kids, so emotionally attached to them, that she'd forget all about the little matter of identifying her husband's murderer?

"It won't work," she said quietly.

"What won't work?"

"I won't forget about Ken's death. I won't drop the investigation."

His unblinking gaze stayed level with hers. "Never thought you would."

Either he was being straight with her, or he was a masterful liar. It was too soon to lay odds on which.

"When do you want to get started?" he asked.

"The sooner the better, but I'll need my equipment."

"Tomorrow, then."

She nodded. "I'll be here first thing in the morning."

"Better wait till afternoon. These kids are supposed to be in school in the morning," he said dryly.

"But those in there—"

"Dropped out or were suspended. We're working on getting them re-enrolled. I don't want to reward them by offering a special class in the morning. Make it four o'clock. That way, more kids will be here and I'll have time to get some work done before I come out to pick you up and bring you in."

"That's not necessary. I can drive myself in."

He shook his head. "I thought we'd settled that. On my turf, I make the rules."

"I'm not one of your strays."

"No, but you are here because I've made it possible," he reminded her in a way that reaffirmed who held the power.

"It's a public building," she countered defiantly.

"You think you can get these old bricks to talk, go right ahead and try," he retorted smoothly.

Dana sighed. "Okay, you've made your point. Four o'clock will be fine. Am I expected to sit in the corner until you're free, or are you taking me home now?"

"No, I am not taking you home now. I'm taking you to lunch. You've lost too much weight. You're obviously not eating."

"How would you know a thing like that? You've never seen me before today."

Before she realized what he intended, he reached out and snagged a chunk of material at her waist and tugged. There was at least an inch or better to spare.

"Evidence, Dana. Solid, irrefutable evidence."

"Maybe I just like to wear my clothes loose."

He grinned. "Give it up. You're not going to win. Ken was very proud of your fashion sense. He often wished he could persuade you to teach these girls a thing or two about style."

He had expressed the same wish to her on several occasions, but she had always dismissed the idea with one excuse or another. She had never realized that he'd shared those thoughts with Rick.

"He said you were too busy with other commitments," Rick said, though it was clear he hadn't bought the excuses.

"Okay, okay. Maybe I have lost a couple of pounds," she conceded. "I haven't felt much like eating."

"Today you will," he assured her. "I'm going to stuff you with black beans and rice, maybe a few enchiladas, maybe a taco or two."

Despite herself, her mouth was watering. "Spicy?" she asked.

"If that's the way you want them."

"Is there any other way?"

He nodded approvingly. "See there, you and I do have one thing in common."

"Don't let it go to your head," she warned.

"Hey, I've always believed that the path to victory was to find the first little chink in your opponent's armor."

"Is that what we are? Opponents?"

"Aren't we?"

For some reason, she didn't care to explore too closely, Dana suddenly regretted the accuracy of his assessment, but she couldn't dispute it.

"Yes," she said softly. "I suppose that is exactly what we are."

It was too bad, too. What she was in desperate need of these days was an ally.

Seven

Rick leaned back in the booth at Tico's and studied the woman opposite him. He'd waited for disdain to fill her eyes all morning, first when she had met the kids at *Yo, Amigo* and minutes ago, when they had entered the tiny, unpretentious neighborhood restaurant. So far, she had surprised him.

She had been polite, if guarded, with the teenagers. Inside the door of Tico's, she had drawn in a deep breath and a positively rapturous expression had crossed her face. Once they'd found an available booth in the crowded room, she had grabbed the typed, laminated menu eagerly. For five minutes after that she had pestered him with questions about unfamiliar items.

She had ordered with such abandon that even the unflappable Tico had been startled. She would be stunned to discover that her meal would be enough to stuff a truck driver. Tico's place might not be much for atmosphere, but he never stinted on his portions, especially not for a customer who demonstrated so much enthusiasm. Rick had had to hide his amusement at his friend's bemused expression.

What a complex woman Dana Miller was, he thought, a little bemused himself as he watched her. This side of her was far too alluring, far too dangerous, when he was already having difficulty resisting the effect she had on his body.

"Didn't anyone ever teach you that it's not polite to stare?" she inquired, squirming just a little under his gaze.

He liked knowing that he could rattle her. "Not that I can

recall," he said, enjoying her uneasiness. She had caught him totally off-guard the night before. He figured it was only fair that he return the favor. "I don't think it applied to circumstances like this, anyway."

She regarded him quizzically. "And what circumstances would these be?"

"Two people trying to figure out what makes the other one tick."

"Is that what you're trying to do?"

Rick smiled. "Aren't you?"

"I already know what makes you tick, Mr. Sanchez," she said with evident bitterness. "You have a passion for just one thing—that program that you have poured your heart and soul into."

It was essentially true, but Rick was vaguely insulted just the same. No man liked to hear himself described as so one-dimensional. "You see no more in me than that?"

"Is there more?"

"Maybe we should let you discover my other passions as we go," he said softly and watched the color climb into her cheeks.

The taunt came as naturally as breathing, before he could stop himself. It drew a spark of pure fire in her eyes that intrigued him, despite his best intentions. Dana Miller was a woman with passions of her own. Whatever they might be, though, they were off-limits to him. Honoring his friendship to Ken demanded it.

"This isn't personal between us," she said, her teeth clenched.

"Oh, no? You blame me for the death of your husband. You want to destroy something I love, something I've worked hard the past few years to get off the ground. I'd say that makes it pretty damned personal, Dana."

"I meant—"

He couldn't resist trying to shock her. "You meant there would be no sex, isn't that right?"

The pink in her cheeks deepened. "How crude of you to put it so bluntly."

"I don't waste a lot of time dancing around the obvious, if that's what you mean." He leaned forward. "As for the sex, I think it's a little too soon to rule anything out."

She glared at him. "You are every bit as despicable as I'd imagined, Mr. Sanchez. My husband is—"

"Dead," he reminded her, then cursed himself when the color washed out of her face. "I'm sorry," he said, and meant it. "I should never have said that."

"I think we should go now," she said, her eyes shadowed with unbearable pain. "I've suddenly lost my appetite."

Rick wondered only briefly whether he should accede to her wishes. Perhaps if she remained very angry with him, if she thoroughly despised him, she would stay away from *Yo, Amigo,* after all. He knew better, though. She wouldn't allow anything—not even her dislike of him—to get in her way. She might avoid him, but she would be back.

He met her gaze squarely. "Suit yourself, but my appetite is just fine, and I'm not about to let Tico's food go to waste."

Their meal arrived as if on cue, plates loaded down with fragrant, spicy concoctions that blended meat and cheese and chili peppers in ways that fast-food chains had never imagined. As furious as Dana was with him, she eyed the plates avidly. He wondered if she would be stubborn enough to leave the food untouched to spite him.

For a moment or two, she did exactly that, hands folded primly in her lap, her chin tilted defiantly, her gaze fixed on some distant point beyond him.

But as he continued to eat, slowly and deliberately savoring each mouthful, he could see her wavering. Finally with a soft sigh of resignation, she picked up her fork.

She took one tiny, tentative bite at first, still resisting the idea of enjoying her meal. That bite was quickly followed by another, larger one, and then another.

"Oh, my," she whispered, more to herself than to him. "This is heavenly."

Rick grinned. "See, not even I can ruin the taste of Tico's enchiladas."

She ignored the comment. "Do you think he would give me the recipe? What's in this mole sauce? How many chilis?"

"I have no idea, and I doubt if he'd tell you. I think he would rather you came here often," Rick said, and immediately regretted his own foolhardiness. He was practically begging to make things more personal, more intimate between them. How many meals could they share without the undeniable sparks between them leading to something neither of them wanted? Her violent response to his taunting comment just moments earlier proved that she was not half as immune to him as she wanted to be. No doubt she believed that such a significant spark of attraction made a mockery of her mourning, whereas he believed it was simply a life force exerting its pull.

"For more of this," she said, holding up a forkful of savory meat, "I would spend time with the devil himself."

For one brief second, Dana Miller was just an attractive, intelligent woman, a woman that his body responded to, even when his head told him nothing could ever come of it. There were depths to her that it would be fascinating to explore, depths he would never know. That being the case, it was better to remind them both of why they were together at all.

"Ken always loved it here, too," he said.

Rather than pain at the mention of her husband's name, though, something soft and wondering lit her eyes. "He came here?"

It was as if he'd offered her an unexpected connection to the man she had lost. "Often," Rick said. "He loved the food and the people. Tico was one of our first success stories when we began four years ago."

Astonishment spread across her face. "Tico was in a gang?"

"He led one of the gangs," Rick corrected, then added somberly, "Until one of the members of his own gang killed his little brother, claiming he was a snitch."

She gasped at that. "How horrible!"

"But out of that tragedy came some good. Tico was ready to listen to what *Yo, Amigo* had to say, to what Ken had to say. His mother was an excellent cook. Tico took her recipes and began to experiment with them. He fixed several suppers for everyone at *Yo, Amigo.* Everyone was wildly enthusiastic. Ken found a few people in the restaurant business, invited them over one night and, after tasting some of Tico's wizardry with Mexican food, they came up with the money to back this place."

"It was a wise investment, wasn't it?" Dana asked.

Rick nodded. "He repaid all of the loans in the first year and he's been in the black ever since. Four of his younger brothers and sisters work here now. His mother comes in to act as hostess in the evening. It's truly a family enterprise."

"You must be very proud," she said with obvious sincerity.

"Not me. Ken had the foresight to see what Tico could be. I was worried only about getting him off the streets. It takes more than that. I can rescue kids every day. I can talk until I'm blue in the face about opportunity and dreams and success. It takes people like Ken to make them a reality, to keep these kids from drifting back to their old ways. Your husband offered more than a moral compass. He offered hope."

He met her gaze evenly. "Can you see now that even though my loss is very different from yours, it runs just as deep?"

He could see the struggle in her eyes, the unwillingness to acknowledge that he might be suffering because of Ken's death, just as she was. Eventually, though, she was too honest to lie, even to herself.

"I think I'm beginning to see that," she conceded, albeit grudgingly. "But don't you see that it was because of that very need you had for him that he's dead?"

Ah, Rick thought, there was the rub. He fought that acknowledgment, denied it. When he did allow it, he could see his responsibility so clearly it kept him awake nights.

"I'm sorry," he told her once more. "But even if I'd known what the outcome was going to be, I wouldn't have stopped him from coming. *Yo, Amigo,* the kids there, kids like Tico, needed him."

"So did I," she said fervently, visibly choking back a sob.

Rick reached across the table and took her hand in his. It was cold as ice, but she didn't pull away.

"I know, Dana," he told her quietly. "I know."

She wasn't through with him yet, though. "Because of you, my kids will grow up without a father."

He could have told her there were plenty of kids here in the barrio who would grow up without a father, as well, but it would have brought her no comfort. He thought of her going home to that empty, silent house in the suburbs and, for once, he didn't envy the life she and so many others had.

Once, not so very long ago, he would have dismissed her as an uncaring, pampered housewife. He had kept that opinion to himself, even when Ken had sung her praises and ignored her shortcomings. Now he was glad that he had. She had loved her husband and her kids. With her misguided notion that she could insulate them from the world, she had wanted nothing more than to protect them. How could he fault her for that? It was exactly what he wanted for so many others.

"I'll take you home now," he said at last.

From the despondent look in her eyes, he suddenly realized that it was a trip neither of them was looking forward to.

With every mile that brought them closer to home, Dana felt the tension inside her mount. It was worse in many ways than what she'd felt only hours earlier, when she had made the reverse trip into Chicago. She had gone to *Yo, Amigo* filled with rage and, perhaps, if she were totally honest, just a modicum of fear of the uncertainties ahead.

Coming home, where she knew exactly what to expect, she felt only this vague tightness in her chest, the far more devastating threat of more emptiness. Even though the winter sky was darkening, it was barely four in the afternoon. A long, lonely evening stretched out ahead of her.

When they pulled into the driveway, Rick glanced at her knowingly. "Are you going to be okay here by yourself?"

"Of course," she said, denying the truth. "I've lived in this house for nine years. It's home." For how much longer? she wondered. She couldn't drag out the move forever. Sooner or later, the board's patience would wear thin.

"I'll be fine," she insisted.

He regarded her with obvious skepticism. "Maybe you should call Mrs. Jefferson."

The thought appealed too much. Kate's cheerful ways and common sense would chase away the shadows. She forced herself to shake her head. "No, this is the way it's going to be. I have to get used to it."

"Not overnight."

"Yes," she said. "The sooner the better." Changing the subject, she asked, "What time will you be here tomorrow?" Only after she'd asked did she wonder if she'd sounded too anxious to escape.

"Two-thirty, maybe three."

"Or maybe later," she said, imagining him to be the kind of man who lost all track of time.

"I said two-thirty or three," he corrected. "That's what I meant."

She shrugged. "Whatever."

He regarded her with a direct look that commanded her attention. Only when he had it, did he say, "Dana, I know you don't want to trust me, not even in so small a detail, but I mean what I say. You'll see."

"It's not important."

"I think it is. Would you like me to come in with you?"

She almost smiled at that. "To chase away the ghosts?"

"In a manner of speaking."

"No," she said too quickly. She didn't want him inside again, in Ken's space. He was the kind of man who could far too quickly overshadow memories. They would fade fast enough without the competition. "I'll be fine. I'll see you tomorrow."

She left the car in a rush, then hurried up the front walk. She fumbled the key in the lock and then she was inside. She closed the door quickly behind her, blocking out the view of Rick Sanchez still sitting in her driveway, his gaze worried as he stared after her.

She didn't want his worry or his concern. The only thing she wanted from Rick Sanchez was entry into the world where her husband had died.

She peeked out from behind a curtain and saw that he was still there. Eventually, though, he started the car and backed out of the drive. Only then did she release the breath she had unconsciously been holding. Relief followed, relief that didn't bear too close an examination.

Fortunately, just then the phone rang. Switching on a light as she crossed the room, she grabbed the portable phone eagerly, glad for anything that would push Rick Sanchez and the disturbing afternoon they'd just shared from her mind.

"Mom?"

She wasn't prepared for her son's whispered voice. It was thick with tears and enough to break her heart. Her oldest prided himself on never crying. Since Ken's death, Bobby had taken his role as man of the house far too seriously. Except at the funeral, he had remained stoically dry-eyed. He had been the one to comfort his younger brothers, to try to explain the inexplicable, when Dana's words had failed. This afternoon, though, he sounded more like a scared and lonely little boy.

"Mommy?"

"Yes, sweetheart, I'm here."

"Why can't we come home? We miss you."

"Oh, baby, I know. I miss you, too. How's school?"

"Awful. It's not like home."

"I know it's an adjustment," she said with a sigh. "But we talked about that. You all said you wanted to stay in Florida for the rest of the school year, remember? You wanted to see if you liked it better there than Chicago."

"Well, I already know. I don't," he said emphatically.

"You haven't given it a chance. I'll be back soon and we'll talk about it some more, okay? In the meantime, aren't you having fun with Grandma and Grandpa?"

"They make us go to bed too early."

"How early?"

"Eight o'clock, like I'm some baby," he said with disgust.

The privilege of staying up until nine had been hard-won. They'd negotiated it on his eighth birthday. She wasn't surprised that he was chafing at an early bedtime.

"I'll speak to Grandma."

"They won't order in pizza, either," he said, apparently encouraged by her response to his first complaint.

"Now that's something with which I totally agree," she said. "We did that too much."

"But they won't do it *ever!*"

She noticed that her little diplomat was quick to switch tactics, seek a compromise. There was no mistaking his father's influence in him. Dana chuckled despite herself. "Okay, I'll see what I can do about that, too. Anything else?"

His already low voice dropped another notch. "Jon wet the bed and Grandma yelled at him."

Dana closed her eyes against a sudden rush of guilt. What had she done by leaving the boys behind? At five, Jonathan was way past bed wetting—or he had been until his world had been rocked by the loss of the father he idolized. That first week, when she'd found it almost impossible to explain why Daddy wasn't coming home ever again, there had been accident after accident. By the time she'd left Florida, though, she had thought the problem solved. Obviously her departure had caused him to regress and her mother's patience to wear thin.

"I'll talk to Grandma about that, too."

"Kevin's acting weird, too. He just stares at the TV until Grandpa makes him do something. It's like he's not even here or something," Bobby said. "I think maybe you'd better come back and get us."

The image of rambunctious, six-year-old Kevin sitting for endless hours in front of the TV brought on the salty sting of tears. She couldn't let it sway her, though. She simply couldn't. "I will, very soon."

"How soon?" Bobby persisted.

"I can't put a time limit on this, sweetie, but I'll talk to you every day."

"It's not the same as you being here."

Dana sighed. "I know. I'll try to finish up here as fast as I can. Now, where's Jon?"

"He and Kevin are with Grandpa down at the pool. Kevin cried, but Grandpa made him go He said we should have a swim before dinner to work up an appetite."

"Where's Grandma? Is she fixing dinner now?"

"No. She's playing cards with her friends."

The thought of Bobby in her parent's condo all by himself frightened her. There was too much mischief he could get into. What had her parents been thinking? Of course, it was entirely possible—no, it was likely, she concluded ruefully— that they had no idea he'd come inside. He was probably supposed to be at the pool with the others.

"Bobby, go back to the pool with Grandpa before he misses you and starts worrying. I'll call this evening."

"Promise?"

"Cross my heart."

"No," he wailed unexpectedly. "Don't say that."

Dana was stunned by the outburst. "Bobby? Sweetie, what is it? What's wrong?"

"Don't you know the rest of that? Don't you remember?"

Dana couldn't imagine what had upset him so about something they'd been saying to each other for years. "What?"

"It's 'cross my heart, *hope to die*,' " he said, sounding teary again. "Don't say that ever again, Mommy. Please. You'll make it come true, just like Daddy. That's what he promised the night he got killed."

His anguished logic stunned her. "Oh, no, baby, it's just a saying. I'm not going to die."

"Daddy said it," he repeated brokenly. "And he died."

"Not because of that," she reassured him. "Bobby, you know what happened to Daddy wasn't because he said some silly words, don't you?"

He gulped back a sob. "A bad guy shot him," he said in a tiny voice.

"That's right. It wasn't because of anything Daddy said or did. It wasn't his fault."

"But why would anyone shoot Daddy?" Bobby asked. "Why would God let it happen?"

Dana couldn't think of how to answer that one. It was a question she had repeatedly asked herself. That bullet that had felled Ken had done more than kill her husband and destroy her life. It had destroyed the faith that had been central to their lives.

If she couldn't see the sense of Ken's death, how could she make an eight-year-old see it?

"I don't know why, baby. Maybe God is just testing us to see how strong we are."

"Mommy?"

"What?"

"Sometimes I don't feel very strong at all."

"Me, neither, sweetie. Me, neither." Shaken by the whole conversation, she tried to figure out how to reassure her son long distance. The answer to that, too, eluded her. "Bobby, go on back outside with Grandpa, okay? I'll talk to you tonight."

"You won't forget to tell Grandma about bedtime, will you?"

She smiled, despite the previously somber mood. "I won't forget. Now, scoot. Love you, Bobby."

"I love you, Mommy."

The phone clattered back into the cradle and left her listening to the faint buzz of a disconnected line. Tears slid down her cheeks, as finally, slowly, she hung up on her end, as well.

Had she been wrong to leave the boys? Had she been wrong to come back here to find the answers the police were unable to find?

The part of her that was a mother said yes. She belonged with her children. They needed her, now more than ever. Her parents had told her that. So had Kate. A conversation like this one only reinforced what she already knew in her heart.

But the part of her that had been a wife, a lover, a friend, said otherwise. She had no choice but to use all of her skills as an investigator to solve her husband's murder. There would be no real adjustment for any of them until the murderer was behind bars.

Eight

The sweat was pouring down Rick's back as he squared off in front of Tico under the hoop on *Yo, Amigo's* indoor basketball court. Gazing straight into the other man's eyes, he kept his body loose as he tried to outguess him.

Tico dribbled the ball slowly, deliberately, between them as if he had all the time in the world. Without the rules of a game, in their one-on-one contest it was a test of patience as much as anything. For two habitually impatient men, it was a real struggle to wait each other out.

Despite the fierce concentration in Tico's eyes, he managed to keep up a steady stream of chatter, alternating between English and Spanish. So far, most of the remarks had been focused on Dana Miller. Tico had more questions and observations than a reporter on a deadline.

"*Que pasa?* Are you two going to become a hot ticket? I saw the way she looked at you. Pure lust."

"Pure hatred is more like it," Rick said, listening to the rhythm of the bouncing ball, even as he kept his gaze steady. These late-night contests had become a welcome ritual, relieving stress with pure exhaustion. Rick had really been counting on its effectiveness tonight, but Tico's remarks were having the opposite effect. Dana's image was staying front and center and growing more provocative by the second.

"Love, hate, sometimes it is all the same, *mi amigo,*" Tico commented.

"Her husband just died," Rick protested. "The only thing

Dana really cares about is finding the person responsible and getting even. Since she hasn't found that person yet, I'm the target of all of her rage."

Shock spread across Tico's face, but he never once lost his concentration. "She blames you for Ken's death?" he asked incredulously.

"She doesn't think I pulled the trigger, but she blames me, yes."

Tico's expression turned thoughtful. "And yet she shared a meal with you today. It could be that she is beginning to see reason." He grinned. "Or she has been charmed by that great wit of yours."

"She ate with me because it suited her purposes. I've promised to help her find the killer."

Tico feinted left, then swiveled to the right and shot. The ball swished through the net. Rick grabbed the rebound.

"Six-four, you son-of-a-bitch," he said.

Tico grinned. "You should pay closer attention, *mi amigo.* Your mind is elsewhere tonight, eh?"

"No," Rick said adamantly, but he doubted he convinced his friend. He certainly wasn't convinced himself. Dana had been preying on his mind ever since he'd left her. She'd looked so lost and alone as she'd walked up the driveway and into the house earlier.

"Not so long ago you feared she or the police would bring down *Yo, Amigo* with all of their questions," Tico reminded him. "What's happened to change your mind?"

"I haven't changed my mind," Rick declared, alternately dribbling the ball with his left hand, then his right. "That's exactly why I agreed to help."

"Was that the reason or was it those sad, blue eyes of hers?"

Rick's hand faltered at that and Tico seized the opportunity to steal the ball, pivot and shoot. Another perfect shot. Two, if the remark about Dana's eyes counted.

"I could really grow to dislike you," he muttered.

Tico laughed, unoffended by the threat. "It is because I see so clearly that which you do not wish to see."

"It's because you beat me every time we walk onto this court. I give up," he said, reaching for a towel and mopping his face.

"So soon?" Tico taunted. "You usually last until midnight."

"My concentration's shot."

"Something else for you to hold against the lovely widow, no doubt." Tico shot him a wry look. "It will not be enough, *mi amigo.* Once a woman is under your skin, blaming her for it accomplishes nothing."

"She is not under my skin, dammit. She's my best friend's widow. Hell, I even thought she was the wrong woman for him."

"But right for you," Tico said knowingly. "It happens that way sometimes."

Rick scowled at him. "Give it a rest, will you? This so-called alliance of ours isn't personal. She made that perfectly clear over lunch today."

Tico's amusement returned. "I know. I heard."

"You know, my friend, you could do me a lot more good if you would eavesdrop on the conversations on the street and help me find Ken's killer."

For once Tico's expression sobered. "I have heard nothing, not since the night it happened. There has not been so much as a whisper."

"Does that make sense to you?"

"No. Frankly, it worries me. There should be more talk. Someone should be claiming credit, gloating."

"What do you think it means, that no one has?"

"That for once the gangs had nothing to do with it," Tico responded readily, confirming Rick's own opinion.

"How can it be that no one saw a stranger, though? Wouldn't word have spread about that? A lot of people here cared about the *padre.*"

"I did not say it was a stranger. I said it wasn't gang-related."

Rick's head shot up at that. "Meaning?"

"Some of those involved in the gangs have ties to important people."

"Such as politicians," Rick said at once, thinking of the voter drives that had been organized and paid for with political money and operated by neighborhood insiders, gang leaders who craved clout at City Hall. The streets had never been safer than they had been on election day. It was an angle he had never once considered.

But what had Ken Miller had to do with Chicago politics? Nothing, so far as he knew. It was a link that made no sense. He shook his head.

"I think we're reaching."

"You'd rather believe it was some kid high on drugs or a stray bullet meant for one of our own?"

"Those would be the obvious answers," Rick said, echoing the police with whom he'd spoken.

"Too obvious," Tico insisted. "I prefer subtleties."

Rick tried to reason it out, but he still couldn't accept what Tico was suggesting. "Ken was from a suburb north of town. Why would he be the target of some Chicago politician?"

"Not Ken, but through him, *Yo, Amigo.* His ties to the program were well-known. Killing him might be expected to create such an outpouring of rage that those in power would be forced to shut the place down. It could be seen as proof that nothing had changed in the barrio."

That, unfortunately, made a terrible kind of sense. And when it came to politicians who disliked the program, there were more than enough to choose from.

Oh, on the record, they said all the right things. They didn't dare publicly decry a program that was already making a visible difference in the neighborhood. But privately they didn't like handing over funds to an ex-gang member with an arrogant streak and unorthodox methods. They didn't like Rick

Sanchez, period. He had tangled with them too often, shown too many of them up for the corrupt fools they were. He never groveled for their money, never sang their praises to the media when they did the right and just thing.

Tico was studying him curiously, clearly aware that his suggestion had struck a chord. "Will you tell Dana what we discussed?"

"Not just yet," Rick said. "Not until I have some kind of proof."

"The smoking gun, so to speak?"

"Exactly."

"I'm afraid any smoking gun is probably at the bottom of Lake Michigan by now."

Rick's expression turned grim. "Then I'll just have to find out who's been out boating lately."

Dana spent another restless night in Ken's leather chair. She was up at dawn, putting together a ragtag assortment of photographic equipment, including every single camera she had in the house. She found Bobby's cheap child's version.

Holding it, she paused to recall their second conversation the day before. It had been no less troubling than the first. To her frustration, her mother hadn't been back from her card game either, so Dana hadn't been able to share Bobby's complaints and work out a reasonable compromise. She considered calling again now, but a glance at the clock changed her mind. It was too early. Instead, she returned to the hunt for cameras.

She found Ken's far more expensive and complex Nikon, plus several of the moderately priced ones she had used on stakeouts. She included her own telephoto lenses, too. She would run out for film and perhaps a few of those disposable cameras as soon as the nearby drugstore opened.

In the meantime, she sat at the kitchen table with a fresh pot of coffee nearby and thought about Rick's comment the day before that perhaps the murderer was closer to home. In other words, someone Ken knew, someone in the neighborhood, perhaps even in his own congregation.

As badly as she wanted to dismiss the notion out of hand, she couldn't. She wouldn't be thorough and objective if she didn't consider each and every possibility. Hadn't that potential lack of objectivity been the very thing Kate had warned her about?

She grabbed a notepad and made a list of places to check, including Ken's office at the nearby church. She would go over before his secretary came in, so no one would realize that she'd been in there snooping. Not that she didn't have a perfect right to collect his personal things, but that wouldn't explain why she was going through church files.

She considered other places to look. Perhaps the morgue at the local paper. Though she read it regularly, it was possible she had missed any articles on people vehemently opposed to Ken's program to bring gang members into suburban homes. She'd check the *Tribune* and the *Sun-Times,* too.

She sat back. There, she'd done it. She had a starting place now, aside from *Yo, Amigo.* That ought to satisfy both Kate and Rick that she was being totally objective. It didn't matter that the list was probably a waste of time. She was all but certain that the answers were right smack in the middle of the gang turf that surrounded the program. The best way to prove that, though, would be to eliminate these others.

Invigorated by having a sense of purpose, she took a quick shower and dressed in jeans, a thick sweater and sneakers for the short jaunt across to the church. She tossed a jacket across her shoulders. She could be in and out easily before anyone showed up at nine.

Or she could have been, she thought with a sigh as she spotted Kate on the front stoop. She opened the door before Kate's knock.

"Eager to see me?" Kate said, then caught sight of the jacket. "Or were you just going out?"

"Actually, I was."

"Where? It's not even seven."

Dana was too exhausted to come up with a quick, evasive retort that would be believable. The truth would have to suffice. "Ken's office. I want to clear out some of his things."

Kate eyed her skeptically. "You want to snoop. I heard what Rick said yesterday. You've been thinking about it, haven't you? You're wondering if someone here could have been behind Ken's murder."

"I have to at least explore the idea," Dana conceded. "But can you see Mrs. Davis or Mr. Worth sneaking into Chicago with a gun and shooting their pastor?"

Mrs. Davis was a 70-year-old retired schoolteacher with a cherubic face and twinkling eyes. Mr. Worth, also retired, had been a librarian at Northwestern. He still had the scent of old books about him. They barely went beyond the corner grocery anymore. Kate knew them both, as well as most of the other regulars at the church.

"It's not as if all of Ken's parishioners were old," she pointed out. "You picked the two people least likely to harm a flea. Now that Mr. Nelson, I wouldn't put anything past him. He has shifty eyes and the build of an ex-boxer."

"He *is* an ex-boxer," Dana said dryly. "His eyes were injured in a fight."

"I still don't trust him."

"Since you seem to have such superior insight into the members of Ken's congregation, would you like to come along and help? Maybe we can sift through the files and get out of there, before we get caught."

Kate's expression brightened. "Really? Let's go."

With startling eagerness, she whirled around and headed back down the steps. A light layer of snow had fallen during the night, then iced over. It crunched underfoot as they took a shortcut across the lawn to the door leading to the office and parish hall portion of the church complex.

Added years after the original church had been built, it was a modern brick structure with a handful of classrooms for Sunday School and other meetings. The parish hall had a small stage facing a cavernous room that was empty now. Folding tables and chairs were set up once a month for a potluck supper and twice a year for pancake breakfasts. They were also used for wedding receptions and other events. Sometimes rows of chairs were lined up instead for a performance by the choir or the various children's Sunday School classes.

Their sneakers made no sound as they hurried across the open space to the set of offices closest to the church. Even so, Dana could feel her heart thumping unsteadily. She couldn't be certain whether it was caused by the fear of discovery or merely dread. This would be the first time she had been into Ken's office since his death. She used to run across once or twice a day to bring his lunch or simply to look in on him.

At the door to his secretary's office, she hesitated. She felt the pressure of Kate's hand on her shoulder.

"You okay?" Kate asked. "We don't have to do this."

"Yes, we do," Dana insisted. She drew a deep breath. "I'll be fine."

She plucked a set of keys out of her pocket and unlocked the door. Kate flipped on the light.

Mrs. Fallon kept her office neatly organized. Dana thought of the chaos in Rick's outer office, despite Maria's valiant efforts, and almost smiled. Perhaps she should loan him Mrs. Fallon for a few weeks. Between her and his lovely Maria, they would make short work of the mess.

Kate glanced around. "No files in here."

"She mainly answers the phone, types and keeps Ken's schedule," Dana said. "Ken liked to keep the files under lock and key with him. Even though Mrs. Fallon was probably in and out of them a dozen times a day, he thought it preserved the illusion of strict confidentiality."

"What the heck's in the files?" Kate asked. "Did he make notes on confessions?"

"Nothing so private, I'm sure. Birth records, marriage records, business stuff, I suppose." She hesitated. "Now that I think about it, I'm not really sure what he would have filed away. Right now, all I'm looking for is a list of church members as a starting point."

At the door to Ken's actual office, Dana halted again. This time before Kate could offer her another excuse for leaving, she forced herself to step across the threshold. She fumbled for the lightswitch, found it, and flipped it on.

"Oh, my," Kate murmured, mirroring Dana's own gasp of shock.

The place had been ransacked. It had to have happened very recently, overnight, perhaps. Mrs. Fallon would never have tolerated such chaos for long.

Dana exchanged a look with her friend.

"Do you think Rick could have been right?" Kate asked in a hushed voice. "Was somebody in here trying to cover his tracks?"

Before she could reply, Dana caught sight of a smashed picture frame on the floor. A choked sob welled up in her throat. Being careful of the broken glass, she picked it up. The picture inside was unharmed. It was a family portrait, taken just last Christmas. Ken had kept it on his desk so he could glance up as he worked and catch a glimpse of the family he loved.

Dana clung to the frame so tightly she could feel the silver digging into her palms. Suddenly the room swam and her knees felt weak. She swayed, but Kate caught her and guided her to a chair.

"Sit. Head between your knees," she instructed briskly. She nodded when Dana complied. "Good. Feel better?"

Dana sat up slowly. "I don't know what came over me."

"Too much stress. Too little sleep. Not enough food. That's just for starters," Kate said. "I think we should get out of here."

"Not without that list," Dana said stubbornly. "It's more important than ever."

"Okay, you sit. I'll find the list."

"We should call the police."

"Let Mrs. Fallon deal with the police. She'll be in her element bossing them around."

Dana glanced around the office. "This will be terribly upsetting for her."

"No," Kate corrected. "It will infuriate her. She'll consider it almost as much of a desecration as if someone had stolen the cross from the altar."

"True," Dana agreed eventually. She still felt terrible about leaving the secretary to deal with the ransacking. "I just don't know—"

"Well, I do," Kate countered firmly just as she reached into a drawer of the desk and nabbed a stack of pages that had been stapled together. She waved it triumphantly. "The list. Now let's get the heck out of here."

Dana reluctantly followed her. They slipped through the parish hall and back outside. Not until they were back in her own yard did she breathe a sigh of relief. The cold air wiped away the last of her queasiness. With that list in hand, she suddenly felt rejuvenated. Okay, it was in Kate's hand, at the moment, but they had it. Kate was demonstrating a remarkable alacrity for investigating. Driven by loyalty and indignation, the woman had absolutely no fear.

"I should have forced you to get your PI license years ago," she told her as they sat down at the kitchen table with coffee and the rest of the pecan coffee cake Dana had made the day before. "You're a natural."

Kate's eyes sparkled. "I've been looking for a new career goal. Maybe I've found my niche. That was invigorating. A real adrenaline rush. I haven't felt this good since the last time I had sex."

Dana chuckled. "And exactly how long ago was that?"

"Never mind," Kate said primly.

"That long, huh?"

Kate made a face, then held out the packet of papers. "Okay, now that we have it, what do we do with it?"

Dana stared at the names and addresses blankly for the space of a heartbeat. It was doubtful that there would be an asterisk by any of the names suggesting he or she was a possible murderer. They were just going to have to use their instincts and some good old-fashioned detective work to discover if there was any suspect at all on the list.

"You've been a member here ever since we met, right?" she asked Kate.

"Yes. I transferred from my old church as soon as I found out your husband was the minister. I liked Ken the minute you introduced us. So did the girls."

"And Ken and I have been here for nine years. Between us, surely we know something about most of the people on that list. How many are there?"

Kate flipped through the pages. "Looks like four or five hundred."

"Holy cow!" she exclaimed, daunted by the unexpectedly high number.

Kate's spirits never wavered. "I guess we'd better get started," she said eagerly "Shall I read the names aloud?"

"Uh-huh," Dana murmured distractedly. She couldn't stop thinking about the size of the task. "If there were that many members, how come Sunday services never drew more than a couple of hundred?"

"Lapsed believers," Kate suggested. "Maybe some of these are dead."

"Mrs. Fallon updates that list once a month. If they're on there, they're alive."

"Maybe some just drifted away and never said anything. Or showed up once every couple of months or at Christmas. They'd still be considered active members, right?"

"Right. Or maybe they split very recently when they disagreed with Ken about the gang members," Dana said. "He might have told Mrs. Fallon to leave them on, in the hope they'd be back. We can probably eliminate anyone that neither of us is familiar with. That should narrow the list down to half, anyway, don't you think?"

"Only one way to find out," Kate offered briskly. "Ready?"

"I suppose so."

"First name, Richard Adams."

It didn't ring any bells at all for Dana. "Do you know him?" she asked.

Kate shook her head.

"Neither do I. Put a question mark next to his name."

They were still at it, with only a handful of recognizable parishioners so far, when Dana glanced at the clock and noted that it was past noon. If Rick kept his word, he would be here for her in a couple of hours.

"Let's get some lunch and call it a day," she suggested. "We've made it through almost half the alphabet, anyway."

Kate stared at her. "Why not finish the rest? Are you going out?"

"Back into Chicago, as a matter of fact," she said, forcing a blasé note into her voice.

"Oh, no. Not again. You cannot be thinking of going back to *Yo, Amigo.*"

"Actually, I am. Rick's coming for me. I'm going to be teaching a photography class."

Kate's mouth dropped open. "You're not!"

"I am. Care to come help?"

"My, my," Kate murmured. "He's even better than I'd imagined."

Dana stared at her. "Meaning?"

"Just that I thought you'd be a tough sell. I'd given him forty-eight hours to work his magic."

"I'm not doing this by choice," Dana protested.

"Yeah, right. He twisted your arm and begged."

"No," Dana said. "He made it a condition of my talking to the kids at the center."

"Then by all means, go, talk."

"I will, but first I'm going to call Mrs. Fallon and see if the police have been there. I haven't seen any squad cars cruising by, have you?"

"No," Kate said. "That seems a little odd, now that I think about it."

"I was thinking the same thing," Dana said as she dialed the familiar number. At the sound of her voice, Mrs. Fallon immediately began clucking sympathetically.

"Oh, you poor darling. I saw the car in the driveway and guessed you were back. How are you?"

"I'm just fine, thanks. Mrs. Fallon, about Ken's office."

"Oh, you saw that, did you? I'm so sorry. I thought I'd have it tidied up before you came over. That's why I didn't call earlier."

"Then the police have been there to investigate."

"Investigate, my eye," she said with disgust. "The police are the ones who left it that way."

Nine

"Dana, what on earth? Where are you going?" Kate demanded as Dana hung up the phone and grabbed her jacket.

"Back to the church."

"Why?"

"That mess we found over there was caused by the cops."

"You're kidding." Kate reached for her own coat and followed Dana out the door, jogging to keep up with her.

Dana had never been so angry in all of her life. It had been one thing to think that the destruction in Ken's office had been caused by an intruder of some kind. It was quite another to realize that the people responsible for it were supposed to be the good guys.

There was nothing surreptitious about the entry she made this time. She slammed open the door and ran across the parish hall. Mrs. Fallon was waiting for her, her distress plain.

"See, there, I've gone and upset you," she murmured apologetically. "I never meant to do that."

"You're not the one who upset me," she reassured the flustered older woman. "Did the police give you a card? Do you know which officers were here? How many were there?"

The barrage of questions only added to her already visible distress. "Now, wait a minute," Mrs. Fallon said. "Let me think. This whole thing has me so rattled I can't string two words together that make any sense."

"I'm sorry. Let's sit down," Dana suggested.

"No, no, I'll be okay. There were two of them," she said

eventually, "though now that I think about it, one of them looked as if he were from Chicago. I was so frantic when they came barging in here, I didn't focus on that at the time. I'm almost certain he wasn't wearing a local uniform." She opened her desk drawer and nabbed a card. "Here, this is the card the one from our department gave me. He wasn't in uniform. I believe he was a detective."

"Dillon O'Flannery," Dana read aloud. She glanced at Kate, who'd grown up right here in town. "Have you ever run across him?"

"Not me. I try to stay as far away from cops as I can. They make me nervous, especially when I'm behind the wheel. One more speeding ticket and they'll take away my keys. What about you? I thought you knew most of those guys."

"So did I," Dana said grimly, punching in the number on the card. It looked as if it might be a direct line, rather than the central switchboard.

"O'Flannery."

His voice was deep, his manner terse. Dana took an immediate dislike to him. Of course, her reaction at this point wouldn't have been any more positive if he'd sung his greeting like Pavarotti.

"Officer O'Flannery," she said sweetly, deliberately downgrading his rank.

"It's Detective O'Flannery."

"Not if I get my way," she retorted. "I'd suggest you get your butt over to St. Michael's pronto, buster, or I'll have your badge before the day's out."

"Now wait just a minute! Who the hell is this?"

"This is Mrs. Dana Miller. You recently ransacked my husband's office. I'd like you here with an explanation and a cleanup crew, on the double."

She slammed the phone in his ear before he could respond, then smiled grimly. "That ought to do it."

Mrs. Fallon looked stunned. Kate appeared worried.

"Do you think, maybe, you were just a little too abrupt?"

Kate asked. "Maybe the situation called for a little diplomacy and friendly persuasion. He is the one with the badge, after all."

"Men like Detective O'Flannery do not respond to persuasion. You have to match their Gestapo-like tactics to get their attention." The police station was only blocks away. The sound of a siren's blare getting closer by the second proved her point. "I believe that would be Detective O'Flannery now."

Kate and Mrs. Fallon stared toward the door, as if waiting for a vision to appear. Sure enough, a man wearing black slacks and a grey tweed blazer came charging through like a lineman for the Chicago Bears. He was a vision, all right, the epitome of seething male.

He pulled up short at the sight of the three women. He seemed to zero in on Dana at once as the culprit behind the phone call. She wasn't quite sure what that said about her appearance. Maybe she was the one who looked as if she were about to flip out.

"You would be Mrs. Miller," he guessed.

"And you're Detective O'Flannery," she said, then added pointedly, "For the moment, anyway."

Blue eyes the color of a very deep lake locked on her. He seemed to be struggling with his temper.

"I know what a strain you've been under," he said eventually.

His tone was so patronizing she wanted to slug him. "You have no idea," she shot back. "Finding that my husband's office was leveled by two cops hasn't improved my mood any." Hands on hips, she squared off in front of him. "Exactly what did you hope to find in there?"

"Something that might help the Chicago police with their case," he said. He turned to Kate, as if to appeal to her more reasonable nature. "We like to cooperate with other departments whenever we can."

"Assuming that a search of my husband's office was critical

to the investigation," Dana shot back, "do you have any idea why it took them over a month to get around to it?"

"They didn't share that with me. They sent an officer and I came along for the ride."

"What a prince," Dana said sarcastically. Between this man and Rick Sanchez, her normal good nature had taken a serious beating. She was turning into a first-class bitch. Unfortunately, this wasn't the time to worry about correcting that shift in her personality. She had a hunch getting a few straight answers would eventually take care of the problem, anyway.

"Tearing things up around here must have made your day," she accused.

Mrs. Fallon swallowed hard and sank into the chair behind her desk. She looked as if she feared Dana's arrest was imminent. After working for a man as even-tempered and gentle as Ken, seeing Dana in action had to be a shock.

Dana glanced at Kate and saw that she looked just the teensiest bit shell-shocked herself, although her state seemed to have more to do with the detective than with Dana's behavior. She took her own survey of O'Flannery. She supposed that someone with eyes that blue and mussed hair the color of coal might have that sort of effect on some women. It was a pity Kate was one of them.

"Did you find anything?" Kate asked in a breathy voice that Dana had never once heard come out of her mouth before.

Detective O'Flannery was either a sucker for a smitten woman or just plain relieved to have someone address him in a friendlier tone than Dana had. He beamed at her.

"Why don't we all sit down?" he suggested. "Let's talk about this."

"Did you find anything?" Dana snapped.

"Sweetie, I think he was just about to tell us," Kate soothed. She latched onto Dana's hand with a warning grip so tight Dana's wedding ring dug into her finger.

"Fine," Dana said, but she refused to sit.

Her stubbornness seemed to amuse the detective. He and

Kate exchanged commiserating glances. Dana concluded she was going to have to fire her new assistant investigator, since her hormones seemed to be getting in the way of her better judgment.

"Did you find anything in my husband's office?" she repeated in a more patient tone.

"Nothing conclusive," he equivocated.

"Meaning that you found nothing or that you found something, but you just haven't figured out yet what it means?"

He seemed taken aback by the question. Maybe he hadn't figured she had the intelligence to realize there was a difference.

"Very good, Mrs. Miller," he praised.

There was that condescending tone again. Dana gritted her teeth and forced herself not to fly off the handle again. "Which is it?" Just in case he couldn't manage to answer a direct question, she tried another angle. "Did you remove anything from the office?"

"Your husband's calendar," he conceded grudgingly.

There was no need to ask why. If Ken had had meetings in the hours or even days immediately preceding his murder, it was entirely possible that one of those might point toward a killer. She should have thought of that herself right after his death, but she'd been too distraught then. She'd been thinking like a grieving widow, not like an investigator.

Given his overall attitude, she gathered there would be little point in asking Detective O'Flannery what names were on the calendar. It wasn't necessary anyway. Mrs. Fallon kept a duplicate schedule on her desk. A quick glance in the secretary's direction drew a subtle nod, indicating that she knew precisely what Dana was thinking and that she was still in possession of the second calendar.

Dana returned her gaze to the detective. "I assume my husband's calendar was in the middle of his desk, where he always kept it," she said blandly.

He nodded. "I believe it was."

"Then would you mind telling me why the hell you had to tear the office up to find it?"

He regarded her blandly. "We didn't go in specifically looking for a calendar."

"What, then? What else were you hoping to find? What was on the warrant? I assume you had one."

"We had one," he said grimly. "Mrs. Miller, really, why don't you just leave the investigation to the Chicago police? Let them do their jobs."

"If one more person suggests that, I'm going to scream. If they were doing their jobs, they'd have the killer behind bars by now. Even a halfway decent cop knows that leads start turning cold after a few days. It's been weeks now, and the Chicago cops have done diddly-squat, as far as I can tell. Now are you going to tell me what you were really looking for in my husband's office, or am I going to have to sue you for violation of his civil rights, trespassing, and anything else I can come up with?"

He exchanged another look with Kate, but for once Kate didn't appear overly sympathetic. He sighed heavily.

"Okay, you asked for it. We were looking for drugs, Mrs. Miller. And, yes, indeed, the search warrant mentioned drugs specifically, in case that was going to be your next question."

If the idea had not been so totally preposterous, Dana might have grabbed the vase of flowers off Mrs. Fallon's desk and cracked it over his thick skull. As it was, she laughed.

"You think my husband, a respected minister, had drugs in his office? His *church* office? Are you out of your mind?" she inquired.

"The Chicago police had a tip from a very reliable source that your husband was dealing drugs and that *Yo, Amigo* was the front for his operation."

Speechless, Dana sank onto a chair.

"You're a goddamned liar."

Rick Sanchez's voice cut through the already charged air like a whip. Dana hadn't heard his approach. She doubted if any of the others had either. Grateful for once to see him, grateful to have such a vehement ally, she didn't flinch when he put his hand on her shoulder and squeezed reassuringly. In fact, she found the murderous glint in his eyes rather satisfying. Let these two males go *mano a mano* for a while and see which one came out the winner. She'd put her money on Rick.

"Who are you?" Detective O'Flannery asked in a quiet tone clearly meant to defuse the rapidly escalating situation.

"I'm Rick Sanchez, the coordinator of *Yo, Amigo*. And this source of yours better have a name, or I'll start by suing you personally for slander."

Mrs. Fallon, who hadn't spoken since they'd been seated, rose unsteadily to her feet and walked over to the detective. She barely came to his shoulder, but that didn't seem to intimidate her one whit.

"Young man, I will not allow you to come in here and defame the name of a decent, kindhearted man. It was bad enough that you tore the place apart, but saying such things about Reverend Miller puts you in cahoots with the devil, as far as I'm concerned, and I won't stand for it."

"Amen, Mrs. Fallon," Kate said.

Dana observed that Detective O'Flannery was looking considerably less sure of himself than he had when he'd walked in. He appeared to realize that he'd lost his sole ally.

"I know that all of you admired and respected Reverend Miller," he said gently. He looked at Dana. "And you loved him. But no one knows everything there is to know about another human being. I've talked to parents whose child has just committed murder, and they will give testament that no child of theirs would ever do such a thing. It's a defense mechanism. We don't want to see evil in those we love."

Dana shot out of her chair at that. "My husband was not evil, detective. If you think we're biased on the subject, then ask any member of his congregation. Ask the kids in Chicago whose lives were turned around because of him. Ask the patients in the hospital who sat beside their beds when they were ill. Ask some of our elderly parishioners whom they called in the middle of the night when some noise frightened them. It wasn't the police, dammit. It was my husband. If you think that man could ever, *ever* sell drugs, then you are so delusional you're a danger to the community."

"Amen," Kate said again.

Detective O'Flannery looked more distressed by Kate's defection than by Dana's actual tirade.

"I'm just telling you what was in the warrant," he said defensively.

"Was the source named in the warrant?" Rick asked. "I'll bet I already know the answer to that. He wasn't. Because he was too much of a coward to come forward publicly with such ridiculous charges. He would have been laughed out of town. I could give you a list, though. There are half a dozen people in Chicago with the clout to convince a judge that what they're saying should be taken seriously enough to justify a search warrant in another jurisdiction. We could start with the mayor. Now there's a man worthy of a police investigation."

The detective held up his hands. "Whoa, let's not start throwing mud around."

"Excuse me?" Dana protested. "Did I hear you correctly? You come in here slandering my husband, and now you're worried about a little mud being splattered on some other good citizens?"

"Settle down," the detective said sharply. "All of you. First of all, I don't know who the Chicago source was. Second, I didn't say I bought into the theory. I was just telling you what was in the warrant. That's one reason I came along. The charge didn't match anything I'd ever heard about Reverend Miller. I wanted to see that everything was done by the book."

Dana gestured toward Ken's office. "You call that doing things by the book?"

He shrugged. "Thorough searches get messy."

"Not when I do them," Dana countered.

His gaze narrowed at that. "Meaning?"

She decided it might be best if he didn't know that she was launching her own investigation and that it had gotten more urgent in the past half-hour.

"Nothing," she said.

He didn't look as if he believed her, but he apparently decided to let it pass.

"I know you want to believe in your husband, Mrs. Miller. The rest of you, too, but the truth is, it looks as if the Chicago police were onto something."

"What?" all four people in the room chorused in disbelief.

"You can't be serious," Rick said.

Dana felt a huge knot forming in the pit of her stomach. Something was going on here, something dark and dangerous and far more complicated than she'd ever imagined.

"What did you find?" she asked softly.

"Traces of marijuana, a small amount of cocaine, and evidence that he'd had crack tucked away, too," he said unhappily. "I'm sorry."

"Oh, sweet heaven," Mrs. Fallon murmured and sank back onto her chair.

"It was planted," Kate said with absolute certainty.

"You bet your life it was," Dana agreed. She shot a venomous look straight into Detective Dillon O'Flannery's eyes. "You said traces of drugs were found. How much?"

"Not a lot," he admitted. "Just enough to prove it had been here."

"Not enough to cost anyone big bucks, right? Not enough to put a dent into a real drug operation?"

"No."

"Just enough to make him look guilty of some crime," she concluded. "If that doesn't suggest planting, I don't know what would. And I intend to prove it, or die trying."

Despite her trembling knees, she managed to stand and then to walk out the door, head held high. She would not cry in front of Detective O'Flannery. She would not let him see how deeply she was shaken by what he'd said. The thought of so much as a trace of all those drugs in Ken's office made her sick to her stomach.

She felt Kate slip up beside her.

"Are you okay?" she asked in a hushed voice.

"I will be," she said stiffly. "As soon as I see them all in hell for what they're trying to do to my husband."

Ten

As soon as they were out of sight of Detective O'Flannery, Dana whirled on Rick and slapped him with all of her might. Frustration, blind rage, hurt all went into that slap. The force of the blow felt exhilarating. Rick's eyes widened with surprise, but to his credit he held his temper, even as a red mark in the shape of her hand took form on his cheek.

"Mind if I ask what that was for?" he inquired.

"You're the one responsible for this," she accused, refusing to massage her stinging hand or to apologize for using it to strike him. "If Ken had never gotten involved with you, he wouldn't be dead and none of this would be happening."

She was tempted to smack him again, but Kate apparently sensed her intention and slipped an arm around her waist as they walked into the house and began murmuring soothing reminders about using honey, not vinegar, to catch flies. The comment was practical, so very much Kate that Dana managed a faint smile. Her temper calmed. A vague hint of embarrassment stole over her. She had never resorted to physical assaults in her life, but she'd slapped Rick twice now. Obviously, the man did not bring out the best in her.

"Okay, okay, no more physical abuse," she promised.

"Glad to hear it," Rick said, gingerly touching his jaw. "Are you ready to go into Chicago now?"

Dana had forgotten all about the plans that had obviously brought him to the church in search of her in the first place. She wanted to tell him that she wasn't going, that she was going to stay right where she was and think about what the detective had told them, but she couldn't. The answers, including those to this latest twist, were still at *Yo, Amigo*. They had to be. Someone there, possibly even Rick himself, had set her husband up. With the police adding up false information, suppositions, and planted drugs, finding the truth was more critical than ever.

"Just let me freshen up," she said to buy herself a few minutes to compose herself. She couldn't spend five minutes alone with Rick in her current frame of mind or, despite her very recent promise, they'd wind up in a ditch somewhere with her trying to pummel him to death.

"If you'd like," she told him, "you can put the cameras and other equipment in the car. Everything's by the front door. I'm afraid I never made it to the drugstore to get film, though."

When he saw the gathered photographic supplies, he seemed surprised that she'd done as much as she had. "No problem. We'll stop on the way." He glanced at Kate. "Are you coming along?"

Kate looked toward Dana, as if awaiting some sort of signal. Dana said, "No, she can't. She has things to do here."

Rick nodded. "Good to see you again, Mrs. Jefferson. Dana, I'll be in the car, whenever you're ready."

As soon as he'd gone outside, Kate whirled on her. "What things do I have to do here? Are you sure you ought to be alone with that man? There are enough sparks flying between you two to light up downtown Chicago. Why can't you just meet the man halfway?"

"I just can't, that's all. I don't trust him," Dana said defensively. Nor was she willing to admit that she feared letting down her guard for so much as a second around him. Right now, thank goodness, she wanted to kill him, not sleep with him. She wasn't so sure that would last forever, though. At the moment, she'd be grateful just to get through the rest of the day without making a fool of herself.

"Okay, so don't trust him. Just be nice." At a sharp look

from Dana, Kate held up her hands. "Okay, okay, what do you want me to do?"

"Finish going through that list of church members and check off anyone whose name sets off any sort of alarms."

"Such as?"

"Rumors about a sudden change in lifestyle, nasty tempers, shady business dealings, whatever. Anything you've heard that might seem remotely suspicious. If you finish that, try going to the newspaper morgue to see if any of the names show up in articles related to any kind of corruption, drugs, excessive parking tickets, whatever."

"I take it we can exclude those receiving media accolades."

Dana thought about that. "Not necessarily. If they've gotten any kind of positive publicity, maybe they'd go to some extremes to avoid having their reputation tarnished."

"That's pretty twisted logic," Kate said.

"We're dealing with a pretty twisted mind. This person not only killed a minister, but he's trying to frame him in a drug conspiracy to throw the police offtrack."

"Okay," Kate agreed, accepting the theory. "I've got it. What time do you want to get together?"

Dana thought of the trip to and from Chicago, the class she was scheduled to teach. They were already running late. As much as she wanted to know what Kate learned tonight, she knew she'd be too exhausted to absorb it.

"Unless you stumble on something urgent, come over in the morning," she suggested eventually.

"I'll leave a message for you if I find out anything that can't wait until morning," Kate promised. "Now run along. It's not good to keep an impatient man waiting."

"If it were up to me, he could wait until hell freezes over," Dana muttered. But she turned and left just the same.

She slid into Rick's car without speaking. Despite her earlier fury, she felt a renewed surge of guilt when she saw that his cheek still bore traces of her slap. She had never believed that violence solved anything. She had never, ever resorted to it herself. She'd never even gently swatted one of her kids to make a point.

She could blame her behavior on stress, but that would be excusing the inexcusable. She vowed then and there to do as Kate had asked and force herself to give Rick Sanchez a break. She was lucky that he was still speaking to her after the way she'd treated him. He could have reneged on his promise to help her earn the trust of the kids at *Yo, Amigo* and she would have had no one to blame but herself. There were plenty of allies in the world who didn't like each other. She supposed the two of them could fit into that category.

Rick pulled out of the driveway and headed toward Chicago, without breaking the silence. He seemed neither angry, nor upset, merely thoughtful.

When she could stand the silence no longer, Dana decided to take the first step in achieving detente. "I'm sorry I slapped you," she said softly.

"I know."

"I wasn't angry with you so much as the circumstances. It was really Detective O'Flannery I wanted to hit."

"I know."

She frowned at him. "You don't know everything, Sanchez."

He glanced toward her and shrugged. "Maybe not everything," he conceded. "But when it comes to you, I think I know quite a lot. I saw the way you kept clenching and unclenching your fists while O'Flannery was talking. Frankly, I wouldn't have minded taking a shot at the bastard myself."

"I wish you had," she said wistfully.

"We'll get whoever's behind all this, Dana. I promise you that."

She listened to the conviction in his voice and wished she could believe him, wished even more that she could trust him. Unfortunately, she doubted she would ever entirely rid herself of the possibility that he was involved in this investigation only so that he could cover any tracks that might lead back to *Yo, Amigo.*

If she was wrong, though, then Rick suddenly had motives almost as powerful as her own for wanting to know who was behind not only Ken's death, but the defamation of *Yo, Amigo's* reputation.

He had to be insane, flat out, men-in-white-coats insane. From the moment he'd tackled Dana Miller during her middle-of-the-night quest inside *Yo, Amigo,* Rick had been so aware of her, so aroused by her that he could barely think straight in her presence.

And all the while his body was humming with electricity, his mind was reeling with guilt. This was Ken's wife, for God's sake. Ken's widow, he amended with a sigh. And that, somehow, made the lust he was feeling that much worse.

After each encounter, he vowed to rein in his feelings. He was finally forced to accept that it was like trying to rein in a runaway stagecoach. It could be done, but it required almost superhuman, John Wayne-caliber effort.

Even so, even knowing that he was tempting fate by spending one single second in her presence, here he was drawing her deeper and deeper into his world. The stupidity of it nagged at him all during the drive into Chicago. His only consolation was the fact that Ken had believed in *Yo, Amigo* as deeply as Rick did. He would not want to see it brought down as a part of any investigation of his murder.

Ken would also want the people who'd been closest to him—Dana and Rick himself—to work as a team, not as enemies. They needed to be united, if they were going to fight what appeared to be an intricate conspiracy surrounding his death.

The drug charge leveled by that detective was so outlandish that Rick had trouble taking it seriously. But he knew in his gut that it was as serious as a bullet in the chest. Whoever had planted those drugs and leaked their presence to the police was determined not only to sully Ken's name, but to bring down *Yo, Amigo*. If Rick got to that person before the police did, the court system was going to have to wait in line to mete out justice. After he finished, prison would probably look good to the creep.

He glanced over at Dana as he turned into the tiny parking lot beside a neighborhood drugstore to pick up the film she needed. She seemed lost in thought. He was finally coming to realize what Ken had known all along, that she was a loyal, admirable woman. Despite all that crap that Detective O'Flannery had thrown at her, she had never once lost faith in her husband. Rick couldn't help wondering what it would be like to have someone believe in him so thoroughly.

Few people ever had. Certainly not the immigrant parents who'd given up on him when he'd turned to gang life because of the sense of power and belonging it gave to him in this strange new country. Surely not the cops, who'd prayed for just one slip, just one charge against him they could make stick. Even his own followers hadn't believed in him with that kind of blind faith. He'd just happened to be the one who'd ascended to a position of power because he was a little bigger, a little tougher than the rest.

Ken, however, had believed in him from the start. Even though he was still struggling to turn his life around when they'd met five years ago, even though *Yo, Amigo* was little more than an idea, it was an idea that Ken had embraced. He'd had the finesse that Rick lacked to pull the program together. Rick had had the street smarts to attract a few toughened kids into the program, but Ken had been able to handle the powerbrokers, to squeeze dollars out of empty city coffers. The program existed today because they had trusted and respected each other.

Even so, that wasn't the same as having the trust and respect of a woman. Rick wasn't sure why that was so, only that when he'd seen that firm belief shining in Dana Miller's eyes, he had envied Ken more than he could say.

"What kind of film do you need?" he asked, when he'd pulled into a parking space.

"I'll run in and get it," she said at once.

"I'll go," he countered, just as firmly. "My turf, remember?"

The corners of her mouth twitched in the beginnings of a smile. "We'll go together, so I can see what they have. Will that suit you?"

Rick nodded. "I'm relieved to see that you can compromise."

"How about you? Can you compromise?"

"Of course."

She regarded him skeptically. "Sorry. I don't see it."

"Don't see what?"

"You ever backing down, once you've taken a stance. You're too arrogant, too bullheaded."

He grinned. "I've grown rather fond of you, too."

She scowled at that. "It wasn't a compliment."

"I know."

They were still bickering, as they bought the film and returned to the car. Nonsense bickering. Bickering that to Rick seemed almost to border on the affectionate. There was no more venom in it. It was as if that vicious slap had finally cleared the air between them and made peace possible.

"You know, Dana, if you're not careful, you and I might actually wind up being friends."

"No way," she muttered hastily.

A little too hastily, it seemed to Rick. He wondered how long it would take her to accept the possibility that animosity and distrust could evolve into friendship. He could envision it, just as he could almost envision a day when they would become lovers. No doubt suggesting that would earn him another slap, despite the truce they had declared.

Still, he couldn't help wondering what would happen if he

bridged the distance between them and kissed her the way he
wanted to, deeply and thoroughly. Would she slap him for
that, too, or would she melt in his arms?

The temptation to find out was almost irresistible. Fortunately, though, he had a lot of practice at resisting temptation.
He'd had to curb his once healthy appetite for petty theft. He'd
had to tame his violent temper, even in the face of provocation
like that scene in Ken's office earlier.

Surely, he could resist the compelling urge to kiss a woman
whose heart belonged to someone else, a woman who
wouldn't even admit to liking him.

Of course, that was the point, he thought wryly. He wanted
to force an admission that she wasn't as immune to him as
she claimed.

"Are you planning to start the car anytime soon, or shall I
get out and walk the rest of the way?" she inquired tartly,
breaking into his thoughts.

He noticed that she was shifting uncomfortably under his
gaze. He found that telling enough, for the moment. The kiss
could wait awhile longer, he concluded.

But it wouldn't be too much longer. Minutes, maybe.
Hours. Days. A few months at most. Time to find the answers
she needed. Time for her to heal. Time for him to make sure
that more was involved here than his always healthy libido.
Not even a saint could be expected to show much more re-
straint than that. And the word on the street had been pretty
consistent about one thing for years now: Rick Sanchez was
no saint.

Eleven

Dana had the uneasy feeling that something other than cooperating to find Ken's killer was on Rick's mind. It had been a long time since she had been the subject of a fascinated gaze from a man other than her husband, but she hadn't forgotten the signs. There had been a knowing gleam in Rick's eye, an easily recognizable flaring of pure lust. She had trembled under that look. It was a reaction she wasn't crazy about.

Kate had mentioned the sparks in the air between them. They had both interpreted that as pure friction, but what if it were more? No, she thought quickly, she wouldn't allow it to be anything more. She didn't even like Rick Sanchez very much. She certainly didn't trust him. How could she possibly be attracted to him? The lust, if it existed at all, was completely one-sided. It had to be.

Which didn't mean, of course, that she didn't have to deal with it. If Rick were ever crazy enough to try something, if he dared to risk this tenuous truce between them by putting the moves on her, she would simply explain to him, in no uncertain terms, that he was way, way off base.

She found herself grinning suddenly at the image of the prim lecture she intended to deliver. Yes, indeed, Rick Sanchez was definitely the kind of man who'd respond well to being told that something—or someone, in this case—was off-limits. He'd probably try to seduce her just to prove how wrong she was. She didn't have quite enough confidence in her resistance to put herself to that particular test.

"Has anyone signed up for the class?" she asked, hoping the move to a safer topic would alter the sizzling tension in the car.

Rick grinned. "These kids don't exactly sign up for things. They show up or they don't. You could have one kid there today or twenty."

"Or none?"

"That's a distinct possibility."

Her spirits sank. She was counting on this overture to pave the way for her. Frustrated, she met Rick's gaze. "Okay. What then?"

"You'll just have to find another way to win them over."

His nonchalant response grated. "You really don't intend to cut me any slack here, do you?" she asked.

"None," he agreed as he pulled into his space behind the building.

His attitude solidified her resolve. "Don't look so smug," she retorted. "I've always loved a good challenge."

"Then you ought to be in heaven here," he said, leading the way inside.

Instead of taking her to his office, he continued past it to a small classroom. It was filled with a hodgepodge of desks and chairs of various shapes and sizes. Wood and Formica surfaces alike had been scarred with graffiti. The blackboard bore a similar collection of four-letter words in English, along with what she assumed to be the Spanish equivalents.

"English lesson?" she inquired.

Rick muttered something unintelligible under his breath and grabbed an eraser. The blackboard was wiped clean in a matter of seconds. There wasn't anything to be done about the desks.

He looked around the dreary, cramped room with a critical gaze, then glanced at her. "It's not much, but it's the best I can do."

"It'll be fine," she assured him. "We won't be spending much time inside, anyway."

Alarm flared his eyes. "Why not? Where are you thinking of going?"

Dana thought that ought to be obvious. "Outside," she said patiently. "It's the best place to teach photography. All of the classes I took spent at least half the time outdoors and most of the rest in the darkroom. Outdoors is where you find the interesting faces, the best scenery, the architectural curiosities. It's also the best way to work with lighting, to learn to use the camera's settings for the best effects. It's where I have the most experience. I've never done much indoor or studio work."

Rick was shaking his head before she could finish. "Dana, I've told you how I feel about you being out in this neighborhood. It's not safe."

"I'm not going to be alone. The kids will be with me."

"I don't know," he said uneasily. "You'll be the only *gringa* around, an easy target."

His choice of words startled her, but she saw at once that he was right. It was an unnecessary risk, one she didn't dare take with three sons counting on her safe return.

"Can't you teach the class here, indoors?" he suggested.

"For a week or two, maybe, while I go over the basics. But if you want these kids to really get some experience, we'll have to venture out sooner or later. Do you have any kind of van to take them someplace else?"

"Are you kidding? On our budget, we can't afford bus fare. Look, just make it later. I'll rearrange my schedule, so I can come, too."

She found that prospect almost as disturbing as the idea of being a target. She quickly glanced around the empty room. "All of this planning seems like a moot point, at the moment. The room isn't exactly overcrowded with students, and it's already after four."

"Time is another problem," he explained with a grin. "They have no sense of it. Part of that's rebellion, I'm sure. Part of it's because they've never had to adhere to any particular structure in their lives."

"Is there a bell or something?"

"Nope. Around here, when it's time for a class or a meeting, there's only one thing to do—go around the building and round them up."

Dana nodded. "Okay. You do that. I'll get set up."

"Sorry, *querida,*" he said with apparent amusement. "Any rounding up will have to be done by you. I have work to do this afternoon."

She stared at him. "You expect me to go out there and talk those kids into coming to my class?"

He winked at her. "Pick the right kid and the rest will follow."

She scowled at him. "Any hints?"

"Nope. I think I'll let you go with your instincts. I'll see you around five-thirty or so. That should be about as much as you can take, before you start wondering what you've gotten yourself into and whether it's worth it."

With that new taunt left hanging in the air, he was gone. Dana sank down on a chair and stared around her. Even if she thought of this as being some sort of elaborate undercover scheme, it was still, without a doubt, the oddest investigation she'd ever conducted.

Or attempted to conduct, she amended, conceding that she hadn't actually done the first bit of real investigating yet. She'd thrust herself into the midst of potential informants, but until she actually held a conversation with someone, the effort was pretty much wasted.

She could sit here until five-thirty and claim that she'd tried, but Rick would see right through that. Or she could march herself out into the main gym and see who was hanging out. If she ever expected to get any answers, there was only one option. She headed for the gym.

She was barely a few feet from the classroom, when she spotted Maria coming her way. The teen beamed at her.

"*Señora* Miller, you did come back. I had to see it with my own eyes. I was sure you would tell Rick to go jump into a stream."

Dana was so relieved to see a friendly face that she didn't bother correcting the fractured phrase. "Hi, Maria. I'm about to go in search of prospective students. Any idea where I should start?"

"Rick said I shouldn't interfere," she said, then grinned. "But if I were you, I would speak first to Marco."

Dana instantly recalled the young man who had surveyed her so insolently on her previous visit. He'd seemed dark and dangerous to her then, even with Rick beside her. He was not the person she wanted most to deal with. Naturally, though, that made him the obvious choice. She sighed.

"Where is he?"

"In the gym, as always. He may have given up the streets, but he cannot live without turf of his own. In the gym, he is king."

"Exactly how did he claim the title?" Dana inquired worriedly.

"As a lion would," Maria said, innocently creating a very worrisome image. "I must run, before Rick misses me and guesses that I've come to see you."

She vanished almost as quickly and quietly as she'd appeared.

"Ah, yes," Dana muttered with a trace of bitterness. "We wouldn't want to upset Rick."

Sucking in a deep breath, she turned into the gym. Sure enough, Marco was sitting on a bench on the sidelines, holding court. At the sight of her, he fell silent. His sensual mouth curved into a smirk, as he lazily surveyed her from head to toe as she approached.

"I see the *padre's* widow is back," he said when she drew closer. "I did not expect it."

"Life is just full of unexpected twists and turns," Dana replied.

"What brings you back out of your safe little suburban world?"

As an investigator who frequently faced belligerent, defensive individuals, she knew there was only one way to deal with a man like Marco. She had to stand up to him and refuse to let his sarcasm get to her. Just as Rick had been doing with her, she couldn't help thinking. He probably thought she had a worse attitude than Marco. Now would be a good time to start changing that, she concluded.

"And here I thought you were so tapped into everything that goes on around here," she said, making the taunt light, but hopefully effective enough to catch his attention. "Haven't you heard? I'm teaching a photography class."

"Now there's something almost as practical as basket weaving," he said, drawing nervous laughter. "Another example of the Anglo notion of keeping idle hands busy."

Dana shrugged off the glib remark. "Who knows? Maybe someone here will have a good enough eye to become a fashion photographer or a photojournalist."

She glanced at the pregnant girl seated next to him. Rosa, wasn't it? Even with the extra weight she carried with the baby, she was a beautiful girl. She had gleaming dark hair, high cheekbones and sparkling eyes that, despite Marco, glinted with interest. "Perhaps Rosa, with the right portfolio to show around, could become a model," she added.

She gave him the same sort of insolent going-over that he'd given her. "Even you, Marco, have an interesting look about you. A bit of attitude . . ." A massive understatement, she thought. "Strong features. With the right pictures, an agency might take a chance on you. Or with your aggression, you could take your camera into places no one else would dare and become a world famous photographer."

A little of his disdain faded, replaced by the tiniest hint of interest. She prayed that the limb she was going out on wouldn't get chopped off behind her. She did know a handful of people in the modeling business and at ad agencies in Chicago, as well as a few journalists. She could get pictures into their hands. She had no idea what their reactions would be, though.

She did know, however, that there was a danger in building false hope here. Already, these young people had seen too many dreams dashed—their parents' and their own.

"Don't get me wrong," she added as a deliberate caution. "Either side of the camera, it's hard work. It's not something for a coward to tackle. It's a risk. If it pays off, it could pay off very well. Or it could amount to nothing at all."

"You know people in this business?" Rosa asked, eyes shining with excitement. Clearly she had been intrigued by Dana's words.

"Shut up," Marco ordered her harshly.

"No, you," the girl retorted, undaunted by the order. "It doesn't hurt to listen, to see what she has to say. That is your trouble, Marco, you never want to listen. You are twenty-two and you think you know everything."

Dana waited to see which one would win the argument. To her astonishment, something in Marco's eyes softened as he gazed at Rosa.

"You would want to do this?" he asked. "You would be a model?"

Rosa rubbed her hands over her rounding belly. "When the baby is born, I would like to know I can support her without taking help from anyone."

Marco said something to her in rapid Spanish, but she refused to back down. Chin up, she faced him defiantly. Eventually he shook his head, his expression resigned.

"Take the class, if it will make you happy," he said, his tone indulgent.

Rosa's expression turned speculative then. "You, too, I think," she told him, clearly not satisfied with her own small victory. "We could do this together."

Dana thought she detected a faint hint of wistfulness in

Marco's expression, but he refused to accede to Rosa's request.

"I am not wasting my time in this way," he said with finality. "The rest of you may do as you like."

Dana seized the concession as the best she was likely to get. "Rosa, come along. If any of the rest of you would like to join us—even if it's just to watch what's going on—we'll be in the classroom for the next hour."

To her disappointment only Rosa followed. Inside the classroom, Rosa regarded her sympathetically. "It is a waste of your time to teach for just one, is it not?" she asked worriedly.

"No," Dana said at once. "I would rather have one person who is truly interested than a whole roomful of people who are just killing time." Plus there would be only one to see how inexperienced she was at this teaching business.

"Now, tell me, would you rather learn how to use the camera or would you rather let me take some pictures and see how they do?" she asked Rosa.

The teenager smiled shyly. "Do you truly think I am pretty enough to be a model?"

"I'm not an expert, but yes, I do."

"Then take the pictures, please. I would like to have one to show the baby someday, even if nothing else ever comes of this."

"Why don't I tell you what I'm doing, as I set up anyway? It never hurts to know a little about what the photographer's job is. I don't have all the equipment that a professional would have, but we can make do," she said, as she set up her tripod, loaded film into the best of the cameras, and mounted it on the stand. "I'll have to use natural light, which puts us at a disadvantage, compared to all those fancy lights in a photography studio, but it may make the pictures more interesting. I'll do a few in black and white, then some in color."

Rosa watched what she was doing with obvious fascination. As soon as everything was set up, Dana pointed her toward the teacher's desk. "Let's try something up there," she suggested.

Rosa touched her face worriedly. "My make-up and hair, they are okay?"

"You look beautiful," Dana assured her. "Very natural." She just prayed she could capture that beauty on film. Though she'd taken more than one photography class for the pure enjoyment of it, she had very little experience with anything remotely like fashion photography. She was far better at catching an errant husband sneaking into his lover's apartment, or an insurance cheat playing volleyball, when he should have been flat on his back. Those pictures needed only to be clear enough to prove deceit, not crisp enough to sell a product or lovely enough for a gallery showing.

Rosa sat stiffly where Dana had directed her. She needed to relax, so Dana began talking, asking questions about the baby. At once Rosa's expression became more animated. No matter the circumstances of her pregnancy, it was clear that the baby was going to be very loved. Only when the talk turned to the future did her brow furrow.

"It is going to be difficult," she said in a whisper. "I have no job. I have not even graduated from high school, yet. I dropped out because of the baby, but I will go back when I can. I want my child to be proud of me."

"How old are you?"

"Seventeen."

So terribly young, Dana thought sadly. "What about your family? Can they help?"

"My family has very little extra, and my father is very angry about the baby. Only my mother has been able to keep him from throwing me out into the streets," Rosa responded matter-of-factly, though the shadows in her eyes made it evident how much this hurt her. "He has not spoken one word to me since I told him. He says I have shamed him."

"Where does Marco fit in?" Dana asked as she clicked the

shutter, shot after shot, trying to capture the lightning-quick shifts in mood on Rosa's face. "Is he the baby's father?"

Rosa laughed. "No, no," she said at once. "Marco is my brother. You must excuse him for the way he is. Macho is very important to him. Inside, though, he is very soft, especially when it comes to me and the baby. If it comes to that, if my father throws me out, Marco will take me in. It will cramp his lifestyle, he says, but he will do it."

"So, Marco has many girlfriends?" Dana asked.

"Very many," Rosa said. "He cannot settle on any one. I tell him he is scared of commitment."

"And what does he say?"

Rosa shrugged. "He says to mind my own business."

"But you don't," Dana guessed.

"Of course not," Rosa said with a grin. "He is my older brother. It is my duty to pester him."

Dana was just wondering whether she had gained Rosa's confidence, whether she dared to venture on to more serious questions, when the girl said softly, "You must miss the *padre* very much."

Taken by surprise, tears sprang to Dana's eyes before she could prevent it. It happened that way sometimes, when she was caught off-guard. For a few minutes at a time, she would almost forget that he was gone and then a reminder would come, just like this, and it would shatter her momentary tranquility.

"I do," she said. "Very much. Did you know my husband well?"

"We all knew him well. He was very much loved here," Rosa told her.

"By everyone?"

"Oh, yes," the girl said fervently.

"So, no one at *Yo, Amigo* would have harmed him?"

Rosa looked shocked by the question. "Never!"

"May I ask you another question?"

"About the *padre?*"

"Indirectly. Is anyone here involved with drugs?"

Rosa looked uncomfortable, and it was a very long time before she finally answered. "There have been drugs," she conceded with obvious reluctance. "But no more. Rick does not allow it. If one of us is caught in the building with drugs, or even high on drugs, we are out of the program. That is the way it is and everyone knows it. It is very strict."

"Has anyone been kicked out?"

"Not for a long time."

Dana wondered whether they measured time the same way. "What do you mean, a long time?"

"A few months," Rosa said. "It was before Christmas. November, maybe."

"Who was caught?"

Rosa's gaze narrowed suspiciously. "Why do you want to know this? It was a long time ago."

A few months, Dana thought, barely two, in fact, before Ken's death. Could there have been some connection?

"Not so very long ago," she said. "Who was it, Rosa?"

Her expression passive, Rosa stood up then. "I think I have said too much already," she said, heading for the door. She paused. "Thank you very much for taking my pictures," she said politely.

Dana knew she would only lose ground if she persisted with her questioning. She smiled. "I'll bring them in for you to see tomorrow."

Despite her evident uneasiness, Rosa couldn't hide her excitement. "So soon?"

"I'll develop them at home tonight," Dana promised, thinking that the time in her makeshift basement darkroom would be more relaxing than many other things she could be doing. "Will you be here tomorrow afternoon?"

"Yes," Rosa said, clearly unable to resist the lure of those photographs. "I will be here."

Then she hurried away, leaving Dana to wonder just who Rosa was trying to protect. Her first guess would have been

Marco, the big brother who'd promised Rosa his protection. But Marco was very much involved in the program. If he'd been banished for drug use, he wouldn't be here now.

Or would he? Was any banishment short-term, no more than a few weeks, perhaps? It was a question for Rick. Would he go as tight-lipped as Rosa had, or would he be honest with her? Maybe this would be the first real test of exactly where his loyalties lay—with his dead friend or with his program. Dana feared she already knew the answer.

When push came to shove, *Yo, Amigo* would win every time.

Twelve

Dana collected her equipment and took it with her to Rick's office. When she entered, Maria glanced up from her work and smiled.

"There you are. How did it go?"

"I had one student," Dana admitted. "Rosa."

"Do not be discouraged. It is a start. Rosa will tell the others and next time, there will be more."

Dana was not so sure of that, given the last words she and Rosa had spoken. "I suppose," she said, trying not to sound too dispirited. "Is Rick free?"

"Actually he had to leave for a bit. There was a meeting he had forgotten. He said for you to hang in." She tilted her head thoughtfully. "Or was it hang out? Anyway, he will be back shortly. You could wait in his office, if you do not mind the clutter. He will not let me touch anything in there. He says he knows exactly where everything is, and if I organize it, he will be lost."

Dana seized the opportunity. At last, she would have free rein to do some serious snooping. "I don't mind at all," she said, trying not to sound too eager.

"Would you like to see a magazine. We have some that were donated. Most are in Spanish, I'm afraid, but there is a *Newsweek* from last December. That is not too old. And a *Reader's Digest*. That is timeless, yes?"

"That's okay. I'll be fine."

Maria's expression brightened hopefully. "Maybe you

would prefer to see some information on the program," she suggested. "We have several papers that were prepared for fund-raising and for grants. The *padre* helped us to write them."

"Yes," Dana said, careful to disguise her eagerness. "I'd love to see whatever you have about *Yo, Amigo.* You don't by any chance have a file of articles that have been done about the program, do you?"

Maria nodded. "Oh, yes, we save them all." She wrinkled her nose. "Even the bad ones."

So not all of the media coverage had been positive, Dana thought. Who were the critics? she wondered. Would they provide some clue about the murder? Or was she grasping at straws to think that opponents of the program might kill as part of some Machiavellian plot to force its closing?

Never before had she been involved in a case in which the victim had been so universally loved. Except for those who disagreed with Ken's philosophy regarding the gangs, there simply were no obvious starting points, at least when it came to identifying people with a motive to do Ken harm.

And yet she couldn't accept the possibility that his killing had been random, even in an area known for its drive-by shootings. Why? Was it simply her own need to put a more meaningful label on the crime? A need to fix blame?

With the quick expertise of a very organized person, Maria put her hands on several thick files and handed them to Dana. "This will keep you busy for a while, yes? Would you like coffee? One of the boys just brought in some *cafe Cubano.* It is very strong, but very good."

"That sounds wonderful." She took a tiny cup of the dark, sweet coffee with her into Rick's office and settled into the chair behind his desk, the file folders spread out in front of her.

Glancing around, she cursed the lack of a copy machine. She'd never be able to read everything in the time she had. Perhaps, though, there would be duplicates of some of the information on the program. She could take a set of those and concentrate for now on the promising batch of clippings.

Sure enough, inside one folder she found several copies of a slick brochure on *Yo, Amigo* that had been designed for fund-raising, along with a printed fact sheet about costs, goals, and achievements. She folded up copies of both and stuffed them in her purse. The grant proposals in another were too bulky to deal with, for the moment, but she made a note of foundations and government offices which had been sent applications for funding.

Then she turned her attention to the articles. One by one, she lifted them from the folder. They were in no particular order that she could discern. They hadn't been sorted by topic or by date. She wondered at the latter. Even if the person filing them, presumably Maria, had simply been stuffing them into the folder, wouldn't they be in something close to chronological order, either front to back or back to front?

Instead, she found articles from two years before filed ahead of those from two weeks ago, followed by one from the program's dedication and grand opening. In fact, rather than being neatly filed, it appeared they had been jammed into the folder hurriedly.

Had someone else searched this particular file and perhaps removed something incriminating? Or, once again, was she grasping at straws? Maybe the person filing simply had no particular system. If Maria had recruited assistance from one of the kids Dana had met, it was entirely possible that the filing had been done haphazardly.

For the moment, perhaps she ought to create a log of the articles by source, date, headline, and topic. Later, she could compare it to a search of the archives of area papers to determine which clipping or clippings might be missing, if any. It might lead her to a clue. It was a slim hope, but it was all she had.

Snatching a notebook from her purse, she made hasty entries, not even pausing long enough to read more than a cursory paragraph or two to familiarize herself with the article's focus. For the most part, there was nothing remarkable about the clippings. In fact, most were glowing accounts of the successes achieved.

There was an intriguing in-depth profile of Rick that she had to force herself not to at least skim. It would be easy enough to track down a copy on microfiche later at the local library. Some stories would also be available on the Internet. She had kept her link to that, even after she had given up her PI practice.

As she reached the last few clippings, she wondered at the lack of negative press, especially in light of Maria's claim that even the bad articles had been kept. The only article that could be considered remotely derogatory was one in which it was charged that the program had exceeded its budget. Even in that one, however, the critics had found that the excesses were justifiable and could easily be made up with the increased cash flow from the following year's contributions.

Just as she was about to replace the clippings, she spotted one tiny article that had been left in the folder. It was little more than a single paragraph with a two-line headline, probably tucked away in the newspaper's pages, just as it had been virtually lost in the folder. The headline made her heart pound.

DRUG CHARGES DISMISSED
AGAINST PROGRAM FOUNDER

Chicago police today conceded that there was no evidence to support drug allegations that had been made against Enrique (Rick) Sanchez, founder of the highly successful gang rehabilitation program. Sanchez was released after questioning.

Dana's hand trembled as she read and re-read the clipping. Rick had been questioned about drugs. Now the police were convinced that Ken had somehow been tied to drug-trafficking. Coincidence? She doubted it.

Why hadn't Rick told her about this after their meeting with O'Flannery earlier? Wouldn't that have been the logical time to explain that this wasn't the first time drug charges had been falsely made about someone connected to *Yo, Amigo?* Or had they been false? Had he just dodged a bullet because the evidence had been too scanty for a conviction?

She was still contemplating the possibilities and clutching the tiny article when Rick walked back into his office. Something in her face must have given her away, because the smile that had been starting at the corners of his mouth faded.

"What's wrong?"

She held out the clipping. "Explain this."

He didn't even reach out to take it. He just sighed. "The article says I was not guilty, does it not?"

"It says there was no evidence," she corrected. "There must have been some reason for the charge being made in the first place."

"As there was in Ken's case?" he asked dryly.

"It's not the same," she argued bitterly.

Rick's expression hardened. "Why? Because he was your husband?"

"Because he was a good and decent man, who deplored the use of drugs."

"And I am not so good and decent?" he asked softly.

Her anger fading just as quickly as it had begun, she stared at him in confusion. "I don't know you that well."

"Exactly, *querida.* You do not know me at all."

Querida, she thought. It was the second time he had used the term of endearment with her. She was not his dear one, his darling, his sweetheart, or his honey. She was nothing to him. And yet she couldn't bring herself to protest. The word was like a caress, impossible to ignore, even more difficult to undo, once it had been spoken. Its casual use inexplicably tightened the bond between them. She drew in a deep breath.

"Will you tell me what happened?"

The smile came back, but it was gently mocking. "Are you

sure you wish to hear the truth? Maybe you would prefer the illusions, especially if they are damning."

"Truth is always better," she insisted.

"Not always," he said. "But in this case, yes." He held out his hand. "Come, I will tell you as we drive."

After a moment's hesitation, she tucked her hand into his and allowed him to gently tug her to her feet. The contact was too fleeting, too tempting. She was glad that she had so many things to carry. Otherwise she might have allowed him to keep her hand clasped in his.

Once they were in the car, however, Rick seemed to forget his promise. Instead of explaining about the drug charges, he asked how her class had gone.

"Only one participant," she said and told him about Rosa.

"Do not look so sad. If you were able to get Rosa, others will follow. Marco has given it his tacit approval by allowing her to come."

"Then Marco has so much power?"

"He is a natural leader, yes."

Putting aside for the moment her determination to learn about those supposedly falsified drug charges, she focused on the opening he had given her to discover more about Marco. "Tell me about him," she said. "He seems like a very dangerous young man."

"Marco is a product of the streets—tough, smart, and far too rebellious to play by anyone's rules."

"And yet he has played by yours, hasn't he?"

"Most of the time," Rick conceded.

"Why?"

"Because I bailed him out of some trouble once."

"With the police?"

"No, with a rival gang. They had him surrounded. I wouldn't have given ten cents for his life at that point."

"Let me guess. You just waded into the fray and evened the odds."

He grinned. "Something like that."

"In other words, you saved his life."

"He believes that I did."

"Which no doubt made it very easy to strike a bargain with him to get him into the program," she guessed.

"Not so easy," he corrected. "But less complicated than it might have otherwise been. He was forced to admit that it is possible to be strong without a gang behind you."

"How many others have you rescued in this way?"

"Fortunately, some of the others have been won over more easily. A few followed Marco. Others came because their parents or a teacher or a priest dragged them."

Dana knew enough about adolescent psychology to guess that those weren't the ones who stayed. "I'll bet Marco's friends have been your greatest successes," she said.

He nodded. "As I said, he is a natural leader. As was Tico."

"Have you ever regretted making Marco part of *Yo, Amigo?*"

"Why would I regret it?"

Dana tried to feel her way cautiously with her response. "Because of things he has done."

"Such as?"

"Drugs, maybe."

"We are back to that again," he said wearily. "Drugs have no place at *Yo, Amigo.*"

"That doesn't mean that drug use never happens, does it?"

"No, but there are severe consequences."

"Banishment."

"Yes."

"Has Marco ever been kicked out for using or selling drugs?"

"Never."

He said it so firmly that Dana was taken aback. "Oh."

"Why so surprised?"

"It was something Rosa said. I guess I misunderstood," she admitted. If not Marco, though, then who would Rosa have been so quick to protect? The answer flashed as brilliantly as neon. Rick, of course.

"Rick, tell me about the drug charges against you."

"There were no charges," he reminded her. "Only allegations."

It was a distinction she couldn't quite grasp. "The police suspected you, right?"

"Because someone fed them false information," he said with transparent bitterness. "They had no choice but to investigate, just as they claimed with Ken. While they did, I stepped down as director. I had to abide by my own rules. Naturally it got blown all out of proportion in the media. Of course, when the investigation concluded there was no basis for the accusations, it was relegated to a brief item buried deep inside the newspaper."

"There was more in the papers than that clipping I had earlier?"

"Exposé after exposé for a few weeks last year," he confirmed. "It could have ruined us, if so many had not had faith in me and in the program."

Dana was puzzled. "Those other articles weren't in the file."

Rick didn't seem especially surprised. "Maria hates anything negative, especially if it's about me. Perhaps she never clipped the articles."

"Do you really believe that?" Dana asked, thinking of Maria's declaration that she had included even the negative press.

"What's the alternative?"

"That someone deliberately removed them."

"Why?"

She shook her head. "I have no idea, but something tells me we ought to find out."

Rick didn't seem nearly as suspicious about the missing articles as she was. "Why take them from the file, when anyone interested could go right down to the papers and pull copies?"

"Maybe the person who took them didn't realize that."

"Anyone knows that newspapers keep files, either computerized or on microfiche."

Maybe it was as simple as someone like Rosa trying to protect a man she liked and respected. "Even the kids at *Yo, Amigo?*" she asked.

He seemed startled by the suggestion. "Okay, no," he finally admitted. "They might not be sophisticated enough to realize that, but doesn't that shoot your theory of some sort of conspiracy all to hell?"

"What theory?"

He smiled. "The one you've been putting together in your head ever since the cops started to toss around allegations about Ken and drugs. Anyone capable of masterminding that kind of conspiracy would have a pretty good idea of how the media functions, wouldn't you say? In fact, they would have to have been manipulating it all along."

"I suppose."

He reached over and clasped her hand. "Don't look so depressed, *querida*. We will find the answers. First, though, we will have a good dinner. Seafood, I think. Brain food. Do you like shrimp?"

Dana nodded, though food was the last thing on her mind.

"Good, then. I know the perfect place."

"Only if it's my treat," she said, thinking of how tight the budget must be for the head of a shoestring program like *Yo, Amigo* must be.

"It was my idea. I will pay," he insisted, scowling at her.

His expression was so intractable that she backed down. She knew enough about machismo not to waste time fighting it.

"Whatever you say," she said.

He chuckled at that. "Ah, I wonder how long I can expect such docility to last?"

"If you're very lucky, until dessert," she said.

"Then I will count my blessings until then."

Thirteen

Dana had kept her word. There had been no more interrogations over dinner, no snide remarks. It was the most pleasant, non-confrontational time they had ever spent together, Rick concluded, feeling oddly out of sorts.

Ironically, he missed the quick-witted arguments, the sizzling tension. He missed the flash of temper in her eyes and even the snap of irritation in her voice. In fact, he found the sudden docility worrisome. It was still bothering him when he took her home.

He had just unloaded her cameras and equipment and tucked everything inside the front door, when he caught her expression. She looked lost, so lost that he found himself inviting himself in for coffee, even though he knew that to stay was dangerous. Too much proximity and he wouldn't be able to resist stealing a kiss, just to know the taste and feel of her lips beneath his.

When she didn't say a word—not *go* or *stay*—he brushed past her and headed for the kitchen, leaving her no choice but to follow.

Since she seemed to accept him taking over, it was fortunate that the automatic coffeepot was in plain view, along with a bag of the gourmet blend he'd already discovered she favored. He busied himself for several minutes with the coffee. He searched the cupboards for mugs and the refrigerator for cream, then put it all down in front of her.

Seated at the table and staring into space, she seemed startled by the arrival of the steaming cup of coffee.

Rick turned a chair around backwards and sat down opposite her. With an expanse of solid oak between them, he ought to be able to keep his hands to himself.

"Where'd you go on me?" he asked eventually.

She blinked and stared. "What?"

"You haven't said much since we left the restaurant. What's going on?"

She attempted to force a smile, but it wavered, then faded. "Just thinking, I guess."

"About?"

When she didn't respond, he hazarded a guess. "Ken, right?"

She nodded and lifted her gaze to his. Her eyes were brimming with unshed tears. "When we drove up here tonight, for some reason, it finally sank in that this was the way it was going to be from now on, coming home to an empty house, living with all this silence. I mean, intellectually I've known it before, but tonight I really felt it. I felt dead inside."

Despite his promise to himself not to touch her, he reached across the table for her hand. It was icy cold in his. "You have three sons," he reminded her gently, as her skin warmed beneath his touch. "Soon they'll be back here with you. The place will be so noisy you won't be able to stand it."

"It won't be the same," she insisted. "And we won't be here, not in this house, anyway. The church has been very lenient about letting us stay on, but we'll have to move eventually. I've already half made up my mind to go to Florida, so we can be near my folks. The boys seem to like it there. The school is good. It would be a solution." She said it without much enthusiasm.

"Short-term or long-term?" Rick asked.

"I don't know," she said candidly. "The choice is too difficult. I haven't been able to deal with it. I managed to get the boys enrolled in school in Florida, because it made sense. They couldn't languish in limbo, while I wrestle with the future."

"Figuring out what's right is never easy," he said.

"And it's harder when you're not the only one involved," she said. "I could come back here and cope somehow. I lived in Chicago before I met Ken. I could do it again. The boys will see him everywhere."

"That's not necessarily a bad thing," Rick suggested. "The memories will be important to them. They'll treasure the unexpected reminders."

Oblivious to the tears that were now tracking down her cheeks, she stared at him hopefully. "You sound so sure."

"I am. You'll never forget, but it will get easier. Just don't look too far ahead. Stick with the moment."

"I guess that's what I did tonight," she said. "I looked too far ahead. I saw our anniversary and the Fourth of July and Thanksgiving and Christmas—all of them without Ken. He made them so special." She sighed, her expression wistful. "He made every day special."

Rick felt a sharp stab of something that might have been pure jealousy. It was inexplicable, but he suddenly wanted to be the one with whom she made so many unforgettable memories. He wanted to make her days—and her nights—so special that she could never forget.

And he felt like the worst sort of traitor for thinking it, especially when he was the kind of guy who didn't make commitments, didn't allow anyone to get too close. Hadn't that been his ex-wife's charge when she left, that she'd felt as if she were living with a stranger. He hadn't thought it possible that he could hurt Dana any more than he already had by inadvertently putting Ken in the line of fire, but he saw now that he could. He could offer her something he wasn't capable of delivering.

"I'd better go," he said and stood up suddenly.

She stared at him in surprise. "You haven't touched your coffee."

"I shouldn't be drinking coffee at this hour anyway. I'll never get to sleep." Not that he'd be getting much sleep anyway. He'd be lying awake, tormented by pure lust for a woman who wasn't his, a woman who'd lost her husband—his best friend—barely more than a month ago. Sick, sick, sick.

"Rick?" she said, her expression quizzical.

"What?"

"Does it bother you when I talk about Ken?"

It shouldn't, he thought, but, by God, it did. "Of course not," he said, denying the truth in order to clutch one tiny shred of honor.

"Are you sure? I guess I thought of all people, you would understand."

He reached down and squeezed her hand. "I do," he said. "I do understand, and it's okay. Talk about him all you want. I swear to you, I'll be a good listener, just not tonight, okay?"

Though her expression remained puzzled, she nodded. "Good night, then."

Impulsively, he leaned down and brushed a kiss across her forehead. "Sweet dreams, *querida.*"

He was almost out the door, almost safely on his way when he heard her footsteps tapping rapidly across the wood floors.

"Rick," she called out.

He hesitated.

"Same time tomorrow? You'll take me back to *Yo, Amigo?* Rosa's pictures will be ready. She's anxious to see them."

He sighed. "Yes. At the same time," he promised, even though it was going to get harder and harder to see Dana and to protect himself and *Yo, Amigo* from the harm she could do.

For the longest time after Rick had gone, Dana sat in the still-dark living room, staring into space. She was more confused, more lost than ever. She needed to make some sort of progress in solving Ken's murder. That would give her a sense of purpose. It would also bring about closure, tie up all the loose ends, and let her move on with her life, get back to her kids and give them the attention they deserved.

A fresh batch of tears leaked out, skimming down her cheeks, until her face and her blouse were both damp. Eventually, she grew impatient with herself, tired of feeling vulnerable, exhausted by the uncharacteristic self-pity.

"Just get on with it," she ordered herself. She grabbed the phone and, oblivious to the time, punched in Kate's number.

Kate's groggy hello instantly filled her with regret. "I'm sorry," she apologized. "You're sleeping. I'll talk to you in the morning."

"No, no," Kate insisted sleepily. "It's okay. Is everything all right?"

"Sure," she lied, "I was just wondering what you'd found out today. I forgot all about the time. I know you like to go to bed early so you can get up at the crack of dawn to see the kids off in the morning."

"It's not a problem," Kate reassured her. "I didn't learn anything earthshaking, though I do have a few people we might want to look at more closely. Do you want me to get the list now? It's downstairs."

"No. We can do it in the morning. Go back to sleep."

"You sure you don't want to talk? You sound upset."

"No, really. I'm fine. I should try to get some sleep myself, as soon as I call the boys to say goodnight. Mother will probably be furious because I'll be getting them out of bed."

"No, she won't. She knows it's important that they hear your voice before they go to sleep. Call, sweetie."

"I will. Good night, Kate. I'm sorry I woke you."

"I'll see you first thing in the morning, and I'm going to want a full report on the kids. Give them my love."

Dana disconnected the call, then dialed her parents' number. Though all three boys were half-asleep and yawning in her ear, she was glad she'd made the call. She felt better, reassured that they were fine.

Afterward, still too restless to sleep herself, she took the film she'd shot that afternoon into her darkroom in the basement. Over the years, between work and shooting pictures of the family just for the fun of it, the process of developing had become a habit, so much so that she was able to do it automatically, allowing her mind to wander.

Had she already met Ken's killer? Was it one of the ex-gang members at *Yo, Amigo?* Or did they merely know more than they were saying? She wanted to believe it was someone like Marco, someone arrogant and rude, whose capacity for violence lurked in the shadows of his eyes.

There was no evidence of it, though. Not yet, anyway. Not even a telltale hint of guilty knowledge in Rosa's eyes under Dana's direct questioning.

When the film was ready, she fit it into the enlarger and made print after print, stunned by the results. She couldn't help smiling at the Madonna-like quality of the pictures, especially those she'd shot in black and white. She had managed to capture the eternal serenity of the mother-to-be in Rosa's expression, as well as an occasional flash of the sexy siren and, in yet another shot, an impish girl.

Pleased with the unqualified success of her afternoon's work, she went back upstairs. She wandered restlessly for a bit, then eventually settled into Ken's chair, the afghan tucked around her. Her body must finally be getting used to the cramped sleeping arrangement, or else she was just thoroughly exhausted. Tonight, for the first time in weeks, she fell right to sleep.

Her dreams, once again, were not of Ken, as they had been ever since his death. Instead, for the second time, Rick Sanchez was there to taunt her. It was one more thing to hate him for, she told herself when she awoke, her body drenched with sweat. He'd stolen the only time she still had left with the man she'd loved—the dark hours of the night.

* * *

In the morning, Dana drank two cups of coffee before making another call to Florida to check in on the boys before they left for school. She'd managed to evade most of her mother's questions the night before, but she knew she wouldn't be able to do it forever.

Her mother picked up on the first ring, as she always did, as though she couldn't wait to hear what the caller had to say.

"Darling, how are you?" she asked, her voice laced with unmistakable concern. "I was hoping to get a chance to talk to you last night, after you spoke with the boys, but you'd already hung up by the time Bobby handed me the phone."

"I'm fine. How are the boys doing? Tell me the truth. Are they okay?"

"They miss you," she said bluntly. "When will you be back?"

"Soon."

"How soon?"

"I can't say for sure."

"Darling, you're not a private investigator anymore. Let the police handle the case."

Dana found the familiar refrain irritating, but managed to keep her tone patient. "We've been over this. I have to do whatever I can to find Ken's killer." She thought of the planted evidence of drugs. "It's gotten more complicated, more important than ever."

"I wish there were some other way."

"So do I, Mother, but there isn't. I'll be back as soon as I can. I promise. As soon as the case is solved, I'll get our things packed up and come back there to start looking for a house of our own to rent," she said impulsively.

"Then you are going to move here? You've decided?" There was no mistaking the excitement in her mother's voice. "Darling, that's wonderful. We'll love having you and the boys close by."

"We'll give it a try, at least until the end of the school year.

If the boys like it, we'll make it permanent," she amended hastily to give herself an out in case they all hated it.

"Oh, I can't wait to tell your father. He'll be thrilled."

Dana closed her eyes and tried to share her mother's excitement. All she felt was the relief of having made some sort of a decision, set some sort of a timetable. She tried telling herself it was the smart thing to do. What was there to keep them in Chicago, really, now that Ken was gone? Nothing.

Still, it was home. It was where she had begun her family, where memories lurked around every turn, just as Rick had said the night before. Good memories, as well as all these recent bad ones.

"The memories will come with you," her mother said gently, as if Dana had spoken her thoughts aloud.

Dana smiled. "How did you know what I was thinking?"

"Because that's how we all react to change. We fear that we'll lose our link to the past. Don't you think Dad and I worried about that when we first came here after he retired? We don't lose those ties, though. I promise you. You'll be happy here. You'll have family close by. It will be good for all of you, you'll see."

"You're sure you and Dad can handle the boys for a little while longer?"

"Of course we can. You concentrate on wrapping up your investigation and getting down here to join us."

"I'll be there as quickly as I can be."

Apparently satisfied with that response, her mother let the matter drop. "I'll get the boys. They're dying to talk to you."

"Wait a second," Dana said, recalling her unfulfilled promise to Bobby. "I told Bobby I'd tell you that he's allowed to stay up an hour later than his brothers."

Her mother chuckled. "So, he did call you. I thought maybe he had. Okay, I'll bend the rule for him."

"He also mentioned that you never, ever give them pizza to eat."

"I thought home-cooked, nutritious meals were better," her mother said defensively.

"They are," Dana agreed. "But pizza won't hurt them once in a while. Do you mind?"

"If you don't object, I don't. I'll tell Dad to order it on my bridge night. I won't have to cook a meal before I go, and he won't have to worry about getting the food on the table. He'll also get to cheat on his diet. That should make everyone happy. I draw the line at anchovies, though. They give your father indigestion."

Dana chuckled at the thought of her boys asking for those "slimy little fish," as they called them. "That won't be a problem, I assure you," she said. "Thanks, Mom. I don't know what I'd do without you."

"Then isn't it fortunate that you don't have to. Love you, baby. Here's Bobby."

Dana talked to each of the boys, reassuring them again, now that they were wider awake and could understand her, that everything was okay back home and that she'd be back with them soon.

"Love you, Mommy," each one said in a rush.

"Granddad's taking us to the pool before school," Bobby explained, sounding more upbeat than he had during their past conversations. "The squirts have turned into little fish. I don't know what they'll do when we get back home and there's no pool. They'll probably shrivel up."

"Will not," Kevin shouted.

Dana laughed at the sound of the familiar bickering. For too long, right after Ken's death, they had been too quiet and subdued. Listening to them now, she honestly believed for the first time that they were going to be okay. Did that mean that she, too, would eventually be okay?

"Bye, sweetie," she said to her oldest. "Keep an eye on your brothers and mind Grandma and Granddad."

"Did you talk to her about my bedtime and the pizza?"

"Taken care of."

"Thanks, Mom. Bye."

"Bye," she said again, but the connection had been broken. Sensing that she wasn't alone, she glanced up and saw Kate standing in the doorway.

"Good girl," her friend said. "Everybody okay?"

"They sound like they're getting better every day. I can't wait to get back and see for myself."

"Then go."

"Not just yet, but soon. If I don't have the answers I need very soon, I'll make a quick trip just to get a look at them. I could use a couple of hugs and some sticky kisses, myself." She stood up, grabbed the coffeepot and poured Kate a cup, then refilled her own. "Okay, let's have it. What did you find?"

"Like I told you last night, not much. I have half a dozen names that triggered some sort of an alarm when I came to them."

Dana's gaze narrowed. "What kind of alarm?"

"That's just it. I'm not sure. Maybe I just have an overactive imagination from hanging out with you. Or maybe there's something in the dim recesses of my mind, a newspaper article or TV report I didn't see yesterday." She shoved her list across the table. "Any of these ring any sort of bell for you?"

Dana scanned the list: Peter Drake, Miriam Kelso, Vincent Polanski, Lawrence Tremayne, Carolina Vincenzi, Gerrold Wald.

"All of these came from the roster of active church members, right?" she asked.

Kate nodded. "Don't you know them?"

"All but one of the women, actually. Who is Carolina Vincenzi?"

"Tall, refined-looking, with an aristocratic nose and oodles of dark hair. Very good face-lift. She hardly looks a day over thirty-five, even though I know for a fact she's at least ten years older than that."

"Is she on here because you're jealous of her looks?" Dana asked dryly.

"No, she's on there because I overheard her talking about the gang kids that Ken was bringing into the community. She looks very much like a lady, but she has a trashy mouth and a streak of prejudice a mile wide. I wouldn't want to tangle with her. She's a tough cookie."

"What about Drake, Kelso, Polanski, Tremayne, and Wald, especially Tremayne? He's head of the church elders, for goodness sake. Surely he's above suspicion."

"I know," Kate said. "He's the kind of upstanding guy that any church would be proud to call its own. Good businessman. Decent father and husband." She shook her head. "I don't know what it is, but I don't trust him."

"He's been very kind to me since Ken died."

"I know. I can't explain my reaction."

"Has he ever said anything, done anything even remotely suspicious?"

"No," Kate conceded. "In fact, when I ran a check on him at the local newspaper, he had nothing but accolades. President of this, chairman of that, honored for something else."

"Maybe he's just a good guy," Dana said, thinking of the very polite man who'd always been eager to help Ken with any church problems. He'd been an absolute whiz at straightening out the mess the church's financial affairs had been in when Ken first arrived.

"Maybe so. Or maybe he has the kind of reputation a man would do anything to protect. Isn't that the kind you said to look out for?"

"He is, indeed," Dana said thoughtfully. She tried to picture Lawrence Tremayne, with his thick, brown hair, perfect features, and expensive wardrobe, tainting his image by committing a murder. She couldn't do it. Still, there was something to be said for finding answers in the least likely places.

She considered the other names on the list. Peter Drake was

a mousy, unassuming little man, but she agreed with Kate that there was something a bit odd about him.

Miriam Kelso was outspoken and highly critical of Ken, as she had been of every other minister the church had had, according to those who knew her best.

Polanski and Wald were in the carpeting business together. Despite that union, they fought loudly and often, always patching things up just in time to save the business from ruin. They had quick, flashpoint tempers, but Dana wasn't convinced they would murder in a fit of rage. They were too used to stopping short of that with each other.

"Maybe I should call and invite them over," she suggested to Kate. "Maybe it's time for everyone at the church to know that I'm turning over rocks to see what crawls out."

Kate seemed a little nonplussed by the idea. "Isn't that asking for trouble? What if one of these people does know something? You could be endangering yourself."

"Very little progress comes without risk."

"I thought you were taking all the risks you needed to by going into Chicago with Rick Sanchez. How did that go, by the way?"

"It was a first step, but I have a long way to go before I gain the trust of those kids. I can't wait for that. I have to keep checking every angle. Will you call these people today? Invite them over for tea tomorrow."

"Why not today?"

"I'm going back to *Yo, Amigo.*"

"Will you tell Rick that you're checking out other leads?"

Dana held up the list of names. "Sweetie, these aren't leads, and that tea tomorrow isn't any more than a chance to float a few theories. It's a little too much to hope that someone will fall to their knees and confess."

"Just in case" Kate said, "maybe you'd better vacuum."

Fourteen

Rosa had almost driven Rick crazy asking about Dana and those photographs she'd taken. From the minute he'd walked into *Yo, Amigo* at 8:30 A.M. until the time he had left to pick up Dana, Rosa had pestered him.

"For the last time, she will be here in a couple of hours," he'd explained at least a half-dozen times. "You can see for yourself."

"You could call her," Rosa had pleaded each time. "You could ask if they turned out at all."

"Patience, angel. You will know soon enough."

"Are you sure she did not tell you they were awful?" the teenager asked worriedly.

"She has told me nothing. She hadn't even developed the film, the last time I talked to her."

Rosa's face fell. "Perhaps she did not have time to develop them. I thought they had to be done at a drugstore, anyway. Perhaps she will not bring the pictures today at all."

For some reason, he had absolute faith that Dana would do as she had promised. He felt confident reassuring Rosa of that. "She promised to bring them, didn't she? She said she was going to do them herself. Even if she didn't have the time, there are many places that have one-hour processing for film. I swear to you that we will stop at one of them, if she doesn't already have the pictures."

"Yes, but—"

"No buts. If she said she would, then you can count on it,"

he said, praying his instincts were right. Maybe he should call to check, just in case, and look for one of those one-hour services in the Yellow Pages.

And maybe he was just looking for an excuse to hear her voice, he had thought with disgust. He had forced himself to resist the temptation to dial her number. He'd been less successful forcing her image out of his head. Fueled by an impatience he could no longer control, he left a half-hour earlier than he'd planned to pick her up.

Even so, apparently Dana was every bit as anxious today as Rosa had been. He found her waiting outside on the front stoop when he drove up. He noted with a sigh of relief that she was carrying a large, flat envelope, along with the camera bag and other equipment she'd had the day before.

He helped her to load everything except the envelope into the trunk.

"Are those the pictures?" he asked, as he put the car into gear.

She nodded.

"Rosa's very excited. I hope they turned out okay. I'd hate to see her disappointed."

"Okay? They're beautiful. Even lovelier than I'd hoped. Trust me, she won't be disappointed."

"May I see?"

She grinned at him. "Now who's anxious? Besides, you're driving. You need to keep your eyes on the road."

"We're still in the driveway," he reminded her.

"Which is no way to get these to Rosa in a hurry."

At the teasing tone, he slanted a look at her. "You sound better today."

"I am better," she said. "I think I'm finally beginning to get a grip on things."

Something in her voice alerted him that she was not referring entirely to her own emotions. "Why? Did something happen after I left last night?"

She said no, but her eyes said otherwise. "Dana? What are you keeping from me?"

"Who said I was keeping anything from you?"

"You weren't out snooping around last night, were you?" he asked, envisioning another foray into the streets surrounding *Yo, Amigo*. He knew she hadn't made it inside, because he'd lain awake all night tossing and turning on that sadistic couch. He would have heard her, just as he had the first time she'd broken in.

She scowled at him. "I don't snoop. I'm an investigator. I investigate."

"Okay. Exactly what did you *investigate* last night?"

"Nothing," she swore. "I printed these pictures, then I went to sleep."

His gaze narrowed. He guessed that might be the truth, as far as it went. Perhaps the question had simply been too narrow. "And this morning?"

"Kate came by," she said nonchalantly.

"And?" he prodded with the sudden sense that he was on to something.

"We talked."

He had to fight a grin at her determined reticence. "About?"

"This and that," she said, continuing the evasiveness.

"Dana!"

"Okay, okay, we talked about people in the church who might be suspicious."

The relief he felt was out of all proportion to the announcement. It wasn't as if she'd proved conclusively that *Yo, Amigo's* kids had nothing to do with the murder. But at least she had opened her mind to other possibilities and was exploring them.

"Anybody look especially guilty?" he inquired.

"No, and don't get your hopes up," she retorted. "So far all I have are hunches and wishful thinking about people who on the surface seem very pious and generous."

"Wishful thinking?"

She sighed. "I don't really want anyone at *Yo, Amigo* to be guilty," she conceded grudgingly, then added hurriedly, "For Ken's sake. I would hate to think he was betrayed by the very kids he'd befriended."

"He wasn't," Rick said vehemently. "I'd stake my own life on it."

"That's very noble, but you're prejudiced."

"I also know those kids better than anyone."

She paused at that. "I hope for your sake that you truly do."

"You'll see," he told her. If she would give the kids a chance, they would win her heart, just as they had Ken's. And they needed her faith every bit as badly as they'd needed Ken's. Far too few people had ever believed in them. He thought again of Rosa and her high hopes.

"Dana, be careful with Rosa. Don't promise her things you can't deliver."

"I'll only tell her what I see."

"And that is?"

"That she is beautiful and photogenic."

"She really is?"

"Rick, I swear to you that even though she isn't professional and I've never done anything remotely like a fashion shoot, these pictures are incredible. I've already called a friend of mine about them. He's promised to take a look at them, if I send them over. As soon as I have Rosa's permission, that's what I'm going to do."

"This friend knows what he's doing?"

"He's with Hanson and Watts. In fact, he's Ted Hanson."

"One of the best ad agencies in Chicago," Rick said incredulously. "I have heard of them."

"The best," Dana corrected. "At least according to Ted."

"You have that much faith in these pictures?"

"I have that much faith in Rosa. If I can shoot pictures like these, a professional would pay a fortune to get her in front of a camera."

He fell silent at that. He couldn't help worrying that Rosa was being set up for a tremendous letdown, but that was one of the risks of dreaming big, and he had always encouraged the kids in the program to dream very big. For too long, most of them had had no dreams at all.

When he pulled into his parking space at *Yo, Amigo,* Rosa was waiting in the doorway, her eyes bright with anticipation, her expression fearful. The contradictory emotions were all too typical. Hopes were shot down here with distressing frequency.

"You'll be lucky if she lets you get inside," he warned Dana, just as Rosa came rushing up to the passenger door and yanked it open.

"Do you have them?" she asked, all traces of her usual shyness gone.

"In the backseat," Dana assured her.

Suddenly Rosa's expression faltered. "They are terrible?"

Dana squeezed her hand. "They are anything but terrible."

"The others are waiting inside to see, even Marco. Maybe I should look at them first, here, so I will not be embarrassed, if they make me look like a huge whale."

"I don't think you will be embarrassed," Dana said. "But let's not look at them out here. We could take them to Rick's office, if you like," she said, glancing at him for approval.

"Of course." He was as anxious to see them as the others. Thanks to Dana, he might catch one of the first glimpses.

But at his office door, after running past a gauntlet of kids with expressions ranging from eager to sullenly distrustful, she put a hand on his arm. "Not yet," she told him. "Just Rosa for now."

"Hey, it's my office," he protested. "That ought to count for something."

"It does. We appreciate it, don't we, Rosa?"

"Yes, very much," Rosa said distractedly, her avid gaze locked on that large envelope.

Rick sighed and settled for perching on a corner of Maria's desk to wait. He kept his gaze fixed on the door, wishing he had the power to see through it or the skill to eavesdrop. Not that the place was all that soundproof, but Rosa and Dana were keeping their voices low.

The first hint he got of Rosa's reaction was a faint squeal, then another, and finally a burst of joyous laughter. He glanced at Maria.

"She sounds happy, yes?" Maria said.

"That's an understatement." He pinned his gaze on the door handle and waited for it to turn. At the first hint of a twist, he was on his feet. So was Maria. He noticed then that Marco had edged into the room and was waiting as well, though his expression feigned indifference.

The door opened and a beaming Rosa beckoned to them. As he passed her, Rick thought he detected traces of tears in her eyes. He glanced hurriedly toward Dana for some indication of what those were all about, but she never even glanced his way.

Rosa grabbed her brother's hand and tugged him inside. "Oh, Marco, wait till you see."

The pictures had been spread across the desk top, Rick noticed. Far larger than snapshots, there were so many they could have filled a model's portfolio. He glanced at the first one and smiled. The second one quite simply took his breath away. In fact, he concluded, even though he was by no means an expert, it seemed that each one was better than the one before.

He turned and saw that Marco's expression was every bit as astonished as his own must be. The hard lines of the young man's face softened ever so slightly.

"She has made me look beautiful, hasn't she?" Rosa asked shyly.

"You are beautiful," Marco said emphatically, then turned

to Dana. "But you have captured it on film. *Gracias*. You have made my sister very happy. My parents will be pleased as well. They have nothing so fine as these at home of any of their children."

"She says that an advertising agency president will look at them, if it is okay with me," Rosa said. "Isn't that incredible, Marco? An actual advertising agency."

Marco, rather than demonstrating the excitement that Rosa so clearly expected, frowned. "Mama and Papa will never allow it."

"It is not their decision," Rosa said angrily. "Papa would have me on the street, if not for Mama stopping it. He will be pleased when I can afford to go."

"But you are under their roof now," Marco reminded her. "You must obey their rules."

"As you did?" Rosa said derisively.

Marco reacted angrily with a spurt of Spanish that brought bright patches of color into Rosa's checks. Her eyes flashed with fiery temper. She didn't back down.

"I will do this, Marco."

He seemed taken aback by the defiance, but then, as suddenly as they'd fought, he grinned. "Yes, little one, I believe you will."

Rosa expelled a sigh of relief and turned to Dana. "You will take these to your friend today? Right now?"

"Perhaps we should let the others see them first," Dana suggested, gesturing toward the young people crowded into the doorway. "In the meantime, I will call for a courier to pick them up."

"I can show them to the others?" Rosa asked, as if they were too precious for her to handle.

"Of course."

When Rosa had gone, leading a parade of curious friends, Marco lingered. He fixed a steady gaze on Dana. "Perhaps I owe you an apology, *señora*."

"It's not necessary," Dana assured him graciously. "You were just protecting her interests."

"And my own," he said wryly. "I do not trust outsiders easily." He hesitated, then added, "If I knew something about the *padre's* death, I would tell you, *señora*. We respected him. None of us wished to see him harmed. And if anyone here had information, I would find out about it. I would take care of it. Do you understand?"

"Yes," she said, clearly shaken by his vehemence and his obvious meaning. Rick knew full well that Marco meant every word.

Marco looked for a moment as if he might say more, but then he turned and followed his sister, leaving Rick alone with Dana.

"He meant that, you know. He confirmed what I also believe."

She nodded. "Yes, I believe he did."

"Your answers aren't here, *querida*."

She lifted her gaze to meet his. Despite his reassurances and Marco's, she still looked doubtful. "Time will tell, won't it?"

"You will be back, then?"

"Until Ken's murderer is behind bars, yes," she said vehemently. "I will be back. For him and for them."

Rick sighed. Heaven protect them all from a woman as hellbent on revenge as Dana was.

"Then I suppose we should go back to Tico's for dinner tonight and formulate some sort of strategy," he said.

"You don't have to help."

"Yes, I do," he insisted. "I owe it to Ken to protect you, while you are on this fool's mission."

She bristled visibly at that. "Is it a fool's mission to want to know who killed my husband?"

"No, of course not, but I believe with everything in me that you will not find the murderer here, but the longer you go on stirring things up, the more danger you are likely to put yourself in," he said. "Right now, the murderer is probably feeling fairly complacent, fairly certain that he's home free. When he discovers that you have not let matters die, you will become the next danger to him. This is a person who eliminates threats."

She didn't so much as blanch at the harsh warning. "Then I will just have to work very quickly, won't I?"

He shook his head. "I don't know whether to admire your tenacity or fear it for the danger it could bring into your life."

"I can take care of myself," she insisted. "You needn't worry about me."

"But I do," he said. In fact, the truth was, he thought about little else these days.

Fifteen

The meal at Tico's had been every bit as wonderful as the first Dana had shared there with Rick. Burritos stuffed with succulent meat and cheese and spicy jalapenos had been washed down with icy beer. The conversation had been pitifully short on answers, though.

Tico had joined them for a time, but he knew no more than Rick claimed to about the murder. Rick had leaned back in the seat across from her and kept quiet, as she cross-examined his friend. There was an expression of tolerant amusement on his face that she had hated.

"This just doesn't make sense," she had cried out at one point in frustration. "No one is more likely to be tapped into the underground network around this part of town, but neither of you has turned up so much as a whiff of information. Why is that?"

She noticed that the two men exchanged a significant look at the question, but both remained stubbornly silent. "What is it that you're not telling me?" she asked again, certain that they were holding back, protecting someone or something— *Yo, Amigo,* for instance.

Both had denied they were hiding a thing, but she knew a cover-up when she saw one. Neither of them could look her in the eye when they said it. She had vowed to take the subject up with Rick again on the way home, but he was prepared for her questions. He fielded them with vague replies that left her feeling more irritable than ever.

She was still trying to make sense of their odd behavior the next day, as she prepared for the arrival of the group from the church. She had baked all morning and hauled out her grandmother's silver service, the one she used only for formal occasions. She'd washed all of her best china cups and set them up on the gleaming dining room table, along with platters of triangular, crustless sandwiches, scones, tiny cakes, and delicate almond cookies. She had held enough of these formal teas that she was able to do most of it by rote, while her mind toyed with interpreting those undercurrents the night before. Unfortunately, no new spin came to her.

She spent a solid hour dressing for the occasion, more time than she'd spent on herself since Ken's funeral. She chose a soft grey suit, a prim white blouse, and grey pumps. Her sterling silver necklace and earrings had been a gift from Ken on a trip they'd taken to Mexico to celebrate their first anniversary.

As she touched the cool metal at her throat, tears stung her eyes and her gaze drifted toward the window overlooking the church cemetery. A huge knot formed in her throat as she looked at the snow-covered gravesite, where long-dead flowers poked through the blanket of white. The sight of the neglected plot saddened her.

Suddenly frantic to see it cared for, she ran downstairs and toward the kitchen door, almost plowing into Kate, who was just coming up the back steps carrying an armful of fresh flowers to brighten the table.

"Hey, where's the fire?" she asked, studying Dana worriedly.

Dana paused and shook her head, unable to get the words past the knot in her throat. Kate followed the direction of her gaze.

"Oh, no," she said softly. "Not now, sweetie. You can't go out there now."

Gently she took Dana's arm and guided her into the house

and into a seat at the kitchen table. She set the flowers in the sink and poured Dana a cup of tea, adding lots of sugar.

"Drink this. It'll make you feel better."

Dana realized then that her teeth were chattering, not so much from the Arctic air outside, but from the deep chill within. She closed her eyes and sighed, as she swallowed the first warm sip. After several more swallows of the overly sweet liquid, she met Kate's gaze.

"I'm sorry. I don't know what came over me. All of a sudden I was frantic to clear away the dead flowers on Ken's grave. It looks so desolate out there."

"We'll do it tomorrow," Kate promised. "I'll help. We'll buy some fresh flowers, too. Or we can take the ones I brought today."

"They'll just wither and die."

"Then we'll get bright silk ones that will last until spring. That's only a couple of months away, you know. By April, there will be tulips and daffodils blooming all over the cemetery."

Dana smiled at the quick, determined responses. "You're a very good friend."

"And why wouldn't I be?" Kate demanded. "You saved me from financial ruin by getting that evidence against Peter. If it hadn't been for you, I'd be working at some fast-food place for minimum wage and struggling to support the girls. College for them would be out of the question. With luck and tenacity, maybe I'd even be a manager by now."

"Who are you trying to kid?" Dana teased. "You'd be running the whole darned chain by now."

"You always did have more faith in me than I had in myself. Speaking of faith, how did yours in those pictures turn out? Was Ted as over-the-moon about them as you were? Have you talked to him?"

"He called me five minutes after the courier put them on his desk. Rosa has a meeting with him tomorrow. Rick and Marco and I are taking her. She's so terrified and excited, she's sure she'll faint when she walks into his office and mess up the opportunity of a lifetime."

"How did her friends take the news that she was getting such an incredible break?"

Dana chuckled at the memory of the aftermath of Ted's phone call. "Let's just say that registration for my photography class has gone through the roof."

"Uh-oh," Kate said. "Doesn't that terrify you? What if lightning doesn't strike twice?"

"Rick's worried about the same thing. I told him and the kids that there are lots of things they can do besides modeling. Not all of them will be suited for it, anyway. I'm hoping I can use the class to get a fix on what they will be good at and steer them in the right direction. I'm not sure if I'm qualified to do career counseling, but I'm going to try."

"Rick must be pleased that you're fitting in so well," Kate said, her expression sly.

"Let's just say he's trying very hard not to say he told me so," Dana replied dryly. She glanced at Kate and thought she detected a new glimmer of excitement in her eyes. She suspected it had nothing to do with the kids at *Yo, Amigo.* "What's going on with you, by the way?"

"Actually, I have a date," Kate said. "That is, I do if it doesn't upset you."

"Why would it upset me for you to go on a date?"

"It's with Detective O'Flannery."

Dana tried not to stare in open-mouthed shock. Of course, she shouldn't be all that stunned. She had seen the sparks flying between the two herself. Even so, she felt somehow as if Kate were betraying her, shifting allegiance to the enemy.

"You are upset," Kate said at once, interpreting her silence as condemnation. "I was afraid of that. I'll call him and cancel."

"You will not," Dana insisted, trying to put her friend's feelings above her own. She owed Kate that after all she had done for her the last few weeks. When Kate seemed about to argue, she silenced her. "Besides, you can pump him for information about the investigation the police are supposedly conducting into this drug business."

Kate grinned. "Obviously he's a very smart cop. He told me you were going to say that."

"Did he also tell you whether he was prepared to lie through his teeth?"

"No. Actually, he said he intended to use the occasion to pump me for information about *our* investigation."

Dana stared. "What? Kate, tell me you didn't blab to him about what we were doing?"

"Of course not, but he's no fool. He figured it out. You dropped enough hints yourself over at the church the day we met him."

"Does he know about this afternoon?" she asked, just as the doorbell rang.

"Not from me, he doesn't," Kate assured her, as Dana headed for the living room.

"I hope you're right," Dana said. "I'd really rather not have the cops turning up in the middle of this little tea party of ours."

She opened the front door to admit Lawrence Tremayne and Gerrold Wald. As she greeted them, she noticed the others arriving in separate cars. While Kate took the coats the two men were wearing, led them inside, and offered them tea, Dana waited to greet the new arrivals.

"My dear, how are you?" Miriam Kelso asked. "I've thought of you so often the past few weeks."

"Thank you. I'm doing the best I can."

"And those darling boys of yours," a glamorous, middle-aged woman said, "how are they?"

Judging from the tautness of her skin, this had to be the very well-preserved Carolina Vincenzi, Dana concluded. "They're still with my parents in Florida," she replied. "We thought that would be best for the moment."

She led the newcomers in to join the others. "Please, allow

me to get you all some tea and you can help yourselves to scones and sandwiches, or whatever you'd like."

As the guests chatted in low voices suitable for an occasion in the home of the recently bereaved, Dana went into the kitchen, closed the door and drew in a deep breath. "Courage," she murmured, then plastered a smile on her face and rejoined the others.

When everyone was seated in the living room, she was about to speak, when Lawrence Tremayne cleared his throat and regarded her solemnly.

"Mrs. Miller . . ."

His sudden formality made her stomach clench. She had the distinct feeling she wasn't going to like what he was about to say. He was the kind of man who normally presumed to call every woman by her first name.

"Dana, please," she reminded him.

Color bloomed in his pasty cheeks. "Yes, of course. I know that you invited us here to discuss certain things, but there are a few things that I wanted to pass along to you, on behalf of the elders."

Dana glanced at Kate and saw that her gaze had narrowed suspiciously, as she watched the normally slick church leader try to impart some apparently unpleasant news.

"Of course, you first," she said with as much grace as she could manage, when she was overcome with a sense of impending doom.

"It has been several weeks now since . . ." He uncharacteristically fumbled for words. "Since your loss."

Dana remained silent and waited.

"We don't want to rush you into a decision about the future, of course." He looked to the others for support, but their expressions were carefully guarded. Most had their gazes cast toward the floor or ceiling. "Actually, it's about the house."

"The house," Dana repeated blankly, then realized exactly where he was heading. "This house." She swallowed back panic. Even though she'd known it was coming, it was too soon. They couldn't force her out, yet. She needed more time.

"You would like me to move, is that it?" she asked, her voice shaky.

Relief spread over his face. "Yes, that's it exactly."

"How soon?" she asked.

"As I said, we don't want to rush you. We haven't settled on a new minister yet, but we expect to have a decision soon. Of course, he will need a place to live."

"Of course," she agreed, then repeated, "How soon do you anticipate needing the house?"

He glanced at the others, but they continued to avoid his daze. "A few weeks, a month perhaps, if that wouldn't be too difficult for you to arrange. I know I had told you to take all the time you needed, but it's just not practical to let you stay indefinitely."

"Of course not. I can be out of here by the weekend, if that would help," she said, fighting an unreasonable fury.

Of course, this was the church's property. She had known that sooner or later she would have to leave it, had already begun making mental, if not practical, plans, but she hadn't expected it to be this soon. She hadn't expected this callous announcement in her own living room with others staring on in uncomfortable silence. She especially hadn't expected it coming from a man who had shown her such compassion right after Ken's death.

"Don't be silly," Miriam Kelso soothed, scowling at Lawrence Tremayne. "You take all the time you need. If the new minister arrives, we can certainly make arrangements to accommodate him, until you're able to make your plans. Your life has been disrupted enough without us adding to it."

"Thank you," Dana said, all too aware that Miriam Kelso's kindness wouldn't fare well against the grim determination she had seen on Lawrence Tremayne's face. She couldn't allow that to matter, though. She had to remain focused on the reason for this gathering. She had brought them all here to ferret out information, to get their uncensored reactions to the news that the matter of Ken's death was far from over. This discussion about her moving on was untimely, but irrelevant.

"I would like a little more time here," she said, injecting a dutiful note of gratitude into her voice. She deliberately glanced in the direction of the cemetery. She didn't have to feign the tears that formed in her eyes. "I'm not quite ready to move on and leave Ken behind."

In truth, she hadn't even considered that aspect when she had made the decision to bury him right here, rather than somewhere else. The church had offered the burial plot, and she had seized the offer, because it was one more detail she wouldn't have to attend to.

"Of course, you're not ready to make a move yet," Mrs. Kelso declared sympathetically. "We understand perfectly. It was all so sudden, so terribly tragic."

The others chimed in dutifully. Dana wondered if they'd heard yet about the latest phase of the investigation. Apparently not, since none of them brought it up. If they'd known about the drugs, they might very well have ordered her off the premises that very afternoon.

She managed a weak, placating smile. "I also would like all of you to know that I am doing everything I can to solve Ken's murder," she said, as if assuming the news would delight them. She watched their reactions very closely, as she added, "The police have essentially back-burnered the case, but I have not."

"I thought it was a drive-by shooting in that terrible neighborhood," Carolina Vincenzi said, sniffing as if she could smell the bad odor all the way out here in the suburbs.

"The police are inclined toward that theory," Dana admitted. "I'm not convinced. As many of you know, I was a licensed private investigator for some time before Ken and I married. I am conducting my own investigation."

The guests did gape at that, even Mrs. Kelso, who'd been doing her best, up until that moment, to be supportive of Dana.

"My dear, are you sure that's wise? Isn't it terribly distressing for you?" she asked.

"It's not only wise, it's necessary," Dana said firmly. "For one thing, the reputation of *Yo, Amigo* has been tarnished in a way that could lead to its downfall. Ken believed in that program . . ."

"Begging your pardon, Mrs. Miller, but your husband was a fool," Lawrence Tremayne declared so vehemently that everyone in the room gasped with dismay.

All except Dana. She rose to her feet and stood over him. Her voice quivering with barely suppressed rage, she said, "I will not allow you to slander a man who is no longer able to defend himself, and I certainly will not allow it here in his home."

"It's the church's home," Tremayne retorted tightly. "You would do well to remember that."

She stared at him in shock. It appeared the kid gloves had been removed. "Is that a threat?" she inquired. "May I remind you that you hold nothing over me. You've already told me that I'm being kicked out of here. My husband's insurance will see that my family is provided for. The church doesn't owe me one single dime of compensation. So what, exactly, are you threatening to do to me, Mr. Tremayne?"

Peter Drake interceded. "I think we should all settle down," he said in the soothing manner of a man used to dealing with warring factions. "Lawrence, mind your tongue. You always did have a tendency to run off at the mouth, without giving a thought to what was coming out."

"Lawrence was just saying what many of us thought," Carolina Vincenzi stated haughtily. "There were quite a few of us who thought Reverend Miller was crazy for defending those hooligans."

"He was defending young people who'd never been given a chance in life," Dana reminded her, aware that not so long ago she had shared Carolina Vincenzi's attitude. Her resentment had begun to fade, as she had started to put faces to the names Ken had mentioned so often. "Isn't that what Christian charity is supposed to be about? Or haven't you read a Bible lately?"

"Okay, okay," Kate said, giving Dana's shoulder a warning squeeze. "I think perhaps we've all let our tempers get in the way of good judgment this afternoon. Obviously, this is a very trying time for Dana. Perhaps, it would be best if you all leave and we postpone this conversation for another time."

"Not just yet," Tremayne said defiantly. He scowled at Dana. "I would like your assurance that the church will not be dragged into this so-called investigation of yours."

Dana met his gaze evenly. "The first rule of any investigation is not to rule anything out, Mr. Tremayne. I will follow whatever leads are necessary. If that brings me to the church's doorstep, then so be it."

"Surely you don't think anyone here had anything to do with your husband's death," Vincent Polanski asked in a shocked tone.

"It's not important what I think," Dana told him. "I will go wherever the evidence takes me."

"Then you'll be dead yourself within a month," Tremayne said with a certain amount of satisfaction.

Dana stared at him. "I beg your pardon?"

The others seemed equally startled by the blunt claim. "Lawrence, shut up!" Peter Drake warned in a tone so uncharacteristically fierce that everyone stared at him in shock.

"No, please," Dana said. "Let him finish what he began. Is that another threat, Mr. Tremayne?"

He flushed. "Of course not. I just meant that you'll be hanging around in that violent section of town, just as your husband did. You're bound to meet the same fate."

After the past hour, Dana wasn't so sure that the real nest of vipers wasn't right here in her living room.

Sixteen

Dana was still pacing the living room, ranting and raving at Kate about the gall of their recently departed guests, when the phone rang. She snatched up the receiver and snapped a greeting.

"Uh-oh," Rick said warily. "What has your drawers in a knot, *querida?*"

With his faintly accented voice, the question had a certain intriguing panache. "Sorry," she apologized. "It's been a lousy afternoon."

"What happened?"

She thought about what actually had happened and concluded that none of it was likely to seem so terrible to an outsider who wasn't living the nightmare. "Nothing, really."

"Tell that to someone who'll buy it. Try again, *querida.* The people from the church came to call, yes?"

"Oh, yes," she said, unable to keep a note of bitterness out of her voice.

"And? There were problems?"

"You might say that."

"Tell me," he said.

He spoke in a gentle, patient way that suggested whatever she described would be made better for the sharing. Dana wasn't convinced, but she told him anyway. "They kicked me out of the house."

"What?"

He sounded satisfyingly incredulous. Dana sighed. "They

have the right to do that. It is their house. And I was expecting it. Just not so soon."

"I'm coming out there," he announced, and hung up before she could argue that there was no point.

She slowly replaced the receiver in its cradle and turned to find Kate regarding her speculatively.

"Rick, I assume."

"How did you know?"

"Your color's better."

Dana scowled at her. "Oh, go suck an egg."

Kate burst out laughing. "Sweetie, you're going to have to do better than that, if you're going to be any match for those jerks who were here this afternoon."

"Believe me, that was just a warm up," Dana assured her, grinning. "I had a very tart tongue before I married a minister and decided I'd better learn to express myself more politely."

"Spending time with Rick Sanchez ought to help. He is charmingly rough around the edges, wouldn't you say?"

"Meaning?"

"There's an aura of barely leashed, street-tough danger about him," Kate said. "In other words, he's sexy as hell. I love it that he's rushing out here to your defense."

"Who said anything about him rushing out here?"

"Your expression gave it away," Kate explained cheerfully. "You looked very put out when he hung up on you."

"How did you know he'd hung up on me?"

"Nobody said goodbye," Kate replied.

Dana scowled at her. "You really do need to get an investigator's license. You're very good at this."

"It comes from having to be one step ahead of two secretive teenagers." She tilted her head to one side. "Now, what do you intend to do with him once he gets here?"

"I don't intend to do anything. I didn't ask him to come. He invited himself."

"So, you intend to toss him right back out on his ear?"

The prospect of that sight seemed to amuse Kate no end.

Dana was thrilled she could provide her friend with so much entertainment.

"No. That would be rude," she said stiffly. "You, on the other hand . . ." She allowed the threat to remain unspoken.

Kate chuckled. "I was thinking of going home anyway, but I've changed my mind. I think I'll hang around for a while."

"Suit yourself," Dana grumbled.

She really was getting tired of all the bossy, presumptuous people in her life. Rick topped the list, but Kate was a very close second. Not that she normally didn't count herself very lucky to have Kate around. Kate didn't bullshit her the way so many of the other women in the church did. Kate had apparently never bought the ridiculous idea that getting into heaven had anything whatsoever to do with tiptoeing on eggshells around the minister's wife. She viewed Dana as a human being in her own right, rather than one half of some sort of holy alliance.

None of that mattered at the moment, anyway. She was losing her focus on the investigation again. For several moments, she tried to concentrate, but everything that had happened remained in a muddle. She finally met her friend's still amused gaze. "Kate?"

"Yes?"

"Did we learn anything here this afternoon?"

"Sure," Kate said, sobering at once.

"Care to share your insights with me?"

"Lawrence Tremayne is a bully. Peter Drake, contrary to all appearances, is a born mediator. Carolina Vincenzi is a biased snob. Vincent Polanski would jump at his own shadow. And Gerrold Wald has been rendered speechless in their presence."

"What about Miriam Kelso?"

Kate's expression turned thoughtful. "She's the strangest one in the bunch. I know for a fact that she criticized Ken behind his back. In fact, she tried to stab him in the back and have him removed, but today, she was so warm and understanding, it made me want to throw up. With that kind of duplicity, she may well be the most dangerous one in the bunch."

"Who's dangerous?" Rick inquired, causing both Dana and Kate to jump.

"How did you get in here?" Dana demanded, as she tried to coax her heart back to its normal rhythm.

"You left the front door unlocked," he chided.

"And how would you know that? Didn't you even consider knocking first?"

He grinned unrepentently. "Given the dangers which you persist in ignoring, I was doing a very necessary security check."

"And your qualifications for that would be?"

"Concern," he replied.

He said it in a simple, straightforward way that sent goosebumps dancing along her spine. Dana swallowed hard and tried not to let him see how affected she was by that sincere declaration.

"Breaking and entering by any other name is still a crime," she pointed out.

He chuckled out loud at that. "You might do well to remember that yourself, *querida.*"

Dana winced at the reminder of her failed break-in attempt. "Sorry. I lost my head for a moment."

"Would you like some tea?" Kate asked him, obviously seeking to smooth over the awkward moment. "Or something to eat? We have scads of food left over. People seemed to lose their appetites this afternoon."

Dana tried to envision the very masculine man standing before her balancing a delicate tea cup and a plate of tiny sandwiches on his knee. She couldn't do it. "Maybe Rick would prefer a beer," she suggested.

His expression brightened. "A beer sounds great."

"I think there's a bag of tortilla chips around here somewhere," she added.

Kate scowled at her. "With all that good food left over? I don't think so. I'll get the beer. Rick, why don't you check out the sandwiches and desserts? There's a plate on the table. Dana never did get around to eating, either."

The last was clearly meant as a very broad hint. Rick took it. He held out a hand.

"Come, then," he urged. "We will all get something and sit in the kitchen, yes? I like the cozy atmosphere in there. A place like that is the heart of a family."

Dana wanted to resist, but her hand seemed to have a will of its own. It slipped into his much larger one and settled comfortably against the faintly calloused palm. He closed his fingers around hers and tugged her to her feet.

"We have been over this before. You have to eat," he chastised her. "You have to keep your strength up."

"You sound like my mother."

"A very wise woman, obviously."

Dana smiled ruefully. "She likes to think so." She regarded Rick curiously. "What about your mother? Is she very wise?"

"She was," he said quietly. "She died several years ago."

"I'm sorry," she said, instinctively squeezing his hand. "You miss her, don't you? I can hear it in your voice."

"Every day," he agreed. "I admired and respected her, even when we were most at odds. I'm not sure she knew that, though. It is my greatest regret."

The admission told her quite a lot about Rick, things she would never have expected from this man who'd once embraced gang violence as a way of life. It proved that even the strength and compassion of a caring parent might not be enough to counter the allure of the gangs. She had always assumed that only those who were unwanted or unloved or disenfranchised would turn to gangs for support and acceptance.

She started to ask Rick why he had chosen the path he had, but held back instead. Why wasn't important. It was because of the choices he'd made that he'd wound up creating *Yo,*

Amigo. That was all that mattered. She cared about him only in so far as he could shed light on Ken's death. Asking for intimate details about his life would only muddy the waters. It would make their relationship into something personal, when it needed to remain adversarial.

As it was, she was already all too aware of the effect of something as simple as having her hand clasped in his. She was drawn to the warmth he offered in ways that she found both confusing and very troubling. Sharing his secrets would only compound the effect.

Reacting to that rush of confusion, she suddenly withdrew her hand from his, using the pretext of gathering food to make the withdrawal seem less abrupt. The amused glint in his eyes told her that he knew exactly why she'd pulled away.

Settled in the kitchen, where, more and more, Rick seemed thoroughly at home and memories of Ken's presence were gradually fading, the three of them examined the afternoon's events and tried to make sense of them.

"Do you suppose this sudden notice of eviction has something to do with panic that you're going to stumble onto the truth about Ken's death?" Rick asked thoughtfully.

Dana shook her head at once. "They informed me they wanted me to go, before I ever said a word about the investigation."

"What about Mrs. Fallon?" Kate asked. "She might have said something about you being in Ken's office. They could have leapt to the conclusion that you were snooping for clues."

"I doubt it. There was nothing odd about my being in his office to gather his personal items. The only thing odd was the police tossing the place."

"Maybe they heard about that," Rick suggested.

"If they had, they never mentioned it. Besides, I think Mrs. Fallon would go to great lengths to protect Ken. I'll bet she has the office spotless again already, and she'll never say a word about the drugs they found in there. The church officials won't know, unless the police question them."

"I agree," Kate said. "But I do have to wonder at the timing of today's little bombshell, especially after Tremayne himself had made a point of telling you a few weeks ago to take your time. I agree with Rick that this turnaround came out of the blue. I think somebody wants you gone before you discover the truth, somebody powerful enough to make Tremayne change his tune."

"What truth?" Dana demanded impatiently. "That underneath that smooth facade, Lawrence Tremayne is a pompous ass? Who would dare to try to push him around? He'd make mincemeat of anyone who tried."

"He shut up when Peter Drake told him to, didn't he?"

"That's true," Dana conceded thoughtfully.

"Tell me about Tremayne," Rick insisted. "That name sounds familiar."

Kate listed all of the man's personal and professional accomplishments, as gleaned from the newspaper files. Dana added her own insights from seeing his work on behalf of the church.

"A model citizen," Rick concluded.

"Until he slipped and told me Ken was a fool and that I was likely to wind up dead," Dana said.

"He threatened you?"

"I'd say it was more like a generous warning that I was treading on thin ice."

"How charitable," Rick said with sarcasm.

"Indeed," Kate agreed.

"Yet he would toss three children out of the only home they have ever known," Rick said with derision. "Already I do not like this man."

"That's two of us," Kate said vehemently.

"Three," Dana added.

"Let me see what I can find out about him tomorrow," Rick offered, his expression thoughtful. "Maybe there are some skeletons hidden in the closet we ought to know about."

Dana had the feeling he already knew exactly where he

intended to look, which once more aroused the suspicion that Rick was keeping something from her. It was pointless to ask him, though. Maybe she should give some thought to tapping his phone and shadowing him.

"Anybody else strike you as especially suspicious?" Rick asked, bringing her attention back to the moment.

"Oddly enough, Miriam Kelso," Dana said, drawing a startled glance from Kate.

"Why?" Kate asked. "I know I said she was behaving strangely, but suspicious? That's a little extreme."

"Not really," Dana disagreed. "We both know she was being insincere and two-faced the whole time she was here. I have to wonder why she bothered?"

"Maybe she was just playing good cop to Tremayne's bad cop," Kate suggested.

"Maybe, but my gut tells me she was overcompensating for something else."

"Maybe she just felt guilty for being such a thorn in Ken's side," Kate said. "She might have wanted him booted out, but she probably didn't want him dead."

"She wanted him out because of the gang issue?" Rick asked.

"No, general principle," Dana told him. "She found fault with every minister the church ever had. That's just the way she is. We heard about her from the last pastor, before we ever got here."

"What about this Drake character?" Rick asked, then. "You said he ordered Tremayne to shut up and that Tremayne listened, right?"

"Actually, that was a bit of a shock," Dana said. "I've always thought of him as such a mousy little man. I couldn't believe it when he snapped at Lawrence Tremayne like that."

"What I couldn't believe was that Tremayne actually shut up," Kate said.

"Maybe Drake has something on him," Rick suggested.

"Oh, please," Dana protested. "We're getting carried away.

Kate, you know Peter Drake. Can you envision him virtually blackmailing anyone, much less Lawrence Tremayne?"

"Not before today, I couldn't. Now?" She shrugged. "I'm not so sure."

"That's three people we should check out more thoroughly," Rick said. "And the others?"

"Polanski and Wald said almost nothing. Carolina said nothing today that she hasn't said a million times in public, according to Kate. I may not be crazy about her viewpoint, but I don't think there are any deep dark secrets there," Dana conceded.

Rick glanced at Kate. "Do you agree?"

"Pretty much."

"That doesn't sound very wholehearted," he said, seizing on the hint of doubt that Dana had also detected. "What's troubling you?"

"Vincent Polanski's reaction to the news that Dana was investigating," Kate said slowly, as if she were still formulating the thought. "Didn't you notice, Dana? He was the only one here who seemed genuinely distressed that you were going to be looking in our own backyard, rather than in Chicago. The minute he spoke up, I had the feeling that he was the one with something to hide"

"Gut instinct?" Dana asked dryly.

"As a matter of fact, yes," Kate retorted defensively.

Dana grinned at her. "Then I guess we'd better pay attention. These days your gut seems to be more reliable than mine."

"That's because you're not feeding anything to yours," Rick pointed out, gesturing toward the untouched food on her plate. "Eat."

"Maybe you ought to whip up a batch of burritos for her," Kate said innocently. "I understand she eats well enough when she's with you at that place called Tico's."

Rick regarded Dana speculatively. "That's true. Perhaps I should call and have him send an order out here. In fact, I am sure he would be delighted to bring it personally. He finds you enchanting." The last was said with an intriguing hint of irritability.

"That's ridiculous," Dana objected, focusing on the plan to have Tico come all the way from Chicago to bring Mexican food and leaving the hint of jealousy in Rick's voice for another time. "There's enough food here already to feed an army."

"But perhaps you have discovered that Mexican food feeds the soul, as well as the body," Rick suggested.

"I've never heard anybody rhapsodize over tacos before," Dana said.

"Then I should have taped your comments the first time we walked into Tico's," he taunted. "Even the aroma sent you into raptures."

Dana laughed, despite herself. "Okay, okay, he does make delicious food, but that doesn't mean I have to live on a steady diet of it." She deliberately picked up a little sandwich and popped it into her mouth. It tasted like so much sawdust. She made a face.

"Perhaps what it needs is a few jalapenos," Rick suggested.

"It was tuna," she protested.

"You could tell that?"

"Okay, so it was a little bland. My tastebuds have just been deadened by all those peppers you've been feeding me the last few days."

"I know of a way to bring them alive again," he said, regarding her mouth so intently that heat climbed into her cheeks.

Kate bounced up. "Well, on that provocative note, I guess it's time for me to go. See you tomorrow, Dana. Nice to see you again, Rick."

"Kate?" Dana stared after her departing friend with a sense of desperation. Kate never even slowed.

"She has quite a sense of timing, wouldn't you agree?" Rick asked, a smile on his lips.

"Oh, yeah. It's lousy," she retorted.

"Not from where I'm sitting."

"Rick, I think you ought to go, too. It's late and you have to drive back to the city."

"Kicking me out? After I came all this way to prevent the same thing from happening to you."

The reminder of what had brought him dashing out here tonight made her sigh. "You can't stop me from being tossed out of this house."

"Maybe not indefinitely, but I'll bet I can slow the process down."

She chuckled. "Do you always jump at the chance to tackle any old challenge?"

"Only those that matter," he assured her.

His gaze locked with hers in a way that left her trembling. Apparently satisfied that he'd rattled her, he stood. "Come. Walk me to the door."

Her knees felt weak as she stood, but she walked with him, fighting a ridiculous sense of disappointment that he'd taken her at her word. She did want him to go, didn't she? Of course, she did. He was just an irritant that had to be tolerated for the moment. No more.

At the door, he paused and looked into her eyes. She thought she detected a hint of uncertainty in his, just as he shook his head. "Ah, *querida,*" he whispered. "What have you done to me?"

Dana swallowed. All of a sudden she was having a very difficult time remembering that she hated this man. "I don't understand."

He framed her face with his hands. His thumbs skimmed lightly across her cheeks, leaving fire in their wake. Just when her breath caught in her throat, just when she was all but certain that his mouth was descending to claim hers, he brushed a soft and tender kiss across her forehead and released her with a sigh.

"*Buenos noches, querida.* Sleep well."

He was gone before she could gather her composure. As he disappeared into the darkness, she whispered, "Good night," and wondered why she suddenly felt bereft all over again.

Seventeen

It was barely dawn when Dana's phone rang. She answered groggily.

"You were sleeping, *señora*. I am so sorry," a soft voice said.

"Rosa?"

"Si, it is Rosa. I did not mean to wake you."

Dana grinned at the barely contained excitement in the teen's voice. "Today's the big day and you're nervous, right?"

"How do you say . . . petrified? These people, do you think they will like me?"

"Of course," Dana reassured her. "You already have Ted Hanson in your corner, and he is a very important man."

"Are you sure it is okay to wear what I wore in the pictures? Maybe I should find something else nicer. My Sunday dresses no longer fit, but perhaps Mama would lend me the money to buy something."

"It's not necessary. If I thought it were, I would take you shopping myself." She paused, thinking of the endless stretch of hours between now and their appointment at the ad agency. If they would be empty for her, they would be excruciatingly slow for Rosa. Maybe shopping wasn't such a bad idea. It would take her mind off the stalled investigation into Ken's murder for a while, too. Sometimes a distraction allowed the head to sort through the facts and put them into some new order.

"Rosa, let's do it. Let's go find something special for you to wear."

"Oh, no," she objected with feeling. "I could not take a gift from you. You have already done so much."

"No arguments. It would be my pleasure. Think of it as my very small contribution to your future," she said, then added briskly, "I'll pick you up at ten at the center."

Rosa hesitated. "You will drive here alone?" she asked worriedly.

"Of course."

"But I do not think that is such a good idea," she protested. "It can be very dangerous here for you. Rick would not be happy if I let you do that."

Rick was not king of the world, not her world anyway. "It's not his decision or yours," Dana said testily. "I'll be fine. Ten o'clock, Rosa. I'll pick you up in the alley by Rick's parking place."

After she'd hung up, Dana concluded that this was the best thing that could have happened. She needed to prove once and for all that she could operate independently of Rick's influence. Perhaps people who wouldn't open up in his presence would admit things to her, if they saw that she wasn't afraid to be in the neighborhood alone. This was not a time to turn into some sort of timid soul. She was intrepid. At least, she always had been before. She just had to hone that side of her nature again.

Of course, she might get her fool head shot off, she conceded. Still, she felt more optimistic than she had in weeks. She felt in charge again. It was a great feeling.

Despite the traffic, she found the drive into the city exhilarating. The air was frigid, but the sky was a brilliant blue, and the sun sparkled on Lake Michigan.

The closer she came to the barrio, the greater her sense of anticipation. Some of that was on Rosa's behalf. More of it was on her own. She would prove to Rick, once and for all, that she was capable of handling herself, even in this dangerous and somewhat alien environment.

Why she felt she had to prove anything to him was beyond her. She didn't care what Rick Sanchez thought of her. He was simply a means to an end. Even as she thought that, though, she sighed. It was getting more and more difficult to convince herself of that with each day that passed. There was an undeniable connection between them, and it seemed to be growing stronger every minute.

Still, she was in a cheerful frame of mind, as she cut through the narrow, crowded streets of the barrio. In the daytime, they were alive with activity. It was hard to feel any sense of the danger that darkened the same streets at nightfall.

As she made the turn into the alley behind *Yo, Amigo,* she saw a large shadow detach itself from the wall. A faint chill of apprehension washed over her, ruining her earlier mood. The test of her newfound determination was coming a little sooner than she'd hoped.

Even so, she forced herself to drive forward. She refused to let anyone intimidate her within a few yards of her destination. She could always scream bloody murder at this point and someone from *Yo, Amigo* was bound to come running to her rescue.

Just in case, her right hand folded around the grip of the gun she'd brought along. Registered and totally legal, she'd owned it since her investigating days, but it had been years since she'd had it out of her safety deposit box. She'd picked it up this morning on her way into Chicago. How fortuitous, she decided, as the shadow ahead began to take the shape of a tall, broad-shouldered man.

She was so intent on him that she never even saw the second man slip up beside the driver's-side door. When it was wrenched open, she gasped with shock and instinctively swerved the car to the right.

The man muttered an oath, but his grip on the door never loosened. Dana was about to hit the accelerator, when a hand stretched across and yanked the keys from the ignition, stopping the car in its tracks.

She whirled in the seat, gun in hand. The barrel was pointed directly at the intruder's midsection.

"Holy Mother of God, point that thing some other way."

At the sound of the voice, she glanced up, straight into Rick's furious face.

"You," she said, shocked and furious herself. "I ought to put a bullet through you, just to teach you a lesson about scaring a person to death."

"Let's just call it even," he suggested dryly.

"Was there a point to your little exercise here?" she inquired.

"I was hoping to show that you were no match for the neighborhood."

"So far, the only times I've been threatened and assaulted here, it's been by you," she reminded him. "I'd say you're the real danger to me."

"You bet, *querida,*" he said in a way that didn't sound half so much like the endearment it usually was.

He wrapped a hand around the back of her neck and dragged her half out of the car, then delivered a bruising, punishing kiss that both infuriated and alarmed her. Why alarmed? Because she enjoyed it far too much. She thrilled to the overwhelming passion behind it. Her mouth stung. Her blood roared. And she hated herself for it, hated feeling so alive, hated that another man could make her feel that way.

Still, she couldn't resist. The gun slipped from her grasp, as she reached up to touch Rick's cheek. When it did, he released her and seized it before she could blink.

"Never let your guard down with the enemy," he reminded her softly, as he unloaded the bullets from the gun, then stuck it in the waistband of his jeans.

"That kiss didn't feel as if it were between enemies," she said, more shaken than she wanted to admit.

"Sex can be as potent a weapon as guns. You would do well to remember that."

An awful lot of people had been handing out free advice to her lately, and she found it damned irritating. Backing away, she sank back behind the wheel and gestured up the alley, where there was no longer any sign of the man who'd distracted her.

"Who was your decoy?" she asked.

"Marco," he admitted readily enough. "He told me of the plans you had with Rosa. We decided you should be made aware of the risk you were taking."

"What a pair of sports!" she said derisively. "Are you coming along on our shopping expedition to protect us from the sales clerks?"

"Though I would like nothing more than to spend the day watching you choose the clothes you will put next to your body, I'm afraid I have work to do here. Marco will accompany you. I will join you later, in time for the meeting at the advertising agency."

"I would hate to disrupt your day. If you're busy, you could skip that, too."

His lips quirked at her testiness. "And miss out on Rosa's big moment? Never. I would not disappoint her that way. Nor would I let you down."

"How sweet!"

"Stick around, *querida*. You will discover there are many sides to me, before we are through."

"And not all of them attractive," she retorted.

He grinned. "But the others compensate, yes?"

Dana wouldn't have answered that if an armed mob had demanded it. The man was already entirely too smug as it was. And she was not prepared to give him a totally honest answer. She couldn't even give one to herself.

Rick's stomach still clenched when he remembered the sight of that gun being aimed so steadily at his gut. Dana had surprised him and, though he would have died before admitting it to her, she had delighted him. She was clearly very brave, even if far too impetuous for her own good.

He was not sure yet which of them had learned the more valuable lesson in that alley. He knew, without a doubt, that he could no longer underestimate her. She . . . well, who knew what she had taken away from the experience. Perhaps an awareness of just how powerful the chemistry was between them.

He would have loved to take the time to pursue the raw emotions unleashed by that kiss he had initiated, but he'd promised Tico he would stop by the restaurant before it opened. He'd said it was urgent and too risky to be discussed on the phone, when anyone might pick up an extension, either at *Yo, Amigo* or in his own kitchen.

Maybe this was the break they'd been looking for, Rick thought, as he walked the few blocks to the small restaurant. Perhaps Tico had found the link they'd sought to some nefarious Chicago politician.

He slipped in the back door, just so he could inhale the aroma of meat cooking with cumin and other spices. He snatched a jalapeno from a huge bowl as he passed and bit into it, as he winked at Tico's mother who was overseeing the lunch preparations.

"Out," she shouted at him, shooing him toward the door. "You pay, like everyone else." She was laughing, though, as she said it.

"Te amo, Mamacita," he called back. He paused to give her a smacking kiss on the cheek. Other than his own mother, there was no one he adored more than this woman with the greying hair and aristocratic features, which had been softened by age, but blessed with wisdom.

"When are you going to marry me?" he asked.

"You want my cooking, not me," she retorted.

"Not so. Tico cooks as well as you, and I do not wish to marry him."

She laughed. "Out of here with your foolishness. Tico is

waiting for you. He is very anxious." Her expression sobered. "There is no trouble for Tico, is there, Rick?"

"No trouble. I promise."

"Muy bien. Vaya. Go. You are in my way."

Rick found Tico in his office, surrounded by mounds of paperwork. He was on the phone, arguing with a supplier in rapidly escalating Spanish. Rick almost pitied the person on the receiving end of the tirade. It sounded as though he were very close to losing Tico's very lucrative business.

"Give the man a break," he mouthed to his friend.

Tico slammed down the phone, with nothing apparently resolved. "A break? He is my cousin, and he is trying to cheat me and you would have me give him a break? I should cut off his *cahones.*"

Rick winced. "That ought to improve family relations no end. When your mood improves slightly, perhaps you would like to tell me why you had me rush over here. In the meantime, I will remain very quiet. I would prefer not to endanger my own manhood by crossing you."

Tico sighed and slugged back a tiny cup of the thick, sweet Cuban coffee he preferred. The man must live with a perpetual caffeine buzz, Rick concluded, watching him try to get a grip on his temper.

Finally, Tico smiled. His shoulders relaxed visibly. "It has been a bad morning. I'm sorry."

"Thanks, but I'm not the one who deserves an apology. In the interest of family harmony, perhaps you should be saying that to your cousin."

"I will," Tico promised, then grinned. "Eventually. In the meantime, he deserves to sweat."

"Now, since your mood seems to be improving, tell me," Rick said. "What have you found out? I assume this has something to do with Ken's murder.

The younger man nodded. "Someone came to me yesterday. He said he had heard that I was interested in information on the *padre's* death. He wanted money, so at first I wasn't sure whether he was desperate or trustworthy. In the end, we came to terms."

"Did he have information?"

Tico shrugged. "You will have to decide that for yourself. He says that a thug named Carlos Hernandez was involved."

The name meant nothing to Rick. He looked at Tico. "Do you know him?"

"I know of him. He runs a gang of sorts, though it is closer to a ring of criminals, if you ask me. They are for hire to do a variety of jobs that are not exactly legal. They stay away from drugs, but they are very adept at everything else, from arson to murder."

Rick considered the information. Was it possible that someone had hired this Carlos to hit Ken? But why, dammit? Why would anyone want to see Ken dead? He thought of the drugs that he didn't doubt for a minute had been planted in Ken's office. Was there a link there?

"You say this Carlos has nothing to do with drug trafficking, but would he be above planting drugs to turn someone into a suspect?"

"He will shoot a man in cold blood," Tico said dryly. "I doubt he would blink at the thought of framing someone. Why? Did someone try to pin a drug charge on Ken, as well?"

"Looks that way," Rick admitted. "Where can I find this Carlos?"

"I figured you would want to see him, so I asked my contact if he could arrange a meeting. Carlos will be dropping by for a beer around four this afternoon. The restaurant will be quiet then. You will not be interrupted."

Four? Damn, he was supposed to meet Dana at the ad agency at four for Rosa's big meeting. In the meantime, with the two of them chasing from boutique to boutique, he had no way to get in touch with her to let her know that there'd been a change in plans. And he had just promised her that he always meant what he said.

Still, there wasn't a doubt in his mind that she would want

him to meet with Carlos, if it would offer them any information at all about what had happened to Ken.

"I'll be here," he told Tico. "But this guy better have something for me, because I'm canceling a very important engagement for this."

"With the lovely *señora?*"

Rick nodded.

"You are treading on dangerous turf with that one, *mi amigo.*"

Tico wasn't telling him anything he hadn't already thought a thousand times. "Tell me about it," Rick said with an air of resignation.

"It happens that way sometimes," Tico observed wryly. "All you can do, then, is hang on for the ride."

Based on the ups and downs so far, Rick was pretty certain it was going to be a roller coaster.

Eighteen

"He said he would be here and he will be," Marco insisted, as Dana muttered under her breath about Rick's failure to appear at the ad agency at four o'clock.

"I'm delighted you have such faith in him," she retorted, "but it's after four now. Where is he?"

"Caught up in traffic," Rosa suggested distractedly as she peered at her faint reflection in the glass covering a huge poster of one of the agency's hottest current print campaigns. "Are you certain I do not look like a blimp in this dress?"

Though she wanted to rail against broken promises, Dana forced herself to concentrate on the nervous young woman. "You look like a beautiful woman who is carrying a baby."

Rather than being reassured, Rosa sighed. "I do look like a blimp."

"I promise you your figure will come back right after the baby is born," Dana told her.

"Maybe we should make this appointment for then," Rosa said worriedly. "No one will hire me looking like this."

"A maternity clothes manufacturer would," a male voice interrupted with quiet authority.

Dana glanced into the opened doorway and saw Ted Hanson grinning at her. He was an extraordinarily sophisticated man with an eye for beauty and a genius for selling, but he looked like anything but that.

His prematurely grey hair was curly. Blue eyes twinkled mischievously behind wire-framed glasses. When he wasn't making major presentations to stuffy corporate officials, he dressed as he had today—in jeans and chambray shirts over colorful T-shirts. Today's shade was purple. Not mauve or eggplant, but brilliant purple.

He crossed the room in three strides to scoop Dana up into an exuberant bear hug.

"I'm so sorry about Ken," he told her again, his eyes reflecting a genuine sorrow. "When I heard about it, I was just sick. I apologize again for not getting back for the funeral. I was on a photo shoot in Italy. It just wasn't possible."

"I got the flowers and the note. That was more than enough."

He examined her face intently. "You're doing okay?"

She flushed under the knowing scrutiny. "Well enough," she said. "Come, let me introduce you to two friends. Marco, this is Ted Hanson." She put an arm around Rosa's ample waist. "And this is Rosa."

Ted's practiced gaze swept over the teenager, assessing her with an instinct he'd been honing for the past twenty years. "You're perfect," he said. "Every bit as lovely as the pictures Dana sent over. Let's go inside. I'll show you around and then we can talk about your future."

Looking more than a little awestruck by Ted's whirlwind approach, Rosa followed in his wake down a wide corridor covered with thick mauve carpeting. They passed an astonishing array of award-winning print ads immortalized in giant posters that had been lit with a touch many museums would envy.

Marco glanced at Dana as they walked, his brown eyes reflecting his own barely concealed awe. His usual arrogance and distrustfulness were nowhere in evidence. "He is very good, isn't he?" he asked, gesturing toward the posters.

"The best." She glanced sideways at him. "You should consider talking to him in your own behalf, as long as we're here," she suggested casually.

"No," Marco said fiercely. "This is my sister's day. She should have his undivided attention."

Dana appreciated the sentiment, but was almost certain she heard a little wistfulness behind the words. "We'll see," she said.

Fighting her fury at Rick's failure to join them, she forced herself to concentrate on the upcoming meeting. It was mostly up to her to protect Rosa's interests, though she didn't doubt for a minute that Ted would be fair, if only as a favor to her. They had known each other a very long time, ever since she had successfully investigated the leaks of some of his presentation plans to a competing agency. She had caught the insider who was betraying him within two weeks, preventing the loss of yet another major account.

Ted's bouncing energy and enthusiasm were catching, as he took them on the promised tour, showing them the art department, the copywriters, the small studio where some television spots were actually shot, even an animation department, which so captivated Marco that Dana wasn't certain they'd ever get him away from the room. Watching the work going on there, his usual sullen expression vanished, and his eyes lit with an eagerness she found charming. Then and there she resolved to encourage that unanticipated excitement. For the first time, she truly realized the seductiveness of helping someone to discover a new future. No wonder Ken had gone back to *Yo, Amigo* again and again.

In Ted's office, the talk turned to jobs and fees and all of the mundane contractual details that Rosa really needed an agent or attorney to oversee.

"If she agrees to any of this today, it will have to be on the condition that a lawyer goes through every word and has the opportunity to challenge any aspect of the deal," Dana said.

"Agreed," Ted said at once. He turned to Rosa. "So, young lady, what do you say? Would you like to come to work for us on an exclusive basis, for say three years?"

"One," Dana corrected. "With options."

Ted scowled. "Two, he countered. "We discovered her. We deserve time to make sure our investment pays off."

Dana grinned at him. "Okay, two," she conceded grudgingly. She had expected him to ask for five in an attempt to tie up a potentially hot commodity for the longest time possible. That he'd been more than fair proved her faith in him had been justified.

"Marco, what do you think?" Rosa asked, her eyes flashing with excitement.

He regarded her with an indulgent smile. "Mama and Papa will go ballistic, but I think you should do it, if it will make you happy and will secure a future for you and the baby."

Rosa jumped up and threw her arms around her brother, her expression relieved. "Thank you."

Dana knew by now that Rosa would have defied him if she'd had to, but today's thrill was even greater, because Marco had joined in with his approval.

Ted looked jubilant. "Then we have a deal?"

"Looks like we do," Dana said.

As if he'd read her mind, Ted turned to Marco. "Now what about you, young man? You have the same excellent bone structure and interesting look as your sister. Can we sign you up today, as well?"

Even though Dana had told him the same thing, Marco looked stunned at hearing it from a professional for whom he'd already expressed admiration. "Me?" He glanced at Dana, clearly bemused that she had been right about his own potential. "Is it possible?"

Dana nodded at him encouragingly. "You should at least think about it, Marco. It's a golden opportunity." She slid in a suggestion she hoped would prove too alluring for him to resist. "Perhaps, you could even convince Ted to let you train in animation techniques at the same time."

"I could do this?" Marco asked, gazing at the agency president with obvious disbelief. There was no mistaking the hint of eagerness in his expression, though.

Ted picked up on Dana's less-than-subtle hint at once. "Absolutely. We could work it into the deal."

"I was not so good at school," Marco confessed. "I have no college."

"This would be on-the-job training," Ted reassured him. "I've found that it's always easier to learn something that fascinates you. I can't tell you the times I barely scraped by in math and science classes."

"You?" Marco asked, shocked. "But you are a very successful man."

"I could show you the report cards," Ted assured him. "My mother waves them under my nose whenever she thinks I'm getting too big for my britches. It keeps me humble, she says. Think about my offer, Marco."

Marco's shoulders squared proudly. "I do not have to think, *señor*. I would be proud to accept this opportunity. I hope that I will not give you cause to regret it."

"I'm sure you won't. I look forward to working with both of you," Ted said, coming out from behind his desk to shake Marco's hand. Rosa jumped up and gave him an impulsive hug, then squeezed Dana hard as well.

"You have changed our lives, *señora.*"

"No," Dana insisted. "I have just given you a helping hand. Return the favor someday to someone else."

"That is what the *padre* always said," Rosa said, her expression suddenly sad. "I wish he could know about this."

"He does," Dana said with confidence, thinking it more than likely he had guided her into the lives of these two promising young people. "I am certain that wherever he is, he knows and he is very proud of both of you."

Rick would be proud, too, for that matter. Maybe she would tell him . . . right before she strangled him.

Rick sat in the most secluded booth Tico's had to offer and kept his gaze fixed on the door. Even though the restaurant was virtually empty, except for a handful of men sipping *cafe*

Cubano at the counter, he wanted privacy, should anyone else come in while he was talking to Carlos.

He repeatedly glanced at his watch, noting when four o'clock came and went. Dana was going to have his head for abandoning them with no notice, especially if this Carlos person never showed and he had no news to report to her.

It was four-fifteen by the time an obviously nervous young man entered the restaurant. His gaze darted from table to table, assessing the risks, Rick imagined. When Tico broke away from a conversation behind the counter, Rick knew that the new arrival was Carlos. Tico gestured toward the booth, and the man swaggered down the narrow aisle and slid in opposite him.

His face was pock-marked and a line of tattoos ran up his forearm, but otherwise he was unremarkable. With his olive complexion, black hair, and dark eyes, he was interchangeable with half of the twenty-five-year-olds on the streets of the barrio. Even his dress was moderately conservative—chinos and a T-shirt worn under a leather jacket.

"You are Carlos?" Rick asked.

"Sí."

"I'm Rick Sanchez."

"I recognize you."

"Tico tells me you might know something about a matter that is of great importance to me, the murder of a friend of mine."

Carlos shrugged. "I might. Tell me about this person."

"He was a minister from the suburbs. He became a friend to all of us at *Yo, Amigo*. He helped many of the young people here. He was a good man, Carlos, a decent man. He didn't deserve to die. The police believe he was a victim of random violence, a drive-by shooting that went awry."

Carlos gestured dismissively. "The police are idiots. It is easier to blame chance, than to admit they do not control these streets."

"Have they questioned you?"

A smirking grin played about the other man's lips. "I am very careful. They do not even know I exist. I prefer to keep it that way."

Rick wondered about that. In his experience, the police frequently knew—or at least suspected—far more than they were able to act on. He had been surprised to discover just how much they knew about the inside workings of his own gang, once he had eventually broken free of its ties.

"What have you heard about this shooting?" he asked, careful not to imply that Carlos had any direct responsibility for it.

Carlos studied him intently, as if sizing him up and analyzing the dangers he might represent. "You say this man was good, but he had at least one enemy," he said eventually. "Someone was willing to pay a lot of money to see that he died."

"How much money?"

"Fifty thousand."

Rick had to work to cover his astonishment. He had anticipated some penny ante crime, a quick hit for enough money to buy another supply of crack. Fifty thousand dollars was big business. How the hell had Ken Miller made such a deadly serious enemy?

"Who, Carlos? Who was behind this?"

"I cannot answer that."

Rick's last thread of patience snapped. He reached across the table and grabbed a fistful of the other man's shirt. "Who, dammit?"

Carlos's eyes darkened dangerously, as he broke Rick's grip. His fingers dug into Rick's flesh painfully in a duel for supremacy.

"You will never do such a thing again, *comprende?*" he demanded in a tight voice.

For the moment, because it was prudent, Rick backed off. "Sorry. My friend is dead. I'm sure you can see how I might overreact. Tell me everything you know. I will keep you out of it. You and I . . ." He shrugged. "If anyone asks, we have never met."

"That is very wise, but I am afraid I have no other answers for you. I never saw this person who paid so much for your friend's death. I heard only a voice on the phone. The money was where I was told it would be. Anonymity protects everyone when you conduct business as I do. I am sure you can see that."

Every fiber of Rick's being wanted to grab this slime by the throat and squeeze the information out of him, but he knew it would be of no use. Carlos had told him as much as he would, perhaps even as much as he could.

He knew far more than he had a half-hour ago. He knew that Ken had had a powerful enemy, someone who had intended that he die that night. Carlos had confirmed once and for all that Ken's murder had not been an accident, a case of mistaken identity.

And if those drugs that had been planted in Ken's office were any indication, the danger hadn't died with him. It was still very much alive, and that meant that Dana could very well become the next victim.

Nineteen

It was dark by the time Dana arrived home, but a full moon created eerie shadows on the snow-covered ground. The unsettling atmosphere suited her mood perfectly. Her emotions were all over the place. She was ecstatic for Rosa and Marco one minute and furious with Rick the next, then despondent when she thought of what Ken had missed today, of all that he would miss in the future.

The first was understandable. The two young people were getting the chance of a lifetime, and she knew in her heart that they would make the most of it. She felt a deep sense of satisfaction that she had played some small role in changing their lives.

She could almost feel Ken beside her, reminding her that good deeds built character and made the world a better place. It was almost as if by helping Rosa and Marco, she had given a gift to Ken as well—an admission that withholding her support from his work at *Yo, Amigo* had been wrong. Her understanding of his commitment had deepened, and her love for him had never been stronger.

And yet . . .

She sighed. And yet there was Rick Sanchez, infuriating her one minute, making her feel alive the next. His failure to show up—more importantly, his failure to keep his promise—had been both disappointing and unnerving. She shouldn't be counting on him so much. He shouldn't even be capable of disappointing her. A few days ago, he had been a despised stranger. Now . . .

Again, she sighed. Now, he mattered in some way she couldn't define, didn't want to define. She feared that to do so would prove her to be disloyal to Ken.

Still feeling that vague stirring of guilt, she put the key into the lock. Then, before she could turn the key, her gaze was drawn toward the cemetery beyond the house. A stronger wave of guilt sent her in that direction. It was an overwhelming, weighty sense of guilt that led her directly to Ken's grave. She desperately needed to connect somehow to the man she had adored, to remind herself of the eternal promise of love that had bound them.

With shaking fingers, she reached out and touched the cold marble tombstone—an open-armed, welcoming angel—that a stone mason in the congregation had worked lovingly, day and night, to be ready for the funeral. She traced the smooth surface, remembering, as she skimmed each indentation, the words that had been carved there: *Here lies an angel of God, a man of faith. Beloved husband. Beloved father.*

The dates below spanned a too-brief lifetime, less than forty years. That saddened her more than anything. The world needed men like Ken, men who put others first and themselves second, men who taught compassion and understanding, men who lived by their words.

She glanced toward the bright, starlit sky and asked again, for the thousandth time, "Why?" It was a plea for understanding, a ritual incantation by now.

No answer came, though, no illumination that could make sense of the incomprehensible. There was just this terrible sense of loss, an ending that had no meaning.

She knelt in the snow, oblivious to the dampness soaking through her slacks, oblivious to the howling wind blowing off the nearby lake. Frantic now, she dug the withered flowers from beneath the snow and tossed them aside. In a motion as old as time, she smoothed the snowy surface as she would the blanket on a child's bed. Tears tracked down her cheeks, freezing in the icy air. Her skin burned with the cold. Her fingers went numb.

"Why, dammit? Why?" she cried, pummeling the ground, the tombstone.

She waited and waited, but only the cry of the wind answered, not God. Never God.

Dimly, she became aware of a muttered curse, then the warmth of arms surrounding her, of soothing words and the whisper of breath against her cheek.

"It's okay," Rick murmured. "Everything is going to be okay."

She felt herself being lifted, held against a solid chest. Instinctively, she snuggled into the heat and clung, as she was carried quickly back to the house.

"Keys?"

She struggled to remember. "In the door," she finally admitted, teeth chattering.

Inside, she was deposited in Ken's chair. The afghan was wrapped around her, the fire lit, and still she shivered.

"Don't move," he ordered.

As if she could, she thought, almost numb with the cold. Only when he returned did he turn on the light, as he handed her a mug of steaming coffee. It had been laced with brandy, she realized as she gulped the fiery liquid and felt the heat shimmer through her.

"More," he insisted.

She drank again and the feeling slowly began to come back. First in fingers and toes, then deeper inside, bringing with it an agonizing pain that no amount of heat could salve.

She finally dared to meet Rick's gaze and was stunned by the anger blazing in his eyes. There was so much fury there, fury and something else. Fear, she concluded with some surprise.

She reached out and touched a finger to his cheek. "It's okay. I'm okay."

He shuddered, but the fear didn't disappear, as she'd intended. "What were you thinking?" he demanded. "You could have died out there."

"It was just a few minutes," she argued.

"It's nearly midnight."

"Midnight?" It couldn't be. She had gotten home hours ago.

"I've been looking for you everywhere. Your car was in the driveway, but you weren't answering the doorbell. Thank heaven I never opened the storm door and spotted the keys, or I really would have gone nuts. You scared the hell out of me, as it was. I've talked to Kate. She's the one who suggested I look in the cemetery. She's frantic, too. I tried to stop her, but she's on her way over."

"Sorry," Dana whispered, teeth chattering. "I had to tend to the grave."

He stared at her incredulously. "In the middle of the goddamned night? If I hadn't found you, you'd have been dead by morning. Are you out of your mind?"

Maybe she was, Dana thought. She thought she had reached rock-bottom the day they buried Ken, but maybe she hadn't. Maybe this was it, this not caring if she lived or died.

Rick watched her intently. "I won't let you do it, you know."

"Do what?" she asked shakily.

"Kill yourself. You're going to live, dammit. And we're going to find the person who killed Ken, and we're going to go on, both of us."

"I wasn't trying to kill myself," she said, shocked by the suggestion. She might not care if she lived or died, but she would do nothing to hasten the process, not with three sons counting on her. She would find some way to be whole again, for their sake, if not her own.

"Well, you could have fooled me," he said, still furious. "If I have to move in here and stay with you twenty-four hours a day, you will live, Dana Miller, because that's what Ken would want."

As suddenly as the tirade had begun, it ended, and he dragged her into his arms. "It's what I want, *querida*," he said softly.

Surprised by the admission, Dana pulled back gently and looked into his eyes. "You?"

"Yes, God help me."

He didn't sound pleased about it, she concluded, somehow amused that this tough, streetwise man had finally come up against something he couldn't control, namely his feelings for her. It gave them something in common. Gazing into his eyes, she admitted finally and only to herself, that she had no more control over her own growing feelings for him.

Since she couldn't—wouldn't—confess as much to him, she settled for going on the attack instead. "Where were you today? You promised to meet us at the agency. You let Rosa down."

"I let you down, too," he pointed out, clearly grasping the real source of her irritation. "When you hear where I was, I think you'll forgive me."

She wouldn't be persuaded so easily. "Don't count on it," she muttered.

He shrugged. "If you don't want to hear . . ." he taunted.

She scowled at the teasing. "Of course, I want to hear. Tell me."

He examined her intently. "Are you sure you're feeling up to it?"

"I'm well enough to flatten that attractive nose of yours, if you don't start talking."

He grinned. "In that case—"

Before he could begin, the doorbell rang and Kate came rushing inside. She tossed her coat over a chair, revealing a mismatched outfit of sweatpants and T-shirt, proof that she'd been in a hurry. Not until she had examined Dana from head to toe and concluded that no permanent damage had been done, did they get back to Rick's news.

He described his meeting with the mysterious Carlos. Dana

gaped when he told her how much had been paid for the hit on Ken.

"So much," Kate breathed. "We're talking serious money here."

"Which means that we've stumbled into a genuine hornet's nest," Dana concluded, her excitement for the hunt returning. At last there was progress, a hint, if not proof, that Ken's death had been calculated.

"But Carlos has no idea who this person was?" she asked.

"None, or so he claims," Rick said.

"Do you believe him?"

"He's probably telling the truth. Anyone with enough cash to pay for an execution isn't going to want anything to connect him to it. There won't be a paper trail, probably not even phone records. Whoever delivered the payoff is probably so far removed that even he can't identify the person ordering the hit."

"Do you think we're talking drugs?" Kate asked. "Or some kind of criminal organization?"

"Drugs would be my guess," Rick said. "Especially in light of the so-called evidence planted in Ken's office."

"I don't think so," Dana said slowly, her expression thoughtful. "It's too pat, too obvious. Somebody wanted to muddy the waters by destroying Ken's reputation. My guess is it's somebody with something else to hide."

"Such as?" Kate asked.

Dana sighed. She was too exhausted to take the next leap in logic. "I wish I knew," she said wearily.

"So, what's the plan for tomorrow?" Kate asked, putting her coat back on.

Dana glanced at Rick. "I think it's time we began to take a closer look at the people right here, starting with Lawrence Tremayne," she said, knowing that her words were bound to make him happy.

To his credit, he didn't gloat. He merely nodded his agreement. "I'd like to talk to him," he suggested. "I have a few things I'd like to say about his plan to boot you out of this house."

"Maybe not," Dana said, even though she rather enjoyed this fierce, protective streak he'd developed. "This conversation requires finesse, not blazing guns."

"I don't even own a gun," Rick protested.

"It was a figure of speech," Dana told him.

Kate regarded them both with amusement. "I'll let you two wrestle with the semantics and the details. I need my beauty sleep. See you in the morning, sweetie." She glanced pointedly at Rick. "You, too?"

"Go," Dana instructed before Rick could reply. "It's already after two. Try to sleep past six, for a change."

"Sorry. My internal alarm clock can't be re-set," Kate said. "But I will call before I come dashing over here." She winked. "Just in case."

When she had gone, Dana looked at Rick. "You can leave, too."

"No way, *querida*. Not tonight. You go up to bed. I will sleep right here on the sofa."

The proposal raised an interesting quandary, though obviously not the one Rick assumed, judging by the determined glint in his eyes. Eventually she shook her head.

"It won't work."

"What won't?" The jut of his jaw suggested he was ready to battle with her, if necessary. "If you knew how many nights I've slept on a far worse sofa at *Yo, Amigo*, you wouldn't worry about this."

"It's not that."

His expression puzzled, he waited.

Dana drew in a deep breath. "I haven't slept upstairs since Ken died. I've been sleeping right here."

"In the chair?" he asked incredulously.

She nodded.

"Oh, baby," he whispered and scooped her up.

Once more, she nestled against him, not even questioning

what he intended. He crossed the room in three strides and started up the steps.

"Which room?" he asked at the top of the stairs.

Dana couldn't bring herself to answer, wasn't sure she could bring herself to cross that threshold, even with Rick's strong arms around her. *Especially* with Rick's arms around her.

Ignoring her silence, he simply peeked in room after room, until at last he reached the cramped master bedroom with its awful gold carpeting. He paused in the doorway and gazed into her eyes.

"Okay?"

"I can't," she whispered. "We can't. Not here."

"Sssh. Nothing's going to happen. I'll just stay here with you until you fall asleep. You need to do this, *querida.* You need to move on."

"I'll be moving out soon. I'll buy a new bed, something with a frilly canopy that Ken would never have set foot in. Then it won't even matter."

"It will," he said with certainty. "I think you must face the fact that Ken is gone, that he won't ever be back to share the most intimate part of your life."

She understood the symbolism, the need to let go, to accept, but she wanted to protest that it was still too soon, the wound was still too raw. She could never sleep here, not with the place beside her cold and empty.

But of course, it wouldn't be. Not if she understood what Rick was proposing, that he lay down beside her, perhaps even hold her, until sleep claimed her.

No matter how innocent the offer, though, she couldn't accept it. It would be sacrilege to allow another man into Ken's bed, especially a man she wanted as desperately as she wanted Rick Sanchez tonight. She couldn't allow him to displace Ken's memory here, of all places.

"No, please," she protested again. "We can't do this.

There's a guest room next door. I'll sleep there." She smiled wryly. "At least I'm up the stairs. It's a start."

Rick's gaze locked with hers and, for a moment, she thought for sure that he would argue, but finally his expression softened, and he carried her to the nearby room.

The decor was spartan, a simple double bed with a beige chenille spread, a small oak dresser with an antique pitcher filled with dried flowers on top.

Rick gently lowered her to her feet, then reached past her to pull down the spread.

"Can I get you a nightgown?" he asked. "A glass of water? Anything?"

Looking directly into his eyes, she shook her head and reached slowly and deliberately for the buttons of her blouse. His gaze locked on her shaking fingers as first one button, then a second and a third came undone. The dawning awareness of what she intended had his breath catching. She stared at him in mute appeal and waited. Eventually he swallowed hard, as he pushed aside her hands to finish the task.

When his knuckles skimmed over bare skin, Dana's heart leapt into her throat. She was caught halfway between panic and excitement, but the brush of his fingertips across her silky bra had her nipples tightening and the blood roaring through her veins as it hadn't in too, too long a time. The thrill of feeling alive again, of feeling whole, overwhelmed her.

She didn't hesitate to weigh right or wrong. She simply gave herself over to sensation, the shimmering heat, the wild ricocheting of her pulse.

She refused to allow herself comparisons as Rick's hands danced across her flesh, inciting passion. There was joy in his touch, a promised ecstasy that came with each quick, deliberate caress.

Clothes magically disappeared right along with inhibitions. There was a surprisingly easy familiarity between them and none of the edginess of first-time lovers.

He made love with every part of his body, with the shifting

of a leg, the stroke of his palm, the lingering touch of his lips. And everywhere he left fire and a wicked yearning in his wake.

Dana's soft pleas counterpointed his harsher moans as they joined, retreated, then came together again in a tantalizing ritual. She blocked out memories and grief, everything but this exquisite present and the man who was making love to her with such life-affirming tenderness and passion.

It was his name she cried out when release came, his name that echoed in her head as sleep finally stole over her.

But tonight, of all nights, it was her husband's face that slipped into her dreams and made her cry.

Twenty

Rick stood in Dana's kitchen, coffee mug in hand, and stared out the window at the destruction she had managed to wreak the night before on her husband's grave. Wilted, frozen flowers were strewn in every direction. The once-glistening blanket of snow was littered with clumps of dirt and brown petals. Tears welled up in his eyes, as he thought of his friend buried deep within that cold earth.

"Ah, *amigo,* she is going to hate me this morning," he murmured ruefully. "And you? How would you feel if you knew?"

He wanted to believe that his friend would understand, that he would give them his blessing to go on living, but he wondered if Ken wasn't a man first and a saint second. Could any man forgive so easily what had happened between his wife and another man so soon after his death?

And yet, Rick couldn't regret the night before any more than he could stop mourning the loss of his friend. Dana touched something deep inside him, a part of him that he'd thought incapable of feeling. She was fiercely proud, defiantly strong, and yet there was a vulnerability in her, a neediness that reached out to him. He wanted to protect her, even though he knew she would never thank him for it. It was enough to do it because he had to—for himself and for Ken.

He was more troubled than he had dared to admit by what Carlos had told him. As badly as he had wanted to protect *Yo, Amigo,* as desperate as he'd been to believe that no one in the barrio was responsible for Ken's death, he wondered if that wouldn't have been preferable to this callous, unknown villain.

What kind of person paid fifty thousand dollars for the murder of a minister? Someone who was beyond desperation, someone with something evil to hide, something dangerous to protect. And how would such a person react to the discovery that Dana was more determined than ever to ferret out the truth?

He didn't have to think long and hard about the latter. He'd had waking nightmares about it until dawn. Most frustrating was knowing there was nothing he could say that would dissuade her from continuing the search. Pleas, demands, all would fall on deaf ears. She felt she owed answers to her children and to her husband. After spending last night in his arms, he guessed that her fervor would only be magnified. It was an understandable sentiment, but a risky one.

Something of what he felt must have shown on his face. When Dana walked into the kitchen dressed in jeans and a T-shirt, she regarded him warily, far more warily than a woman should a recent lover.

Unless, of course, she was filled with regrets. He gazed into her eyes only to have her look hurriedly away. Despite his anticipation of the reaction, it hurt just the same. Putting his coffee on the table, he reached out and touched a finger to her chin, forcing her to turn toward him.

"Don't," he said, more harshly than he'd intended.

Her gaze met his, then skittered nervously away. "Don't what?" she asked.

"Pretend that nothing happened. Pretend that it didn't matter."

She kept her gaze steady, then. "It didn't," she said vehemently. "It was a—"

"No," he protested, cutting her off. He didn't want to hear that it was a mistake, even though he'd mentally prepared himself for her saying exactly that.

She wouldn't let it drop. "I was feeling lost and alone last night, that's all. I needed to feel alive."

He regarded her knowingly. "And you did, did you not, *querida?* You felt very much alive in my arms."

She closed her eyes, as if to block out the truth, but Rick knew that she couldn't deny it. Neither of them could. What had happened in that bed last night had been more than just sex. A bond had been formed. Where it would lead, he had no idea, but it was as strong as any he'd ever felt.

Few people in his life had really mattered to him—his mother, Tico, Ken, and now Dana. He would have given his life for any of them. Instead, two were lost to him forever. He was left to honor their memories and to go on.

"There will be time enough to figure out what it all means," he promised her. "Just don't deny that it was important. Don't lie to either of us that way."

She glanced toward the window, then back at him. "How can you?"

"How can I what?" he demanded. "Stand here in my best friend's kitchen, talking to his wife about making love to her? How can I live with the fact that I'm alive and he's dead? How can I look you in the face, knowing that despite last night, despite everything that has happened between us, you still hold me responsible for his death?"

She started to protest, but he cut her off again. "No, if you're being totally honest, you know that you still blame me simply because of where he was when he was killed. It doesn't really matter who pulled the trigger, does it?"

"Of course it does. That's what this whole investigation is all about."

"Really?" he asked doubtfully. "Or is it about punishing me for living, while your husband is dead?"

"This isn't about you, you egotistical jerk," she said with quiet rage. "None of it is about you. It's about justice."

"Justice?" he asked softly. "Or vengeance?"

She hesitated just long enough to prove his point.

"Leave that to God, *querida*."

"I don't believe in God," she insisted. "Not anymore."

Shocked by the response, he said, "You dishonor your husband's memory when you say that."

She slapped him then, her hand connecting with his cheek with such unexpected force that it snapped his head back. His skin smarted, but no more than his pride. She had taken him by surprise a second time, something no one had done since his teens, something no woman had ever done.

When she would have slapped him again, he grabbed her wrist and held it, his gaze locked with hers.

"Once I can forgive," he said. "Not twice."

Her eyes filled with tears. She would have turned away, but his grip on her arm held her in place.

"This is wrong," she murmured.

"What?" he asked, his voice turning gentle at her evident distress.

"That I want you so badly."

He tugged gently until she came into his loose embrace. "No, *querida*. It is not wrong. It is life. You and I are alive. We cannot be blamed for that. Ken would not blame us for that. He, more than most, understood the cycles, the need for the living to hold onto each other and move on. How many times have you heard him counsel others to let go of their grief and live?"

She sighed, acknowledging the truth of his claim, and relaxed against him. Her arms crept around his waist. He could feel her tears on his bare chest and wondered if she knew that his own cheeks were damp with tears that were part sorrow, part relief.

They would survive, the two of them, because they had to. They would go on. Perhaps together, perhaps not. He had never gazed into the future before, because he hadn't dared. Now, with Dana in his arms and his heart pounding in his chest, he wished he could see what lay ahead.

Unfortunately, the only image that came readily to mind

was trouble, spelled out in neon and flashing with savage intensity.

As if to confirm his prescience, the phone rang, shattering the momentary calm between them. With lifted brow, Dana informed him it was Maria, as she handed him the receiver. He vowed to strangle the woman when he got back to *Yo, Amigo.* Dana signaled that she would be back and left the room.

"Yes?" he said.

"Sorry to interrupt," Maria said, sounding more amused than apologetic.

"I'll bet. What is it?"

"You'd better get down here right away."

Rick sighed. "Another break-in?"

"Si."

"What did they take this time?"

"It's impossible to tell. The place has been turned, how do you say, turvy-topsy?"

"Close enough," he said. "I'll be there as soon as I can. Don't touch anything in the meantime."

"But it is a terrible mess," she protested. "I cannot leave it this way."

"You can until I see it," he told her. "Don't call the police yet, either."

"You know they would take forever to come, anyway," she said wryly. "We are not a priority, unless they wish to hustle someone here."

Rick grinned. "Hassle," he corrected.

"Whatever." She paused. "By the way, how is the *padre's* wife this morning?"

"Mrs. Miller is just fine, thank you."

"She did not sound pleased to hear from me. I interrupted something? The two of you are playing toesie?"

He didn't point out that it was footsie, because he didn't want to belabor the direction of her thoughts. "You are entirely too nosy, Maria," he said, instead. "I will be very glad when you go off to college."

"You say that now, but I know better," she said confidently. "You would be buried under paperwork in a week and cursing the day I left. That is why I must come back every day."

She was probably right, unfortunately. Rick would have died before telling her that, though. She was entirely too sure of herself, as it was.

"I'll be in soon. If you're tempted to clean something, run home and help your mother."

"My job is here. I will be waiting for you."

When he'd hung up, he glanced up to see that Dana had returned. She was watching him curiously.

"Problems?"

"A break-in at the center."

"At least this time you know I had nothing to do with it."

He grinned. "That is some consolation, yes."

"You didn't sound especially surprised when Maria told you. How come? Has it happened before?"

He saw no point in keeping the past problems from her. "A few times."

"Is that why you were there the night I broke in?"

He nodded, without adding that this latest invasion did not appear to have followed the pattern. Earlier thieves had taken whatever valuables they could find. Although it was possible that this one had ransacked the place because there was nothing of value left to steal, he suspected that wasn't the case. This one, he believed, had been looking for something less obvious than computers or VCRs.

"I'd better get back into town. Will you come with me? The sign-up sheet for your class has gotten very long, thanks to your success with Rosa and Marco, and that was even before they heard about the deals that were struck yesterday. Everyone is eager to see you."

"Tomorrow," she promised. "Today I want to see what I

can dig up on Lawrence Tremayne. He's the only person I can think of who might be able to come up with fifty thousand dollars for a hit."

"You will take Kate with you?"

She shook her head. "No, this is something I have to do alone." She smiled. "Don't look so worried. I investigated dozens of cases without the people having any idea whatsoever that I was digging around in their lives."

"You'll pardon me if I only recall that I caught you red-handed trying to sneak into *Yo, Amigo*."

"I was in a rush to do something. I was careless," she conceded. "It won't happen again."

He framed her face with his hands. "See that it doesn't," he said softly. "Before each step you take, think of your sons. Think of me. We are all counting on you remaining in one piece."

She made a face at him. "Gee, thanks. With that in mind, I won't dare to take any risks at all."

"That's the general idea." He pressed a quick kiss against her lips. He wanted to linger for more, but didn't dare. One thing would lead to another and the day would pass. It would be a far more pleasant alternative than his current plan for the morning, but he knew in his gut that they would not find peace in each other's arms until Ken's murderer was behind bars and the past could be well and truly put behind them.

"I will call you later," he promised.

She gave a little shrug of indifference that suggested she would not be counting on his keeping that promise any more than he had kept the one he'd made the day before. Her lack of faith, though well-deserved, stung.

He forced a smile. "You'll see, *querida*. I am a man of my word."

"Whatever," she said, her voice laced with disbelief.

He saw then what he should have seen sooner. As important as that meeting with Carlos had been, he had paid a heavy price for choosing that over keeping the commitment he had made to Dana. In time, she might forgive him. Trust would not come so readily.

Twenty-one

Dana didn't realize how tense she had been all morning, until Rick finally left and she felt her breath ease out of her in a deep, heartfelt sigh. The cramped muscles in her shoulders relaxed as well. The burning sensation in the pit of her stomach slowly disappeared.

Ironically, she couldn't place the blame for the tension on him. She was the one who'd been tied up in knots, trying to resist throwing herself straight back into his arms. She had awakened in torment, as images of her wanton behavior the night before came back to her.

Rationally, she knew it was not possible to betray a dead man, but in her heart, she felt she had. She might tell herself again and again that even the marriage vows said only "until death do us part," but she had always believed they were meant to last through eternity.

Surely they should at least last beyond the first-year anniversary of her husband's death. What she had done was unforgivable. Ken had been gone less than two months and already she had been with another man. Far worse, it had been a man who had played at least some small role in her husband's death, even if she was coming to admit that the role was only indirect.

If she were ready to be totally honest, she'd have to admit, though, that it had been good. More than good. She had been more uninhibited with Rick in some ways, than she had been with her own husband. Maybe that had to do with timing and desperation, or a million-and-one other things, but she couldn't help wondering if it meant she had always held back subtly with Ken, simply because of who he was . . . a minister. If that were true, she could come to hate herself for cheating them both that way. Or was it simply that each experience in life, each person, paved the way for the experiences and people to come?

What kind of a woman was she? The question tormented her.

Rick would have said she was merely human. Ken, she thought with a rueful smile, would have said the same. He had been exceedingly non-judgmental about human frailties. There had been no fire and brimstone sermons about dire consequences spoken from his pulpit. He had preached compassion and love. His God was a kinder, gentler one than the one she'd been brought up to believe in. As a child, she had sometimes quaked at the images of hell her pastor had managed to evoke on Sunday mornings.

So, where had Ken's God been when someone had pulled a gun and aimed for Ken's chest? she wondered angrily for the thousandth time. What was the purpose of the test He had designed for those left behind? What was the morality lesson when evil triumphed over good?

As ever, no answers came to her. She forced herself to push aside the questions and concentrate on those she could answer. Reaching for the pad of paper she kept by the phone, she began jotting down the background information she wanted on Lawrence Tremayne before she faced him again and confronted him with her suspicions.

She was determined to conduct the remainder of this investigation slowly and methodically. Up until now, the impulsive decisions she had made had skirted disaster by a very narrow margin. No more. From vast experience, she knew what needed to be done and how to do it, so that it would hold up in court. It was time she started acting like the trained detective she was, rather than a grieving widow.

Lawrence Tremayne owned a large company with its own office tower in downtown Chicago. She had no idea what sort of business it was or what its holdings were, and it was about time she found out.

She would start with a broker, who had handled investments for her after she had sold off her investigating company and put the money into a joint account with Ken for the future of their children. If Tremayne Industries was traded on any of the stock exchanges, Jean Bragg would know it. Dana picked up the phone and called her.

She waited impatiently through the expected expressions of sympathy and gave terse replies to Jean's questions about the boys. Apparently, her abrupt answers alerted the other woman that this wasn't a social call.

"Okay, Dana, what can I do for you?" she asked, her tone changing to brisk formality. "Are you worried about the status of your investments? I can assure you that everything is in order in both your names with right of survivorship. There will be no problems getting access to anything, if you need to liquidate. I'm sure things must be unsettled for you financially now."

"Thanks, Jean. I'm not worried about that. Ken had insurance and I have some savings. We're set, until I can get back into my old business. Actually, I called for some information."

"Sure. If I have it, it's yours."

"What do you know about Tremayne Industries?"

The broker's hesitation was barely perceptible. "Why? You aren't thinking of moving some of your money into it, are you? I can tell you right now, you have far better stock in your portfolio already."

Jean's worried reaction set off alarm bells. "Then it wouldn't be a good investment?" Dana probed cautiously, trying not to arouse suspicion with her questions. It would be far better if the broker merely thought she was checking out a prospective addition to her stocks.

Again, there was the slightest hesitation before Jean said,

"It's a local company, as you probably know. It's had some rapid growth in the past. Long-range, maybe it's still a good investment."

She paused, as if she weren't sure how to proceed. "Okay," she said finally. "Here's the deal. I don't like to bad-mouth a local company, but in the short-term, I'd say Tremayne Industries is very risky."

"Why?"

"Tremayne has had some bad luck with a few of its properties lately. A couple of huge development deals fell through in Latin America."

Dana seized on the last. "Tremayne does business in Latin America? Why?"

"Growth. Opportunity. At least, I'm sure that's what he anticipated."

"But it was a bad call?"

"So it seems."

"But how can that be? By all accounts, he's a savvy businessman."

"I honestly don't know. All I've heard is that he's heavily in debt, because these deals went sour. You know I like to support local firms. There's plenty of information readily available. I know the people firsthand. Some of these companies are on the cutting edge, which I find very exciting. But the bottom line is I'd think very seriously before putting a dime into Tremayne Industries right now."

Dana decided she had all of the information she was likely to get without giving away her real interest in the company. "Thanks, Jean. I'll give it some more thought."

"Call if you need anything else. I'll give you the best advice I can."

"I know you will," Dana said. "Thanks, again."

As she slowly replaced the receiver, she pondered what she'd discovered. Lawrence Tremayne's business was in trouble, maybe not in dire straits, but trouble enough that a cautious broker was recommending against investing in it.

What was the significance of the fact that the trouble had begun with a Latin American connection? Was that and the fact that Ken had been shot in a heavily Latino neighborhood pure coincidence? Dana didn't believe much in coincidences.

She also knew there was a danger in leaping to conclusions. Fortunately, the ringing of the doorbell kept her from doing just that.

She opened the door to find Detective Dillon O'Flannery on her porch. His expression—never especially cheerful in her brief experience with him—was very grim. He looked as if he'd rather be almost anyplace else on earth.

"What?" she demanded, her heart thudding dully, as she considered what his presence meant.

"I'm sorry. I really am," he began.

She reached out and clutched the door for support. What had happened? One of the boys? Her parents? What? Images from that night just over a month ago flooded back. Two policemen had stood on her doorstep, then, their expressions every bit as tormented as O'Flannery's was now.

"Just tell me," she whispered, fighting panic.

He held out a piece of paper. Startled, she simply stared at it. She recognized what it was at once, but she couldn't quite believe it.

"It's a search warrant," he explained, confirming her guess.

"A search warrant?" She almost laughed, giddy with relief that no one else she loved was dead. Then, as the implications sank in, she stared at him. "Why?"

"Probable cause to search for more drugs."

"I don't believe this." Her temper rose. "How dare you? My husband was not dealing drugs. He abhorred drugs."

"We found evidence of drugs in his church office," O'Flannery reminded her, his voice oddly gentle. "Look, I know this is upsetting, but why not let us in and get this over with."

"No," she said, standing squarely in his path. "Who's behind this?"

"It was the next logical place to look, after what we turned up at the church."

"Logical?" Her voice climbed. "There is nothing logical about any of this. Someone is campaigning to destroy my husband's reputation and I want to know who. More anonymous sources?" she suggested derisively.

Because it was inevitable anyway, she moved aside and gestured expansively. "Go on. Search to your heart's content. You'll be wasting time and taxpayer dollars. You won't find a damn thing."

He turned then and gestured to the uniformed officers waiting behind him, men she'd been too blinded by fury to even notice before.

With O'Flannery on her heels, she returned to the kitchen and sank down onto a chair. He refilled her cup with coffee, rinsed out the mug Rick had left on the counter, and poured another for himself. He sat down opposite her.

"I'm not taking any pleasure in this," he said eventually.

"I'm thrilled by your sensitivity," she said bitterly. "Tell me, did Kate know you were coming over here this morning? Does that explain why she hasn't shown up yet?"

He winced a little at that. "No. Obviously, I couldn't say a word to anyone until we had the warrant in hand."

"I'm sure she'll be impressed with your dedication to duty. I'll pass along the word."

Blue eyes locked on hers. "Let me do the explaining, okay? Your spin might be just a little biased."

Dana studied his expression. "Don't tell me she actually matters to you. I thought perhaps she was just a source you planned to pump for information about the evil, drug-dealing pastor."

"She's a nice woman," he said simply. "I don't run across too many of those in my line of work."

"Yes, she is nice," Dana agreed. "Too nice to get mixed up with the likes of you."

He looked offended. "Hey, I'm one of the good guys, remember?"

"I suppose that depends on where you're sitting, doesn't it? From where I sit, your white hat is decidedly dirt-streaked."

He shrugged. "I guess it is a matter of perspective. I'd still like to have a chance to get to know Kate better. That won't be possible, if you condemn me in her eyes. She cares too much about your feelings. She's already made that plain. I suppose that puts me at your mercy. It's a damned awkward position, one I'd rather not be in, to tell you the truth."

He actually did sound vaguely unsettled by the power she held over him. Dana sighed. Maybe Dillon O'Flannery was a decent guy. Maybe it was just circumstances that were no fault of his own that put them on opposite sides, for the moment. She could be reasonable enough to concede that Kate had the right to make up her own mind about him.

"I won't interfere," she said at last, drawing a relieved smile. "But you upset her and I will personally rip your heart out."

"I'll consider myself forewarned," he said, just as one of his men came to the door and gestured for him.

"What?" Dana demanded, when the detective would have walked off with his colleague.

O'Flannery met her gaze evenly, then nodded to the other man. "It's okay. What have you found?"

"Two very small packages of what appears to be cocaine."

Dana stared, open-mouthed. "No," she protested. "That's not possible. Where?"

"In a small room at the end of the hall upstairs. It was taped behind the dresser."

In the guest room? Dana thought wildly. Where she had spent last night in Rick's arms? Where no one else had been in weeks?

There was no way in hell that her husband had brought cocaine into their home, any more than he had taken it into his office at the church. She would have staked her life on that.

But if Ken hadn't brought the drugs into the house, then who had? The most obvious answer, the one she didn't like one bit better than the one the police were coming up with, was Rick.

Had he used the opportunity she had so eagerly given him the night before to plant more evidence against her husband? If not Rick, if not last night, why the guest room? Who else had had recent access to it?

"Mrs. Miller?"

She blinked and stared at Dillon O'Flannery.

"Has anyone else been in that room lately?"

She thought of the two people who had spent last night discovering passion in that very room. "No," she said slowly. "No one."

She told herself that the lie wasn't meant to protect Rick. If he were guilty, he didn't deserve protection. The lie was only meant to buy time, until she could look him in the eyes and make the accusation herself.

And if she didn't like what she read there, she would strangle him with her bare hands. *Then* the police could have at him with her enthusiastic blessing.

ner they were about and free wander[illegible]. Even
later, she soaked him. Some wanted [illegible] over the eyes when
suddenly [illegible]

Rick wasn't [illegible] it. "Your [illegible] he's staring?"
[illegible] to it warned [illegible].

"[illegible]" she said [illegible]. "[illegible] won't stare for
now.

Twenty-two

Maria's neatly arranged stacks of files had been strewn from one end of *Yo, Amigo's* offices to the other. Rick surveyed the mess and patted the distraught young woman on the shoulder. It had taken her months to get everything organized. The prospect of doing it all over again clearly daunted her.

"It's okay. I'll get some of the others in here to help you straighten everything out," he promised, more irritated than worried about the ransacking, now that he'd seen it. It didn't look like the work of a professional who was out to discover some specific, incriminating piece of paper. It looked more like kids up to mischief.

"What about the police?" Maria asked indignantly, clearly ready to condemn the perpetrator to prison for life.

Rick shook his head. "Not for this. It will only bring us to their attention. We don't need any more unfavorable publicity downtown. I'll get the word out that we don't appreciate this. That ought to prevent a repeat."

"How will you spread the word?" she asked suspiciously. "Will you talk to Tico?"

Something in her voice caught his attention. She had sounded almost derisive. He studied her intently. "That's what I was thinking of doing. Is that a problem?"

She shrugged. "Not to me. It is your choice, as always."

Her attitude spoke far more loudly than her words. "Maria, what is it between you and Tico?"

She looked slightly flustered at having been caught sounding disparaging about a man she knew was his friend. "Nothing," she declared, though she wouldn't meet his gaze when she said it.

Rick wasn't buying it. "What nothing? It's something. I can hear it. Have you two argued?"

"Never," she said dismissively. "I would not waste my time."

"Has he done something?"

"Nothing," she insisted.

"If you don't tell me, I'll ask him."

"He will only lie," she said. "Leave it alone. I should not have said anything."

"Believe me, Maria, you have said nothing, at least nothing that made any sense."

He shook his head. Women! He would never figure them out. Perhaps his friend could make sense of the mystery. It had been days since he and Tico had played basketball one-on-one. He resolved to invite him over tonight after the restaurant closed. He would grill him until Tico shed some light on this animosity Rick had detected in Maria's voice.

"If you do not need me, I will begin cleaning," Maria said stiffly.

"Fine. If you discover that something's missing, let me know."

"Why? You will do nothing about it, except perhaps talk to Tico."

She said it with a reappearance of that same subtle disdain. This time, however, it was directed at him. Rick stared as she left his office and deliberately allowed the door to slam behind her.

"Now what the hell was that all about?" he muttered.

He was still pondering that when the door whipped open and hit the wall behind it. Dana came in, fury radiating from her in waves he could feel across the room.

"Hi," he said cautiously. "I didn't expect to see you again this morning." He decided not to mention his displeasure over the fact that she had obviously gone against his frequently expressed wishes and made the trip to *Yo, Amigo* alone.

"I didn't expect to be here," she said. "Then I had a visit from Detective O'Flannery."

Rick stood up. He would have rounded his desk to comfort her, but a warning look stopped him in his tracks. "Okay," he said slowly. "What did the detective want?"

"He had a search warrant to look for more drugs. Imagine my shock when he found more cocaine."

He stared at her. "You're kidding? In the house?"

"In the damned guest room," she said, visibly shaking with rage. "Taped to the back of the dresser. Now, how do you suppose it got there?"

"I have no idea," he said, then stared at her in shock, as her meaning sank in. "You think *I* put it there? Is that what you're telling me?"

Her gaze never wavered. "I think it's awfully damned suspicious that you were in that room just last night and now the police have found drugs in there."

"You were in there, too," he pointed out quietly. "You've had ongoing access to that room with no one around to observe your actions, while I was there only with you. You also had access to Ken's office at the church. I did not."

She stared at him in visible horror, as he turned the tables on her. "You believe that I . . . that I could have planted those drugs?" she demanded.

"It is a more reasonable assumption than the one you're making," he said, forcing himself not to shout.

She shivered violently, then covered her face with trembling hands. "Oh, God, I'm sorry. The whole damn world is going crazy. *I'm* going crazy. I didn't want to believe you could do something so despicable, but nothing else makes any sense."

Rick crossed the room in three quick strides and put his hands on her shoulders. He was relieved when she did not pull away. "Are you sure now that it was not me? Do you trust me at least that much?" he asked gently.

She lifted a tormented gaze to meet his. "I want to believe that."

He sighed at the doubts still apparent in her voice. "But you can't be sure."

"Can you blame me?" she asked angrily. "The timing . . ." She let her voice trail off.

"The timing sucks. I'll admit that. But I swear to you, Dana, I had nothing to do with those drugs. You know what the policy is around here. I instituted it. I enforce it. Where would I even get the drugs to plant them?"

"I imagine that would be easy enough," she said, gesturing toward the window. "You could confiscate them from half a dozen kids right outside the door, more than likely."

Rick couldn't deny that, as much as he wanted to. In fact, she sounded so rational even he began to doubt himself. "But why?" he asked. "Why would I do that?"

"I don't know. I've been thinking about that ever since I left the house, and I just don't know." She stared at him bleakly. "Did you hate Ken for some reason? Was last night part of some revenge, too?"

"Never!" he practically shouted, then tried to calm down.

He hated having to try to explain away her doubts, hated even more that she still harbored such deep distrust of him. That she would accuse him of sleeping with her as an act of revenge infuriated him, but he couldn't blame her for it, not entirely. The arrival of the police and the discovery of more drugs would have tested the faith of almost anyone.

"You know I didn't," he said very softly. "Ken was the best friend I ever had. If I'd had the choice, I would have given my life for him."

"Someone hated him," she said. "Someone here. It had to be."

"Why?" Rick asked, fighting bitterness that, after all they'd shared, they were back to this. "Because the kids in the program would be able to get their hands on drugs?"

She nodded.

"Dana, anyone can get their hands on drugs, if they want them badly enough. They can score right out there in the suburbs, if they know where to look. They don't have to come into the barrio. You know that." He leveled a look directly into her eyes. "Don't you?"

"Yes," she admitted finally. She moved away from him and sat down. "Dammit, it's just so frustrating. Rick, I can't for the life of me figure out what's going on. I was one of the best investigators in the business. I could unravel mysteries that stumped my colleagues. But this one is beyond me."

"You're just too impatient and too involved. You haven't been able to step back and look at what you know objectively."

"Because I don't know a darned thing."

"Didn't you find out anything about Tremayne this morning?"

"Just that his company is having financial trouble," she said dismissively.

"That's something."

"I thought so, too, at first, especially since the deals that went sour had a Latin American connection. Then I really thought about it. If he were having financial problems, where would he come up with fifty thousand dollars to have Ken killed? And why would he do it? It's not as though Ken might spread the word and ruin him, or something. It wouldn't have been a big secret for long, anyway. My broker told me about it. If she knew, then surely others do, too. So what danger would Ken pose to him?"

Rick settled against the edge of his desk, his knees brushing hers. "Maybe that wasn't the danger. There could be more to this than we know. Don't rule Tremayne out just yet. I still don't like him."

"Now there's an objective opinion, if ever I heard one," she taunted.

Rick grinned. "You're the one who's supposed to be objective. I get to react from the gut."

"What an interesting distinction."

He met her gaze evenly. "Are we okay now?"

"Yes," she said, though her voice lacked real conviction. "I'm sorry I rushed down here to accuse you of planting those drugs."

"It's not a total loss. I need to talk to Tico. You can come with me. It's almost lunchtime. He will be happy to see you again. Perhaps that will distract him sufficiently, so that I can get some straight answers."

She hesitated, then nodded. "Maybe a little salsa will clear my head."

Rick grinned. "It couldn't hurt. I've always been of the opinion that salsa has hidden medicinal qualities."

"And jalapenos?"

"Better yet." He urged her through the outer office, before she could get a good look at the mess that Maria and several helpers were attempting to straighten up. Clearly she had been too upset to pay much attention to it on her way in. It would be just as well if she didn't start asking too many questions about what he'd learned about the break-in. It was possible she would be no more impressed than Maria by his plan of action . . . or inaction, as Maria saw it.

Though it was after noon, the restaurant was not yet crowded. Most of the customers came later. By one o'clock it would be jammed. Now, though, Tico turned over the hosting job to one of the waiters and followed them to a booth. To Rick's irritation, he squeezed in beside Dana.

"It is a pleasure to see you, as always," Tico told her, deliberately ignoring Rick's scowl, or perhaps choosing to exacerbate his apparent irritation.

"Your chef performs magic. How could I resist coming back? Besides, you refuse to give me the recipes," Dana replied.

"Naturally," Tico said. "Then you would stop coming."

"Okay, okay, you're glad to see her," Rick groused. "She's thrilled to be here. Can we cut the chit-chat and get to the point?"

Tico regarded him with amusement. Dana merely looked puzzled by his irritability.

"I didn't know there was a point," she said. "I thought we came for lunch."

"We did. I also told you I needed to speak to Tico."

"I am right here," Tico said reasonably. "Tell me what's on your mind."

"I was hoping we could play a little basketball tonight, after you close."

"*Si*, I have no other plans," Tico said readily. "And the rest?"

"What makes you think there is more?"

"You do not come here just to see if I can come out to play, my friend. There are phones for something so trivial."

Rick sighed. Tico wouldn't let it rest, until he knew precisely why Rick was so eager to see him. He decided to leave news of the break-in for later, when they were alone. Dana might seize on the details of that and obsess on its possible connection to the murder. He was all but certain it would be a waste of her energy.

Instead, he brought up Maria's name, just to see what sort of reaction he would get.

"What about Maria?" Tico asked blandly, his eyes wide with an innocence that Rick suspected was feigned.

"Have you two argued recently?" he asked bluntly.

Tico's gaze narrowed. "Why would you ask such a thing? What did she say?"

"It's what she didn't say that concerns me," he said, watching Tico's expression closely. It gave away nothing. "I always thought you two got along just fine. Today I got a different impression."

Tico laughed. "That is what this is about? One of your impressions?" He glanced at Dana. "Rick believes he has deeper insights than the rest of us, that he is attuned to the subtleties of conversations. He prides himself on this sensitivity."

Dana's lips quirked, but she managed to keep from smiling. Rick was impressed with the attempt. He was less thrilled with his friend's observation.

"You're avoiding my question," he accused. "Has something happened between you and Maria?"

"If it has, it is personal, *mi amigo,*" Tico said lightly. "It is not for you to interfere."

"I believe it is. I introduced the two of you. Maria is a good girl. I would not like to see anything upset her, *comprende?*"

For just an instant, Tico's expression hardened in a way that startled Rick. It reminded him that Tico had once been one of the street's most dangerous young men. Then he smiled, once more the jovial host. The transformation was so swift, Rick thought he must have imagined that momentary flash of pent-up violence.

"No harm will come to your precious Maria," Tico informed him. "I will see to that."

Dana had watched the exchange very closely. As soon as Tico had excused himself to get their meals, she stared at Rick. "What was that all about?"

"You heard."

"I heard what you said, but the undercurrents were extraordinarily tense. I thought you two were good friends."

"We are." He waved his hand dismissively. "It's a guy thing. Don't worry. We're not going to come to blows over Maria."

"Are they dating?"

Rick had wondered that very thing, but he'd never heard any rumors to that effect. Then again, Tico's private life was pretty much an enigma to him. It might have been a carryover from his days on the streets, when secrecy had been essential. But Tico guarded his privacy fiercely.

"I don't have any idea," he admitted.

She looked straight into his eyes then. "Why didn't you mention the break-in to him?"

Rick swallowed hard and hoped that the fire he felt in his cheeks wasn't visible to the woman opposite him. Unfortunately, she seemed able to read even what he tried hardest to hide. "I didn't want to get into it with him, just yet."

"You've been avoiding the subject with me, as well. What have you learned?"

"Nothing. I am all but certain it is the work of vandals."

"Nothing was stolen?"

"Not that we've discovered so far."

"How are you handling it?"

Apparently there were to be no secrets between them. "I was going to have Tico put out the word on the streets that we're not happy about what happened. The culprit will turn up."

"The culprit or a scapegoat?" she inquired thoughtfully.

He stared at her. "Meaning?"

"That someone hoping to please you or Tico might very well make a sacrificial lamb of an innocent party."

"I hadn't thought of that."

She grinned. "That's why you have me around, for the subtleties."

"Quiet. You'll ruin my reputation. Everyone around here thinks I grasp those on my own."

"Then you would truly be a rarity among men," she said. "The only man I ever knew who could read between the lines so well was Ken."

"Yes," he agreed, reaching for her hand. "He often saw things that the rest of us missed."

She regarded him with puzzlement. "It sounds as if there's a story behind that."

He thought of his initial impression of her as a suburban snob with little redeeming social conscience. He had wondered at Ken's judgment in marrying such a woman. Clearly, though, his friend had known that there was far more to this woman, a rare depth and complexity that Rick was only now discovering for himself.

"Maybe someday I'll tell you," he said.

"Not now?"

He shook his head. "No, it reflects too poorly on me, I suspect. We have reached a rapport, you and I. I don't want to do anything that might cause you to question that. Your faith in me has been shaken enough for one day."

"You want to be sure you can remain a spy in the enemy's camp?" she asked tightly.

"Never that," he said. He grinned wickedly. "So that I might be invited to share her bed again."

Color flamed in her cheeks at that, but she didn't pull her hand away, not even when Tico returned and stared at the two of them with blatant amusement.

"Perhaps I should warn you about my friend here," Tico said lightly.

Rick was about to respond to the taunt, when Dana spoke up. "No need," she assured him. "I know exactly what I'm doing."

"I wonder," Tico said enigmatically.

Then, at a harsh scowl from Rick, he retreated and left them alone, but not before a faint shadow of doubt crossed Dana's eyes. Rick vowed to soundly thrash his old friend at the first opportunity. The stakes in this game were far too high for his kind of taunting interference.

Twenty-three

Dana returned home to find Kate and Detective O'Flannery engaged in full-scale warfare on her front stoop. She gathered that Kate had heard about the drug raid.

"Stay out of it?" Kate shouted.

She poked her finger directly into the man's very broad chest. He withstood the gesture with obvious amusement, which no doubt only served to inflame Kate further.

"With people like you ready to crucify Ken Miller, there's not a snowball's chance in hell that I'm going to stay out of it," she told him emphatically. "In fact, I might just organize a rally, a protest march on the police station. We'll demand your resignation. Maybe that will teach you to have some respect for the decent people of this community."

Telltale patches of red climbed into his cheeks. The show was so good, Dana decided to sit in her car and watch the rest of the performance. She leaned back and waited to see what would happen next. She doubted the policeman would allow the threat to his livelihood go unchallenged.

"Decent people pay me to keep this community safe," O'Flannery barked back, taking an intimidating step in Kate's direction. She held her ground as he added pointedly, "That means following up on evidence of criminal activity."

"Criminal activity, my Aunt Bessie. It's slander, that's what it is."

They were toe-to-toe now. Unless Dana was very much

mistaken, there was enough sexual energy charging the air to send them both up in flames.

"We found drugs," he countered quietly.

"I don't care if you found an armed militia in the basement and enough guns and drugs to supply the entire Midwest. Ken Miller had nothing to do with any of it," she said so emphatically that she was practically vibrating with indignation.

O'Flannery obviously wasn't impressed. "Your faith in him is touching, but compared to the evidence, it doesn't amount to a hill of beans."

"I'm telling you that you don't have any damned evidence," Kate said, her voice climbing another decibel level, "except that someone was out to get him."

"I agree."

He said it so softly that it apparently took several seconds for it to register with Kate. When it did, her furious expression faltered. "You agree?"

O'Flannery grinned and nodded. "I would have told you that, if you'd taken a deep breath and listened for half a minute, instead of trying to blast out my eardrums."

Dana had to admit the effect of that grin was fairly devastating. Even she got a tingle, and she was clear across the yard and immune to the charms of all cops. Kate was absolutely no match for it. She flat-out wilted at the sight.

"Oh."

The smile broadened. "Care to apologize?"

"When hell freezes over," Kate said staunchly. "You still conducted the stupid search."

"It was my job," he explained patiently.

"Then it's a stupid job," Kate said, still defiant.

"Remember you said that the next time you're in trouble and need a cop."

"I don't get into the kind of trouble that requires the Gestapo."

He sighed heavily. "I can see there's only one way to shut you up," he said with an air of resignation, just before he bent

down and planted a kiss on Kate that generated enough heat
to melt the snow drifts in the front yard.

Dana waited for a full sixty seconds, expecting steam to
rise at any moment, before concluding it was time to make
her presence known before the elderly neighbors saw more
than their hearts could take. She deliberately bumped the horn
as she exited the car. Kate jerked out of the detective's embrace, as if she'd been shot. He looked as thoroughly unflappable as ever. In fact, he seemed so thoroughly amused that
Dana had a sneaking suspicion he'd been aware of her arrival
all along.

"So we're all agreed that someone has been planting the
drugs, correct?" Dana demanded, as she opened the front door
and led the parade inside.

"Yes," Kate declared firmly.

"Agreed," O'Flannery said.

Dana beamed at them. "Now all we have to do is figure
out who's behind it."

"You make it sound as if that will be a stroll in the park,"
the detective said. "Do you already have some idea of where
to start looking?"

She debated filling him in on the preliminary suspect list
she and Kate had drawn up, but decided that would be a tac-
tical error. He'd probably laugh his head off, if he heard some
of the names on that list. Respected community leaders, one
and all. And when it came to a lack of solid evidence, she and
Kate were in an even weaker position than the police were,
with regard to Ken.

"Not really," she demurred.

He looked skeptical. "Okay, let me ask a few more questions, then. Who has access to the house?"

"Just me," Dana said. "The boys are in Florida."

He glanced at Kate. "You don't have a key for emergen-
cies?"

Signs of her hair-trigger temper flared in Kate's eyes.
"You're accusing me now?"

"Simmer down. I just want to know exactly where we stand, okay? Do you have a key?"

"Yes," Kate acknowledged irritably.

"Is it still in your possession?"

"Yes, dammit."

"You're sure?"

With a defiant scowl, Kate flipped her purse upside down on the kitchen table, dumping the contents into a heap. She plucked the key out of the mess. "Here. Satisfied? See anything else suspicious? Maybe that lipstick is an illegal weapon. Or the comb? I could do a lot of damage with that comb, I'm sure."

He turned on his full kilowatt grin again. "I'm sure you could."

Kate rolled her eyes. Dana gathered the detective's charms were beginning to wear a little thin.

He fixed his gaze on Dana again. "What about the church? Does anyone there have a spare key?"

She almost said no, then paused. Had there been a master key in Ken's office, along with all the others to the parish hall and the main church? It certainly made sense that there would have been. As had been so recently pointed out to her, after all, it was the church's property.

"I'll call Mrs. Fallon to check," she said, reaching for the phone.

The secretary confirmed the existence of a master set of keys. She checked and reported that it was still locked in a small, fireproof safe, along with important church documents.

"Who has the combination to the safe?" O'Flannery asked, when Dana repeated what the secretary had said.

Dana asked.

"Reverend Miller did. I do. And Mr. Tremayne, of course, since he frequently has to attend to church business."

Dana tried not to react to the mention of Lawrence Tremayne. "I see," she said quietly. "Thanks, Mrs. Fallon. You've been wonderful through all of this."

On an impulse, she added, "I hope you'll come to lunch tomorrow so I can thank you properly." The suggestion wasn't made entirely out of generosity. Dana had the feeling that Mrs. Fallon knew more about church politics than anyone else. She'd been observing them from the inside for years now, longer than Ken had been pastor of St. Michael's.

"Why, thank you, dear. I'd love to."

"About noon, then?"

"I'll be there."

When she'd hung up, she noticed that O'Flannery was regarding her impatiently. "Sorry," she apologized. "That was long overdue."

"Who has access to the safe?" he repeated.

She debated lying to O'Flannery and keeping Tremayne's name to herself, but decided maybe it was time for the police to put a little pressure on the church elder. If they considered him a genuine suspect, they had the means to conduct a far more thorough survey of his background than she could.

She told the detective the three names. "Mrs. Fallon would die before she would let anyone into that safe."

"And Mr. Tremayne?" he asked, watching her intently. "You think he's capable of this, don't you?"

Dana winced. Apparently O'Flannery was a better detective than she'd given him credit for being, or else she was more transparent than she'd prided herself on being. "Let's just say, I don't like him and leave it at that."

"To your knowledge, has he been in the house recently?"

"Actually, he was here for tea, just the other day," she admitted, regretting the fact that she hadn't recalled that herself earlier. In fact, there had been a whole bevy of people right here at her invitation, all of them suspects, for one reason or another.

O'Flannery's expression brightened. "Now we're getting somewhere. Did he ever leave the room, say, to go to the restroom?"

Dana slowly shook her head. "I don't think so." She glanced across the table. "Kate?"

"No," Kate said with obvious regret. "He was in plain view the whole time." Suddenly her expression brightened. "But several of the others used the facilities."

The detective regarded her expectantly. "Who? What others?"

At a subtle nod from Dana, Kate said, "Miriam Kelso, Peter Drake, and Carolina Vincenzi. I remember each of them excusing themselves at one time or another." She paused, her expression thoughtful. "Actually, I take that back. Carolina never said a word. She just slipped out of the room, right after Peter Drake left."

"So each of them had the opportunity to have planted those drugs," O'Flannery said. "Interesting."

Dana found it interesting, but far from conclusive. She still thought Tremayne made an excellent prime suspect. "Don't forget, I was out of town for weeks after the funeral. Tremayne had access to the key. He could have come in here undetected at any time and planted those drugs. I haven't cleaned since I've been back. I doubt I would have looked behind that dresser, even if I had."

With Tremayne and the three who had excused themselves during the tea the only ones with probable access to the upstairs bedroom, the suspect list was shrinking. There was still one on it that Kate and O'Flannery didn't know about, and Dana intended to keep it that way.

As desperately as she wanted to believe that Rick had had nothing to do with Ken's death or the drugs, she couldn't help thinking about the access she'd innocently given him to the very room in which the cocaine had been found. Until she had a truly viable alternative, her awareness of that fact would always stand between them.

* * *

Tico was charging the basket with far more force than was necessary, Rick concluded, when he'd taken his third elbow to the gut. He backed off.

"Hey, man, what's with you tonight?" he demanded. "You're playing like a spot in the NBA finals is at stake."

Tico grabbed a towel and wiped his face before replying. "Just trying to work off a little steam," he said.

"Is that it, or do you still have a problem with the fact that I asked about you and Maria?"

Tico shot him a look of undisguised disgust. "Not that again. I don't need this. I have a mother who cross-examines me, if I so much as frown. I have employees who think they can run the business better than I can. I have a kid brother who'd rather get high than wait tables."

Rick sensed that this last was the real source of Tico's short temper. "Joey's using?"

"José," Tico corrected. "He's discovered his roots. Latino pride has kicked in with a vengeance, thanks to that worm, Carlos."

"He's running with Carlos?"

"He thinks he's some kind of god," Tico said. "Nothing I say can convince him that at the first sign of trouble, Carlos will drop him like a sizzling fajita pan. He'll give him up to the cops, if it'll save his own sorry hide."

"Is Joey the one who tipped you that Carlos might know something about Ken's murder?"

Tico shrugged. "Not intentionally. I heard him and his buddies. They said enough for me to add two and two. I had a little talk with Carlos and convinced him that he should clear his conscience by talking to you."

"I'm sorry I missed that conversation. I didn't see any war wounds when I talked to him."

Tico shrugged. "There are other ways to convince a man to do what is right."

Rick's gaze narrowed. "You have something on him, don't you?"

"What I know about Carlos is between us, *mi amigo*. I would not tell anyone—even you—unless it became necessary."

"Dammit, a decent man is dead, a man who helped you get straight, a man who put his word on the line to set you up in business," Rick snapped. "Isn't that enough to make it necessary? Carlos is slime, Tico. He doesn't deserve your protection."

"I am not protecting him. I am maintaining my leverage."

Rick muttered an oath under his breath. Tico's expression hardened.

"Up until now, you have been my friend," Tico said, his tone lethal. "Do not say anything to make me regret that."

Rick really didn't like being warned off by a man who owed his salvation to *Yo, Amigo*. He whirled on the other man so quickly that Tico was forced to back up a step, straight into the wall. Rick crowded in close, a subtle reminder that he had twenty pounds of solid muscle on the wiry younger man.

"Do not threaten me, Tico. There is too much history between us. I would not like to have to remind you who controlled these streets before you."

Fury flashed in Tico's eyes. "That was a long time ago. You are out of practice."

"There are some things a man never forgets," Rick said.

Sweat beaded on Tico's brow, but his gaze remained defiant. "I like threats no more than you do, *amigo*."

"Then do not make them necessary again," Rick suggested, backing away.

Tico snatched up his gym bag and left, without another word. Rick had the feeling that the exchange had just cost him another friend. What he didn't understand was why it had happened in the first place.

Back in his office, he went over the conversation, word-by-word, trying to see why Tico had gotten so riled and so defensive so quickly. Was it Joey? Was Joey inadvertently dragging his big brother back into gang life, if only to serve as his protector?

And what were the links between Tico and Carlos? At one time, he supposed that they had been kingpins of rival gangs, though Carlos's name had never surfaced in any of the usual street talk. When Tico had walked away from the streets, the rivalry should have ended, anyway.

Or did such things ever end? Perhaps Carlos's recruitment of Joey had been deliberate, a slap at an old enemy. Not even his recent successes in mainstream society would be enough to keep Tico from reacting to such a taunt.

Damn, where were the answers? Rick had been so sure, when he steered Dana's investigation into her own backyard, that he'd been right. Now he was beginning to have doubts. Some kind of turf war was building right here in the barrio, and his old friend Tico appeared to be smack in the thick of it. Had Ken been one of its innocent victims, after all?

Twenty-four

Dana was awakened by the shrilling of the phone before dawn. Her heart slammed against her ribs, as she anticipated bad news. It was always bad news at that hour.

"Mom?" Bobby's voice sounded plaintive.

Back in Ken's chair again—now there were two rooms upstairs she couldn't bear to sleep in—she sat straight up. Her grip on the receiver tightened. She forced herself to keep her voice calm. "What is it, baby? Is something wrong? You're up awfully early."

"I didn't want Grandma and Grandpa to hear. They're still asleep."

"What didn't you want them to hear?"

"Me and Kevin and Jonathan want to come home."

Dana closed her eyes in a futile attempt to block out the image of her son's pitiful expression. When she couldn't, she sighed. "Not yet, sweetie. I'm sorry."

"When?" he asked, suddenly defiant. "It's not fair that we have to stay here and you get to be at home. We miss our school. We miss our friends."

"You have friends there. Grandma told me that kids are running in and out all the time."

"Babies," Bobby said derisively. "There's nobody my age."

"Not even at school?"

"Oh, sure, but they treat me like I'm some kind of weirdo, just because I'm new."

Dana sensed there was more to this sudden desire to return

to Illinois than homesickness. Bobby was also the kind of kid who adapted readily to new situations. Of course, that had been before his very stable world had collapsed.

"What happened at school?" Dana asked, virtually certain that something there was at the root of the problem.

The direct question was greeted with silence, indicating that her guess had been accurate. Bobby had always hidden his feelings. He'd taken his role as the oldest very seriously, especially since Ken's death. He would never have called, if this worry, whatever it was, weren't too heavy for his young shoulders.

"Bobby? What happened?" she persisted. "Something must have. Last time we talked, you were okay with staying in Florida for the rest of the school year. Come on, sweetie, tell me. I can't help, if you don't."

"One of the kids . . ." His voice cracked. "Never mind. It's not important."

She'd been through this kind of hurt enough times to guess at the source of it. "If it upset you, then it is important. Did somebody say something mean?" she asked, anticipating some typical remark about an unfashionable, dorky shirt, or her son's thick-lensed glasses. "You can tell me anything, you know that."

"Not this time. I don't want to say."

"It's okay. Please tell me."

There was another long hesitation before he finally began in a voice that faltered, "He said . . ."

She could hear him swallowing back tears, and it killed her that she wasn't there to gather him into her arms. "Take your time," she soothed.

"He said . . . he said my dad was murdered because he was a dope pusher."

Dana gasped, stunned not only by the unexpectedly terrible cruelty of the remark, but by the content. How the hell had a child all the way in Florida known about the rumors all the way up here? When she'd left them there, she'd thought her

kids would be safe from wild speculation and all the fall-out
from their father's death. Sure, parents talked, but the discovery of drugs in Ken's office and at the house hadn't been
publicized.

Or had it? She realized she hadn't been paying much attention to the papers or to TV news. Whoever had gone to the
trouble of planting the drugs might very well have leaked it
to the media.

Damn whoever it was to hell, she thought fiercely. She
didn't care for herself, but this was different. Her kids were
being hurt by the lies now. And when it came to her kids, this
sleaze was walking on very thin ice. She would destroy anyone
who attempted to hurt her babies.

"Is it true?" Bobby asked in a tiny, scared voice. He was
obviously as shaken by her silence as by the original accusation.

"No, baby, it is not true," she said adamantly. "Your daddy
was a fine man and he hated drugs. Remember, he talked
about that all the time, so you and your brothers would know
just how bad they were."

"Then why would somebody say that?" he asked plain-
tively. "He didn't even know my dad."

"People like to spread gossip. They don't care about the
facts. And kids your age can be especially cruel without even
meaning to be. Whoever said that about your dad probably
didn't know what he was saying. He didn't realize how badly
it would hurt you."

"He did, too, know," Bobby insisted. "He laughed, Mom.
He told all the other kids, and then he laughed. I want to come
home NOW!"

Suddenly, Dana wanted nothing more than to gather her
children close and hug them. She wanted to be there to protect
them from vicious lies, even though she knew rationally that
that was impossible. Maybe leaving them in Florida had been
a terrible mistake, after all.

Even after all the second-guessing, though, she knew she

couldn't bring them home yet. If they were being taunted hundreds of miles away, then what would happen to them right back here in their own community, where gossip was bound to flourish? Life couldn't possibly go back to being the way they'd remembered it. Even in Sunday School in their father's church, there would be subtle, but unmistakable, shifts in attitudes. There was no way on earth to prevent it. How would they feel the first time one of their old friends was forbidden to play with them, because of the rumors and innuendos circulating? They would be devastated.

No, this was no safe haven for them now, either. In the long run, they were better off right where they were, at least for the moment.

"I'm sorry, sweetie, but you can't come home yet," she said, bracing for more tears. "I'm trying really hard to clear up all these terrible lies about your daddy. All of my energy has to stay focused on that. I need a little more time."

"But Kevin and Jonathan and me could help. We could tell people the truth."

"I know you could, and that would be a huge help, but it's going to take more than just our word. I have to find out who's behind this, and that takes time. I wouldn't be able to be home with you."

"Grandma could come with us. She would, if you asked her to. Please," he pleaded.

"Soon," she promised. "I'll be down there before you know it."

Her vow was greeted with shocked silence.

"You're coming here?" he asked eventually. "We're not coming home?"

She heard the panicked note in his voice and tried to reassure him. "That's something we'll all have to decide together."

"No, it's not," he shouted. "You've already decided. I can tell. We're never coming home again. I hate you. I hate you. I wish you had died, instead of Daddy."

"Bobby," she whispered, shattered by the harsh words. As

the phone clattered to the floor, she shouted one last time, "Bobby!"

She could hear his footsteps, as he ran away from the phone. Her eyes swimming with tears, she listened to her mother's sleepy attempt to soothe him, to find out why he was so upset.

Sweet heaven, she had made a mess of things. His angry words echoed in her head as she waited, praying that her mother would notice the dangling receiver and grab the phone.

The minutes ticked by. Silence fell on the other end of the line. She could only guess that her mother had taken Bobby back to his room. Was he still sobbing? Had she been able to console him at all?

Eventually she heard the faint padding of bare feet on the tile floor.

"Dana?"

Dana choked back a sob. "Oh, Mom, what have I done to him?"

"It's not you. It's just the circumstances. The teacher told me what that awful child said to him yesterday, but Bobby wouldn't talk about it. I should have called you myself last night, but I thought maybe he was handling it okay. He was so stoic. I didn't want to upset you by repeating such vicious nonsense."

"Was there something about Ken's death in the papers down there? Is that how that child heard about it, from some news report?"

Her mother hesitated. "Now that you mention it, no. There wasn't a word. I was as stunned as Bobby by what the child said. I was sure he'd just made it up to taunt him. Are you saying there's some truth to it?"

"Of course not, but drugs have been planted." She described what the police had found and the theory that she and Detective O'Flannery shared that someone had deliberately set out to destroy Ken's reputation.

"Well, how on earth would a third-grader down here know about that?" her mother asked indignantly.

"That's a good question," Dana said. "Any idea what the kid's name is?"

"The teacher never said. She was protecting the little darling, I suppose. I'll do my best to get it out of Bobby, if you think it's important."

It was a longshot, but Dana was grasping at straws these days. "Please," she said. "Just try not to upset him any more than necessary. He's furious with me, as it is."

"He'll settle down, as soon as he sees you again. He's just frightened. His whole world has shifted, and he's struggling to make sense of it."

"So am I," Dana said with a heartfelt sigh. "So am I."

Dana spent the rest of the morning in emotional turmoil, torn between her children's needs and her duty to straighten out this mess and clear her husband's name. Nothing Kate said could placate her, so she finally sent Kate off to do more digging into the backgrounds of their four local suspects—Carolina Vincenzi, Miriam Kelso, Peter Drake, and Lawrence Tremayne.

"I want to know if any of them has so much as a parking ticket on their record, okay? Take my laptop and modem. I just reconnected this morning with some of the financial records services I used to use. You can access those and check their credit, too."

Recalling her conversation earlier with Bobby, she added, "And see if any of them has any ties whatsoever in Florida."

"What will you be doing?" Kate asked.

"Mrs. Fallon's coming to lunch. I'm going to call her right now and ask her to bring along Ken's calendar. I want to check the entries for the last few months before he was killed. Maybe there will be something there, a suspicious pattern of meetings or something."

Kate nodded as she shrugged into her jacket. "Okay, sweetie. I'll check in with you later."

"Do you want to have dinner tonight?"

A guilty expression spread across Kate's face. "I wish I could, but I've already made plans."

"With the cop?"

"Don't say it like that, please. He's a good guy. He really is on our side in this."

"You could have fooled me," Dana retorted, then forced a smile. "Sorry. Go and have a great time. You deserve someone special in your life."

"And you? Where do things stand with the sexy Latino?"

"There's nothing between us. How many times do I have to tell you that?"

"As many as it takes to make it sound convincing. You're not even close yet."

When Dana would have protested, Kate hugged her. "Never mind. Go on denying it, if you like. Just don't shut the door on whatever's happening out of loyalty to Ken. He wouldn't have wanted that. Remember something else, too. He respected Rick. He thought he was a very decent guy. He would be happy, I think, if the two of you found something together. He'd give you his blessing, you know he would."

Dana couldn't tell Kate that she was holding back out of fear. Not fear of commitment. She already knew that a committed relationship was important. She believed in marriage with all her heart. Not even fear of leaping so quickly into a new relationship, even though she thought that showed evidence of disrespect for Ken's memory.

No, what she was terrified of was discovering that the man she was falling for might have had a hand in her husband's murder. No matter how many times she told herself that wasn't possible, no matter how badly she wanted to trust Rick, she couldn't overcome all of the doubts. The seed of distrust had been planted, and it seemed to be flourishing, fed time and again by some new piece of information just when she thought things might be okay.

"Just think about it," Kate pleaded.

"I will. I promise."

After Kate had gone, Dana made a quick call to the church to ask Mrs. Fallon to bring her copy of Ken's calendar. No sooner had she hung up than Rick called.

"How's it going out there this morning?"

"Well enough," she said tersely.

"Doesn't sound like it. What's wrong?"

The genuine caring in his voice had her spilling out what had happened with Bobby earlier. "Am I being selfish to leave him down there, so I can finish this investigation?" she asked.

"No. You're just doing what you think is best. Parents make that kind of call all the time. Sometimes they're right, sometimes not. You just have to go with your instincts. Even after this incident, his life is more stable there than it would be here at the moment."

She sighed. "I don't know why, but it helps to have you say that."

"You should listen to me all the time. I am very wise."

"You also have a very large ego."

"Confidence," he countered. "I hear most women consider it very sexy."

"And then there are those who consider it a challenge to destroy it," she shot back.

"Which are you?"

"Oh, I think I'll let you worry about that for a while," she teased.

"So, tell me, what are your plans for the rest of the day?"

"I'm having Mrs. Fallon over for lunch shortly. She's going to bring Ken's calendar, so I can see what was going on the last few days he was alive."

"Are you sure that is wise? Won't it upset you?"

"Yes, but it may also give me some new leads."

"Okay, then. You will do as you wish, anyway."

"That's true. By the way, how did your game with Tico go?"

"Not well," he said, his voice sobering. "There is something going on with him, but I can't figure it out."

"Maybe he's in love with Maria, and she's giving him fits."

"No, this has to do with his brother. Joey is tied up with Carlos in some way, and Tico is obviously frightened for him."

"You don't think it has anything to do with Ken's death, do you?"

"I'm not sure, *querida*," he said, sounding genuinely distraught. "I wish I were. I will call you later, if I learn anything new that might link Tico's brother to all of this. Joey's not a bad kid, but I don't like his new associate one bit. Carlos is not a man to have as an enemy or as a friend. If there's money to be made, he will use anyone."

"Wait a second," she protested. How could he drop a bombshell like that and then hang up on her? Was he beginning to suspect Tico's brother of pulling the trigger for Carlos? Is that what Tico suspected that had him behaving so defensively?

Unfortunately, Rick didn't seem eager to share his speculations with her. The phone connection had already been broken.

"Well, hell," she muttered, putting the receiver back on the hook.

Thank goodness she had lunch to prepare. That would keep her occupied for the next half-hour or so, until Mrs. Fallon's arrival. It had been weeks since she'd actually prepared a meal, not that chicken salad in half an avocado was exactly gourmet cuisine, but it kept her attention off of the case for a bit.

She had just put the finishing touches on the plates, when she glanced at the clock and realized it was already well past noon. By the time she'd filled the coffeemaker and turned it on, it was almost twelve-thirty. It wasn't like the secretary to be late. She had always prided herself on being prompt, even when Ken had told her time and again, especially during blizzards, to take her time getting to work on icy roads.

Dana went to the living room and glanced across the grounds toward the church. There was no sign of Mrs. Fallon on the path. The first faint stirring of concern crept over her, as she went back to the phone and dialed the office. The phone rang and rang, unanswered.

Panicking now, Kate grabbed her coat and keys, and raced toward the church. The side door to the parish hall was standing wide open, despite the freezing temperature.

"Oh, dear God," she murmured, sure now that something was terribly wrong.

"Mrs. Fallon!" she shouted, as she ran toward the office. "Are you here? Mrs. Fallon, it's Dana."

The door to the outer office was slightly ajar. After opening it wide, a quick, sweeping glance revealed nothing amiss. The room was as tidy as ever. A cup half full of coffee was cool to her touch. Had Mrs. Fallon left the building, though, that cup would have been rinsed and set neatly into her desk drawer. It was possible she'd gone into the restroom down the hall and fallen ill, Dana speculated, then dismissed the idea. She would have taken the cup with her to wash.

Dana glanced to her left, then, and saw that the door to Ken's larger office was closed. With a sick feeling in the pit of her stomach, she opened it, then cried out in shock.

Mrs. Fallon was sprawled unceremoniously across Ken's desk. A bloodstain ran down her back from a bullet wound in the center. Fighting back nausea, Dana rushed to her, searching frantically for a pulse. There was none.

She hadn't been dead long, though. Less than an hour, Dana guessed from her body's temperature and based on the last time she'd spoken to her.

Tears welled up in her eyes. Mrs. Fallon would have hated the uproar that would ensue the moment the police came. She would have hated being the center of attention, especially in this undignified position. If she hadn't known how critical it was to leave everything exactly as she'd found it, Dana would have straightened the woman's dress and laid her carefully on her back.

Who would do such a thing? Who would kill a sweet, gentle

woman who had never had a harsh word to say to a soul? There was no question that Mrs. Fallon's death and Ken's were linked. Why? Because she had known something, of course, and because she was going to share that with Dana today.

Was that it? Had someone learned that Mrs. Fallon was having lunch with Dana and feared what she might reveal? Only three people that Dana could think of knew about their plans—Kate, Detective O'Flannery, and Rick.

It was the last that had her shuddering and weakened her knees so badly that she had to sit down. She calculated the time from the moment she'd spoken to him until she'd discovered the body. There had been time enough for him to make the trip, if only by the skin of his teeth. A desperate man would make sure it was enough time.

Twenty-five

Dana had to force herself not to think about Rick's possible involvement in Mrs. Fallon's murder. She reminded herself that suspicions and doubts were not evidence, and then tried to push him completely out of her head. If she were to dwell on Rick's whereabouts right now, she would fall apart, and there was no time for that.

With every second that passed, the chances of someone else discovering Mrs. Fallon's body with Dana herself in too close a proximity to it increased. She really didn't want to have to explain her presence to anyone.

Before she called Detective O'Flannery, Dana wanted to see if she could find Ken's calendar, the one Mrs. Fallon had kept for her own record of his daily schedule, so she could pencil in appointments for him.

It wouldn't have been in any obvious place in Ken's office. She was confident of that, so she backed out of the room and gently closed the door, leaving it precisely as she'd found it.

To her disappointment a thorough examination of the secretary's desk revealed nothing. Would Mrs. Fallon have put it with her purse to make sure she didn't forget to bring it along? Or was she so fearful of its contents being discovered that she might have hidden it in the safe?

Dana prayed it wasn't the latter. She didn't know the combination, and though she'd had some experience with breaking into safes, it wasn't a skill she'd actually perfected. She didn't have time to try out her amateur technique right now. The purse was her only bet.

She knew that the secretary routinely changed her hiding place for it, from the supply closet to the filing cabinet in Ken's office to her desk. Since she already knew it wasn't in the desk, she took a deep breath and returned to Ken's office to try the drawers in the file cabinet. There was no sign of either purse or calendar tucked behind the neat rows of folders. For the second time, she closed the door carefully behind her, as she left.

The supply cabinet in the outer office was next. If the purse wasn't in there, it was also possible that it had been stolen. Perhaps Mrs. Fallon had merely interrupted a thief, who'd panicked and shot her. Thieves were common enough in churches these days, though until now, St. Michael's had been spared. Of course, most of them didn't go out of their way to shoot an old woman in the back—especially when it was fairly obvious that she couldn't have seen him with her back turned toward the outer office.

Dana tried the door to the supply cabinet and found it locked. No doubt Mrs. Fallon had the key in her pocket. Swallowing her distaste for the task, Dana retrieved the key. She was shaking uncontrollably by the time she returned to the cabinet.

She fumbled her first several attempts to unlock the door, but eventually she was able to get it open. Sure enough, there on the bottom shelf was Mrs. Fallon's purse and under it, Ken's calendar. Dana grabbed the daybook and ran.

Only when she was back at home with the calendar safely secreted away under her mattress did she call the police.

"Where are you now?" Detective O'Flannery asked, when she told him what she'd discovered.

"At home. I didn't want to touch anything in the office," she explained dutifully.

"Good thinking," he praised.

She might have felt guilty about her lie, if he hadn't sounded so darned condescending.

"Stay there," he added. "I'm on my way."

Within minutes, the church and the grounds were swarming with police. Detective O'Flannery, after a brief visit to the church, rang Dana's doorbell. She had seen him coming and reluctantly opened the door before the second screeching chime could sound.

His gaze swept over her. "You okay?"

"Just peachy."

He grinned and took her elbow. "Come on. Let's go into the kitchen. You'll feel better after you drink a nice, hot cup of tea."

"I already have coffee made," she protested.

"And I'll drink that," he said. "You need tea, preferably loaded with sugar."

"When did you go into medicine?" she grumbled, but she found that she sat willingly enough and let the detective wait on her. He found the tea readily, indicating that he'd been observing her very closely on past visits. Just thinking about it made Dana jittery. She wondered how Kate was going to like being involved with a man who noticed every little detail. Maybe to her it would be a pleasant change, after being married to a man who had hardly noticed her at all.

When O'Flannery handed her the sweetened tea, Dana wrapped both hands around the cup, absorbing its warmth. She hadn't realized how very chilled she was, chilled and heartsick.

"Better?" he asked eventually, his gaze steady.

Dana nodded, resisting the desire to squirm under his penetrating observation.

"Tell me what happened."

She took a deep breath, then recited the information she'd been subconsciously preparing ever since she'd found the body. "I'd invited Mrs. Fallon to lunch." She met his gaze. "You were here yesterday when I talked to her."

He nodded.

"Anyway, I spoke to her again just before twelve, actually closer to eleven-thirty. Then I fixed lunch. When I had it on the table, I glanced at the clock and realized that she was almost a half-hour late."

"And that's unusual?"

"Very. We could have a foot of snow on the roads and Mrs. Fallon would be at her desk precisely at nine A.M. She prided herself on punctuality. She thought it was a matter of courtesy and a tidy mind."

He jotted down a note. "Okay. What did you do next?"

"I had a really bad feeling about it, so I called. When no one answered, I ran over to check on her. She wasn't at her desk."

"Was your husband's office door open or closed?"

She thought of her repeated trips into that office. "Closed," she said. "Just the way I left it for you."

He'd been scribbling down her answers again, but his head jerked up at that. "Closed? It was open when we got there."

Dana's heart thundered wildly at that news. Had the killer still been there when she'd been in the office? Had he or she seen Dana steal the daybook? Or had someone else come along and stumbled on the murder scene, then fled in a panic?

"Think very carefully. Are you sure you closed it again?" O'Flannery demanded.

Again and again, actually. "I'm positive," she said.

He grabbed his two-way radio and barked out an order to the officers at the church. Then he turned back to Dana.

"You didn't see anyone? Hear anything?"

"Nothing," she swore. "Believe me, I was so scared I think I would have jumped if a pin had dropped."

"Did you notice any fresh footprints in the snow on your way over?"

"The snow's been on the ground for days. The kids play out there sometimes. There's no way to tell which footprints might be fresh."

"Okay, then. After you saw the body, what did you do?"

"I checked for a pulse, then I ran back here and called you."

Unlike his response on the phone, this time he stared at her with blatant skepticism. "Isn't there another phone around the church you could have used?"

Dana had figured he'd ask that, once he'd had time to think about it. She was ready with another dutiful recitation. "As far as I was concerned, the whole church was a potential murder scene. I didn't want to disturb anything."

He still appeared skeptical, but he let it pass. "Can you remember anything else? Anything that struck you as odd, before you ever got to that office?"

The question triggered a memory. "The side door was open," she said at once. "I had my key with me, but I didn't have to use it. No one uses that door except those of us with keys. It's a fire exit. It's kept locked from the outside. If it's opened from the inside, it should set off an alarm."

"But you never heard an alarm?"

"No."

"Which means that more than likely whoever used that door before you had a key and used it to enter," he said thoughtfully.

Dana felt as if a tremendous weight had been lifted off her shoulders. It couldn't have been Rick, then. It had to have been someone connected to the church, someone in that group of suspects she and Kate had already been considering. Lawrence Tremayne, for example.

As if she'd conjured him up, the church elder came bursting into the kitchen just then. Apparently, he'd seen no need to bother knocking or ringing the doorbell.

"What the hell is going on here?" he demanded indignantly. "I drop by the church to check on things, and I'm told that I can't go inside." He scowled at Dana, as if she'd had something to do with the presence of the police. "Is there some new scandal? Ever since your husband came here, we have been mired in controversy."

Detective O'Flannery shot a sympathetic look at Dana, then slowly rose to his feet. He scowled at the irate man.

"I don't believe I heard you knock," he said quietly. "That's breaking and entering."

"Who the hell are you?" Tremayne asked. "This house belongs to the church, I can come in here anytime I feel it's necessary."

"Oh, really? I think there are a few laws on the books that might say otherwise, as long as Mrs. Miller is in residence."

The detective was doing such a good job on her behalf that Dana saw no need to enter into the fray. She sat back and watched the two men go at it. Tremayne seemed only mildly intimidated by the mention of the law.

"I suppose you're some legal flack she hired to protect her own interests the minute we told her we wanted her to get out. Well, you can just check the terms of the contract we had with her husband. He was expected to be out within thirty days of being dismissed or leaving for any reason. We have been more than lenient with Mrs. Miller, due to the tragic circumstances."

O'Flannery tried hard, but he couldn't entirely mask his disdain. "Actually, I'm Detective Dillon O'Flannery. And while I'm fascinated with the arrangement you had with Reverend Miller, it's hardly any of my business. And you would be?"

The color washed right out of Lawrence Tremayne's face. He seemed to be having a difficult time recalling his name, so Dana supplied it.

"Ah, yes," O'Flannery said. "I've heard quite a lot about you. In fact, I've left several messages at your office. Don't you check in?"

"How I run my business is no concern of yours," Tremayne said scathingly.

"We'll see about that," O'Flannery replied. "In the meantime, perhaps you'd like to wait in the living room, while Mrs. Miller and I conclude our business."

The church elder didn't take kindly to being summarily dismissed. He huffed and turned on his heel.

"Mr. Tremayne?" O'Flannery said.

"Yes?"

"In case there's any doubt in your mind, that wasn't a request, that was an order. Don't even think about budging out of that living room."

Tremayne stared at him, practically quivering with indignation. "You're actually detaining me?"

"In a manner of speaking. I'm sure, as an official of the church, you'll want to cooperate, won't you?"

"Cooperate in what? More of this damnable mess that Miller left behind?"

O'Flannery started to reply, but Dana shot him an oh-please-let-me look. He nodded.

"They're investigating a murder," she told him, her gaze locked on Tremayne's smug face for any change in expression that might betray him. "Mrs. Fallon has been killed."

To her deep regret, his shocked reaction seemed genuine. In fact, his eyes practically bugged out of his head.

"Mrs. Fallon is dead?" he asked, his normally forceful tone gone. In fact, he sounded a little lost.

"I found her body earlier," Dana told him.

He stared at her, looking truly shattered. "Oh, my God, this is terrible, just awful," he murmured, then looked at O'Flannery. "Who would do such a thing? I have to tell the others. They'll want to be here."

"No," O'Flannery said. "Any notifying that gets done for the time being will be done by me. If you'll just go into the other room and wait, I'll be with you in a minute."

All of the fight seemed to have drained out of the other man. He simply nodded. "Yes, yes, of course. Whatever will help."

When Tremayne had gone, O'Flannery looked at Dana. "What did you think?"

"I think he was stunned."

"Me, too. Unfortunately, there's nothing on the books that lets me run a man in just because he's an arrogant jerk."

"He does have a key to that exit, though. And he knew the combination to the safe," Dana reminded him. "Maybe he's also a consummate actor."

"Maybe's don't win convictions. You sit tight, okay? Let me go see if I can pump any additional information out of him."

"Can't I sit in?"

"Not a chance." He grinned. "Of course, if you happened to be passing nearby and eavesdropped, there wouldn't be a thing I could do about it."

She returned his grin. "You know, you may turn out to be okay after all."

"Put in a good word for me with Kate, that's all I ask."

Dana doubted Kate needed any good words from her on the subject of the sexy detective. She seemed smitten enough, as it was. Besides, the man needed to worry a little about his prospects.

"We'll see," she said.

He frowned at the lack of commitment, but he didn't argue with her. When she rose to follow him, he warned, "Stay out of sight and keep quiet."

"You'll never know I'm there," she promised.

"I will," he said. "Just see to it that Tremayne doesn't."

Dana tiptoed into the dining room and crept along the wall, remaining just out of Tremayne's line of vision from his position on the sofa on the same side of the living room. To her everlasting regret, O'Flannery kept his voice pitched deliberately low. She couldn't hear half of the questions he asked, but she had no problem at all with Tremayne's responses. He bellowed most of them, growing more and more outraged with each apparent hint that he had access to several crucial pieces of information related to both Ken's murder and now Mrs. Fallon's.

He had just leapt up and declared an end to the interview,

when Dana felt a hand close over her shoulder. She whirled around and came face to face with Rick. Her heart ricocheted around in chest like a Ping-Pong ball.

"Dammit, you scared me to death," she muttered.

"What the devil's going on?"

She touched a finger to her lips, then led him back into the kitchen. When the door was closed behind them, she explained about Mrs. Fallon's murder and her own discovery of the body. Although it seemed like an eternity had passed since then, a glance at the clock on the stove indicated it was only mid-afternoon.

"What are you doing here?" she asked, unable to keep a lingering hint of suspicion out of her voice. "You didn't say anything about coming out when I spoke to you earlier."

"Maybe I just got lonely."

"And maybe you knew about the murder," she blurted without thinking.

He went very still at that. "What are you suggesting?"

His anger was almost palpable. Her suspicions withered under his hard look. "That it had already made the news," she improvised hastily. "What did you think I meant?"

He regarded her silently, as if he was struggling with his temper.

"You thought I was suggesting that you had something to do with it, didn't you?" she asked.

"It wouldn't be the first time," he retorted.

A telltale guilty flush crept into her cheeks.

"You did, didn't you?" he asked incredulously. "You thought I killed her."

"No," she protested, then sighed. It was absurd to try to lie to him. "Okay, for just a minute, it crossed my mind that you were one of the few people who knew I intended to see her this afternoon and what I hoped to get from her."

Before Rick could respond to that, O'Flannery interrupted. She hadn't even heard him return. "And what would that have been, Mrs. Miller? What did you hope to get from Mrs. Fallon?"

"Information," Dana said at once. Her gaze pleaded with Rick not to contradict her, even though she could see how furious he was with her at the moment. "I was sure she would know who Ken had been spending time with lately, if he'd argued with anyone. Secretaries know far more than we credit them with knowing, especially one as observant as Mrs. Fallon.

"Now we'll never know what she knew," she concluded, her voice breaking.

"Perhaps we will," O'Flannery said, holding out an all-too-familiar black daybook.

"Where did you get that?" Dana demanded, even though she had a pretty good idea. She had placed one just like it beneath her mattress less than two hours earlier.

"You didn't think I bought all that crap about you racing back here to phone us just to avoid contaminating the scene, did you? There had to be another reason you wanted to get back here, such as hiding some piece of information you wanted all to yourself."

Dana couldn't deny it, so she settled for regarding him sourly. She supposed this wasn't the time to mention that he'd found it without a warrant.

"Anything in here?" he asked.

"I haven't had time to look at it," she admitted grudgingly.

"I should just take it down to headquarters and go over it there," the detective said, then grinned slightly. "But, since you went to so much trouble to get it, I won't."

He joined them at the kitchen table, then cast a look at Rick. "I assume you're interested in what's in here, too."

"Of course. I want to find Ken's killer as badly as Dana does." His gaze locked on hers. "I have my own personal reasons for wanting to prove that neither I, nor anyone at *Yo, Amigo* was involved."

O'Flannery watched the byplay between her and Rick, then nodded. "Okay, then let's see what we have."

He flipped the daybook open to January. Meeting after meeting had been entered in Mrs. Fallon's neat, precise handwriting. There was nothing unusual about any of them. As far as Dana could see they were the usual assortment of meetings necessary to conducting the business of the church, plus the regular weekly notation of Ken's commitment to spend the evening at *Yo, Amigo.*

Most of the meetings had times dutifully noted, but toward the beginning of February there were several entries which did not. Just a name had been jotted down.

"What do you suppose this means?" O'Flannery asked. "Are these people who dropped by without an appointment?"

"Exactly," Dana said. "She always found that extremely annoying, even though Ken welcomed drop-in visits. I guess she dealt with her frustration by putting the names down after the fact."

Tremayne's name had been entered repeatedly, indicating his arrogant habit, which Mrs. Fallon's scowls had obviously failed to correct. So had Peter Drake's name and Miriam Kelso's. Mrs. Fallon had always grumbled that people like that should have known better. "No one would walk into *their* offices uninvited and unscheduled," she had protested often enough.

Some of the names entered were kids, including several visits by Juan Jesus in the days right before Ken's death. Since there had been no mention of his dropping by in January, his repeated visits in February seemed especially suspicious to Dana.

"Could he have known something?" Dana wondered aloud. She glanced at Rick. "Maybe he'd heard something on his weekends at home and it worried him."

Rick looked doubtful. He also looked as if he could cheerfully strangle her for dragging the teenager into this.

"Only one way to find out," he said eventually and with

obvious reluctance. "He's staying just a few blocks away, isn't he? Let's go talk to him and clear this up right now."

"Fine," Dana said, facing Rick defiantly. It wasn't as if she'd accused Juan Jesus of killing anyone, just of knowing something about Ken's murder.

"Hold on, you two," O'Flannery said, as they both stood up. "This is a police investigation, remember? If anybody's going to talk to the kid, it'll be me."

Dana glanced at Rick and suspected he was about to argue, which would only cause O'Flannery to dig in his heels and start citing all sorts of ethical considerations. She jumped in first. "Couldn't we all go? Rick knows him. Maybe Juan Jesus will be less frightened and more forthcoming with a familiar face in the room."

The detective scowled. "I really hate it when civilians make sense. Okay, let's do it."

To her regret, he tucked the calendar under his arm. Apparently, he had no intention of letting her hang onto the lone piece of potential evidence she'd discovered.

"Shall we all go in my car?" O'Flannery asked.

"Fine," Dana said, just as Rick said, "No."

She stared at him.

"Dana and I will take my car," he said tightly. "We'll meet you there."

Judging from the tightening of his jaw and the fierce expression in his eyes, Dana had the feeling that for once in her life, she ought to jump at the chance to have police protection. Unfortunately, O'Flannery merely waved his agreement and headed for his car. She shot a tentative gaze at Rick.

"Okay, whatever's on your mind, let's hear it," she said, bracing for a tirade.

He glanced at her. "What makes you think there's something on my mind?"

"You didn't arrange to get me all to yourself, so you could chat about the weather or kiss me senseless."

His lips almost quirked into a smile at that. "Don't be so

sure about the kissing. There are times when you do tempt me beyond endurance."

Despite her suspicions, despite everything, she was intrigued. "Really?"

"Really," he confirmed. "Don't let it go to your head, though. There are also many times I'd like to throttle you, *querida*."

"And this would be which?"

He did smile at that. "Perhaps I'll let you think about that for a bit." His expression sobered. "In the meantime, I will try to think how to protect a good kid from the kind of interrogation you've drawn him into."

"You blame me for drawing Juan Jesus into this?" she asked incredulously.

"I didn't hear anyone else suggesting he might be involved, did you?"

"But I was just . . ."

"Just what? Trying to cast blame on the outsider, yes? You are more like the others than you would care to admit, I think. Maybe worse, because you hide your prejudice."

"No," she retorted defensively, shocked by his interpretation of her actions. "His name was there. I was just speculating out loud."

"To a police officer," he reminded her. "Not to me. Not to Kate. To a cop."

She winced at his accusatory tone. "I want answers."

"Any answers?" he asked. "Or the truth?"

"The truth, of course."

He regarded her with obvious sorrow. "Sometimes, I wonder, *querida*. Sometimes, I wonder."

Twenty-six

Juan Jesus Villanueva was a skinny and, at the moment, frightened sixteen-year-old. His eyes widened with alarm, and he literally shook when Rick introduced him to O'Flannery and explained that he was a detective.

"I didn't do nothing, man." He gazed beseechingly at Rick for support. "Ever since the *padre* brought me out here, I've played strictly by the rules. I swear it."

Rick put his hand on the boy's shoulder and squeezed reassuringly. "It's okay. We just wanted to ask you a few questions. Nobody's accusing you of anything," he said with a pointed glance at Dana.

She smiled at Juan Jesus. "Truly, all we want is some help in trying to figure out what happened to my husband. Can you try to remember what was going on back in February, right before he was killed?"

Rick felt him shudder, but the kid bravely forced a nod. "The *padre* was good to me. I'll tell you whatever I can, if you think it will help."

"Thank you," Dana said. "Maybe we should go inside, where we'll be more comfortable."

Juan Jesus shook his head. "I'd rather stay out here. There's no point in dragging the Wilsons into this." He gazed at Rick, studiously avoiding making eye contact with O'Flannery. "What did you want to know?"

Rick glanced at the detective for permission to do the questioning. The other man nodded.

"Do you remember back in February if you were stopping in to see the *padre* a lot?" Rick asked.

The boy looked relieved by the question. "Sure," he said without hesitation. "A couple of times a week."

"Why?"

"Is it important?" he hedged.

"That depends on the answer," Rick told him. "Do you have something to hide?"

"Not the way you mean." He looked chagrined. "Okay. You're not going to believe this, but I was having trouble with Spanish. I mean I can speak it and all. Hell . . ." He glanced at Dana. "Sorry. I mean that's all anyone talks at home, but I never learned to write or read the stuff, not the way you have to to pass a class."

"Why didn't you ask your parents or Maria for help?" Rick asked.

Juan Jesus regarded him with disgust. "You gotta be kidding. I'd never have heard the end of it. Mama would have had me at the kitchen table all weekend long with all the old books she brought from Mexico. I didn't want to waste my time like that."

"So you went to Ken for help?" Rick asked.

"He'd told me from the start I could always come to him, if I had a problem. Believe me, this was a big problem. He tutored me a couple of hours a week." He grinned. "Brought my grade up to a B-minus, too."

"And that's the only reason you were spending time with him?" Rick persisted.

"Sure." He stared at them all curiously. "Why? What did you think was going on?"

"Never mind," Rick said. "You've been a big help."

"Wait," Dana said. "Could I ask one thing, Juan Jesus?" Rick scowled at her. "Dana . . ."

"It's okay. I don't mind," the teen said.

"Thank you. I was just wondering if anything unusual ever happened while you were with my husband."

Juan Jesus looked perplexed. "Unusual how?"

"A phone call that seemed to upset him, maybe, or an argument with someone. Did anyone drop in unexpectedly?"

Rick had to admit the questions were logical ones. Other names had been noted on those days when Juan Jesus had been in Ken's office. Perhaps he had overheard or seen something.

"People dropped in all the time," the teenager said. "It made Mrs. Fallon loco. She used to get this pinched expression on her face, like she'd smelled a dead rat or something."

"So you didn't find anything odd about any of these drop-in visits?" Dana persisted.

"Not really," he said. Then his expression turned thoughtful. "Except this once. I got there and heard somebody inside crying. I figured somebody had died, the way they were wailing. Mrs. Fallon hurried me out of the office. She made up some errand for me to run. In fact, she couldn't hustle me out of there fast enough."

Dana's shoulders sagged with disappointment. "So you never saw who was in the office?"

"Sure, I did. She was too rattled to think clearly, so the errand was a snap. It only took me a minute, and by the time I got back, the crying had stopped, but the door was still closed. Just when I thought Mrs. F was going to send me off on another errand, the door opened and this lady came out. She practically knocked me down, she was in such a hurry. I've never seen anybody look so furious in all my life, not even on the streets back home. She looked mad enough to kill somebody."

As if he realized what he'd said, his eyes widened with shock. "You don't think? . . ."

"We don't know what to think," Rick insisted quickly. He didn't want Juan Jesus to start speculating. The rest of them were doing quite enough of that. "That's why we're exploring all sorts of possibilities. You don't know who this woman was, do you?"

Juan Jesus shook his head. "Nah. I'd never seen her before. And the *padre* had this confidentiality thing. He acted as if it had never happened. So did Mrs. F. I figured it was none of my business."

"What did she look like?" Dana asked.

"It was kinda hard to tell. She was tall and skinny, I remember that, but she was wearing this big, floppy hat. It covered up most of her face."

Rick glanced at Dana to see if the description rang any bells. He recognized a spark of excitement in her eyes and gathered it had, though she was remaining tight-lipped about her suspicions.

"Anything else?" he asked O'Flannery.

"No." The detective smiled at Juan Jesus. "You've been a big help, son. The *padre* would be proud of you."

Juan Jesus glanced at Rick for confirmation. Rick nodded. "He would be, you know."

"I owe him a lot," the boy said, gazing at Dana. "You must miss him a lot, huh?"

"Yes," she said softly. "A lot."

"If you'd ever like me to come by, maybe help out with your kids or something, I could. I hung out with them sometimes at the church, after my lessons. They're pretty cool for little guys. I'm the youngest in my family, so it was kinda fun to be around kids younger than me. I felt like a big brother, instead of being the baby."

Rick saw that Dana was genuinely touched by the offer. Tears sparkled in her eyes.

"They would like that," she said. "And so would I. When they come back from Florida, I'll call you."

"They're in Florida? Awesome. Frankie's down there, too."

All of the color seemed to wash out of Dana's face at that. "Frankie who?" she demanded so harshly that Juan Jesus looked taken aback.

"Frankie Vincenzi," he responded at once. "He's in my

class at school, or at least he was, until his mom sent him and his kid brother off to Florida to stay with his grandparents."

"When was that?"

"A couple of weeks ago, I guess. Maybe longer."

"Do you know where in Florida?"

He shook his head. "I don't remember. Geography was my second worst subject. Maybe if I heard the name, it'd come back to me."

"Orlando? Miami? Tampa?" Dana suggested.

Rick stared at her, stunned by the desperation he heard in her voice.

"Nah, it wasn't any place that big."

"Think, please. Was it Clearwater? Fort Myers?"

Juan Jesus's expression brightened. "Yeah, that's it. Fort Myers. I knew it sounded like some military base or something."

Rather than looking relieved that Juan Jesus had remembered, Dana looked as if she might faint. Rick touched her arm. "Are you okay?"

"I have to get home," she said, shakily. "Right away."

Rick glanced at O'Flannery, who was watching Dana intently. "Are we through here?" he asked him.

"For the moment."

"Are you coming back to the house?"

"No. I have some things I want to follow up on at the station. I'll catch up with you two later."

The minute they were back in the car, Rick turned to Dana. "Okay, *querida,* what's going on?"

"Just take me home, please. Hurry. I have to call my parents."

Suddenly it all added up. Her panic. The mention of Fort Myers. Frankie Vincenzi. He turned on the engine and sped out of the Wilsons' driveway.

"You are leaping to conclusions again, *querida,*" he said, even though he'd just done exactly the same thing.

"What conclusions?"

"That Carolina Vincenzi's children are the ones taunting your boy."

"It has to be," she insisted. "But it's more than that. You heard Juan Jesus's description of the woman in Ken's office that day. It had to be Carolina."

He regarded her with confusion. "And if it was?"

"Didn't you hear what he said? He said she looked mad enough to kill."

"And from this you've concluded that she was behind Ken's murder?"

"It makes sense," she insisted.

"No," he argued. He tried to inject a note of reason. "What was her motive?"

"I don't know," she admitted with obvious reluctance. "Whatever they were fighting about."

"Do you know a court of law that would permit this as evidence?"

She scowled at him. "I don't give a damn about evidence. I want to protect my boys. She knows where they are."

"So do dozens of other people," he reminded her. "Everyone in the congregation knows that you took them to Florida to be with your parents. It would not be so difficult for anyone to get the address from the church office. I'd be willing to bet you even received condolence notes down there, didn't you?"

She shuddered at that and covered her face with her hands. "Oh, God, why didn't I think of that? I should never have told anyone they were there."

"You weren't thinking clearly."

"But I should have been. From the beginning I believed that Ken's death wasn't an accident. I should have been more cautious. What kind of investigator am I, if I can't even think to protect my own kids?"

"You were not thinking as an investigator at the time," he reminded her gently. "You were thinking exactly as you should have been, as a grieving wife and worried mother."

She sucked in a deep breath and visibly steadied herself.

"Yes," she said, her tone suggesting a strengthened resolve. "That was exactly what I was doing, but no more." She peered out the window, then pointed. "Take a left at the next corner."

"But that's the opposite direction from your house."

"I know."

He regarded her suspiciously. "Where are we going?" he asked, while he made the turn she'd indicated. Apparently he had no willpower at all where she was concerned. Going along with her hare-brained schemes was a habit he really should concentrate on breaking.

"Where else?" she said. "We are going to pay a call on Carolina Vincenzi."

That was not exactly what Rick had had in mind when he'd cautioned her against leaping to conclusions, but he could see from the determined set of her jaw that there would be no talking her out of it. She'd decided to go straight to the source for her answers and, unfortunately, he couldn't fault her logic, even if he did question the impetuous timing of her decision.

"Do you have a plan?" he inquired.

"What sort of plan?" she replied testily.

"Do you know what you intend to ask her? What are we looking for?"

"For starters, I want to know what she was wailing about in Ken's office that day, to use Juan Jesus's phrase."

"And if she chooses to lie?"

She sighed at the suggestion. "Hopefully, my gut instincts will kick in, and I'll be able to tell."

Resigned to helping her in this folly, he said dryly, "Just in case, perhaps you should settle for keeping Mrs. Vincenzi occupied, while I poke around elsewhere in her house."

She gaped at that. "You're going to search the house, while she's in it? No, it's too risky."

"And what you intend is not?"

She had no argument for that. "But how?" she asked eventually.

"You leave that to me," he said, figuring it was best she not know exactly how skilled he was at breaking and entering. Maybe he'd lost his edge, anyway. It had been a long time. Perhaps he would be caught red-handed, just as she had been at *Yo, Amigo*.

"Does she have a housekeeper?" he asked.

"No. I think she has a maid, but not full-time."

"Well, hopefully the maid will be off."

"And if she's not?"

He grinned. A maid was the least of his concerns. "I can be very persuasive, when I put my mind to it."

She scowled. "I'm not so sure I like the sound of that."

"No need to be jealous, *querida*. I will always save my best efforts for you."

"I am not jealous," she insisted indignantly. "For some reason, I'm just worried about your sorry hide."

"You leave the worrying to me. I will drop you at the corner, then circle the block to park in the back. Keep your eyes open. When you see the car in the front again, then you can wrap up your conversation with Mrs. Vincenzi."

"What if she happens to hear you creeping around inside?"

"She won't," he assured her. "Not if you irritate her sufficiently. She will, perhaps, be wailing again. That should cover any noise I might make."

"Not that I doubt your snooping skills," she said, "but do you have a plan? Do you have any idea what you're looking for?"

"Same as you, *querida,* something that would give her a motive to kill."

"Or the weapon," Dana suggested belatedly. "My God, Rick, what if she has a gun?"

"If it's THE gun, then we're in great shape."

"Not if it's aimed at us," she said, her expression suddenly dire.

"Don't chicken out on me now."

Her chin rose. "I am not chickening out," she insisted. "You're the one who's always preaching caution."

He grinned, as he slowed at the corner. "What do I know?" he asked with a shrug. "Go, *querida*."

She opened the door and slid out, casting a worried look back at him, as she slowly closed the door.

"Be careful," she said, then turned and marched intrepidly down the block.

Rick watched her go with a renewed sense of admiration. She truly was a remarkable woman. With a sudden flash of insight, he realized that he had fallen in love with her. Despite her infuriating habit of blaming him for murders he hadn't committed, he wanted to spend the rest of his life with her.

Only after he'd driven away did he begin to get that first nagging sense of impending disaster burning a hole in the pit of his stomach. Had he just sent the woman he loved off to get her head blown off?

Twenty-seven

Carolina Vincenzi lived in ostentatious style. The heavily wooded lots in her exclusive development were an acre or more. With the exception of one or two towering old oak trees, which had the audacity to shed an occasional dead leaf, her grounds had been trimmed and manicured as tidily as any formal garden Dana had ever seen on an English country estate. Even the days-old snow looked clean, as if it had been swept free of soot.

The house, which had been built in no discernible style, had touches of Art Deco, a little taste of country French, and a hint of Frank Lloyd Wright. It was ugly as sin, too big for the lot, and every bit as tasteless as Dana would have anticipated, right down to the gargoyle knockers on the double front doors.

To Dana's frustration, pounding on that massive front door with that hideous knocker and ringing the bell drew no response. The place was as silent as a tomb—an image she wished hadn't come to mind.

Foiled in her plan to cross-examine Carolina, she crept behind the bushes to peer in the closest window, a narrow floor-to-ceiling panel of glass beside the door.

The foyer was practically the size of her living room, with an Oriental carpet in bright reds and blacks covering most of the wide plank oak floor. An Oriental vase, probably from some ancient dynasty, sat atop a gleaming mahogany table in the center. Someone had devoted hours of elbow grease to getting that deep shine on the wood.

Dana had seen exclusive hotel lobbys that had been decorated with less attention to effect. In her house that table would have been cluttered with mail and keys. Not here. She doubted there was so much as a speck of dust on it, or even swirling in the air above.

Just as she was debating whether to try some makeshift means of picking the lock, she saw a stealthily creeping shadow toward the back of the foyer. Rick, no doubt. She tapped lightly on the window to try to attract his attention.

Rather than Rick, however, it was another man who slipped into view. Peter Drake. Dana stared at him incredulously.

Fortunately, he either hadn't heard her tapping or was too absorbed in his own invasion of the place to give it any attention. He edged into a room on the left and disappeared from view.

Dana practically trampled some kind of thorny bush in her haste to get around to the back of the house, so she could intercept Rick, before he inadvertently joined Drake inside. She rounded the corner in such a rush that she ran smack into the very man she'd hoped to warn.

"What the hell?" Rick muttered, his arms closing around her. "Dana?" He scowled at her "Why aren't you inside? You've had plenty of time."

"Because no one answered the door," she said simply.

"Ah, I see. Well, good," he said, not wasting time on questioning what he obviously viewed as their good fortune. "Then we should have free run of the place."

When he would have moved toward the door, she held him back. "Not exactly."

"What do you mean, not exactly?"

She described what she had seen. "I guess he figured whoever had been ringing the bell had left."

"Or he was trying to get to a window so he could check," Rick suggested.

Just then they heard an engine starting. Apparently there had been another alternative.

"Or he was trying to get to a door, so he could beat a hasty retreat," she said. She took off for the front, with Rick right beside her. They were just in time to see Drake's familiar and very expensive sports utility vehicle speed away.

She glanced up into Rick's puzzled eyes. "Curiouser and curiouser, yes?"

"I'll say. What do you want to do now? Shall we leave or check out the inside and see if we can figure out what Drake was up to?"

She regarded him with suspicion. "It's my call?"

"*Querida,* you're the investigator."

"Yes," she said, grateful for the acknowledgment. "Yes, I am." Excitement shimmered through her. "Let's do it. Can you get us in? I don't have my lock picks with me."

"Perhaps we should just try the door Drake used. I doubt he was locking up on his way out."

Naturally, though, that would have been too easy. The house was locked up tighter than Fort Knox, complete with an alarm system that warned Rick off.

"It's too advanced for my skills," he conceded, after studying the wiring.

"Which raises an interesting point," Dana said. "How did Peter Drake get past it?"

"Maybe Carolina let him in."

Dana recalled the weird feeling she'd gotten as she'd approached the house, the image of the place as a tomb. "You don't suppose . . ." She let her voice trail off, but Rick caught her meaning.

"That she's inside," he said. "Unfortunately, there's only one way to find out. I don't have a problem setting off the alarm to find out, if you don't. We can always say Carolina expected us and that we saw someone sneaking around on the property and decided we'd better investigate."

"Think that'll fly with Detective O'Flannery?"

Rick shrugged. "I suppose it depends on whether or not we find Carolina dead."

Dana shuddered. She'd really stumbled upon all the dead acquaintances she wanted to, when she'd discovered Mrs. Fallon's body. "Maybe we should look in the garage first, see if her car's here."

Rick grinned. "Turning cautious, *querida?*"

She scowled at him. "You should be pleased."

"I am," he assured her, leading the way to the double garage on the far side of the house.

To Dana's regret, the builder had inconveniently neglected to put any window into the garage. Dana stared at the impenetrable-looking doors, while Rick searched for some indication of whether the alarm system extended to this part of the structure.

"Is it wired?" she asked.

"There's no evidence of it, but anything is possible."

The lack of conviction in his voice set off her own mental alarms. That prickling on the back of her neck had once been very familiar. It had alerted her to impending disaster.

"What now?" she asked.

"Now we see if lifting weights has paid off for me," Rick said, grabbing the handle and trying to heft one of the doors up. Apparently locked, it stayed firmly in place. In fact, it didn't so much as creak on its hinges.

"Very solid," he muttered, then brightened. "But no shrieking alarms have gone off, because I tried to lift it. I would have expected a very sensitive motion detector."

"A very good sign," she agreed. "Then we move on to plan two." She dug around in the bottom of her purse for a paper clip. She waved it under his nose and knelt down to fiddle with the lock.

"You expect to break in with a paper clip?"

"No, I *hope* to break in with a paper clip," she said, trying to delicately nudge the lock's tumblers. Her fingers weren't nearly as deft as they'd once been, but the skill hadn't entirely abandoned her. She felt the precise instant when everything clicked into place. The handle turned easily and the door began to glide up smoothly. Adrenaline pumped furiously through her veins. Damn, but it felt good to be back in action. Her confidence soared.

"That's far enough," Rick said, bending down to peek through the opening. "No need to have the neighbors wondering why the garage door's sitting open."

"What neighbors? The nearest one is half a block away, behind a quarter-acre of trees."

"You're assuming he never leaves the house to walk the dog I hear barking."

Dana frowned. "Okay, your powers of observation are very good."

"Better than yours, perhaps?"

"Don't rub it in. It might make me start to wonder how you honed them."

He chuckled. "Yes, we definitely would not want that."

"So, is there a car inside or not?"

"Two of them. A Mercedes and a very expensive sports car, a Lamborghini, perhaps, though I have never seen one up close."

"That's Carolina's," Dana confirmed. "Which means she could be inside."

"Or in Florida with her children," Rick reminded her. "She would not leave a car like this in the lot at O'Hare. She would take a limo to the airport, yes?"

The reminder that at this very moment Carolina might be near Dana's children frightened her even more deeply than the possibility had earlier. Finding Peter Drake sneaking around inside the house had only confirmed that something very strange was going on and that Carolina was involved in it.

"Are you ready to check inside?" Rick asked. "If the garage alarm was off, then my guess would be that the whole system is down."

"No," Dana said at once, oblivious to the golden opportunity they had to sneak in undetected. "I want to check on my kids. I have to warn my parents to be alert, in case Carolina shows up there."

"Not even a quick peek?" Rick asked. "You could use the phone inside and charge it to your calling card, so there would be no record of it on their bill."

Tempted, Dana stared at him, intrigued with the devious workings of his mind. There had been a time when she would have hired an intrepid, quick-thinking man like that on the spot to work for her. Now she couldn't help worrying just a little about all that she didn't know about the darker side of Rick's past. Was he merely indulging her in this quest to keep her from once more focusing on him as a suspect? At the moment, there was enough to intrigue her right here. She would worry about Rick's motives later.

"Okay, you win." She wiggled the paper clip in front of his nose. "Your turn," she suggested, when they reached the front door.

To her chagrin, he was even more adept than she had been with the garage door. They were inside that pretentious foyer practically before she could blink.

"You call. I'll look around," Rick said. "Make sure you don't leave any fingerprints on the phone."

She tolerated the warning because it made sense. "Be careful," she whispered. "This place gives me the creeps."

"It is good to know you don't need a mansion to be happy," he said in an enigmatic way that raised goosebumps and some fascinating speculation.

"Not this mansion, anyway." She left the room before he could respond to that. She headed straight in the direction she had seen Peter Drake taking. Maybe he had only been looking for a nearby exit, or maybe he'd been doing a quick scan for something important.

The room she entered was very masculine and, indeed, it did have its own exit. Perhaps so Carolina's husband could slip in and out late at night? she wondered. It was an intriguing possibility.

She knew next to nothing about Tony Vincenzi, except that he'd made his money with a string of upscale pizza places. He rarely attended church with his wife, except on special occasions, such as Christmas Eve services. In fact, Dana realized, she had heard once that he and their sons attended the nearby Catholic church, which would explain why Bobby hadn't known the boy who had taunted him down in Florida . . . if that's who it was.

Although she was itching to poke through the desk, she took a handkerchief out of her purse, picked up the phone, and dialed her parents' number, using her calling card to do it, just as Rick had suggested.

Her father answered on the first ring. It was an old habit, indicative of his impatience. He was usually curt to the point of rudeness on the phone, except with her. His greeting now was as abrupt as always.

"Hey, Dad, it's me."

"Dana, baby, how are you?" he asked, his tone softening.

"I'm fine. Are the boys there with you?"

"They went shopping with your mother. Why? You sound worried."

"It's nothing specific, just a mother's intuition, I suppose."

"A mother's or a private investigator's?"

"A little of both," she admitted. "Did Mom ever find out the name of the kid who'd been tormenting Bobby at school?"

"Bobby wouldn't say. She hasn't pursued it with the teacher, as far as I know. Is it important?"

"It could be. I just heard that a couple of kids from the area are down there."

"So you think they picked up that garbage about Ken from home?"

"Exactly."

"But who would say something like that, unless they knew about the drugs being planted?" He hesitated. "My God, you think that that kid could know the person who planted the drugs, don't you?"

She wasn't surprised by how quickly he'd grasped the problem. "It's possible. Please, Dad, don't alarm them, but keep a close eye on the kids, okay? This whole thing really has me spooked."

"What do the police say?"

"They're doing the best they can," she said, feeling more generosity toward them than she had when she'd rushed home to pick up their slack. "They agree with me that it looks as if Ken was framed by somebody hoping to destroy his reputation after his death, probably so the police would dismiss his murder as a drug deal gone sour or something."

"Honey, you do what you have to do. I know you're torn about leaving the kids down here with us, but they're fine. They're adjusting to school. Even Bobby's getting along okay now. Ken was the best son-in-law a man could ask for. You clear his name, okay?"

"I'm trying."

"Just don't put yourself in danger. The boys need you safe and sound. We all do."

Dana thought of the man in the house with her and wondered if the warning hadn't come too late. She trusted that Rick wouldn't harm her, at least not physically. But in making him her ally, she had placed her heart at serious risk.

How would her father feel about this man who was so very different from Ken? she wondered. Would he welcome him, as he had the quieter, gentler man she'd married? Or would his old instincts about troublemakers kick in? Would he view Rick as an ex-street kid who'd flouted the law for too many years? Fortunately, the need to answer that was a long way down the road.

"I love you, Dad."

"Love you, too, baby. Take care of yourself. I'll see to it that no harm comes to your sons."

"I know you will," she said. After she'd hung up, she prayed that he could do as he'd promised. Was he any more of a match for a murderer than Ken had been?

Yes, she concluded. Because unlike her husband, who had trusted everyone, her father had no illusions about human nature. He'd been a prosecutor for too many years, seen too many supposedly reformed criminals released back on the streets to commit more atrocities. He was the one who'd fueled her desire to become an investigator, in the first place. On occasion, she had even been fortunate enough to work for him, before his retirement. He'd had a cop's instincts and a passion for seeing justice done.

"Dana?" Rick called in a hushed voice.

She went into the foyer and saw him standing at the top of the stairs.

"I think you ought to come up here."

Her heart thudded dully. "It's not Carolina, is it?"

He shook his head.

"Then what?"

"Not what, who. My guess is it's her husband. He looks just like the guy in the wedding picture on the nightstand."

Dana sucked in a deep breath and squeezed her eyes shut. When she opened them again, she forced herself to climb the steps.

"He's dead?" she asked when she reached the top.

"Oh, yeah," Rick said softly. "He is very dead."

In fact, Tony Vincenzi looked as if he'd been dead for some time—a day or two, perhaps—which brought into question who had killed him. It hardly seemed likely that Peter Drake had done it days earlier, then returned to the scene of the crime for another search of the premises—not unless he was a total idiot, anyway.

Had he even seen the body? He'd been downstairs when Dana had spotted him.

She glanced at Rick. "Shall we call O'Flannery from here or tip him off after we make a getaway?"

"Your call."

"My gut is practically screaming that we should get our butts as far away from this place as possible," she said.

"And your head?"

"For once, it concurs. Let's go." At the foot of the stairs, she hesitated and glanced around wistfully. "I never got to look around down here."

"I think we can safely assume that if there were anything incriminating in the place, your friend Mr. Drake would have found it. Whoever killed Vincenzi, my guess is that Drake was here to tidy up."

"You think Carolina asked him for help?"

"Or whoever ordered the hit, in the first place."

"Hit? Why did you say it like that?"

"His hands were bound behind him. It looked to me as if he'd been kneeling on the floor when he was shot. Classic hit."

Obviously she'd been too rattled by the sight of yet another body to analyze the scene. "Of course," she said, recalling the image of the way his body rested against the foot of the bed, almost as if he'd been saying his prayers when he was shot. It didn't surprise her, as it once might have, that his prayers hadn't been answered.

"Two minutes in that den, that's all I ask," she pleaded.

"I don't think so," Rick said.

He suddenly grabbed her hand and practically dragged her toward the back of the house with an urgency that startled her.

"Would you mind telling me what's going on?" she said, balking at the door.

"We're leaving."

"By the back door? We came in the front."

"Just as Detective O'Flannery is about to do," he noted with some urgency. "Apparently your Mr. Drake wasn't quite as oblivious to our presence as we might have hoped. My guess is he gave us time to get well and truly implicated in the crime, then called the police and reported prowlers."

Dana didn't waste time cursing Peter Drake or the possibility of a silent alarm, which neither of them had considered. She raced out the back door, one step behind Rick.

Fortunately, he'd had the foresight to park on an undeveloped piece of land, just beyond the Vincenzis' property line. They disappeared into the woods almost at once, making it a virtual certainty that O'Flannery couldn't spot them, not without bloodhounds anyway.

Dana's adrenaline was pumping fast and furiously as they pulled away.

"Remind me to take you on a nice, tame date, once all this is over and done with," Rick suggested a few minutes later, when they'd both caught their breath.

"You sure you wouldn't get bored with me?" she asked.

He gazed into her eyes. "Never, *querida*. Never."

The wicked desire she saw blazing in his eyes made her tremble. Oh, yes, she thought, she was in this—whatever *this* turned out to be—way, way over her head.

Twenty-eight

There was no time to ponder what they might have done about the desire darkening Rick's eyes, because they found Kate waiting impatiently for them in the kitchen. The aroma of food was in the air and the table had been set for four. Dana had a pretty good idea whom she'd been expecting.

"Where the devil have you two been?" Kate demanded when they crossed the threshold.

"You wouldn't believe me, if I told you," Dana replied. "Have you made coffee, by any chance?"

"I've had time to make a whole gourmet meal," Kate retorted irritably. "Yes, there's coffee and a roast and baked potatoes and fresh green beans. I was just thinking of baking a damned cherry pie."

Dana grinned at Rick's incredulous expression. "Kate cooks when she's anxious," she explained.

"You would not like to visit *Yo, Amigo* when these attacks come on, would you?" he asked, sniffing the air appreciatively.

Kate frowned at him. "I don't expect another one. I'm demanding that the doctor give me tranquilizers, as long as Dana and I remain friends."

Dana regarded her suspiciously. "Are you sure I'm to blame for this? I thought you had a date with O'Flannery tonight. Did you have this meal planned for him?"

Kate scowled. "Okay, yes, but the dutiful detective got a call, so I hauled everything over here, figuring maybe you could fill me in on what's been happening. O'Flannery is as tight-lipped as a clam. He said he would come by here, when he could, if he could, whatever. I got the distinct impression that there is news."

"You could say that," Dana agreed. She described the assortment of dead bodies that had recently come to light.

"Holy mackerel!" Kate breathed, when she was done. "What do you suppose it all means?"

Dana glanced at Rick, then said, "Actually, I've been thinking about that. As weird and unlikely as it seems, I think maybe Carolina and Peter were having an affair."

"Oh, yuck," Kate said. "He is so . . ."

"Bland," Dana supplied.

"No, slimy, smarmy, whatever."

"Not a good candidate for an affair with the elegant Carolina?" Rick interpreted.

"Exactly."

"So, if it wasn't romantic, what was it?" Dana asked. "What connected them?"

"The obvious," Rick said. "The church. They were all on the board, were they not?"

"Yes," Dana said. "So what?"

"Have you seen any financial records from the church?" he asked.

Dana stared. A familiar tingle began, and for once it wasn't the least bit sexual in nature. It was the reaction she always had when she finally discovered the thread that would start to unravel a complex mystery. "What exactly are you thinking?"

"Were these two in a position to embezzle church funds?" he asked point-blank.

Dana was at a loss. She had never interfered in that part of Ken's life. "I have no idea how that part of the church's business was conducted. The only person besides Ken who could tell us that would be Mrs. Fallon."

"And she is conveniently dead," Kate said. "I think Rick might be on to something."

Dana held up her hands. "Okay, I see where you're going with this, and it's certainly worth checking out. It would explain why someone planted drugs. They probably figured it would make it look as if Ken embezzled the money to buy drugs, right?"

"Exactly," Rick said.

"Okay, then, why is Tony Vincenzi dead? He didn't even attend this church."

"Wild speculation?" Rick asked. "He found out what his wife was up to and ratted her out to Ken. That's why she was wailing in his office that day, because she'd been caught. In her case, confession apparently wasn't good for her soul."

As badly as she wanted to tie up all the loose ends, Dana couldn't entirely buy Rick's not quite far-fetched theory. "Why would they need to embezzle church funds? Carolina's loaded. You saw her house. And Drake does okay."

"Are you sure about that?" Rick asked. "Appearances can be deceiving. Maybe Carolina's husband kept her on a tight budget. Maybe Drake lived beyond his means."

"And Tremayne? Where does he fit in?" she asked.

"Maybe he doesn't," Kate chimed in. "Maybe we've been focusing too hard on him, because we don't like him."

"Or maybe he's behind it all, to get money for his failed development deal in South America," Dana said slowly.

"We need to see the books," Kate concluded. "Or bank records. Do you have any of that stuff around the house?"

Dana shook her head. "It's all in the church office. Even if we found the books, do either of you know anything about accounting? I certainly don't. It's not the kind of thing I ever investigated."

"I do," Rick said. "I've had to take a crash course since opening *Yo, Amigo.* The government demands very accurate records for the funding it provides."

Kate cast a resigned look toward the stove. "That roast was destined to taste like sawdust, wasn't it?"

Dana grinned "Then it will be just right for that cop who stood you up."

Kate visibly perked up at that thought. "Yes, it will."

"Which cop would that be?" a familiar voice asked just as they reached the front door.

They found themselves facing a very disgruntled-looking O'Flannery.

"Whoops," Dana murmured under her breath.

O'Flannery didn't wait for a reply to his question. "Now just where would you all be off to this time?" he inquired cheerfully.

"A walk," Kate said at once. "We were just going for a walk to work up an appetite."

"I thought we had dinner plans," he said.

"We did. You canceled," she reminded him. "Your message said you'd catch up with me here."

"And take you out," he elaborated.

"You didn't say that. Besides, I'd already cooked. I brought the food over here."

He beamed. "Terrific, then we can all eat together." His gaze settled on Dana, then skipped over to Rick, and back again. "Maybe over dessert you two can tell me what you were doing sneaking around inside the Vincenzi home just prior to my arrival there."

Dana sighed. Rick scowled.

"Who is this Vincenzi person?" he asked.

"Oh, give it up," O'Flannery said. "I know you were there. I saw you as you made a dash for the woods. I didn't waste time giving chase, because I knew exactly where to find you."

Dana's expression brightened. "Precisely. Would you have felt the same, if you'd seriously thought we were fleeing felons?"

"Felons? Maybe not, but you were fleeing a crime scene. How'd you get in and why were you there?"

"Do we have to do this standing in the middle of the living room, while my roast dies a little more with each passing minute?" Kate grumbled peevishly.

O'Flannery sent a warm smile her way. "Of course not. I'm sure we'll all be much more relaxed over a nice, hot meal."

"Speak for yourself," Dana muttered.

"Hush, *querida,*" Rick whispered as O'Flannery followed Kate toward the kitchen. "You will stir his suspicions."

Dana stared at him incredulously. "His suspicions are on full alert, as it is. I don't have any explanations I care to share with him, do you?"

"No, but I am very quick on my feet. There was a time when it was the only thing between me and prison."

"How reassuring."

He caught her hand in his and squeezed it. Oddly enough, she felt better almost immediately. Not relieved exactly, but warmer. Hotter, in fact. No, she corrected at once, that was another reaction entirely, and one that was growing increasingly troublesome.

"Ah, I see the table is already set for four," O'Flannery said jovially. "What good planning. Or were you expecting someone else?"

"It would serve you right, if we were," Kate muttered, as she began shuttling dishes of food to the table—enough food for an army, which only confirmed her earlier agitation.

His gaze narrowed. "I thought you understood that I had to go out on a call."

"That was before I knew you were going to try to pin a crime on my friends."

"Nobody said anything about locking your friends up for a crime," he protested. "Besides, Tony Vincenzi was long dead by the time they broke in."

Dana exchanged a congratulatory look with Rick. Obviously, she knew more than she'd ever wanted to know about dead bodies. A few more and maybe she'd qualify for a career in forensic medicine.

She was so intent on patting herself on the back that she apparently missed the significance of the rest of O'Flannery's statement. Kate hadn't.

"Are you going to charge them with breaking and entering?" she demanded.

"Not if they open up and tell me what they were doing there," he said, then gazed first at Dana and then at Rick. "Well?"

"Do you actually have evidence that we were ever in that house?" Rick queried quietly.

"An eyewitness, namely me."

Dana gathered from the question what Rick's strategy was going to be. She chimed in. "Where were we when you spotted us?"

"Hightailing it across the backyard toward the woods."

She grinned. Rick looked complacent.

"Interesting," she said. "That would be outside the house, then, correct?"

O'Flannery scowled. "Oh, no, you don't. You two were inside. There's not a doubt in my mind about that."

"But you just said that you didn't actually see us inside," she reminded him. "You're making an assumption based on circumstantial evidence."

He didn't look nearly as rattled or as defensive as she might have liked. He turned calmly to Kate, instead.

"Did these two happen to mention anything about Tony Vincenzi when they arrived here?"

"You mean that he was dead?" Kate asked.

Rick groaned.

"Oh, Kate," Dana murmured.

Kate stared at them. "What did I do?"

"They would only have known about Vincenzi, if they were in that house," O'Flannery explained gently.

"Oh, hell," Kate muttered, glaring at the detective. "You tricked me."

"I was only able to do it because you're an honest woman.

Thank you. You'll make a terrific witness." He paused and stared pointedly from Rick to Dana and back again. "If it becomes necessary."

Dana broke first. "Okay, okay. I'll tell you why we were there."

He chuckled at the belated and very reluctant offer. "No need," he said indulgently. "Remember, I was there when Juan Jesus described the woman who'd been crying in your husband's office. I knew you'd head straight over there to confront her. I parked a block behind Rick and waited to see how things would play out."

Dana regarded him incredulously. "You tailed us?"

"You bet."

There wasn't so much as a hint of repentance in his voice, which irritated her no end. "Well, given the number of reinforcements you obviously called in," she said sarcastically, "did anybody think to tail Peter Drake, when he slipped out of the place?"

The detective's smug expression slipped just a little at that. "Who the hell is Peter Drake?"

"He's the man who was inside Carolina Vincenzi's house when we got there," Rick supplied. "Too bad you missed him. I suspect he could tell you quite a lot about who murdered Tony Vincenzi and why."

To Kate's obvious irritation, O'Flannery shoved aside his plate and leaned forward, elbows on the table. "Maybe you'd better start at the beginning," he suggested, glaring at Dana. "And this time, don't leave out any of the significant details, okay?"

Something in his impatient tone suggested that there would be dire consequences for jerking him around again. Dana took the hint seriously. After a quick glance at the others for approval, she elaborated on the skimpy story they'd sketched for him earlier. When she was finished, the detective sighed heavily and stood up. After casting a regretful look at his untouched plate of food, he motioned toward the door.

"Let's go, all of you."

"You're taking us to jail?" Kate asked. She seemed to have lost a little of her righteous indignation.

"Not yet," he retorted. "Right now, we're all going over to the church office. While you're in the vicinity, you might want to say a prayer or two that I don't charge the whole bunch of you with obstructing justice and anything else I can dream up."

Her temper clearly revived, Kate planted herself in his path and glared up at him defiantly. "You wouldn't dare."

He scowled right back. "Try me."

Dana had the feeling that a very promising romance was about to go up in smoke, unless someone stepped in to prevent it. Against her better judgment, she interceded.

"Kate, he's just doing his job."

"Well it's a lousy job," Kate grumbled.

"Could we debate the merits of my career choice some other time?" O'Flannery asked. "Or, if you'd prefer, you three can stay here and argue about it, while I go over to the church."

"Not a chance," Dana said, heading for the door. She smiled at him smugly. "Besides, I'm the one who has the keys."

"The lack of keys doesn't appear to be a real impediment with this crowd," he retorted dryly. He reached in his pocket. "Besides, I have a set, too. It's a crime scene, remember? Only the police have access for the moment."

Check and checkmate.

Everyone dutifully trailed after the detective. Dana was so irritated, she was oblivious to the biting, bitter cold wind. She was imagining all sorts of dire fates befalling him and enjoying each and every scenario, when Rick tugged her to a halt.

"What?" she asked, lifting her gaze to meet his.

"You go on. I'm going back into town."

Given the circumstances, the announcement stunned her. She studied his face intently, but his expression was unreadable. "Why? I thought you were going to help us interpret the books."

"I'm sure O'Flannery can do that."

Her suspicions mounted. "And you can't bear the thought of letting another man steal the limelight?"

"Hardly."

"What, then? Why run out now?" She fastened her gaze on his, or tried to, anyway. He continued looking everywhere but directly into her eyes. Either they were getting too close to a solution he didn't like or . . . She regarded him with excitement. "You've thought of something, haven't you?"

"Maybe," he admitted.

"Then I'm coming with you," she said at once.

"No. O'Flannery's going to be ticked enough, when he realizes I'm gone. He'll blow a gasket, if you pull a vanishing act, too. He'll come charging into the city, instead of staying out here and examining those books."

"But you don't think he's going to find anything in the books, do you?"

"I honestly don't know."

"Rick, if you know something, you have to tell me."

He touched a finger to her lips to quiet her. "That's just it, *querida*. I don't know anything. I am only guessing. I will call you as soon as I have something concrete. I swear it. Just cover for me now, okay?"

When it became obvious that he wasn't going to relent and tell her a thing, Dana shrugged indifferently, vowing to herself that she would join him the very instant it was safe to leave Kate and the detective. "Fine. Go."

"What will you tell O'Flannery?"

"Let me worry about that. Get out of here, before he realizes that something is up."

"With Kate beside him, I don't think the investigation is all that's on his mind. He will remain distracted for a moment or two longer. He leaned down and brushed a slow, lingering kiss across her lips.

"I will call you," he whispered eventually. "I promise."

As he turned and hurried swiftly out of sight, Dana sighed.

Didn't he understand that that was another thing Ken's death had accomplished? Ken had left her with very similar words on the night he'd been shot. She no longer had any more faith in promises than she did in prayers. The streets of the barrio almost guaranteed that even the most honorably spoken vows couldn't be kept.

Twenty-nine

Something had been nagging at him from the minute he'd stumbled on Tony Vincenzi's body, but not until they'd been playing mind games with Detective O'Flannery had it come to Rick what it was. If he was right . . .

Madre de Dios, he hoped he wasn't. He also hoped like hell that Dana would be able to keep the detective off his tail. She could do it, if she felt so inclined, but he'd seen the doubts in her eyes, the fear that he was about to betray her to save either himself or *Yo, Amigo.*

Right now, he needed luck and time. He needed to buy a few hours to see if he couldn't straighten this mess out on his own . . . if he was right that there was a mess and that his old friend, his triumphant success story was smack in the middle of it.

His first stop was *Yo, Amigo* headquarters. With any luck, the information he was after would be in the files, files that Maria kept so organized that he should be able to put his finger on it in a heartbeat. Even after the office had been ransacked, she had managed to put everything pretty much back in order by working day and night, with help from Rosa, Marco, and the others, who would have walked through fire for her.

He went straight to the alphabetized stacks of files, searching until he found the G's. He went through the pile twice before determining that the file for Tico Garcia was missing. Though he knew he would have no better luck there, he also searched the T's, in case it had been misfiled by someone uncertain of correct filing procedures.

In the end, there was only one conclusion. It was gone. And with it, the only solid piece of evidence linking Tico's restaurant and Tony Vincenzi, if Rick's guesswork was correct.

He sank down into the chair at Maria's desk with a heavy sigh. The fact that the file was missing was as much confirmation as he needed that he was on the right track. Oh, he didn't have all of the pieces of the puzzle just yet, but he didn't like what he did have: one chunk with his old friend's angry face on it and another he was all but certain would have Tony Vincenzi's signature on a loan guarantee.

Only a handful of people knew who had been in on that deal. The investors had insisted on anonymity. They had shunned publicity.

Ken had been one of those who knew. In fact, he had been the one who had organized the backers in the first place. Had he subsequently stumbled on something questionable about the operation? Was that what had put his life at risk? Had the killer also suspected that Ken might have duplicates of the loan papers in his *Yo, Amigo* files at the church?

There was only one place to get answers, and it was the last place on earth Rick wanted to go, the last person he wanted to confront. Feeling bone-weary and heartsick, he walked the few blocks to the restaurant.

At this hour of the night, business was booming. The salsa music was lively, the aromas mouth-watering. Tico's mother greeted him with an exuberant hug.

"Think you can squeeze me in, *Mamacita?*"

"For you, there is always room. I save the best table for special friends." She bustled down the narrow aisle toward a small table for two, where she usually sat herself when business was slow.

"Sit. I bring you chips right away and a margarita, perhaps? You look as if you need to have your spirits brightened. Tequila is very good for that."

"No margarita, *por favor.* Is Tico around?"

"Not just now." She studied his face and frowned. "Is something wrong?"

Rick wasn't ready to answer her questions. "When will he be back?"

Her expression faltered, then turned to worry. "I do not know. He has gone after Joey."

Something in Rick's stomach went ice-cold at that. "Gone after him where? *Mamacita,* this is important. Please, where are they?"

She hesitated, clearly torn between the two sons she adored, and the man who had given her oldest a chance at a better life.

"You want to help them?" she asked, a soft, pleading note in her voice.

"If I can."

She sighed. "Florida. Joey went to Florida. Tico went after him. He was a wild man when he heard his brother had gone there. What is happening? I don't understand this."

Neither did he, not entirely. He closed his eyes against the sick sensation that washed over him. Eventually he forced himself to stand. As he stood, he squeezed Mrs. Garcia's trembling hand. "Don't worry, *Mamacita.* I will do what I can for them."

"This is very bad, isn't it?"

Thinking of Dana's sons, who were now very much in the path of a man on the run, Rick could only nod. "Yes, I think it may be very, very bad."

He debated taking action alone, keeping silent until he had all the facts. He weighed Dana's frantic worry against her right to know, and saw what he had to do. He owed her the truth. Honesty, in fact, might be the only chance at salvaging whatever there was between them. If he kept silent and anything happened, she would blame him forever.

"Can I use your phone?" he asked.

"Of course. It is in the kitchen."

He called the church office, a number he knew by heart from calling so often to talk things over with his old and trusted friend.

O'Flannery answered. It wouldn't have been his first choice, but maybe it was for the best. A lot of things needed to be set in motion in a hurry and who better to do it than a cop?

He explained his theory and the admittedly sketchy proof he had. "All I do know for sure is that Dana's kids are down there and somebody needs to be alerted to protect them, in case I'm right, and Joey's desperate enough to try to grab one as a hostage."

"Isn't that a big leap?" O'Flannery asked.

He sounded so skeptical that Rick was sorry he'd involved him. "Not if he doesn't get what he wants from Carolina Vincenzi," he explained impatiently. "He's going to be after some other way to get money to get out of the country, and kidnapping would sound like a sure bet if you're a scared kid who's not thinking too clearly."

"I suppose I'll have to trust your instincts on this one. I'll get on it right away," O'Flannery said tightly.

"Let me talk to Dana."

"No."

"Dammit, let me talk to her."

"There's no point in upsetting her with wild speculation," the detective countered. "At this point, we don't have squat."

"They're her kids. She has a right to know what's going on."

"What you think is going on," O'Flannery countered.

"Put her on the phone, or I'll just have to drive all the way out there to tell her in person and waste more time, when both of us could be catching a flight to Florida."

"Dammit, Sanchez!"

Rick remained silent until finally O'Flannery sighed heavily. "Fine. Here she is."

"Rick? What's wrong?"

He filled her in as hurriedly as possible. "O'Flannery's going to get police protection for the boys. In the meantime, I'm calling to book seats on the next available flight out. You call your father to warn him and then meet me at the airport. Okay? Have you got all that?"

To his relief, there was no hysterical outburst, just a terse, "Fine. I'll be there as fast as I can."

He had never been more admiring of her strength. "Dana, try not to worry. This is just a precaution. I may have gotten it all wrong."

"No," she said, sounding exhausted and terrified. "I think you've gotten it right. It's the only thing that makes sense."

"Querida?"

"Yes," she said in a flat tone.

"I hope to God I'm wrong."

She never said a word. All he heard was the quiet click of the phone disconnecting. He wondered then if she would someday thank him for solving the case, or if she would only hate him forever for inadvertently setting the whole series of tragic events into motion in the first place.

From the moment Rick told her what he suspected, Dana felt as if her world began moving in slow motion. Realistically, she knew that phone calls were made hurriedly, that the drive to O'Hare took a fraction of its usual time, with O'Flannery's siren blaring the whole way, but it all seemed to take an eternity—too long, by far, when she imagined her boys in harm's way.

Maybe, though, it wouldn't come to that. Maybe Joey would get what he needed from Carolina and be long gone when they got there. Maybe Tico would greet them and fill in all of the missing pieces of the puzzle, ending weeks of terrible uncertainty and speculation.

For one fleeting instant, she thought of the cost to Rick. He had been forced to admit that his shining example of *Yo,*

Amigo's success was at the heart of some kind of scandal that had led to the murder of three people, so far. No sooner had the stirring of sympathy come, than she angrily dismissed it. It was, after all, because of him that Ken was dead, just as she had believed in the beginning.

And she had slept with him. Worse, she had begun falling in love with him. She sighed. Why not admit the truth now, at least to herself? She had fallen in love with him, against all odds, against all reason.

When this was over, though, she would walk away from him. It was the only choice she had, she concluded with devastating finality.

He was waiting for them outside the terminal at O'Hare. After a quick glance at her, he stepped away with O'Flannery, so the detective could brief him on all of the arrangements that had been made with law enforcement officials in Florida.

Dana felt Kate's hands on her shoulders and dragged her gaze back from the two men to meet her friend's deeply troubled expression.

"Don't blame him," Kate said, reading her as clearly as if she'd spoken her thoughts aloud. "He didn't kill Ken."

"He didn't pull the trigger, but he might as well have. Ken is dead because of the world Rick dragged him into."

"No," Kate said sharply. "Ken is dead because he cared so much for helping others that he took risks. He weighed them and he took them anyway. The risks didn't matter to him."

Dana stared at her incredulously. "You want me to blame Ken for getting himself killed?"

"Haven't you been doing that from the beginning? Rick is just a convenient target, sweetie. The person you're really furious with is your husband."

She couldn't be mad at Ken, Dana thought, as tears stung her eyes. Ken was dead, gone forever. It would be wrong to be so terribly angry with him.

And yet, wasn't there a nugget of truth in what Kate said? From the instant she'd been told about the shooting, hadn't she really wanted to shout and curse at the man who'd left her alone with three young sons, who'd put strangers' needs above his own family's?

She pushed aside the anger. What did it matter now? She couldn't think about any of this now, not while events were still being played out hundreds of miles away. Not while her babies were in danger.

Again, Kate squeezed her shoulders. "Promise me you won't slam any doors," she said urgently. "Promise me."

"It doesn't matter now. I have to concentrate on Bobby, Kevin, and Jonathan."

Kate sighed. "Yes, of course, you do. They're going to be fine. I'll be praying for them every second until I hear from you."

Before Dana could reply, Rick was beside them, his expression serious, his eyes wary. "We have to go or we'll miss the flight."

Dana nodded, then gave Kate a quick, final hug. She gazed up at O'Flannery. "Thank you for everything you've tried to do."

"It hasn't been enough, but everything's in motion. Your boys will be safe and sound when you get to Florida."

"Dana?" Rick said.

"Yes, I'm coming." She turned and walked into the terminal without another backward glance.

"I have the tickets. We can go straight to the gate."

He led the way and she followed, bitterly aware that he hadn't touched her, hadn't really even looked directly at her since her arrival at the airport. It was as if he already knew, as she did, what the future held for them: nothing.

Thirty

Fear overcame despondency very quickly as the flight touched down in Tampa. A connector flight to Fort Myers was available almost at once, but after they were on board, the plane sat parked at the ramp for what seemed an eternity.

"What's happening?" Dana asked. "Why aren't we leaving?" She reached for the call button to summon the stewardess.

"Weather," Rick said, putting his hand over hers to prevent it. "There's a bad storm passing over. I'm sure we'll take off as soon as it's safe."

Until he mentioned it, she had been oblivious to the raging rain and wind and the occasional violent bursts of thunder. "Dammit, we can't wait," she said unreasonably. "What if . . . ?"

Rick quieted the question with a touch of a finger to her lips. "Sssh, *querida*. Use that brilliant head of yours. We won't get there at all, if we take off, only to crash. You know that. We have to rely on the pilot's judgment."

Of course, she understood that, but it didn't matter. Not knowing what was happening to her children was killing her. Her own safety didn't matter at all.

She suspected Rick was just as worried about his friends, although, at the moment, she didn't give a rat's ass if Tico and his brother went down in a burst of gunfire. Still, she knew how hard it must have been for Rick to admit that Tico was implicated in the crime. Yet he hadn't hesitated. He had told her at once. She supposed he deserved some credit for that.

"What made you think Tico might be involved in all of this?" she asked eventually, hoping that conversation would keep her mind off of the inevitable delay.

Rick sighed, his expression filled with sorrow. "The way he's been acting lately, for one thing. He's been tense and defensive. He said it had to do with Joey, but a part of me wondered if that was all there was to it. Then today, when we were at the Vincenzi place, I started thinking about the consortium of investors that Ken had put together."

"You'd never met them?"

"Never. I'd never even heard their names, because they insisted on anonymity. I wondered about that at the time. In my experience, most people wish to take credit for their good deeds. I went back to *Yo, Amigo* to see if the paperwork was in the files, to see what, if anything it might reveal. It was gone, which explained that ransacking. To my regret, too many things added up."

"I'm surprised you didn't fly down here on your own to check it out, without telling me what you suspected," she admitted. "Tico is your friend, after all."

He gave her a rueful grin. "I considered it."

"And?"

"I figured you would never forgive me if something happened and you believed you could have prevented it, if only you'd known the truth about what was going on. You deserved to hear everything from me." His gaze locked with hers. "Don't forget, *querida,* you and I are friends, too. Perhaps even more than friends."

"It really matters to you what I think of you?" She supposed it shouldn't have, but it surprised her.

"This is not news," he said dryly. "It has always mattered, *querida*. You were the wife of a man I respected, a man I thought of almost as a brother. Even before we met, it bothered me that you hated me so."

"How did you even know I hated you?"

"It wasn't too difficult," he said with a sad half-smile. "Never once, in all the time your husband and I were working together, did you invite me to your home. Ken grew uncomfortable whenever I suggested we all get together. Since he and I spent a great deal of time together, it didn't require a tremendous mental leap to realize that you were the one who wanted no part of me."

"It wasn't personal," she said. "It was never personal."

"You were afraid for him," Rick said wearily. "I understood that."

"I was right," she pointed out.

"Does that make you feel any better?" he asked softly. "Or did it only create a rift between you when he was still alive, one that you will never be able to heal, now that he is gone?"

The truth of that hurt. "Yes," she acknowledged. "It created a terrible tension and that makes me feel unbearably sad."

"Me, as well. I regret that I inadvertently came between you." He glanced out the window. "It looks as if the storm is over. We will be taking off soon and then all of this will end."

"You don't have any doubts at all about what we will find, do you? Do you think Tico will fill in the blanks, once he is caught?"

"Despite what you think of him, he is an honorable man. He is only trying to save his brother. However that turns out, he will tell you what you need to know."

And then, Dana thought, the nightmare would finally be over.

The instant the plane touched down in Fort Myers, Dana rushed for the door. Her father was waiting for her inside the terminal and she could tell at once from his drawn expression that the nightmare wasn't over, after all.

"Dad, what is it? What's happened?" she asked, as he enfolded her in a tight embrace.

When he released her, he met her gaze evenly. "Now, baby, I don't want you to panic. The police assure me that they have the situation well in hand."

She could feel her already frazzled nerves snapping. "Dammit, what situation? Please tell me."

Her father exchanged a look with a man standing quietly nearby. He walked over to join them.

"Mrs. Miller, I'm Detective Hanson. If you'll come with me."

Dana balked. "Not until I know what's going on, all of it."

"Just tell her," Rick said. "She needs to know everything. She's a very strong woman. She won't fall apart on you."

Her father nodded. "That's right, detective. My daughter is a professional investigator. She's been working on this case for weeks now. She might be able to help."

"It's your son," the detective said, his voice gentle, his gaze obviously watchful for any sign that she was about to fall apart. "He's being held hostage, we believe by a man named José Garcia."

"Where?" she asked, fighting to keep her voice from shaking. She had anticipated this possibility, but the reality of it was devastating. Her whole body suddenly felt ice-cold with dread.

"At the Vincenzis," her father said, his expression filled with guilt. "It's our fault. We didn't know. Bobby asked to go to play with one of the boys from school. We didn't realize which boy it was, until it was too late."

Not again, she thought. Please, God, not again. She couldn't bear to lose another person she loved to this kind of insane violence.

And for the first time since Ken's death, she began to pray. It was pure instinct. She didn't know if there was a God, or if He would hear her this time, but at the moment, prayer and faith were all she had.

Thirty-one

The Vincenzi home in Fort Myers must be a considerably more modest one than the monstrosity they had searched in the Chicago suburbs, Rick thought, as they drove into the neighborhood of small Spanish-style stucco structures on postage stamp-sized lots.

Dana hadn't said a word since they'd left the airport. She had sat huddled between him and her father on the drive, seemingly oblivious to their presence. She hadn't reacted in any way when he'd taken her icy hands in his and rubbed them to restore the warmth. From time to time, he could feel her shivering, even though the tropical air was warm and muggy.

He glanced at her father and saw that he hadn't missed Rick's gesture. It would have been too much to expect approval in his eyes, but there was no censure either, just questions that would remain on hold, for the time being. Rick could respect a man for wanting to wait and see, before giving his blessing to a relationship.

If there was to be a relationship, he reminded himself. That was very much in question, for the time being. Dana was allowing his touch at the moment, because she was, quite frankly, oblivious to it. Later, he had no idea what to expect. He prayed for the best and feared the worst.

In the meantime, there was Bobby to worry about. He was convinced that Joey wouldn't harm the boy. No matter how panicked he was, how cornered he was feeling, he was a decent kid at heart. Rick conceded reluctantly that his opinion was based more on desperate hope, than facts. Joey had been in a gang for a long time before Tico had forced him out after his own redemption. He'd been in there long enough to become desensitized to violence. Who knew what effect Carlos's ugly influence had had.

There was a crowd gathered on the street just down the block from the Vincenzi home, though the police had done their best to keep neighbors and others drawn by the unfolding drama at a distance.

"You okay?" Detective Hanson asked Dana, after pulling to a stop behind a line of police vehicles.

She nodded, though her complexion was pale and her eyes darkened by fear. Unshed tears made them shimmer like deep blue pools.

"Let's go, then," her father said. "Let's let Bobby know that his mom is right outside."

As Dana and her father made their way to the SWAT team coordinator, Rick held back and surveyed the throng, searching for Tico. If Joey was inside, Tico wouldn't be able to stay away. Nor would he have gone in with his brother. Rick still believed that his friend would fight to the end to prevent a tragedy.

Eventually he spotted Tico lurking in the shadows, two houses down, standing all alone. Rick slipped through the darkness and came up behind him.

"We've got troubles, old friend," he said softy.

Tico jerked at the sound of his voice, but he never turned. He kept his bleak, tortured face focused on the house where his brother was holding an innocent young boy hostage.

"I was too late," he said, in a voice quivering with emotion. "As soon as I knew, I came after him, but I was too late. If all of this comes to a bad end, I will kill Carlos with my bare hands."

"It's time for the truth. Did Joey kill Ken?"

Tico's head snapped around at that. "Never!" he said furiously. "It was that gringo, that slime who is inside at this very moment holding Joey and the others hostage."

Rick gaped at the totally unexpected reply. "Gringo? Who?"

"Drake."

"Peter Drake?" he asked, incredulous, even though he'd seen that very man at the scene of another murder.

"*Si.*"

"How the devil was he involved?"

"From the beginning, he was demanding payoffs," Tico said, obviously aware that it was too late now for denials or evasions. "He said I should be pleased to become a front for a money-laundering operation, since he had made it possible for me to open."

"I don't understand."

"He and the woman were having an affair. She used her influence with her husband and with the *padre* to put the loan deal together for me. As far as I knew, it was a straightforward deal. Then this Drake came to me and explained the facts of life, as he called them. He had this little drug operation, he and some others."

"Lawrence Tremayne?" Rick guessed, thinking of the Latin American connection that they'd never been able to make sense of.

"He was one. There were more, I suspect, though I never met them."

"Did you cooperate?"

"For a while, until I could think what to do." He regarded Rick wryly. "With my past, I didn't think I could go to the police."

"You could have come to me," Rick said.

"No, my friend. I could not involve you. For once, I needed to solve this problem on my own. You were counting on me to be a success story, yes?"

Rick guessed the rest. "You talked to Ken."

"*Si.* It was the worst mistake of my life. I should have

known how he would react. He went loco. He threatened to blow the whole operation out of the water. He was incensed at the betrayal of men he'd thought to be honorable. I tried to calm him, to make him think rationally, but he insisted on doing it his way, on confronting them with what he knew, on giving them a chance to make things right."

"Right how?"

"By turning themselves in." Tico shrugged. "He was a very naive man, yes? It was his charm, but also his downfall."

"How did Carlos and Joey fit in?"

"Drake went to Carlos with his little problem. Carlos decided it would be a fascinating test of Joey's loyalty to him to ask him to shoot the *padre*. Naturally he did not trust him to do it. When Joey refused, Carlos pulled the trigger, then placed the gun in my brother's hand. Do you think the police would have believed that, though?"

"And today? What happened to bring you down here today?"

"Joey told me earlier that Drake had had Vincenzi killed, too, and that he was planning to fly here, get Carolina, and leave the country. We concluded, once more, that the police would not believe such a story. We decided to try to stop them ourselves. Joey, however, was too rash. He went in before we could think of a plan. Drake has them all now."

"Including Ken's boy," Rick concluded quietly.

Tico stared at him. "The *padre's* son is in there?"

"Yes." He met Tico's gaze. "Perhaps you and I should do what the police do not dare."

"Go in?" Tico replied, looking doubtful. "I do not think this is such a good idea."

"We don't have a choice, my friend. If we don't, they may harm the wrong man. They think Joey is behind this, and Drake will be eager to serve him up as the culprit."

"You would do that for me? You would risk your life to save my brother?"

"I would do it for you," he said readily. "And for Dana."

"I saw her arrive," Tico said. "I did not guess that you were with her."

Rick shrugged. "Where else would I be?" he said wryly. "Though at the moment I doubt that she appreciates it."

"You have it very bad, don't you, *mi amigo?*"

"*Si.* Very bad."

Tico grinned at him. "So, you and I are together again. You have a plan?"

"As I recall, we were once very good at improvising."

"True, but there is danger in that."

"There is danger in living," Rick told him. "And even greater danger, sometimes, in doing nothing."

They moved in tandem, then, slipping around behind the house, staying in shadows, alert for the presence of the SWAT team that had every door and window under surveillance. Breaking in without being detected, either from within or without, was not going to be so easy.

"Do you know exactly where they are being held?"

"At the far end of the house, I believe. The garage protects it on one side, and the windows are smaller. I have seen no movement through any of the sliding glass doors. It seems to me it would be foolish to hold them where they can be readily seen, and this Drake is no fool."

Rick regarded the house thoughtfully "Perhaps we can change that. Wait for me here."

He circled to the front of the house and slipped through the crowd, until he could catch Dana's father's eye. The older man joined him at once.

"Tell Dana to insist on seeing her son, preferably through that sliding glass door in the living room. Once he's there, ask her to try to keep him in view as long as possible. Cry, plead, whatever it takes, okay? Make sure she keeps Bobby where he is plainly visible, so there will be no mistakes."

Her father didn't waste time asking a lot of unnecessary questions. He seemed to know intuitively what Rick was planning. He, too, seemed to accept the limitations of the police.

He met Rick's gaze with an unblinking look. "Are you sure you can do this?"

"I have no choice but to try."

"You could leave it to the police."

"And while they debate the alternatives, the man inside could begin to get very jittery. I have to do this for Ken's sake."

"And for my daughter's," the older man guessed. "God speed, son. Thank you."

Rick hated expressing any hint of doubt about the outcome, but he needed Dana to know what she had meant to him. He met the other man's gaze. "If anything should happen to me, would you . . . ?"

He smiled and squeezed Rick's shoulder. "I will tell her that you love her very much. I think, though, that you should come back to her safely and tell her yourself."

Rick grinned. "I'm going to do my damnedest to do just that."

Dana's eyes were gritty from staring so hard at the tiny house, trying to catch a glimpse of her son. He must be terrified. So far, though, the police hadn't let her make an appeal to Joey Garcia, nor had they let her speak to her son.

She was dimly aware of her father having a hushed conversation with Detective Hanson, then of several policemen huddling together, as her father returned to her side.

"You doing okay, baby?"

"Dad, I am so scared," she admitted. "I don't think I have ever been more terrified."

"Not even when Johnny Payne locked you in that steel vault?" he asked, referring to a harrowing incident that had taken place while she was an investigator.

"Not even then."

"He's going to get out of there," her father reassured her. "I believe that with all my heart."

"But we've been at a stalemate for hours. I don't think the police are even negotiating for his release."

"That may be about to change."

She stared at him. "What do you know?"

"Here comes Detective Hanson now," he said, evading her eyes. "Let's see what he has in mind."

"Mrs. Miller, we have phone contact with the kidnapper. Do you think you could talk to him?"

The very idea of chatting with the person who was terrorizing her child made her blood run cold, but she nodded. She tried to remind herself that Joey was little more than a boy himself and that he was Tico's brother.

"What do you want me to do?" she asked.

"Ask to see Bobby. Tell him you want to come up to that front window and see your boy. If he agrees, keep Bobby and the kidnapper there as long as you can."

"What if he refuses?"

"Keep at him until you wear him down. Plead. Cry. Whatever it takes."

She nodded.

"Okay, then, let's do it."

He spoke to the SWAT commander, who relinquished the phone to her.

Dana forced herself to remain calm, as she clutched the receiver as though it were a lifeline to her son. "Joey?" she said softly.

A sinister laugh made her stomach plummet. Instantly alert, she said, "This isn't Joey, is it?"

"How brilliant of you to conclude that, Mrs. Miller. You were always far too smart for that saccharine husband of yours."

"My God," she murmured, instantly recognizing Peter Drake's voice, even though she had heard him use that tone only once before, at the meeting at her house with the church elders. "It's you."

"Right again. I was afraid you'd put it together. Those stupid policemen don't have a clue who they're dealing with. I've had them on the phone with Joey all evening. I couldn't resist the chance to talk with you, though."

"What do you want?"

"My freedom," he said simply. "Carolina and I want to leave the country and live quietly."

"I can make that happen," she said impulsively. "But first I want to see Bobby."

"Sorry. Not possible."

Terrified of the answer, she asked the obvious questions, anyway. "Why? Have you killed him already?"

"Killed my ace in the hole? Perhaps you're not as bright as I thought."

"Then why can't I see him? You could bring him into the living room. I'll stand right outside the window."

"And I will make myself the perfect target for some sniper."

"No," she insisted. "You can stay out of sight. Just let Bobby come where I can see that he's all right." Though she'd vowed not to cry, she couldn't help the sobs that rose in her throat. "Please, Peter. I have to see him. I have to let him know I'm here."

"You can speak to him on the phone."

"No," she repeated. "It won't be the same. Look, I can help you get away from here, but not unless you do this for me."

"What makes you think you can get the police to let us go?"

"I'm a minister's wife. They'll believe me when I tell them you had nothing to do with this, that it was all Joey Garcia. That's what they think, anyway."

"They are idiots, aren't they?" he said, sounding thoughtful. "Okay, I will bring Bobby to the window. Don't try anything crazy, because I will have a gun on him the whole time. You come up to the house alone. If I see anyone else close, the deal's off and your boy is dead. Are we clear?"

She swallowed hard. "We're clear." She handed the phone back to Detective Hanson and gave him a curt nod to indicate that the kidnapper had bought the plan. Then she began moving very slowly across the street and onto the Vincenzis' front lawn. With each step she took, her heart pounded a little harder and sweat beaded across her forehead.

Was she doing the right thing? She had blindly accepted the police plan without asking what their intentions were. Would they be rushing the house from another direction, even as she herself approached? Was she only putting her son into more danger? It was too late for second thoughts now, though. She was only a few yards from that window and a precious glimpse of Bobby.

There was a neatly tended flower bed outside the sliding glass doors, which substituted for windows around most of the house. Oblivious to the destruction, she stepped on bright pink impatiens, until she was close enough to touch the glass.

And then she waited. She waited for so long, she was certain that Peter Drake had only meant to torture by making a promise he had no intention of keeping.

Then suddenly Bobby was there, shoved from behind so hard that he stumbled as he came into view. Dana pressed her hands to the glass.

"Mom!"

He sounded on the verge of tears, but he squared his shoulders bravely. He stepped closer to the doors and blinked at her through his glasses. She noticed one lens was cracked.

"Are you okay?" he asked.

Dana's own tears spilled down her cheeks unchecked. "I'm doing just fine, now that I see you." She pressed her hand against the glass and Bobby placed his against it on the other side. "I love you, sweetie. We're going to get you out of there."

Bobby swallowed hard, his chin wobbling. "I'll be okay, Mom. Try not to worry."

Just then the pane of glass between them shattered. Dana didn't hesitate to consider what had caused it or whether she or Bobby were likely to be cut. As the shards fell away, she snatched him into her arms and ran. Before she'd taken two

steps, they were surrounded by half a dozen officers in bul-
letproof vests.

Even as they escorted her and Bobby to safety, she could
hear the two-way radios blaring with confused exchanges.

"What the hell happened?" the SWAT team commander
was demanding. "Nobody had an order to shoot."

Dana glanced up then just in time to see Peter Drake being
led away in handcuffs, as two very familiar men looked on.
She guessed then who had come up with the daring rescue
plan. She glanced at her father.

"You knew, didn't you? You knew what they were going to
do? How did they manage it?"

The color had finally come back into her father's face in
the past few minutes, but his expression remained totally
bland. "I think you'll have to talk to Mr. Sanchez about that."
He leaned down and scooped up his grandson in a bear hug.
"Come on, boy. Let's let your mom have a minute of privacy."

Bobby stared, as Rick left the house and crossed the yard.
A furious SWAT team commander was about to intercept him,
when Dana stepped between them.

"In a minute," she told the policeman. "I have a few words
to say to Mr. Sanchez."

"One minute," the man replied tersely. "Then I get a crack
at him."

Her gaze never left Rick's face. "I will never forget what
you did here today. I have no idea how you accomplished it,
but I don't care. I will always be grateful."

"I owed you one." His eyes locked on hers. "What will
you do, now that you have all your answers?"

"Not all of them," she replied, "but I'm sure the police will
fill me in."

He nodded. "Are you going to stay here?"

She hadn't thought past this moment, but she nodded
slowly. "For a while."

His expression blank, he said quietly, "Yes, that makes
sense. The boys will need you with them."

Suddenly, she felt as if she were talking to a stranger, making small talk, when far more important things remained unspoken.

Before she could say precisely that, the patience of the SWAT team leader snapped. "You'll have to excuse us, ma'am. This man has some explaining to do."

"Where are you taking him?"

"To headquarters for a little chat."

Dana turned to her father, who was waiting nearby. "Dad, go with them."

Rick's mouth quirked into a full-fledged grin at her protective tone. "I do not need an attorney, *querida.*"

"Humor me," she countered. "And if there's anything else I can do for you, *anything,* you can always call."

His dark eyes challenged hers. "Then this is goodbye?"

Tears stung her eyes, and her heart felt like lead, but she forced herself to nod.

Rick's steady, dark-eyed gaze locked with hers. *"Adios, mi amor."*

Only after he had walked away without a backward glance did she reply softly, *"Adios, mi amor."*

Thirty-two

Dana couldn't seem to let Bobby out of her sight, much to his chagrin. He finally told her to lay off, or he'd wind up being known all over Florida as a mama's boy.

"I won't even be able to show my face on the streets. I'll have to quit school," he warned.

"Okay, okay." She studied him worriedly. "Are you sure everything's all right with you, though. No nightmares or anything?"

He rolled his eyes. "Mom, I've told you and told you, Mr. Drake never hurt me. Mrs. Vincenzi threatened to cut off his . . ."

"Never mind. I know what she threatened."

In fact, if Peter Drake ever left jail and got together with Carolina Vincenzi, Dana wasn't sure which one she'd pity more. She had heard a few days ago that Carolina had put her house in Illinois on the market, as well as the house in Fort Myers. She and her sons had vanished. Some thought they were living in Grand Cayman on money Tony had stashed away, before his death.

As for Rick, he and Tico had flown back to Chicago, as soon as they'd been released by the police. Her father had stayed with them the whole time and reported back that both men had been cleared of any possible charges, even though the local police were mad as hell that a couple of vigilantes had jumped into the stand-off with a daring rescue attempt.

Rick had shattered the window, so that Dana could grab her son, while Tico had jumped Drake from behind.

Joey had gone back on the same flight, in police custody, until he could make his statements to the Chicago police about Ken's murder.

She had heard from Kate the night before that Lawrence Tremayne was in custody, as well, though the infamous Carlos had conveniently disappeared. When she'd asked about O'Flannery, Kate had been coy, but she sounded happier than she had been since that sleaze of a husband had run out on her.

Her own world should be settling back into something resembling normalcy, Dana thought, as she sat on the beach with the boys playing nearby. It seemed like a lifetime since she had sat in this very spot and made up her mind to go home and solve her husband's murder. She had her answers now, but she was no less restless. The longed-for peace of mind continued to elude her. This time, though, another man was at the center of her thoughts.

She had her eyes closed, when she sensed someone standing over her. She glanced up, just as her father dropped down to the lawn chair next to hers.

"When are you going to tell me what's going on between you and Sanchez?" he asked.

So much for pussyfooting around the touchy subject, she thought resignedly. "There's nothing between us," she said.

His eyebrows rose skeptically. "Really? I wonder, then, why he told me to tell you that he loved you, if anything happened to him when he was playing hero the other night."

She removed her sunglasses and peered at her father. She wasn't sure which stunned her more, that Rick loved her or that he'd told her father. "Rick said he loved me? You're not just putting words in his mouth?"

"No, and even if he hadn't said the words, it was plain as day, when he looked at you. I know the signs, baby. The man's a goner." He regarded her intently. "How do you feel about him? No evasions this time."

She sighed. It was a question she had asked herself, repeatedly. "I don't know," she said, being as honest as she could. "For a time, I thought I did. But before that, I had so much anger and resentment where he was concerned. Then, while I was investigating Ken's death, I kept bumping into more suspicions and doubts. How can I get past all that?"

"Maybe you can't," her father said simply. "But you won't find out by hanging around down here on the beach."

She grinned at him. "Are you kicking me out?"

He studied her face for a minute. "I love you, baby, but yes, that is exactly what I'm doing. Go home. Find out what's left there for you."

For some reason—fear maybe—she was reluctant to make that commitment. She lifted a handful of warm sand, letting it sift through her fingers.

"Mom thinks we should move down here," she said eventually, testing the idea on him. "She thinks it would be good for the boys to have family nearby."

"True, but your mother doesn't know what I do."

"Which is?"

"That your heart's still in Chicago."

"Where do you want this?" Kate asked, precariously balancing a huge box.

"What does it say?" Dana asked. "I marked everything."

"If I could see what you wrote, do you think I'd be asking?" Kate retorted.

Dana stood on tiptoe to peer at the top of the box. "Kevin's room. I think those are his stuffed animals."

"What does he have, a blessed zoo?" Kate grumbled as she headed for the stairs. "And would you tell me why you had to buy a three-story townhouse and put the boys in the top floor?"

"Just to torment you on moving day," Dana replied.

She had been back in Chicago for three hectic months. She had spent most of that time settling Ken's legal affairs and house hunting. Though she'd looked at several places within blocks of the church, time and again, she had been drawn into the city, into a neighborhood of old townhouses that had been gentrified in recent years.

Before she had made the final decision, she had gone into the cemetery by the church to talk it over with Ken, as she had any major decision she'd made since they'd married. As she'd planted daffodils and tulips around his tombstone, she'd told him about all of the emotional upheavals that had happened since he'd left them.

"I'm not angry at you, anymore," she had said finally. "I've made peace with what happened, though I'll go on missing you until the day I die." And then, after taking a deep breath, she had told him about her feelings for Rick. "I'm scared, though, scared of moving on, scared of losing another person I love. He's right out there, you know, right in the thick of the very neighborhood where you were killed. How will I be able to stand knowing that something could happen to him at any second?"

She touched the cold marble of the angel and, ironically, it was that fleeting contact that gave her the answer she'd been seeking. Soon enough, they would all die, but for now, she and Rick and their passion were very much alive.

She had glanced up at the sky, a smile on her lips. "Thank you," she whispered to Ken, or God, or whoever had led her to the answer she'd been so desperately seeking.

She hadn't told Rick yet of her decision, had made no overtures of any kind to bring him back into her life. She had wanted to get settled in her new home and bring the boys back from Florida, first. Her parents would be arriving with them next week. They were bursting with enthusiasm about coming home and about living in the city. She wanted Rick to see that she had made her choice to stay because it was the right one for all of them, and not solely because of him. Soon, though. Very soon.

She caught Kate staring at her curiously. "What did you do with O'Flannery?" Dana asked her. "He's supposed to be hauling the big stuff."

"Last time I saw him, he was sitting in a chair on the sidewalk cursing the day he ever met the two of us."

"Uh-oh," Dana said. "That doesn't bode well for your future."

"Sure it does. He complains about everything he loves—his job, me."

Kate started up the steps with Dana right on her heels. "He loves you? When did that happen?"

"It happened the day he set eyes on me." Kate grinned. "He just got around to figuring it out the other day, though. Some men have to be blindsided by a bat before they get it."

"If you two would stop gabbing, we would finish this move a whole lot faster," the man in question announced from downstairs. "Where do you want this blasted sofa?"

Dana rushed back down. "How did you get the sofa in here by yourself?" Her voice trailed off when she saw Rick standing silently at the opposite end of the sofa, his expression wary. O'Flannery glanced at Dana, then back at Rick.

"I guess the sofa can wait," he said, lowering his end to the floor. He brushed past Dana to head upstairs.

"How did you get here?" she asked eventually just to break the silence. "I mean, how did you know we were moving?"

"O'Flannery and I have stayed in touch. He filled me in. I thought maybe you could use some extra help." He watched her warily. "Do you mind?"

"No, of course not. It's . . ." Her voice faltered. "It's kind of you."

He regarded her wryly. *"Por favor, querida,* enough of the polite small talk. You look wonderful."

She glanced down at her filthy jeans and baggy T-shirt. "Oh, I'm a beauty, all right."

"Yes," he said fervently, "you are. I've missed you."

It couldn't have been even a quarter as badly as she'd missed him, she thought, remembering the lonely nights when all she'd been able to think about was the single time they'd made love. She had wondered if they would ever risk a second chance. If she dared.

"I've missed you, too," she said in a choked voice. "I, um, I saw that Rosa had an ad in the *Tribune* last Sunday."

He grinned. "She was over-the-moon, as they say."

"And her father? What did he say?"

"He bought up every copy he could find and gave them to all his friends."

"Then I guess it was a good thing it was an ad for cosmetics, instead of lingerie."

"Or maternity clothes," Rick said. "Though I think he is coming to terms with her pregnancy. It's just in the nick of time, too. The baby's due any second."

"And Marco? I've been meaning to check on him, too."

"Marco has gone to Hollywood," he said proudly. "Your friend sent his pictures out there to a co-agent, and he got him a commercial two days later. I think maybe Rosa will join him eventually. You did a good thing for them." He fastened his gaze on hers. "The others ask about you, you know. They are waiting for you to come and help them."

She was surprised by that and pleased.

"Will you come to *Yo, Amigo* again? Maybe teach another photography class? Ileana has been taking pictures like a crazy woman. She says she wants to have a portfolio ready when you come back."

"Ileana? With the scorpion tattoo?"

He grinned. "She pretty much terrorizes her subjects into sitting for her, but she's actually gotten some interesting results."

"I'd love to see them."

"I could pick you up tomorrow. We could have lunch at Tico's. He's been asking about you, too." He shrugged. "Bullying me, actually. He thinks I've been wasting too much time before coming after you. Was he right?"

She shook her head.

"I thought maybe you needed time to get your bearings," he explained.

"I did," she admitted.

"And now? Do you know what you want, *querida?*" His hands were shoved into his pockets, as if he feared he might reach for her, only to have her slip away.

She nodded. If she had doubted it before, she would have known it the minute she had seen him in the living room, filling the room with his very masculine presence, just as he had the house she had shared with another man she had loved heart and soul.

She realized then that she had bought this townhouse with him in mind. She had chosen the vibrant colors for the walls and selected huge pots of hibiscus and bougainvillea to sit beside the French doors in her den, because they reminded her of the passionate man who'd brought her senses back to life. She had especially liked the privacy of the master suite on the second floor, far from the prying eyes of little boys.

"You," she confessed softly. "I want you."

A smile began slowly at the corners of his mouth, then spread. His hands came out of his pockets, and he opened his arms. She flew across the room into his embrace. As his arms closed tightly around her, it was like coming home again, finding a safe haven in the midst of turmoil.

For a long time, neither of them spoke. It was enough just to know the comfort of being held. Then he pulled back and gazed into her eyes.

"We'll fight," he warned her.

She laughed. "But you'll let me win."

His expression rueful, he nodded. "Sometimes. Because there is very little I could deny you."

She touched her fingers to his lips. "Making up will be extraordinary."

"You are extraordinary." He stepped backwards, deliberately tumbling them, onto the couch with her on top. His mouth sought hers, slowly, gently, and then with a passion that made her blood roar. Everything, their surroundings, the noises from the street, the proximity of Kate and O'Flannery, all of it faded away. The only thing real was Rick and the hunger of his kisses, the heat of his body.

"Think they've forgotten that we're here?" Kate whispered.

The softly spoken words broke the spell. Dana chuckled. "A good friend would have slipped discreetly out the door."

"And left all the rest of the furniture sitting in the street?" O'Flannery asked, then added pointedly, "Including the beds?"

Rick sighed, his gaze locked with hers. "They have a point."

"Yes," she conceded. "Especially about the beds."

"The faster we move, the sooner we'll have this place to ourselves," Rick added. He was already lifting her to her feet as he said it.

But as Dana started to follow Kate and O'Flannery outside, Rick caught her hand and tugged her back. "In case I didn't mention it, I love you, *querida*."

"I love you," she said quietly.

He had been with her in twilight and in the darkest moments of her life. With any luck, the shadows were gone and the rest of their days would be all sunshine. And if that was too much to hope for, at least they both knew with absolute certainty that their love was strong enough to weather the most volatile of storms.

Dear Reader:

When I was writing **TEMPTATION**, my first book for Zebra, I became intrigued with a very minor character, Dana Miller. In that book she was brought in as an old friend of the hero's for a couple of scenes to do some minor private investigation work. A retired PI, married to a minister, a mother of three boys, something about Dana stuck with me. In the way of all authors, I began to wonder *what if* . . .

What if Dana's kind, decent husband were killed? What if they had disagreed about the work that had put him in danger? How would that test her faith? What if the man she had to turn to for help was the very man she blamed for putting her husband in harm's way? And what if she began to fall in love with that same man? Could their feelings survive the anger and distrust?

Thus **TWILIGHT** was born. I hope you enjoy this very emotional story about two very different people who must overcome the past and tremendous odds to be together.

As always, I'd love to hear your reactions. You may write to me at P.O. Box 490326, Key Biscayne, FL 33149. I'm usually abysmally slow, but I do answer and I am always appreciative of the time you take to write. ANd if you're ever in Virginia on any weekend between April and December, stop by my bookstore and say hello. Potomac Sunrise Books is located across from the Potomac River at 308 Washington Avenue, Colonial Beach.

With all good wishes,

Sherryl Woods